Also by Alyson McLayne

THE SONS OF GREGOR MACLEOD

Highland Promise
Highland Conquest
Highland Betrayal
Highland Captive

HIGHLAND CAPTIVE

ALYSON McLAYNE

Published by Sourcebooks Casablanca, an imprint of Sourcebooks
P.O. Box 4410, Naperville, Illinois 60567-4410
(630) 961-3900
sourcebooks.com

Printed and bound in Canada.
MBP 10 9 8 7 6 5 4 3 2 1

To my husband, Ken, who supports his family with his whole heart—through long work hours, toy explosions, and chronic pain—and all he asks for in return is a cuddle, a coffee, and that I occasionally wash his jeans. Loving you lots and lots.

One

Gleann Moireasdan, Scotland, 1453

Deirdre MacIntyre leaned back against the tent pole and tried to take ten slow, steady breaths—a trick taught to her by her old nursemaid—but nothing worked to calm the panic and dread welling up inside her.

His eyes.

She pressed her fist to her lips to stop their trembling and again peeked around the tent flap into the crowded market. The man she'd been watching for the last ten minutes had disappeared. She broadened her search, casting her eyes over the groups of people milling around the square. The spring gathering of the western clans brought everyone together for selling wool, livestock, and other Highland wares, like the fine plaids in the tent in which she'd taken refuge.

Her husband had insisted she come to the gathering this year, feeling guilty, perhaps, for all the time he'd spent away from her and Ewan the past few years. She hadn't wanted to go; her stomach had been tied in knots for weeks, imagining the crowds and the mistakes she might make—and be judged for. But worse than that, he'd also insisted she leave Ewan behind.

Now she was glad her son had stayed home.

She scanned the crowd, not seeing her target. He couldn't just blend in—he was possibly the biggest man she'd ever seen. It was an unusually warm day, and he'd rolled up his linen sleeves, the tie at his neck undone. The material had hung open, revealing muscles that rippled and bulged in his arms and chest.

Developed wielding the huge broad sword that hung down his spine, no doubt.

The muscles weren't what frightened her the most—nor the sword. It was the grim intensity in his face and eyes that promised retribution…eyes that were the exact same color as her son's.

That scared the life out of her.

"Where are you?" she whispered, hearing the desperation in her voice, the fear that howled like a wounded animal through her body.

"I'm right behind you, lass, and wondering why the wife of Lewis MacIntyre, son and heir of the ruthless Laird MacIntyre, almost ran me down in the middle of the market and has been unable to keep her gaze off me since. You're a lovely lass, for sure, but you doona stare at me with lust in your eyes. 'Tis not a swiving you're after."

Deirdre's stomach clenched, and she would have run—like a mouse, never the lion she wanted to be—but his hand landed on the swell of her hip. The pressure of his palm silently ordered her to turn around.

She did. And when she stumbled, his fingers tightened on her body and steadied her. He watched her with narrowed eyes, his gaze landing on the pulse that she could feel beating wildly in her neck and on her trembling lips. She knew that luminous stare—the bright, dazzling blue that verged on crystalline sea-green. But the eyes she'd been staring into for the past two years looked back at her lovingly, adoringly. Not with suspicion and barely hidden enmity.

For him, she stiffened her spine. For the sake of *her* son.

"Let go of me. I doona need your help."

The man's gaze flicked to hers, and she saw a growing interest. Speculation. He withdrew his hand and took a step back. She stared up at him, this time trying to look past those familiar eyes and see what other similarities she could find in his frightening countenance.

The same long, thick lashes fringed his piercing gaze; the same shallow dent marked his chin. His hair formed a downward peak in the middle of his forehead, the same as her son's. Except Ewan's hair was longer and lighter, almost a white-blond. This man had hacked his blond hair short, so it looked darker and stood up in ragged bristles.

Her eyes drifted down to his mouth. He had lips like her son's too, but while Ewan's were soft and childlike, his had firmed with age while still keeping their full shape.

That's where the similarities ended. Her son's welcoming smile was nowhere to be seen. Nay, this man looked grim and possibly cruel. It was there in the twist of his lips, the harshness of his countenance, the quickness with which he was ready to condemn her.

He expected betrayal, and she suspected he'd even welcome it, because then he could punish whoever had crossed him.

Aye. A cruel man, indeed.

"Is your husband here, Lady MacIntyre?"

"He's here…somewhere." Just where, she had no idea. Truth be told, she didn't expect to see him for days yet, if not weeks. Which made his insistence that she accompany him to the festival even more surprising. "You know a great deal about me, but I am at a disadvantage. Who are you?" she blurted out.

"I'm Gavin MacKinnon, Laird of Clan MacKinnon. Did you come here looking for me, lass? Is there something you want to tell me? Some information you want to share?"

The last words sounded almost hopeful, eager, and that disturbed her as much as the color of his eyes. Hope implied faith and dreams. Cruel men did not dream—and she wanted him to be cruel. Aye, if he was a blackheart, she could turn away and never look back.

"Nay," she said abruptly, her panic rising again. *What information was he looking for?* "And you're mistaken. I wasn't looking at you. I was just…looking."

The eagerness faded from his eyes, replaced by disappointment and frustration, even bitterness. It caused an unexpected pang in her heart. She didn't like that she'd somehow hurt him and put that bleakness back into his gaze.

"Aye, you stared at me for a long while. Did you like what you saw? I'm a big man. Some women mistake that to mean the same as rough. Is that what you were hoping for, lass? A hard tupping? Did I misunderstand your interest?"

His tone was harsh, the words callous.

Shock flooded her senses. Especially as she could see he didn't mean what he said. He was deliberately trying to hurt her. To diminish her. And it worked. As much as she tried to fight it, shame and fear invaded her body. As quick as that, she was back to being five or ten or thirteen and at the mercy of her mother and siblings.

No one but her family had ever tried to wound her deliberately. Marrying Lewis and coming to the MacIntyres, despite her young age, had turned into a blessing. Her husband was distant but not unkind, and his clan was respectful. They'd even become friendly since she'd been given Ewan. Her son's laughter and love had opened everyone's hearts.

"I doona wish *that* from you, sir. I doona wish anything from you other than to be left alone."

"Everyone wants something, Lady MacIntyre. And eventually I'll discover what you want too."

He nodded once—a curt dip of his head—then moved past her into the gathering. She held her breath and closed her eyes, making herself stay still, no matter how much she wanted to turn around and watch him leave. Her throat tightened, and she felt the pressure of tears building behind her eyelids.

She would not let them fall. She'd promised herself she'd never cry again over the hurtful words of cruel men—and women too. Aye, her mother and siblings had been experts at saying hurtful things.

But this was different. *This* was about Ewan.

God almighty, Lewis. What have you done?

The panic she'd been trying to hold at bay rose without warning and threatened to strangle her. With a desperate sob, she darted to the back of the weaver's tent and slipped out an opening, then ran through the crowd. She passed pens of goats and pigs, a tanner's stall filled with sheets of leather, and a tinker's cart covered in metal pots and pans. At any minute, she expected a hand to land on her shoulder and wrench her back, a harsh voice demand she tell him where to find Ewan. Her heart pounded in her chest, and her breath sawed through her lungs—not from exertion, but from fear.

She couldn't do it. Ewan was *her* son. Maybe her husband had lied to her, maybe Ewan was not his, but all children deserved a happy home with a loving parent—and that's what she provided. Ewan was worthy of every happiness she could bestow upon him. Not a cruel father who would beat him down.

She would break the chain of abuse she'd been subject to. She would teach her son to hold his head high and know he was worth everything.

When she reached the outskirts of the gathering, she wove her way through several campsites before spotting her own. Harold, the guard who protected the camp, appeared to be sleeping, and she yelled at him as she ran past. "Bring the wagon around, Harold! We're leaving!"

His eyes popped open, and he staggered in alarm. Harold couldn't protect her from a fly that had drunk its way out of a mug of ale. It was a joke she even had a guard. She might be the wife of Laird MacIntyre's only son, but her husband stayed as far from his father as he could—and sometimes, she thought, as far away from her as he could. No one paid any attention to Deirdre or Lewis in their small keep on the edge of MacIntyre land.

Which suited both of them just fine.

Harold hurried after her as she darted into her tent. She didn't wait for Magda to appear and help her pack. She opened her wooden chest with the shell inlay on the top instead and began throwing clothes inside after just a cursory folding.

"My lady, we canna leave yet. Your husband isna back," Harold said, his eyes wide and concerned.

She could understand his confusion. Deirdre had never been one to raise a fuss or make important decisions unless pressed. Nor did she ever raise her voice or dart around in a panic like a bee had flown under her skirts.

Nay, she didn't like the attention any of that brought—especially if she made a mistake. Although the last two years with Ewan had taught her a lot about standing her ground. When it came to her son's well-being, she'd found she could become a lion in the blink of an eye. She'd even gone against the nursemaid's wishes when it came to how much affection she showered on him. And almost every night, Deirdre allowed him to crawl into bed with her after everyone had fallen asleep.

Deirdre didn't mind. She liked pulling him close for a cuddle. And it wasn't as though Lewis ever appeared to stake his claim to her bed.

Her mouth tightened, and she stopped to stare directly at Harold, fighting that innate need to drop her eyes. "Then why doona you tell me where he is, and I'll go tell him we're leaving? I'm sure he willna mind me showing up and disturbing…whate'er it is he does when he's away from me."

Color washed up Harold's cheeks, and he was the one to drop his eyes. She felt a moment of triumph but also relief that her insolence hadn't been punished. For Ewan's safety, she would face all the fears her family had instilled in her.

"That willna be necessary. Did something happen at the gathering to frighten you?"

This time she dropped her eyes. And closed them for an instant. Aye, something had happened. Her whole world had been pushed to the brink—and she was facing a great chasm filled with heartbreak and despair.

"'Tis naught to worry you, Harold. I just wish to leave. My husband can follow on his own when he's…done."

She turned away and moved to the makeshift bed in the corner, which was covered by a soft, wool blanket in the familiar colors of her old clan—the only thing she had left from her time as a MacColl. She'd become a MacIntyre at just fifteen years old, sent to marry a man she'd never met, with only her nursemaid and lady's maid as company. Deirdre'd loved both women dearly, but they'd left her now—her nursemaid to the grave nearly five years ago, and Arline, her maid, to marry a lowlander she'd met at another gathering last summer. Deirdre had attended the wedding with Ewan, and she'd wished Arline the very best.

She knew better than most that marriages—and families—were not always what they seemed.

A wooden toy horse sat on her pillow, given to her by Ewan when she'd left to make sure she wouldn't get lonely. She picked it up and squeezed it tight. Thank goodness she'd be able to return it to him soon.

Finally, a tear did slip through. She wiped it away and breathed deeply to restore her equilibrium. She'd heard of the MacKinnon clan and Gavin MacKinnon. Everyone had. He was one of five lads fostered by the great Gregor MacLeod. The fostering had intended to bring the five boys together to become brothers and allies and bring peace to the Highlands. Although the last thing Gavin had made her feel today was peaceful.

She was probably overreacting. She had no idea if Laird MacKinnon was Ewan's father or not. Aye, they looked alike, which indicated some shared ancestry, but she knew that Gavin had a sister. Maybe she'd birthed Ewan out of wedlock, or one of Gavin's cousins had done so. It wasn't unheard of for a laird's daughter or niece to carry a bastard.

Still, she couldn't imagine her quiet, unassuming husband as one to inspire Gavin's sister, Isobel, a renowned beauty, to invite him into her bed without the benefit of marriage. Or imagine him even going to her bed at all. Deirdre *did* have the benefit of marriage, and he still wouldn't come.

"My lady?"

Deirdre turned to see her maid, Magda, standing at the tent's entrance, looking worried. She dredged up a reassuring smile. "Naught has happened. I just wish to return home. I doona know why my husband insisted I come when he wouldnae be here himself. The gathering is smaller than I imagined, and I confess I feel a wee bit under the weather. I'll help you to pack so we can be home in time to put Ewan to bed—if not tonight, then tomorrow night."

Magda curtsied and smiled. "I thought it might be so. I'll finish up in here, and Harold has brought the cart around. He's laid out the pillows and blankets for you, so you can have a rest as you travel. We'll leave Jordy behind to wait for your husband."

Deirdre dipped her head. "Aye, thank you. I think I will go and crawl under the blankets." And hide her head like the little mouse she was, so Gavin MacKinnon wouldn't see her leaving.

She couldn't help darting across the campsite to the wagon instead of walking calmly, looking over her shoulder as she climbed on board. Despite the swaying of the wagon and the warm spring sunshine, she knew she wouldn't sleep on the way home. Nay, she wouldn't be able to sleep until they were over her drawbridge, the portcullis locked, and her bedchamber barred with her child on the inside.

She doubted she'd sleep soundly again until she knew Gavin MacKinnon wasn't ever coming for her son.

Gavin raised one disbelieving brow at the tanner trying to sell him a so-called cow's hide that certainly was not from a cow. He ran his fingers over the leather. Aye, definitely a goat. "I didn't know you were a magician. 'Tis an amazing feat you've accomplished, turning one animal into another. Can you turn water into wine too? Verily, you'll be most welcome at my table if you can do that."

The tips of the tanner's ears turned red, but other than that, he hid his emotions well. "You're mistaken, sir. 'Tis a new breed of cow from the continent. A smaller beast with a tough hide and tanned in the Roman way. A favorite of the Italian women."

Gavin just resisted rolling his eyes. Did he look like a man who could be persuaded by the whims of women? As a young man, aye, but certainly not since his terrible marriage.

He reached behind his shoulder, slowly pulled his giant blade from its scabbard, and cradled it in his arms. The weight was nothing for a man of his strength and size, and he no more felt the strain of it than a woman lifting a brush to her hair.

An image filled his head at the slightest prompt… silky strands sliding through the bristles, soft, blue-gray eyes watching him, full breasts pressing against a linen shift.

He stilled at the direction his thoughts had taken, at the scene he'd envisioned as clearly as the loch on a bright summer's day. The same scene he'd dreamed about last night, causing him to wake up hard and wanting.

He'd been thinking of Deirdre MacIntyre. Again.

"God's blood," he cursed, loud and hard. The tanner blanched and pulled a tough cowhide from beneath the table. But it was too late. Gavin was no longer interested. He re-sheathed his sword and turned away with a scowl—something he'd been doing constantly, ever since he'd noticed Lady MacIntyre crossing the market yesterday morning. He'd stopped to watch her, not so much because of her beauty, although that was considerable—fair skin, dark hair, lush, red lips—but because she looked so…vulnerable. And when she'd glanced up and he'd seen those soulful eyes… Her expression had hinted at an uncertainty that made his heart squeeze. He'd wanted to tuck her into the crook of his arm and fight off all her enemies, especially those who'd made her doubt herself.

And more basic than that, he'd wanted to lose himself in her body—bring those rounded breasts to his mouth and suckle them as he tupped her.

Which really was utter shite. That woman was hiding something, and Gavin was a right bastard who didn't want anything from a lass—not even a hot mouth or a busy hand—not anymore, at least. And she didn't have to be beautiful. His wife, Cristel, had been beautiful, and she'd ruined his life. Ewan's too.

She'd taken his almost two-year-old son to the fall festival two years ago—against Gavin's express orders—and she'd lost him. If she hadn't died from the plague, Gavin would have thrown her into his dungeon.

He'd spoken to her maid, the only surviving member of her attendants, who said Cristel had wanted to show Ewan off to some other high-born lasses and wouldn't let the boy's nursemaid accompany them. He'd been missing for hours before she'd told anyone.

They'd looked for him, but by then, people—including Cristel—had started falling ill. Gavin had searched the burned remains of the dead bodies afterward, ankle-deep in ash. Thankfully, he hadn't seen any signs of a child.

So he'd offered a substantial reward and run down

leads for over a year before those had dried up. He'd sent men to every corner of Scotland, looking for a boy with his blond hair and blue-green eyes. He'd even had an artist paint Ewan's likeness and distributed the pictures across the land.

Reports had come in about sightings from as far away as the Orkney Islands.

Gavin was here now because of one such report. He was to meet the woman at the festival this afternoon. For a moment yesterday, when Deirdre MacIntyre had stared at him for so long and so hard, he'd thought perhaps she was the informant he was supposed to meet—the one to give him back his son.

He'd felt a flare of hope as she'd studied his face, but at her denials, that crushing blackness had swamped him once again. He'd been short with her. And crude. He shouldn't have said the things he'd said, but he didn't have the self-control and decorum he once had. Anger and worry, along with years of barely sleeping, had eroded his courtesy and goodwill.

He was trapped in a nightmare, and he couldn't get out.

Ewan had to be alive. Gavin refused to believe otherwise.

"And to think, the lasses used to swarm to see your smiling face."

Gavin turned his head in the direction of the speaker, whose tone had been so deep and blunt. He realized he was still scowling—seemingly his permanent expression now—and grunted in acknowledgement. "They may have flocked to me at one time, but they run from *your* frightening face always."

Kerr MacAlister, Laird of Clan MacAlister, grinned, holding the reins of his huge black stallion in one hand. With the other, he pulled Gavin into a bear hug—an animal Gavin swore his foster brother just might be related to. As big as Gavin was, Kerr was even bigger, with eyes and hair as dark as Gavin's were fair. The long, thick strands of that dark hair had been secured in a leather thong at his nape and fell past his massive shoulders.

The bleakness began to lift as hope and lightness filled Gavin's soul once more—as light as he could be not knowing if his son was hurt or scared or dying.

"'Tis good to see you, Brother," he said roughly.

"Aye. It's been a long winter not having your bonnie face across the table from me or hearing your sister's agreeable, dulcet tones."

Gavin barked out a laugh. Calling Gavin sweet and Isobel agreeable was like calling their foster father, Gregor, dull-witted.

"She missed you too," he said, "although she would ne'er admit it. 'Tis high time you find a way to convince her to marry you. I desire cousins for Ewan to play with when we finally get him back."

"You'll get him back long before then," Kerr said, "And I hear from Darach that cousins are already on their way. Caitlin is with bairn."

A smile cracked Gavin's face, and he felt more optimistic than he had since he'd said goodbye to his foster family last fall. "What a blessing for them and for all of us! Knowing Caitlin, she'll give Darach a daughter. Several daughters. Every one of them as fair and sweet as she, and just as much trouble."

Kerr laughed. "I can hardly wait. Best we find Ewan soon, so he can start training to keep them safe."

The breath caught in Gavin's throat, and he had to remind himself to breathe—slow and deep. Still, his voice rasped with emotion when he spoke. "Aye, best we find him soon."

Kerr clapped him on the shoulder, and they began walking toward Gavin's small campsite. Glancing back, Gavin looked for Kerr's men. "You're alone then?" he asked when he couldn't spot anyone.

"Nay, I have Sorley and Greer with me. I sent them on ahead—told them to look for the campsite in the best defensive position."

Gavin laughed. "Aye, Gregor taught us well."

"You said in your letter you were meeting someone here with news of Ewan. Has that changed?" Kerr asked.

"Nay. She should arrive sometime today. She told my man, Lorne, that she saw a young lad fitting Ewan's description at a recent wedding, but she was nervous and wouldn't say any more." His teeth ground together as he thought about the next part of her letter. "She said it was too dangerous."

Kerr's brows rose. "In what way?"

"I doona know, but Lorne's stuck near her, just in case. He didn't want her to get scared and run. Or be put in a grave before she could pass on the information."

"And he couldn't entice her?"

"I'm sure he tried. Yesterday, I thought maybe..." Gavin trailed off and scratched his hand through the scruff on his jaw, surprised by his reluctance to tell Kerr about Deirdre.

"Maybe what?" Kerr prompted.

"Do you know Lewis MacIntyre? Son of Laird MacIntyre?"

"I met him a few times when we were younger. He's quiet but not disagreeable. A better man than his da, that's for sure. His father and *my* father were friends—if you could call it that—before I killed him."

Gavin knew Kerr referred to his own father. Laird MacAlister had been a degenerate man, and when Kerr was just seventeen, he had killed him. To save his own life, yes, but also to stop the abuse of men, women, and children at Clan MacAlister—and anywhere else his father could find them.

Gregor MacLeod, Kerr and Gavin's foster father, had known that someday MacAlister would make an attempt on his son's life. Gregor had trained Kerr hard to prepare him—even harder than he'd trained the other lads—so Kerr would survive. Each year at harvest time, when the lads returned to their own homes, they'd said goodbye to Kerr with heavy hearts, not knowing if that would be the year he wouldn't return.

"I met his wife, Deirdre, yesterday. She was… watching me," Gavin said.

Kerr raised his brow and gave him a look. "How exactly was she watching you?"

"Not like that. Although…"

"Although…what?"

Gavin shrugged. He took a moment to control his heart rate as he dodged a cart in the crowded market. "'Tis nothing. She's married. I was just going to say she's a lovely lass, but she seems a wee bit broken. And I wondered if Lewis might be the cause."

"I ne'er sensed that in him. His father, for sure, but not him." Kerr furrowed his brow, and Gavin could see he was trying to remember something. "Now that you mention her, I think Deirdre's great-grandmother may have been a MacAlister. That would make Deirdre my cousin. Many times removed, of course."

"Truly? Her hair is dark like yours, but she's fair skinned with light eyes—a gray-blue color with a dark-gray rim. And her lips are red, like the inner petals of a young rose."

Kerr stopped in the middle of the crowd and stared at him, his brow raised high and his eyes wide. Gavin could practically see the gears turning in his head, and heat washed up his cheeks. "'Tis not what you're thinking."

"Inner petals? Young rose? I've been pining after Isobel for five years, and I've ne'er once compared her to a flower."

"Maybe that's your problem. There's no romance in your soul."

"And there is in yours?"

Gavin grinned suddenly. "Apparently."

Kerr shook his head and resumed walking. "Did you romance her, then? Married or not, you obviously wanted to."

Shame flooded Gavin, and he scrubbed his fingers through his beard again. "Nay, I was rude to her. I may have used the word 'swiving.' And 'tupping' too."

"Why? What did she do?"

"She'd been watching me from a distance and then staring at me like she recognized me. I thought perhaps she knew something about Ewan. And I was already thrown because of…"

"Her petal lips?"

Gavin sighed. "I'll ne'er live that down, will I?"

"Nay."

"And you'll tell Darach, Lachlan, and Callum, no doubt."

"Of course. And Gregor too."

"God's blood," he muttered just loud enough for Kerr to hear. "'Tis no wonder Cain murdered Abel, if his brother was as annoying as you." Out of the corner of his eye, he saw Kerr smile. "I was thrown because it's been a long time since I've been so drawn to a woman, and I doona mean just physically. But at the same time, her behavior made no sense. I'd swear on my life, on *Ewan*'s life, that she knows something about his disappearance."

"Then we'll speak to her immediately. I doona need to drop off my bags at your camp. Where is her tent located?"

"I didn't ask. I was afraid I'd become the one watching *her* from a distance. After my talk of tupping, she would have felt unsafe."

"She would have felt unsafe anyway. Have you looked in Isobel's mirror lately? You're a prosperous laird, for Christ's sake. Have someone else trim your hair and whiskers."

Gavin shoved his hands through the short, choppy strands and then scratched over his jaw and under his chin. It felt good. There had been a time—before Ewan was taken—that he ne'er would have had whiskers if he could help it. Now the most upkeep he did was taking a sharp knife to it every few weeks or so. He didn't want to look like the Gavin of old. He wanted to stay rough and raw until he got his son back.

And maybe that was what had bothered him so much about Lady MacIntyre. She tempted him to want warm and soft things again.

"Laird MacKinnon."

Gavin looked over and saw Lorne, a man slightly younger than him with a bulbous nose and heavy brow—which hid a quick mind, no matter what some might think. He also had a fair and loyal heart. Gavin quickly stepped forward, and they clasped forearms in the way of warriors.

"Well met, Lorne. 'Tis good to see you."

"And you, Laird."

Glancing behind Lorne, he saw a no-nonsense-looking woman in her middle years, standing with her arms crossed at her waist. Hope rose in his chest. She didn't look like the type of woman to come forward just for the reward. She would want to do right by his son.

"I'll have my money before I say a word," she said when she saw Gavin watching her. He barely held back a surprised laugh. So much for his keen sense of observation.

"I canna give you the money until I verify your information," he said.

She looked around the market with suspicious eyes, and both Gavin and Kerr did the same, moving automatically into better fighting positions lest they be attacked.

"Would you prefer somewhere more private?" Gavin asked.

"Aye, over by that tree." She pointed to a tall Scots pine near the edge of the market.

Gavin met Kerr's eyes. Was it an ambush? "Nay, come have a meal with us at our camp. It's the least I can do after your long journey."

The woman nodded curtly. Gavin took the lead while Kerr brought up the rear of their group. Nothing seemed out of the ordinary, but he didn't want to take any chances. After arriving at camp and settling the woman on one of the logs around the fire with a hot bowl of cooked oats, Gavin sat down beside her. He couldn't wait any longer. He braced himself for disappointment, knowing that the chances this woman knew anything were slim. Nevertheless, he couldn't stop the hope and eagerness that bloomed in his chest. It reminded him of how he'd felt when he'd spoken to Deirdre in the tent yesterday. Right before she'd said she didn't know anything.

No matter. If this woman's information was good, he ne'er had to think about Deirdre MacIntyre again.

"Can you tell me now?" he asked. "Where have you seen my son?"

"At a wedding I attended last summer. The lad you search for was there with his mother."

"His mother is dead."

"That may be, but the young laddie called her Mama, and she called him Ewan. She certainly watched over him like a mother hen. He's the spitting image of you. Are you sure you didn't get the lass pregnant and not know it? I've heard rumors that her husband is rarely in their bed."

"In whose bed?" Gavin asked, his impatience and frustration making his voice sharp.

"Lewis MacIntyre's, son and heir of Laird MacIntyre. 'Tis Lewis's wife, Deirdre, that you seek.

"I swear on my grave that Deirdre MacIntyre has your son."

Two

Gavin rode Thor, his huge gray stallion, across the hard-packed trail as fast as he could, despite the late hour and only moonlight for guidance. Kerr rode alongside him with five of their men—three MacKinnons and two MacAlisters—trailing behind them on their horses. The moon was full and the night sky clear, but it still didn't brighten their trail enough to show all the ridges, holes, and debris on the road. Especially at the speed he'd set.

And not a single one of the men had protested.

They'd wasted time earlier looking for Deirdre's campsite before learning that she'd packed up yesterday. The woman had headed home shortly after she'd spoken to Gavin.

After she knew Ewan was my son!

She'd looked him in the eye, seen the resemblance—the spitting image of Ewan in his face—and run as fast as a thieving fox back to her keep. He might never have known his child was within a day's ride if the other woman hadn't come forward.

Fury swelled within him again, turning his anger as hot as the blacksmith's forge. The MacIntyres and MacKinnons were now at war, and if any harm had come to his son, whoever was responsible would pay with a sword in their belly.

Deirdre's husband and father-in-law couldn't save her now. Nor could her brother, Boyd.

"Gavin!" Kerr yelled at him, his cry barely discernible over the pounding of the horses' hooves.

Gavin heard his foster brother but kept moving. He knew what Kerr was going to say, and he didn't want to hear it. The big bear of a man lunged forward and grabbed Gavin's reins, slowing his horse. The others skidded to a halt behind them.

Gavin rounded on him, his blood hot, his face tight with anger. "Imagine if Isobel were in that castle! Would you be stopping right now?"

"If it were Isobel, then I hope you'd be riding with me, urging me to be cautious, so we didn't ruin our chances of saving her."

"That woman has had Ewan for two and a half years. She will not have him for one more minute!"

"That woman is my cousin, and she may well be innocent. We will let her explain herself before we do anything that canna be undone!"

"I doona need her explanations! She saw me, she knew who I was, and she ran. She. Is. Not. Innocent! You're either on my side in this or you're against me…Brother."

"Shut it, ye wee *ablach*! Of course I'm on your side. But for the sake of your son, for *my* nephew, we will go in with a plan, and we will go in carefully! Do

I need to bloody well fight you on this? Getting us caught or killed will not save Ewan!"

They were leaning toward each other across their saddles, almost nose to nose. A red haze of anger clouded Gavin's vision, and he almost smashed his fist into Kerr's face.

And Kerr would smash his fist right back, that was for certain. It wouldn't be the first time. Or the last, most likely. And where would that get them? Rolling around in the dirt while Ewan stayed trapped in the MacIntyre keep.

Gavin ground his teeth together, then looked to the rear of the group and locked eyes with Clyde, his second-in-command. Clyde was a short, stocky man with the strength of Goliath and hands the size of dinner trenchers. For a moment, Gavin couldn't decide whether to ask Clyde for his opinion or order him to kick Kerr in the arse.

Not that Kerr wouldn't have kicked the man's arse right back.

Clyde moved to the front of the group to stand his horse beside Gavin's. "Laird?" he asked, his voice gruff.

"What do you know about the MacIntyre's southern keep? I've ne'er been there before. It didn't sound like Deirdre MacIntyre had a large guard with her. Maybe the keep isn't part of their line of defense."

"I know that it's the oldest of the keeps. The castle is small, built on a parapet with a moat dug around it. That moat will be filled with the spring runoff now. From what I've heard, Lewis is not in his father's good graces. The laird has married several times since Lewis's mother died, trying for another son. He's been blessed with one daughter since." Clyde had eight children, all girls on whom he doted, and it offended him when anyone suggested, by word or by deed, that a daughter was less valuable than a son.

He pointed toward a mountain in the distance. "The castle is not far, maybe another hour, and we'll need to breach it without alerting them to our presence. The hill and the moat will make that more difficult. I agree with Laird MacAlister that we should take care."

"And we doona know how many men are in the castle," Kerr said. "You need to clear your head and your heart, Gavin. Think strategically. We haven't alerted Gregor or the lads to our plan. If we're caught, not only will we lose our chance to get Ewan back, but our allies willna be riding to our rescue."

Gavin pressed the heel of his hand into his forehead. He was so close to Ewan he could almost feel the warmth and weight of him in his arms, the tiny puffs of air against his neck as his son slept on his shoulder.

The lad would be different now—over two years older. Two years that Gavin would never get back. He rolled his head and tried to loosen the tension from his shoulders.

"We'll ride until we spot the castle. Then we'll plan. I need to see the keep and know that someone isn't leaving with my boy."

Deirdre woke with a start. Her heart racing, her eyes wide as she listened for whatever had woken her. The fire in her bedchamber had burned down to barely glowing embers, leaving the air cool and the room dark, but she was warm under the covers. Ewan slept soundly in her arms, and he put off enough heat to warm their small keep.

She'd just started to think it had only been another nightmare that had woken her—all of them about Gavin MacKinnon coming to steal her son—when she heard a loud crash outside her window in the bailey. The noise was followed by a man's yell, abruptly cut off.

Untangling herself from her son, she slipped quickly out of bed and darted across the bare, cold floor to the window. She yanked on the shutters to get them unstuck—just one of many ways the keep was falling apart around them—and wedged her shoulders through the small opening to see what was happening. The air outside was brisk. Usually one torch was left burning in the bailey below, but tonight the light was doused. The moon was out, but without that extra light, Deirdre had a hard time distinguishing shapes.

There! She peered into the night at the shadow she was sure had moved. Was that a man? Or a rain barrel? An owl hooted. Seconds later, another returned its call. She heard what sounded like a grunt—but that could have been anything, including the horses.

And then she saw it, the flash of metal in the dark. God help her—Gavin MacKinnon was coming for her son!

Panic engulfed her, and she raced back to her bed, the air rasping through her lungs. She felt for her plaid, found it, and then threw the length around her linen shift. Leaning over Ewan, she gently lifted him into her arms. Soft, whispered words formed on her lips, and he snuggled closer, still asleep. His head rested on her shoulder, and he wrapped warm arms around her neck.

She'd left her shoes by the chair and started across the floor for them. But then remembered Ewan had been playing with them. She'd never find them in the dark!

She couldn't outrun the devil anyway. She had to find a place for them to hide.

"Gavin, wait!" a man yelled outside, just as the door to the great hall banged shut one level down from her. She jumped with a fearful squeak, her eyes filling with frightened tears. Stretching out her free arm, she rushed for her bedchamber door, not stopping until her palm hit the smooth surface. With one hand, she dragged the bar back, cringing as it scraped noisily through the metal loops.

"Ewan!" A voice cried out from inside her home. His call echoed hauntingly in the dark, empty keep. But this was no ghost. She knew who it was: Laird Gavin MacKinnon.

She wrenched open the door and ran in the opposite direction, toward a circular staircase at the end of the hall. It led upward to another level of bedchambers, the laird's solar, and the nursery. When she reached the first step, she looked back. Light from a flickering torch shone on the wall, growing bigger as the torchbearer neared the top of the staircase.

Swallowing her sobs, she climbed to the uppermost level, dragging her fingertips along the stone to orient herself as she raced forward. But to where? Where could she hide that Gavin MacKinnon wouldn't find her?

"Ewan! I'm coming for you, Son!" The disembodied voice thundered and threatened from behind her.

Deirdre wanted to wail, terror thick in her throat. He would take her child and then what? Would he hurt him? Neglect him? Change him into an unloving man who didn't remember her?

God help her. They needed somewhere to hide!

"Gavin, slow down! Where are you?" another male voice cried out.

"She's not in her bedchamber," Gavin yelled back, his voice echoing. "The bed is still warm. I'm going up to the third level! Ewan! Where are you, lad?"

Deirdre stumbled in the dark and almost dropped her son. He woke with a confused whimper. "Mama?"

"Hush, baby. I have you. You must be quiet." She entered the nursery just as the light from the torch grew brighter again behind her. Heavy footsteps pounded up the stairs. Her arms shook so badly she could barely hold on to Ewan anymore, and he began to slide down.

"Mama? It's too dark! Lift me up."

"Ewan?" Gavin yelled. Feet pounded down the hallway toward them. A second set followed behind the first.

She hauled Ewan into her arms and raced blindly forward, but she stepped on something hard in her bare feet and yelped.

"Mama!"

"It's all right." She'd intended to soothe him, but she'd whimpered as she said it. She could hear the heartbreak in her voice, feel the sharp pain of it in her chest. Fear weakened her, sickened her. How could she protect him?

The door crashed open behind her, hitting the

stone wall. She crouched down and pulled the wool blanket from her shoulders, covered her son, then rose to face the fury of his father. If Gavin was going to run his blade through her breast, soak her white linen shift with her blood, she did not want her beloved child to see it.

Gavin raged forward, his huge sword held out in one hand, the flaring, smoking torch in the other. The room came into view, the long, dancing shadows turning the nursery she'd lovingly decorated for Ewan into a house of horrors.

Which was fitting, seeing as she was about to die in it. His lips pulled back in a tormented grimace, his eyes as they landed on her wide and feral. She had no doubt her death would be violent and bloody.

"Where's my son?" he roared.

She couldn't speak. All she could do was shake her head and pray Ewan stayed hidden under the blanket behind her.

Gavin swept the torch in a circle, scanning the room. When he didn't see Ewan, he advanced on her, every step a drumbeat marching her closer to death. She swayed as her knees buckled, and she grasped the back of a chair with one hand for support.

She'd been a mouse most of her life. But now she would stay standing as she defended her son. Be the lion she'd always wished to be.

He swung the torch close to her, and the heat washed over her face. She gasped in pain and horror. Would he burn her instead? What if the blanket behind her caught fire and Ewan was killed?

"No, please!" she cried.

"Gavin, step away from her!" a voice roared from the doorway.

The MacKinnon laird didn't move, just stared at her with death in his eyes, his jaw as tight as a vise and his eyes filled with hatred.

No, more than that…filled with pain.

At losing his son?

"You have him," he croaked, his lips barely moving. "Please," he continued. "Tell me where he is."

His tone scraped at her heart. Her soul. The desperation in his voice shredded her.

But then a small, warm hand grasped her ankle from behind, giving her courage. *My sweet boy,* she prayed, *please stay hidden.*

"I doona have him," she said.

"I heard him."

"Maybe 'twas me you heard. I was frightened. My voice squeaked."

The other man now stood behind Gavin, two massive warriors, armed and deadly, staring down at her. The other man was dark like her, his long hair tied behind his shoulders.

She tilted her chin up, forced herself to meet their gazes. She couldn't help but notice Gavin's identical eye color to Ewan's, but the shine of love and laughter was missing.

"Give me the torch, Brother," the other warrior said as he grasped the long handle. "And put away your sword. This is no way to find your son."

Her lips parted on a silent sob. "*My* son," she whispered bleakly, pain roiling through her. Ewan would never again sleep in her arms, never come running to tell her about his latest adventure, never sit quietly with her after dinner and ask her all his questions. She almost collapsed, the ache in her body was so intense.

But Gavin MacKinnon stepped forward, the rage rolling off him in waves. He grabbed her upper arm with one hand and raised his sword with the other. "You have one chance to live, Deirdre MacIntyre. One chance to tell me. Where. Is. My. Son?"

The hand on her ankle rose higher, and then a small, soft body leaned against her leg from behind. Ewan wrapped his arms around her thigh and pressed his head against her waist. Her hand dropped automatically, and she smoothed loving fingers over his silky hair.

The dark man behind Gavin inhaled sharply and dragged down his brother's sword arm. Softly, he said, "Gavin, look."

Gavin MacKinnon dropped his gaze slowly, his pulse pounding in his throat. When his eyes finally fell on her son, his whole face changed, almost as if the tiny muscles that controlled his expression crumpled. His mouth jerked down at the corners, and his chin trembled. His brow furrowed inward as his eyes scrunched and watered over. When he blinked, tears ran down the hard planes of his cheeks.

He blew out a trembling breath, then crouched down and stretched out a shaky hand to Ewan. "Hello, laddie," he rasped. "I've missed you, Son."

Ewan glanced at Gavin's hand, and then at his father. A frown transformed his sweet face, and he looked even more like the hulking man before him. Suddenly, he stepped in front of Deirdre and pushed

Gavin's hand away. "You're a mean man. Stay away from my mother!"

Gavin stared at his son, feeling like his heart might burst from his chest even as it broke into tiny pieces. His son, who used to toddle to Gavin whenever he saw him, raise his arms to be picked up and swung high into the air, had called him mean. Instead of laughter and adoration, Ewan was angry with him for hurting his…his…

Gah! He would not acknowledge that woman as his son's mother.

Gavin reached out again, wanting to pull his wee lad into his embrace, needing to feel the weight and warmth of his body in his arms. But Ewan pressed back against Deirdre, his face turning fearful. She crossed her hands over his chest and pulled him tighter against her legs.

A spurt of anger surged through Gavin. She'd done this. She'd run away from him, tried to hide Ewan from him. He would never have put his sword to her throat or pushed the torch close to her if he'd known Ewan was there. His son might have been hurt. Or traumatized. He *was* traumatized.

She'd ruined their relationship before they could even get reacquainted.

But the terror on Deirdre's face, especially when he'd pushed the torch close, pricked at his conscience. Kerr held the torch now, almost as if he didn't trust Gavin with it. Gavin didn't blame him. He could control his sword, but fire was unpredictable, and he could have set her long locks on fire. What would have happened to Ewan then, hiding under the blanket behind her?

I could have lost him all over again.

He scrubbed his fingers through his short, bristly hair before making a fist and tugging on the strands. They were too short to get a good grip, which was why he'd chopped his hair off in the first place. Maybe he'd grow it back now that Ewan was no longer missing.

He stilled as the words reverberated in his head. *Not* missing.

He covered his mouth to hide the emotional joy and relief that coursed through him, overwhelmed him. *Thank the angels he's here with me now!*

His son wore a light linen shift that came halfway down his thighs. It was similar to Deirdre's, except hers touched the floor—one reason neither Gavin nor Kerr had seen him. Gavin looked the boy over for signs of injury or neglect, but the lad appeared healthy and well treated. He was taller, leaner, stronger than before, and his hair was shorter and thicker. Those baby-soft curls Gavin had wrapped around his fingers and kissed were gone.

But it wasn't just how he looked that shocked Gavin; it was the words he'd spoken. When he'd been taken, he'd barely started to talk. Gavin had been worried the boy's speech was delayed, but the nursemaid had assured him Ewan would speak in his own time.

She'd been right.

The words he'd said had cut Gavin, but he'd still marveled at the precise way his child talked. In the time he'd been missing, his bairn had become a wee lad.

That ever-present anger surged again. Years he'd never get back! Everything he'd missed!

"How long have you had him?" he asked coldly, without looking at Deirdre.

Her hands clenched the front of Ewan's shift. "I... What do you mean?" Her voice shook, and he could hear the lie in it.

"When did you first meet my son?"

"When I gave birth to him, of course. And I think you've mistaken him..." She trailed off when Gavin raised his gaze to hers. He didn't say the word. He didn't need to.

Liar.

He looked back down at his son. Smiled. "Do you remember coming here, Ewan? It would have been a long trip. Riding on a horse, or maybe you sat in a wagon?"

"Nay," the lad answered, looking confused. "But I've been in the wagon for our picnics. Mama always puts lots of pillows down so it's soft. And next year I can start riding!" His voice picked up excitedly at the end.

"Sooner than that, Ewan. It is Ewan, isn't it?"

"Aye."

Gavin couldn't help glancing at Deirdre again, knowing his enmity raged in his eyes. "You doona have any other names, Ewan? Perhaps a second or third one?"

"People doona have so many names."

"Some do. And as sure as I'm looking at you right now, I know that you have three more names."

"I do?"

"Aye. Ewan Ailbeart Gregor MacKinnon."

The boy's brow furrowed in concentration, and he tried to repeat what Gavin had said. "Ewan Alban—"

"Ailbeart. Gregor. MacKinnon." Gavin helped him say it.

When he was done, Ewan asked Deirdre, "What about MacIntyre?"

Deirdre's lips trembled, but she smiled wanly at him. "'Tis something new to think about, Ewan. I doona know where MacIntyre will go now."

"For you too?" he asked.

Her smile slipped. "Aye, perhaps."

Ewan frowned suddenly and returned his gaze to Gavin. "I doona want more names if Mama doesn't get any."

A hand squeezed Gavin's shoulder—Kerr telling him to choose his words carefully. "Maybe your mother has other names too," he said. He certainly had a few choice ones for her.

When he saw Ewan was about to ask Deirdre what they were, he quickly distracted him. "Ewan, I know you said you had to wait a year before you started riding, but I was younger than you when I first learned. How would you like to ride on a horse with me right now?" He put excitement into his voice and watched his son's eyes light up.

But Deirdre gasped—a tormented sound—and Ewan looked at her. His excitement faded. "Can my ma come? She doesn't know how to ride either."

Gavin stilled. He hadn't considered what would happen after he found Ewan—never imagined that his son might not want to come with him. He glanced around the nursery in the torchlight. It looked old but was filled with enough wooden and stuffed toys to make any boy happy. And someone had taken the time to decorate the chamber with wall hangings to interest a child. In the corner sat a small table and two chairs.

It seemed Ewan was happy here. And he wouldn't want to leave without the woman he thought was his mother.

The last thing Gavin wanted to do was hurt his child. But was he willing to kidnap Deirdre the way Ewan had been kidnapped? Nay. It was not the same at all. No one knew where Ewan had been taken, whereas Gavin would make sure Deirdre's husband, laird, and father all knew he had her and that he wanted them to come take her back—with an army.

Aye, until he knew better, Clan MacKinnon and their allies were at war with Clan MacIntyre.

He looked over his shoulder at Kerr. He knew his brother would be thinking the same thing he was. Kerr nodded.

"Pack a few things for my son and yourself," Gavin said to Deirdre. He smiled again at Ewan and finally he touched him—a brief tousle of his hair. "Deirdre will be coming with us. We wouldnae want her to miss seeing you ride for the first time, would we? We're going to go back to my castle. We doona have a moat, but there's a huge loch where we can swim. And I can hardly wait for you to meet my sister, all my other brothers, and my foster father. He'll want you to call him Granda."

"Granda?"

"Aye. His name is Gregor MacLeod. He's the most powerful laird in all the Highlands and you are his first grandson."

"Oh. I can hardly wait to tell Old Mungo. He said he has twenty grandbairn, and if I wanted, I could call him granda too. I willna have to, if I have my own. But…"

"But what, Ewan?"

"If he's my granda, then who are you?"

Emotion welled in Gavin's chest again, and he had to swallow several times to loosen his throat before answering. Still, his voice rasped. "My name is Gavin Owen Ailbeart MacKinnon. I haven't seen you since you were almost two, lad, but I've thought about you every single day since then. You used to laugh when I tossed you in the air and pretended to drop you. And you'd always sit beside me when we supped."

He took a deep breath, gently grasped his son's hand, and looked him in his eyes. "Ewan, you may not remember me, but I'm your da."

Three

"Where are your shoes?"

Deirdre shifted her gaze to Gavin's as she hurried along the passageway to where he waited for her at the top of the stairs. She held a full leather satchel in one arm and Ewan in the other.

She'd packed and dressed them both in record time, remembering to grab Ewan's favorite toy horse from where he'd left it on her bed, but not much else. Everything was a blur. Her hair hung loose, as she hadn't had time to braid it, and she hadn't remembered to take a ribbon to tie it back, let alone a hairbrush.

Or, apparently, her shoes.

She glanced down at her bare toes poking out from beneath her arisaid. "Not on my feet."

He didn't smile, and she wanted to kick herself for speaking so inanely.

"I suggest you get them before we leave." His words were clipped, the tone neutral, as if he was trying to manage his ire. For Ewan's sake, no doubt. Certainly not hers.

He reached out suddenly, and she flinched. An

automatic response. His eyes widened at her reaction, but instead of his hand landing across her cheek, he lifted her son effortlessly into his arms, tight but not too tight, and stroked a hand up and down his back.

Ewan looked startled, but he also settled into Gavin like he'd never forgotten him. As if his body and heart remembered how it felt to be in his da's arms, even if his mind didn't.

When Gavin pressed a kiss to his head, a lump formed in Deirdre's throat. She didn't know what had happened or how Lewis had gotten Ewan, but she could see that Gavin had missed him.

She could also see how angry he was—at her. She may yet find herself at the end of his sword. Or thrown down a gulley during their ride to his castle.

"Deirdre."

"Aye?"

"Get. Your. Shoes. We'll wait for you."

She hesitated, afraid to let Ewan out of her sight for even one second. What if Gavin was lying, and he ran with her son once Deirdre was gone? *He doesn't need to lie to me to do that. Go!*

She sprinted back toward her room. Ewan cried out, and she heard Gavin calming him.

A torch burned in the sconce on the wall in her bedchamber, but she still squinted as she searched for her shoes. She finally found them on opposite sides of the bed where Ewan had been walking around in them. She grabbed one in each hand and was running out when she spotted her hairbrush and quickly snagged it too.

Gavin saw her coming and turned to go down to

the great hall before she got there, but Ewan let out another shriek, reaching for her. The MacKinnon laird stopped and waited until she was beside him, then wrapped his other hand firmly around her upper arm. Ewan stretched his hand across Gavin's shoulders and held tightly to a lock of Deirdre's hair. The strands tugged, and she winced, but she didn't pull away. She was glad her son wanted her close. Maybe Gavin MacKinnon would show her mercy for Ewan's sake.

They hurried down the stairs and across the open area toward the outside door. She felt immense relief to be going with them to Clan MacKinnon. If Ewan had been taken from her tonight, she didn't know how she would have survived. And he would have been devastated. She would stay by his side as long as possible—despite the fear for her own safety.

Maybe she could petition Gregor MacLeod to intervene in some way. Everyone said he was a good, just man. And she hadn't done anything wrong. All she'd done was love a boy she'd been told was her husband's son.

Gavin shouldered open the door, and the brisk morning air washed over her face, making her realize her cheeks were wet. She scrubbed the tears away with the back of her hand, not wanting to upset Ewan further.

The sun was just cresting the horizon, and not one cloud marked the brightening sky, promising a beautiful spring day. Once she was in the wagon, she would have time to think, to plan how she could win over Gregor MacLeod.

And maybe Gavin MacKinnon too.

If they kept her alive, she could stay at Clan MacKinnon for as long as Ewan needed her. Her husband wouldn't care. Truth be told, if no one told him, it might take him months to notice she was gone. When he was at home, Lewis MacIntyre was kind and respectful, and she enjoyed their games of chess, but their marriage wasn't a real marriage. Still, living with him was better than where she had grown up. For that, she was grateful.

And for Ewan too.

Gavin tugged her down the stairs to the bailey, where four men—including the big, dark-haired one named Kerr MacAlister—stood with the horses. In the distance, two men rode toward the raised portcullis and lowered drawbridge. How had they breached her home? She'd thought herself safe behind her walls, but obviously these warriors knew how to invade a castle—moat or not.

Not that her small, crumbling keep could be called a castle.

Kerr looked up at Gavin. "I've sent Sorley and Greer to Clan MacLean with the news that we've found Ewan—and who had him. Callum will send riders out, and the lads and Gregor will arrive with their forces in no time."

"Forces?" Deirdre squeaked. "We're a small household. We've barely any guards. The men and women here are farmers and crafters." Were her people going to suffer for her supposed sins as well?

"Nay, not here," Kerr said. "At Clan MacKinnon." Then he took her bag and shoes and proceeded to transfer her belongings into his saddlebags, which were already full. When he came across Ewan's toy, Kerr pranced it over to him, huffing and neighing like a horse.

Her son laughed, and Deirdre couldn't help smiling too—albeit a watery smile—her first since she'd hugged Ewan yesterday upon her arrival. But then Kerr pulled out her hairbrush from the bag. He tried several ways to fit it into his saddlebags. When it didn't work, he gave up and tossed the brush onto the steps. Her smile dropped.

"No room," he said. "You can use one of Isobel's combs when you get there."

She stared at her brush, wanting to reach for it. *A strong woman would pick it up and find a way to shove it in his saddlebags—or elsewhere.* But she didn't move.

"What did you say?" Gavin asked.

She glanced up at him, startled. "I said naught." Surely, she hadn't spoken aloud.

"Aye, you did. I heard something."

"Of course she did," Kerr said with a grin. "She's a MacAlister. We ne'er keep our emotions to ourselves."

Deirdre stared at the huge man. He had slanting eyebrows and the fierce eyes of a hawk, although the color was dark like a merlin. Surely, he was daft.

"Did you not know that your great-grandmother was a MacAlister?" he asked. "We're cousins, Deirdre. Several times removed, but still cousins."

"I've ne'er heard this. But I haven't seen my family in seven years, other than one visit from my brother. We did not talk about our ancestry. But if..." She trailed off, as she was prone to do. She'd learned as a girl it was safer to keep her impertinent thoughts to herself.

"If what?" Kerr asked, one eyebrow raising.

She shook her head and felt the heat sweep up her cheeks. She'd been about to say, *but if we had spoken about our relatives, we wouldnae have discussed the scoundrels and black sheep among them.*

How could she have been so addlepated? Men like Gavin MacKinnon and Kerr MacAlister did not want to hear her opinions.

Kerr rested his hand on the back of his horse, and Gavin turned to face her.

"Oh, come now," Kerr said. "You canna start like that and then just stop. There are rules."

"Rules?" she asked, her brow raising.

"Aye, rules of engagement, and I doona speak of war. What were you going to say? I'll let you pack your hairbrush if you tell me."

She looked at the brush, a keen yearning for it almost breaking her silence. But nothing was worth being left behind if by chance she offended him.

She dropped her eyes. "'Twas naught. I only meant to say that if we had spoken about our relationship to Clan MacAlister, it would have been with great respect and pleasure."

Gavin rolled his eyes as Kerr snorted.

"A bad liar too," Gavin said. "Also a trait of the MacAlisters."

It was a jest, but Deirdre could hear the edge to his words. Aye, Gavin was only half teasing, and he wasn't speaking of his foster brother.

Kerr laughed as he checked the straps of the saddlebags on his huge black stallion. She looked around for the wagon she and Ewan would ride in but didn't see one. Alarm grew in her as Gavin put an excited

Ewan on his stallion. He showed the lad how to pat the horse's neck and rub between his ears. "His name is Thor, after the Norse god of war. We're descended from the Vikings who invaded these lands hundreds of years ago."

"Where's the wagon?" she asked.

Gavin looked over his shoulder at her. "You'll ride with Kerr. Ewan stays with me."

His words echoed in her ears. *He's only a wee boy!* Concern made her heart pound and warred with her need to placate the warrior. "But…my son's ne'er ridden. He doesn't know how. He could get hurt."

"*My son!*" Gavin didn't raise the pitch or volume of his voice, but he spoke forcefully, and everyone, including Ewan, stopped what they were doing and looked at him. "Ewan will know how to ride soon enough, and he willna fall, because I'll have ahold of him."

"Well, what about when he's tired?" Deirdre asked, unable to let it go despite Gavin's glower. "And sore? Surely you canna mean to make a young boy ride for hours on end his first time?"

"When he's tired, we'll stop, or I'll hold him. The lad has more resilience than you think."

"Mama, I can do it. Thor is a bonnie horse."

The great, gray beast looked at her—a stallion trained for war—and she shivered.

Kerr mounted his black stallion and reached for her. "Come, Cousin. A wagon isna an option. 'Tis too slow. We need the speed and agility of horses."

"I'm to go behind you?" she asked.

"Aye. You'll hold on."

"But how—"

"'Tis now or never, Deirdre," Gavin said. She could hear his patience wearing thin.

She placed her hand tentatively in Kerr's, expecting him to lift her gently, but he yanked her up toward the horse. She yelped in shock, her arms and legs flying, and the stallion shifted its weight from side to side in alarm. Terror gripped her as old fears from her childhood surfaced.

She was on her belly across the beast's arse, and Kerr kept pulling on the arm she was trying to wrap around the stallion so she wouldn't fall off.

"Christ almighty! Hold on to me, not the bloody horse." Kerr pulled her upward again, and this time, she grabbed on to his waist as she began to fall over the other side. "Sit up, Deirdre. Swing your leg o'er his hindquarters."

"His tail is in the way. He'll kick," she wailed.

"Aye, if you knee him in the bloody arsehole, he will."

Finally, she got her leg over and wrapped her arms around Kerr's waist in a stranglehold. "Thank the bloody saints," he said as he urged the horse toward the portcullis, catching up with the others—Gavin and Ewan on Thor and three other men. Ewan watched them anxiously over Gavin's shoulder.

"You havenae any imagination," she said, speaking through gritted teeth as her bottom slid toward the back end of the horse with every step.

"What does that mean?"

"Everything you say is bloody this and bloody that! Canna you think of anything other than gore and carnage?"

"Nay. I like gore and carnage."

"Another trait of the bloody MacAlisters, no doubt."

"Aye, Cousin," Kerr laughed as they rode under the portcullis and over the rickety drawbridge. The horse picked up speed, racing for the field. "It's in our blood!"

A high-pitched yelp—followed by Kerr's cursing—reached Gavin's ears as they galloped across the open field from Deirdre's keep. He looked over his shoulder in time to see his foster brother rein in his stallion and try to catch Deirdre before she tumbled off the back of his horse. He failed miserably, and Deirdre hit the grass hard at an awkward angle, her ankle rolling beneath her.

Gavin covered Ewan's ears, then whistled to his men. The two in front, Clyde and Lorne, took up defensive positions. His third man, Sheamais, positioned himself in the rear. Gavin didn't think they were in any danger from Deirdre's household—not one of the men knew how to fight—but they were still within range of an archer.

"Mama!" Ewan yelled, and he squirmed so fast that Gavin lost hold of him. The lad tumbled over the side of the big horse. Gavin tried to grab him, but missed, and Ewan almost got stepped on. Before he could blink, the boy was up and running toward Deirdre.

When Gavin saw that Ewan was safely in her arms, he breathed a sigh of relief and then couldn't help grinning. "He's fearless," he said to Kerr.

Kerr grinned back. "Like a wee monkey."

Deirdre glared at them, obviously neither proud nor amused. She was as mad as a badger dug out from its den in the middle of the day. But he preferred her this way than when she dropped her eyes to the ground.

He wanted to fight with her.

Gavin dismounted, and after commanding his mount to wait, he strode toward Ewan and Deirdre.

"You said you'd hold him. You said he wouldnae fall," she yelled, eyes flashing. "He was almost stomped by your great beast of a horse!"

Gavin rubbed his hand across the back of his neck. On second thought, maybe a little meekness wouldn't be amiss. "He's fast. And slippery."

"He's a boy, not a fish." She pushed herself to her bare feet, holding tight onto Ewan and favoring one foot.

Gavin scowled. "I know that." He crouched on the ground and picked up the foot she'd twisted.

She tried to pull it away, but he slid his hand to her calf and held tight, trying to ignore how soft her skin was. And cold. Why the hell wasn't she wearing her shoes?

"What are you doing?" she asked, sounding a little breathless.

"Making sure it's not broken." He rotated her foot and then squeezed down to her toes. She moaned softly, and he looked up to see she'd pressed her lips together as if to hold in any further sound. "It'll heal," he pronounced, then yelled, "Kerr!"

"I'm right here," his foster brother said from behind him, sounding surprised. And no wonder. The first thing Gregor had taught them was always to be aware of their surroundings, including the positions of all the people.

He repressed an irritated sigh. "Can you bring her shoes?"

"Aye." Kerr's footsteps receded as he retreated to his horse.

"I can put them on myself," she said, trying to tug her foot away again.

"Apparently not, or you would have done so already."

"And when would that have been? When you were dragging me down the stairs? Or when—"

She stopped talking suddenly, and he jerked his chin up to see her lips were squeezed tight like before, but not from pain this time. Nay, she was desperately trying to swallow her words. And strangely enough, that irritated him too.

"You could have put them on in your bedchamber before you came out. I gave you my word we wouldnae leave without you, and I meant it. I will ne'er lie to you, Deirdre. You willna always like what I have to say, but 'twill always be truthful."

One of her shoes landed beside him on the grass, then the other, Kerr tossing them from his horse. He saw Deirdre's eyes flash as a clod of dirt flew up from the impact and hit Ewan's cheek. Ewan ignored it, which pleased Gavin. The lad would be taught to lead, and he couldn't do that without learning to fight—and getting hurt and dirty in the process. Gavin and his foster brothers were some of the best fighters in the Highlands. They hadn't achieved that level of skill by shying away from a little mud or pain.

He pushed her sore foot into the boot and tied it tightly in place to help reduce the swelling. She never made a sound, even though it must have hurt. "Keep that on for the next few days unless you're bathing. Cold water will be good for it."

When he rose, he lifted Ewan into his arms—the same position he'd always carried him in before. He loved how his son relaxed against his shoulder—unless Deirdre was out of sight or in distress. Then Ewan tensed and struggled to get down. Which could be a problem. Once his son was comfortable in his true home, Gavin intended to return Deirdre to her family. She wasn't in danger while she was with the MacKinnons, but she also wasn't an honored guest.

"I'll put her in front this time," Kerr said, bringing his big stallion over.

Something welled up within Gavin, resisting the notion of Kerr pressed up against Deirdre in the saddle, and he tensed. "Nay, she'll ride with me. Ewan willna settle otherwise. Besides, there's no room for her with that big arse of yours in the way."

Her lips moved in response, but the words she'd spoken were so soft he couldn't hear them. He wouldn't have even noticed, except he stood so close to her. Ewan was even closer, leaning toward her to grab her hair like he had before.

"You said something—just like at the keep," Gavin said, his tone almost accusatory. Deirdre's eyes widened before she dropped her gaze and shook her head.

Ewan laughed.

"You think my big arse is a jest?" Kerr asked, pretending to stomp toward the lad and sticking his arse out behind him.

God's blood, I forgot how much Kerr likes bairns.

Ewan laughed harder. "Aye. And then Mama said big arse, big head."

Color washed up Deirdre's cheeks. "Ewan, hush!"

But he didn't hush. "Big arse, big head! Big arse, big head! Big arse, big head!"

Kerr clapped his hands over his heart. "Cousin, you wound me!"

Gavin couldn't help the amused twitch of his lips. He rolled his eyes and whistled for his horse. Thor came over immediately, but by the time he could take the stallion's reins in hand, Gavin's unexpected urge to smile had faded. Things were complicated enough without Kerr taking a liking to Deirdre. Especially since they were distantly related. Kerr had killed many of his uncles and cousins after he became laird and the other MacAlister clans attacked him. He would be happy to find a decent, honorable relative—so long as that was what Deirdre was.

It was obvious she loved Ewan and had taken good care of him, but she had run away from Gavin two days ago, all the while knowing he was Ewan's father.

That, he couldn't forgive.

No matter what her story was or how she'd gotten Ewan, Deirdre was not staying.

He sat Ewan on Thor's back, close to the withers, so there was room behind for Gavin and Deirdre. "Hold on to the mane and squeeze with your legs," he told the lad.

Deirdre's eyes had widened and her face blanched, seeing her son up there.

"You're next," he told her. "And if you panic this time, you'll knock Ewan off. Control your breathing,

Deirdre, and you'll control your fear. If you control your fear, then you'll have control of your body. Do not flail about wildly, just swing your leg over Thor's back, grab the mane like Ewan is doing, and squeeze your legs around the stallion's flanks."

Kerr moved to Thor's other side, just in case, and Gavin bent over and linked his fingers together to make a stirrup. Deirdre put her foot in his hands and stepped up. Gavin raised her slowly, and she balanced on his shoulder, then swung her leg over Thor's back. After reaching around Ewan, she grasped Thor's mane tightly. Once she was settled, Kerr offered his hand from the other side, and Gavin quickly grasped it and jumped up.

Then he wished he hadn't.

She was warm against him. And soft. Her hair was silky wherever it touched his bare skin, and she smelled like honeyed lavender.

And she fit perfectly between his thighs. Her plump arse cushioned his cock, and when he slipped his hands around her to grasp the reins, his arms brushed the undersides of her breasts. Their weight rested, full and yielding, against his muscles.

She inhaled jaggedly, and he couldn't help holding her just a wee bit closer, to feel her breathing.

She was well endowed up top and below but narrow through her rib cage and waist. He dug his heels into Thor's sides to stop himself from imagining what she might look like naked. At the pressure on his flanks, the stallion jumped forward and straight into a gallop.

Deirdre let out a terrified shriek, while Ewan yelled in delight.

Gavin grinned again at his son's exuberance, but

Deirdre was soon tilting to one side, and Gavin had to tighten his arms and legs just to keep them all in place.

"Close your eyes, Deirdre."

She stiffened and tilted again. "What? Nay, I canna."

He pulled her upright once more. "Aye you can, or you're going to take us all down with you this time. Close your eyes, lean back against me, and relax. Trust that I'll keep you and Ewan safe. Stop fighting me and let go."

"You're asking too much," she said, and he heard tears in her voice.

He realized she wasn't talking about the stallion anymore, and he felt a strange pressure in his chest. He wanted to wrap one arm all the way around her waist and rest her against his heart—absorb her uncertainty and heartache so she didn't hurt so much.

But how could he do that when he planned to take Ewan away from her?

He couldn't.

"I said I would ne'er lie to you, Deirdre. The only promise I can make right now is that I'll get you and Ewan safely to Clan MacKinnon. Once I find out what happened to my son, I'll hunt down and punish those who took him. That I swear."

Four

"Mama, look! A pattern," Ewan said, holding up a pine cone that he'd pulled off a tree. He had a growing collection of leaves, twigs, and flowers that he'd picked from the foliage as they'd ridden by. Having nowhere to put his treasures, he'd woven the various pieces into Thor's mane so they wouldn't fall off.

Deirdre wagered the stallion had never looked so bonnie.

Grasping her son's hand, she slowly turned the pine cone to see how the buds grew upward in a circular design from the stem. "It *is* a pattern. One we often find in nature. Do you remember what it's called?"

"Aye, it's a…a…" His brow furrowed as he tried to remember the name. "It's the same as the snail's shell we found at the creek. And the seeds in the sunflower."

"It starts with an 's,'" she said. "Sp—"

"Spiral!"

"That's right! And the name of the mathematician who gave us a numerical sequence for the spiral?"

"Fibonacci. 1, 1, 2, 3, 5, 8, 13, 21, 34, 55, 89, 144,

233." He said it in a singsong voice, which had helped him memorize the numbers and their order.

"I'm impressed," she said. "I think I was older than you when I learned the numbers."

"Who taught you that?" Gavin asked.

"Mama. She drawed me a picture of all the different rectangles too, and then we put a line through them until we had a spiral. It works every time! When we stop, she can show you."

What did Gavin think of that? When Deirdre was growing up, her tutor had been her godsend. Spending time with him in the nursery, away from her family, had been long, happy, mostly uninterrupted hours learning mathematical equations, music, language, history, and art. She'd begun teaching everything she knew to Ewan, as the cost of a tutor had been out of the question. Lewis might be the next laird of Clan MacIntyre, but until then, his father was making sure he lived on as little money as possible.

And truth be told, she didn't mind. She loved spending time with Ewan and educating him about the subjects she held most dear. Especially geometry. It wasn't what her sisters had been interested in, and certainly not her mother, whom Deirdre would often watch outside riding her horse. But for Deirdre, inside with her quills, ink, and books, she'd felt safe and happy.

Ewan snagged another flower from the tree and weaved it into Thor's mane behind his ear. Gavin snorted behind her, and she couldn't help smiling. "Such a bonnie lad," she said to Ewan.

"Aye. I'm sure he feels pretty," Gavin replied.

Now it was her turn to snort. And then she wished she hadn't. Who knew what might offend the laird behind her?

Ewan settled down after that, and a few minutes later, he yawned, which made her yawn in turn. She knew, though, it would be impossible for her to sleep. She'd never been in so much pain in her life. It was no wonder she'd rarely ever ridden a horse. Her whole body ached from the tip of her toes to the top of her head. They'd rested twice already, and she'd hobbled like an old woman when she'd dismounted. The second time, she'd fallen when her feet hit the ground. Only the fear of being left behind had made her get back in the saddle.

She'd finally relaxed against Gavin and found that it *had* helped. At least she was no longer petrified of falling off.

And truth be told, she liked the feeling of his arms around her. A strange flutter had started in her belly, and his strength—controlling Thor and holding them all up—made her feel protected. All this even though he was the one stealing her child and dragging her across the Highlands to an unknown future.

It makes no sense.

She'd never been this close to a man before, never mind leaned her body against one. Well, other than that once, and that had been confusing, upsetting—and terrifying in the end. Another reason she'd been happy to escape to Clan MacIntyre, even though it meant leaving her beloved tutor behind.

"Mama, I'm tired," Ewan said as he squirmed around to face her. Fear shot through Deirdre, and she tipped to one side at the sudden imbalance, but Gavin's arms tightened around her until she was settled against his chest again. Safe.

Ewan laid his head on her shoulder, and Gavin pulled her son's legs over either side of their legs. She winced at the jolting pain, but then Ewan settled and quickly drifted off. She slipped her hands beneath his bottom to keep him steady.

Gavin brushed his fingers through his son's silky tresses, then leaned down and kissed Ewan's brow. Gavin's spiky hair tickled her ear, making her shiver. He tightened his arms around her for a moment, and her pulse sped up until she felt it drumming in her ears.

That strange flutter had risen into her chest now, and she couldn't take a full breath. What was wrong with her? She'd never been attracted to a man in her life. Why, when it finally happened, did it have to be to a man who would ruin her?

It wasn't as though he would return the attraction. Gavin MacKinnon was tall and fair like the rest of her family. She was the dark, soft, unattractive outcast even her husband didn't want.

But for just a moment, she thought about what it would be like if Gavin MacKinnon was her husband instead of Lewis—and the son she held in her arms had come from her own body. What if Gavin held her tight like this because he loved her? And after kissing their son, he turned his head and kissed her—the side of her neck, the whorls in her ear?

Aye, what would that feel like?

The flutter in her chest turned into a flood of heat that saturated every inch of her and throbbed between her legs. The tips of her breasts hardened and sensitized, the soft underside rubbing against Gavin's arms with every sway of the horse.

Is this how it would feel to be married to him? To want him?

To welcome him into her body?

Her experiences with men had not been pleasant so far, but she thought with Gavin MacKinnon, that could change.

"Were you at the summer festival when the pestilence hit?" he asked, his words quiet yet clipped, as if he was angry.

And the heat in her body doused with cold. How could she have forgotten?

"Nay. I've ne'er been to a gathering other than the one a few days ago."

"That's hard to believe. You ne'er went with your family to any of the festivals near your castle?"

Heat rose up her cheeks again, but this time from embarrassment instead of desire. How could she tell him that her family had never wanted her with them? And the times she did spend with them were some of the most excruciating in her life—filled with fear and humiliation, but also with a desperate neediness to belong? To be loved?

She shook her head, not wanting him to hear the shame in her voice.

"Then where did you find Ewan?" he asked. "And doona tell me you birthed him. We both know that's not true."

She had to unclench her jaw before she could talk. Force the words past her lips. "I didn't find him anywhere. And he is my son. I know it, and Ewan knows it."

He drummed his fingers on his leg where his kilt had ridden up to reveal brawny thighs. "So, if you didn't find him, someone gave him to you. Your husband, perhaps? Was he mistreated before you got him?"

"Nay!"

"Nay your husband didn't give him to you, or nay he wasn't mistreated?"

"He's ne'er been mistreated in any way. I would ne'er hurt Ewan. I would give my life for my son!"

"Not your son. Do you think people could believe for even one moment that you're his mother? You couldnae be more opposite."

"You wouldnae say that if you met *my mother*. She's as fair as Ewan. All my family is."

"And do they all have my eyes? And the same cowlick that Ewan and I share? The same dent in our chins? Does their hair peak downward in the middle of their brow like mine does? Like Ewan's?"

She stayed silent. This was a pointless discussion. She could agree, confess that Lewis had given Ewan to her and told her he was the boy's father, but then what would Gavin do to him? Lewis wasn't a bad man, and she couldn't imagine he'd deliberately hurt a child in any way. Nay, she'd been fifteen when she'd married him, and he'd treated her like the child she still was instead of taking what was his by rights of marriage. Her life had vastly improved since she'd moved to Clan MacIntyre, and if nothing else, she owed Lewis her loyalty.

"Do you not find it strange that they didn't change his name before they gave him to you?" Gavin asked.

"Someone took him from the gathering before the pestilence hit. They knew his name, so he must have been targeted. And then they gave him to you to raise—to take him on picnics and teach him about spirals and put your life before his—without even trying to hide who he was. Why?"

She shrugged, feeling helpless and confused. Frightened. Her time with Ewan was almost at an end. She knew it. Gavin MacKinnon would not want to keep her around. Her fantasies about them being a happy family were just that—fantasies. Tears pricked her eyes, and her lip trembled.

"I think whoever took him wanted to use him as leverage against me," Gavin continued. "But if that's true, why didn't they? Why give him to a lonely, barren woman to raise instead? To make him happy?"

She blinked, and the tears ran down her face. Aye, she had been lonely. And she'd done her very best to fill her son's days with love, laughter, and learning, which had filled her own life too. A life which now loomed ahead of her as barren as Gavin had described.

He pushed Ewan's hair back from his forehead with his fingers. A small scar marked the center of his brow. "Did you ever wonder how he got that?" he asked. "He fell off a chair in the nursery and hit a jagged edge on the stone wall. I had the mason come in the next day and sand down all the sharp edges on the walls so my son wouldn't be hurt like that again. And this one on his palm?" He turned Ewan's hand over, so she could see, but she didn't need to. She knew the exact scar he referred to. "He grabbed a knife I'd laid on the table. I was right there, watching him, and I only intended to put it down for a moment. I banned all daggers from the keep after that."

He rubbed Ewan's back, down low on the right side. "He has a birthmark here in the shape of a rearing horse, and his wee toes are perfectly shaped—all ten of them—which he did not get from me."

He rubbed his hand on Ewan's back again, soothing but also strong and protective. "I did everything I could think of to safeguard my son. And then someone stole him from me when I wasn't there. And I could do naught to stop it. All I could do was keep looking for him. Keep believing he was alive. I never gave up the search."

Pain radiated off him, and he squeezed his arms more tightly around Ewan. He kissed his head once more, and then nuzzled his face in the boy's hair. Things that Deirdre had also done every day since he'd been given to her.

"He wasn't hurt, Laird MacKinnon, or sad or unprotected. Take comfort in that. He was—*is*—loved and happy." She pressed her fingers over Gavin's and traced the outline of the birthmark that she knew by heart. "We named the rearing horse on his back Dardoo—a made-up name that he liked. And I also didn't let him around knives. He's fascinated by them. You'll have to teach him to use them responsibly soon."

She pushed his fingers back to Ewan's leg where a more recent scar sat. "A weasel bit him here. Ewan found it going after the chickens and chased it out of the coop. He fevered afterward and was sick for a few days. I ne'er left his side." She trailed her fingers up to his knee. "He's scraped and banged these too many times to count. His elbows too. I've held him until he stopped crying and washed, bandaged, and kissed every cut and bruise. And I've kissed all ten of his perfect toes."

She turned her head this time and nuzzled Ewan's hair. "Aye, Gavin MacKinnon, he's your son. But he's my son too."

Gavin led Thor across the wildflower-strewn field to the creek. The gloaming was upon them, and the sky was covered in waves of orange and pink. He crouched down at the stream's edge and drank deeply, as did Thor, then splashed water on his face.

They would make camp here tonight and hopefully cross into MacKinnon land two days hence. He hated to admit it, but the ride had been tough on Ewan. Having to stay on Thor for so long was no easy thing, and Gavin had often wished they'd brought a wagon, as Deirdre had asked.

The ride had been tough on her as well…but that wasn't his concern, no matter how many times he'd considered stopping early so she could rest.

He looked back over his shoulder and saw Deirdre and Ewan walking toward the woods with Clyde—Gavin's most trusted man—at their heels. Deirdre moved awkwardly—in pain from the ride, most likely—and Ewan stepped sedately beside her, carrying a linen that dragged on the ground. Not like the first few times they'd stopped, when he'd darted all over the place, exploring.

Nay, they were both done in.

Kerr approached the creek with his stallion and crouched beside Gavin for a drink. When he finished, he wiped his mouth on his linen sleeve and followed Gavin's gaze to where Deirdre and Ewan had disappeared into the forest.

"Are you expecting trouble?" he asked.

"Not exactly."

"But you doona like Ewan out of your sight?"

Gavin nodded. "Especially if Deirdre is with him."

"She hardly seems capable of escaping—either by herself or with a child. Let alone incapacitating Clyde first."

"Aye, I know. It's not a rational fear."

Kerr squeezed his shoulder. "But understandable. Did she tell you anything further?"

"She said that she did not find Ewan or steal him. Which means someone gave him to her. Her husband, most likely."

"'Tis what the castle folk said when I questioned them. I wouldnae have thought it in Lewis's nature to steal a child, so maybe he found Ewan. Lewis was a kind lad when I knew him and reviled by his father in the same way I was reviled by mine, except he didn't have the stones to stand up to his da like I did—or the support of all of you and Gregor. Doona rush to judgment, Gavin, until we have the full story."

Gavin nodded, but his muscles tensed in resistance. Deirdre had known he was Ewan's father before she'd run from him at the spring gathering. "What else did they say?"

"That Lewis brought Ewan home after one of his

'absences' and said the boy was his son. Deirdre raised him after that."

"Absences? 'Tis an odd word choice."

"According to the groom, who was hushed by the housekeeper, Lewis only lived there periodically."

"Deirdre too?"

"Nay, she was there the whole time. They said her trip to the gathering a few days ago was the first time she'd left. Ever. And according to her maid, she didn't want to go—especially not without Ewan—but Lewis insisted. So she wasn't trying to keep the lad hidden."

Gavin couldn't help imagining what would have happened if Ewan had been at the gathering, if Gavin had seen his son in the middle of the market. Then Deirdre wouldn't have run. And they'd already be home. "Where does Lewis go when he leaves? His father's keep? Or some of the other defensive posts?"

"No one could say for sure. And Laird MacIntyre hasn't been there in years. As Clyde said earlier, his father is trying for another male heir and doesn't seem to want anything to do with his firstborn."

"Well, Lewis obviously has Deirdre's loyalty. She wouldnae spill her husband's secrets, so he must not have treated her poorly."

"And by the looks of it, not your son either. Ewan's a happy and well-loved lad, Gavin. You can put that worry to rest."

Aye, he had, but how could he tell Kerr that even so, he did not want Deirdre to have one extra minute with his son? She'd stolen time from him, whether she'd known it or not. Time with Ewan that he couldn't get back.

If anything, he was more filled with anger than before. He thought he would be happy to find his son, and he was—overjoyed!—but he was furious too. Especially now that he had someone to focus that anger on.

He didn't think Kerr would see it that way—and maybe he was right.

But for now, Gavin couldn't let it go. "I just want to keep Ewan safe. Like I failed to do the last time."

Kerr clapped him on the shoulder, then rose and stretched to the sky with a noisy yawn. "It's been a long couple of days. I shall sleep well tonight whether it's on the hard ground or in a field of flowers."

"'Tis the same thing, is it not? I canna imagine the flowers will be any softer once you've flattened the life out of them."

"Mayhap a patch of moss then." He reached into his saddlebag and tossed Gavin an apple, then took one for himself. "And you, Brother? Will you finally sleep?"

Gavin knew why his foster brother was asking. All the family worried about his lack of sleep the last few years—e'er since Ewan was taken. Before that, even, when the marriage he'd had such high hopes for had withered and died. The Cristel he thought he'd married—a giving woman who loved him and shared common interests, who enjoyed his touch—hadn't existed. Instead, she'd wanted them to live separate lives and had encouraged him to find his pleasure elsewhere.

Gavin had been devastated. And furious. He'd been brought up with loving parents whose only sorrow had been their lack of bairns after Gavin was born. They'd weathered several miscarriages and even a stillborn.

When Isobel had finally come along, healthy and squalling, ten years later, it had been a true blessing.

And he'd seen the love that his foster father, Gregor, had for his wife Kellie. He'd never stopped loving her, even after she was lost to him during childbirth, but he'd sworn he would take their marriage vows to his grave.

Gavin had wanted, and expected, that same happiness with Cristel. She had certainly played the part in the beginning, pretending to love him until after their wedding night.

When she'd birthed Ewan, she'd finally been honest with him: if Gavin hadn't been laird, she would never have married him. And now that she'd given him a son, she would not continue their physical intimacy. She'd trapped him with lies and false intentions, and in so doing, had destroyed all Gavin's dreams of a loving, supportive union.

He thought back to what Kerr had asked him and shook his head. "I doona think sleep will come so easily. Maybe once we're in the keep and I know he's safe."

"Do you think we've been followed?" Kerr asked.

"Nay, it would take the MacIntyres at least a day to organize a search."

"So something else is bothering you then. Deirdre? Aye, I'm worried about her too. It seems an unfair punishment to take her child from her when all she's done is love him."

Gavin rounded on him. "My child!"

Kerr's eyes widened at his outburst before they narrowed on him. "No one's saying he's not your child, Gavin. But you canna deny that she loves him as a mother should, and he loves her right back. To separate them could cause irreparable harm—to both. I doona know what the answer is, but I do know that we shouldnae rush into making a decision."

"'Tis no' 'we' making the decision, Kerr. It falls on my shoulders alone. I am Ewan's father and his laird. 'Twill be my cross to bear."

"Aye, 'tis a burden for sure. And it will only get heavier if you doona allow us to help you carry it."

Kerr spoke the truth—and Gavin remembered saying something similar to Callum's wife, Maggie, last summer. But in this instance, he didn't see any possible compromise. And certainly, no happy ending.

"Why hasn't she had other children?" he asked, flinging his half-eaten apple into the woods angrily. "They've been married for seven years. Surely a woman as young and fertile as her wouldnae be barren?"

Kerr's brow rose. "There's ten years between you and Isobel. You of all people should know that conception is not always guaranteed. Besides, it may be him and not her at fault."

"Aye. 'Tis just...if she had other bairns..."

"She might not feel the loss of Ewan so acutely. I've thought the same thing." Kerr sighed. "No matter what choices are made, good people will be hurt."

Gavin bit his tongue just before he blurted out, *Good people doona run off with other people's bairns.*

Deirdre and Ewan came out of the woods just then, and Gavin found himself scowling at Deirdre. She blanched and took a step back. Ewan looked up and saw Gavin's dark, twisted face and the way he was glaring at Ewan's mother. He quickly grabbed her hand and tugged her away in another direction, looking over his shoulder fearfully at his da.

"God's blood," Gavin muttered, anger wanting to explode from between his clenched teeth.

"He'll ne'er abide you hurting her," Kerr said.

Gavin rounded on his brother, ready to smash his fist in his face. His head felt tight, hot, and every muscle tensed for action. If they were attacked right now, he would happily wade into a hundred enemy warriors.

"Is he watching?" he asked, barely reining in the need to shove his foster brother into the creek behind him.

"Aye. Take a walk, Gavin. Make sure your head's right before you come back, or you may lose your son forever this time."

Gavin met his brother's gaze, saw the steel there, but also the concern and the compassion. He was in trouble. If there was one thing Kerr knew well, it was a lad's need to protect his mother—and the hatred that formed in his breast if he failed.

Deirdre could not stay in Ewan's life, but how could Gavin get her out?

Five

When they crossed the border onto MacKinnon land several days later, with Deirdre and Ewan riding in front of him, Gavin felt an upswelling of exhilaration and joy.

My son is home!

He whistled to the men he knew were hidden in the trees and on the ground patrolling his border. A young, agile warrior dropped to the trail in front of them and ran alongside Gavin's horse.

"Finn!" Gavin cried out, a smile splitting his face. "Well met, lad."

"And you, Laird! You're home early. We weren't expecting you for..." Finn's eyes widened as he took in Ewan. "Is that...is that..."

"Aye, Finn." Gavin laughed. "Let everyone know that Ewan is back!"

Finn let out an excited holler and punched his fist in the air. Other yells and whoops went up around them, and more men dropped down from the trees or appeared to spring up from the ground.

A huge warrior with a bushy beard that rivaled

Clyde's rose up from where he was hidden in a wee gulley. "Laird!" he yelled, leaves and twigs falling from his plaid as he hurried forward. "You've found your son, just like you said you would! Our wee Ewan…returned to us at last. And look at him—so big and braw. Have you fought off any dragons on your trip, lad?"

Gavin slowed Thor to a walk so Ewan could respond to the big warrior, Artair, who was a favorite of Gavin's.

"Aye," Ewan said. "I fighted a hundred dragons and they had giants on their backs!"

The men all laughed, Artair's booming chuckle drowning them out.

Finn slapped him on the shoulder. "Were they as big as this giant here?" he asked.

Ewan's mouth dropped open. "You're a giant? Was your ma a giant too?"

"She surely was," Artair said. "As wide as me and as tall as your horse."

"My ma isn't a giant." Ewan turned to look up at Deirdre, and Gavin tensed. "Are you, Ma?"

"Nay, Ewan," she said softly. "I'm not a giant."

The men around them quieted, giving her curious looks. They knew Deirdre was not Ewan's mother.

Gavin urged his horse forward and whistled ahead to Clyde.

The battle-hardened warrior twisted in his saddle and peered at Gavin. "Aye, Laird?"

"Send Sheamais and Lorne to the castle, so my sister knows we're coming. Have her prepare the nursery."

"Aye, and tell her I'm with them," Kerr yelled from

behind him. "She'll want to use that mirror of hers to look pretty for me!"

The men laughed at the jest. They all knew the only thing Isobel used her mirror for was to blind unwary folk. And she needed no primping to look pretty. Isobel was considered a beauty throughout the Highlands. Gavin wanted her to marry Kerr, the only man he knew who could handle her stubborn nature without crushing it, but Isobel was dead set against him. Neither of them knew exactly why, as she'd been sweet on him when she was younger.

Kerr had his work cut out for him, but if there was one person Gavin knew who was more determined than Isobel, it was his foster brother.

It was almost dark by the time they passed the village, not too far from the castle. Ewan was asleep in Deirdre's arms, and she had gotten more and more tense the closer they drew to Gavin's home. Aye, truth be told, Gavin had too. He'd thought long and hard about what to do with her, and he'd decided he needed to separate her from Ewan as much as possible until he could send her home—starting with nighttime when Ewan wanted to sleep snuggled against her.

And who wouldnae want to sleep in her arms?

She had the kind of beauty and manner that drew you in and wouldn't let go. Like stepping into a hot pool. Warm, lush, soothing—and all-consuming. But he suspected that beneath the luxuriant depths were unseen bubbles of hot mud and simmering geysers, ready to explode at the right provocation. Like when Kerr had pulled her onto his horse or Ewan had almost been trampled by Thor.

She was a married woman and would be lady of her clan someday—if he didn't kill her husband first—but it didn't stop his men from sneaking glances at her whenever they thought they were unobserved.

Everyone except Kerr, who had taken wholeheartedly to being her cousin. It helped that he had eyes only for Isobel.

They passed the cathedral that was being built about halfway between the village and his castle on the loch. Deirdre straightened in the saddle as they rode by, shifting Ewan so he stayed sleeping as she turned her head to see its outline against the moonlit sky.

"What's that?" she asked, her voice picking up in wonder.

"My mother's dream," he said.

"A cathedral?"

"Technically 'tis only a church. Cathedrals are the seat of the bishop, as I'm sure you know. I suspect my mother believed that if she built the grandest church in the area, the bishop would follow. She commissioned work on it a few years before she died. It willna be finished for many years."

"How wonderful," she sighed.

"Are you devout, then?" he asked.

"No more than most, but I've seen drawings of the great cathedrals in Rome and Paris. They are a sight to behold."

"Maybe one day you'll be able to see them in person."

"Maybe. But I'd travel in a wagon. I'm done with horses."

"'Tis because you haven't ridden on your own,

galloping to freedom. The first time you do that, you'll ne'er want to ride in a wagon again."

"I'd end up broken on the ground. If you weren't holding me up, I'd fall."

"Nay. You're stronger than you think."

"Maybe," she said quietly.

She settled against him again. Everyone seemed subdued now that the initial jubilation was over, including Kerr, who'd kept up a lively banter most of the way there.

The lights at the castle were ablaze, and as they neared, he saw the portcullis was open. He whistled again, softly, and this time Clyde rode back to them.

"Laird?"

"Ride ahead and tell them to keep quiet," Gavin said. "I doona want to wake the bairn."

He meant to start how he intended to go. Ewan in the nursery at night, Deirdre in a guest chamber. His nursemaid would be there if he awoke, and she could put the child back to sleep. Or call Gavin, if she needed help.

Gavin still hadn't slept much, even though he'd gotten his son back. Maybe that would change once Ewan was safe in the castle nursery.

He knew there would be much talk about Ewan and speculation about Deirdre, and once Gavin knew the truth, he would tell his clan what had happened. They deserved to know, if they were going to war against the MacIntyres and their allies. That list included the MacColls—Deirdre's birth clan, although she didn't seem to have anything to do with them.

But for now, he just wanted to get them into the castle without any upset.

After they passed under the portcullis, the iron grill shut behind them. When they stepped into the bailey, it was filled with whispering people craning to see Gavin's sleeping lad. Their faces lit up with happiness, many cheeks wet with tears.

Highlanders were a stoic lot, but in this instance, the floodgates had opened—Ewan, the wee lad they all loved, had been returned to them!

Gavin's own emotions surged, and he raised a silent hand of greeting and thanks to his clan as he rode through the crowd—mostly castle folk and warriors not on patrol at this time of night.

On the other side of the crowded clearing, his home loomed. MacKinnon castle was large and impressive, even to his own eyes. They were a prosperous clan with good management the last few decades due to the guidance of a smart, honest steward, Gregor MacLeod's guidance, and a father who'd listened to both.

As he neared the steps leading up to the great hall, Gavin's eyes fell on his sister, Isobel. She stood halfway down the stairs, one hand pressed over her heart, the other covering her mouth, and her face crumpled with tearful disbelief and happiness. Her bright blond hair hung loose down her back, and he heard Deirdre suck in an awed breath—at the same time Kerr, who rode beside him, sighed.

Aye, Isobel was a sight to behold. Tall and willowy, with Gavin's blue-green eyes and the face of an angel. Not that she behaved like one. Nay, as much as she loved him, and he suspected loved Kerr as well, she could be downright disagreeable, fighting with them over every wee thing.

Although Kerr did seem to go out of his way to rile her. On purpose.

She raced down the stairs, eyes jumping from him to Deirdre, to Ewan. "Is it really him?" she asked, her voice shaking. Gavin turned Thor just enough so that she could see Ewan clearly, sound asleep on Deirdre's shoulder.

Isobel moved between the two horses and lifted her hand to stroke her nephew's hair. A sound escaped her throat, halfway between a sigh and a sob, and she leaned back against Kerr's horse with tears streaming down her face. Kerr lowered his hand to her shoulder and squeezed. She raised her hand and grasped his fingers.

"And this is Deirdre MacIntyre," Kerr said. "She's my cousin. She's had Ewan all this time. Made sure he was safe, happy, and loved. She ne'er knew he was stolen." Kerr raised his eyes to Deirdre. They brimmed with sympathy. "Did you, love?"

Her body shuddered in his arms as she shook her head. Gavin didn't want to see her face. Didn't want to see the heartbreak there.

He slipped off of Thor and then lifted Deirdre down. Ewan made a soft sighing sound, but he kept sleeping.

"I'll take him," Gavin said. "You've been holding him for a while. He must be heavy."

"Nay, I doona want to disturb him," she said, her arms tightening around him.

She was delaying the inevitable. Gavin slipped his hands under Ewan's arms and pulled him from her embrace. Deirdre let out a heart-rending sob, but Gavin turned away. He settled Ewan on his shoulder and walked up the stairs to the great hall, Isobel on his heels. He looked down toward the bailey once they were at the top. Down below, Kerr had wrapped one huge arm around Deirdre, who had collapsed against him.

Kerr spoke into her ear as he guided her toward the stairs. Gavin wondered what his foster brother was saying.

"Gavin, what's going on?" Isobel asked as she stepped up beside him.

"I have Ewan back. That's what's going on." He pushed open the heavy door that led into the great hall and waited for Isobel to walk through.

"But that woman—"

"Is not Ewan's mother. She did not birth him, and she kept him from me after meeting me at the spring gathering. I'm grateful for her care of him the last two and a half years, but she'll be returning home soon. Compensated for her trouble." Isobel stood at the door, unmoving, and Gavin's agitation increased as Deirdre neared.

"I doona think giving her gold will ease her pain," Isobel said. "She's heartbroken."

"Aye, so was I for more than two years. At least she'll know where he is and that he's happy and safe. That's more than I had."

Isobel looked at him, her eyes pained. "I love you, Gavin, but you've changed since Ewan was taken, since Cristel turned her back on your marriage—on you. You've become hard. 'Tis not a trait you want to pass on to your son. I hope now that he's back with you—with us—you can learn to feel again."

He rounded on her, his heart beating in anger, his

words clipped. "I feel, Isobel. I've felt naught but pain since Ewan was taken. Deirdre canna stay. She has a home and a husband, whom I will most likely kill, and I will ne'er let my son leave without me again. I'm taking Ewan to the nursery before everyone starts yelling. If you want to help, do your best to keep Kerr calm. His bellows will reach right up to the nursery and wake *my* son."

Gavin grunted—almost a growl—and stepped through the heavy, wooden door.

He'd thought walking into his home with his child in his arms would give him comfort, but he just felt worse. After having Deirdre in front of him for so many hours, learning her scent, hearing her voice, feeling the weight and warmth of her body against his, he just felt empty.

Almost…bereft.

So he hugged Ewan harder and strode across the great hall toward the dark stairwell entrance in the corner. A second stairwell was in the same spot at the other end of the room, the construction similar to Deirdre's keep but on a larger scale. Which was good, because it would feel even more familiar to Ewan.

Fresh rushes crunched under his feet. Light blazed from every candle along the walls and in two large, circular chandeliers that hung from the ceiling on chains that could be easily raised and lowered on pulleys.

Opposite him, a fire burned in a huge hearth used for heating the great room and the castle. Racks sat in it to hold the iron pots of food that came in from the kitchens to feed the castle folk and the warriors who were not away or on watch. The benches and tables used during meals had been stacked neatly against one wall, ready to break the morning fast.

A second, smaller hearth, with a flowered wall hanging above the mantel, also had a fire burning in it. Three chairs with embroidered cushions on the seats sat in front of the hearth, footstools tucked underneath. On a side table sat a tray laden with cups and a pitcher—of mead, most likely—set out for the laird's friends and family.

The ceiling rose several stories, and two-thirds of the way up, a narrow balcony encircled the hall, an access used by archers in defense of the castle. Small murder holes had been carved in the stone walls, allowing the men to shoot the encroaching enemy if they stormed the keep, but also to let in light and air during peaceful times.

Gavin had just reached the stairwell entrance when Deirdre and Kerr entered the keep.

"Gavin," Kerr said, his voice raised, demanding.

Gavin didn't stop. If he answered his foster brother, all he would do was wake Ewan, who would then want to be with Deirdre. Instead, he started up the circular stairwell.

He heard Isobel say, "Calm down, Kerr. You'll wake Ewan. Gavin's just taking him up to bed. Annag is up there, airing the room."

The stairwell was lit every few feet, but it was narrow and low, barely clearing his head. Harder for the enemy to get by you that way. He worried about scraping Ewan's knees on the stone as he continued upward, passing the next level with several bedchambers and the laird's solar, and up to the fourth level where the nursery and additional bedchambers were located.

When he stepped into the passageway, several burning candles in wall sconces chased away the darkness, and the nursery door stood open. Light blazed from within.

Gavin stopped in his tracks, suddenly overwhelmed with emotion. His throat and chest tightened, and he could barely breathe.

He hadn't seen the nursery door open in over two years.

He walked forward slowly, his eyes hot, his skin tight—and this time not from anger but from relief and happiness. And love. When he blinked, tears rolled down his cheeks and soaked into his short, scraggly beard.

He turned into the chamber. The room was large—larger than the nursery at Deirdre's keep—with a canopied bed in the corner. The bed was covered in a light-green quilt embroidered with sword-wielding knights on horses, dogs by their sides, as they fought a great, scaly dragon. A soft, wool rug covered the floor that Ewan used to play on, and a chair sat by the window. He used to stand on that chair to look outside and see what was going on in the bailey and in the fields beyond the castle. The shutters were open to let in the cool night air.

Several chests carved with forest scenes—including fairies and imps—were pushed against the wall across from the bed. In another corner, a small table was the battleground for warriors whittled in soft stone. Ewan had been playing with them the morning he left with Cristel for the festival he'd disappeared from. The maids who had come in periodically to clean and dust the room had left the small figures exactly as they were.

An older woman, her gray-streaked hair pinned back in a messy bun and her shape as familiar to Gavin as his own mother's, crouched down on her hands and knees, searching for something beneath the bed.

"Annag," he said softly, his voice breaking at the end. He breathed deeply to contain the emotion, but when his nursemaid—and Isobel's after him, then Ewan's for too few years—turned her head, it was a losing battle.

She used the bed to help push herself up from the floor, her face crumpling into tears and smiles all at once. In her hand, she clutched a carved wooden soldier that she'd pulled out from under the bed. She raised it to her mouth, forgetting it was there. When she felt it against her lips, she laughed and lowered it, then moved toward them, tears streaming down her cheeks and into her smiling mouth.

"I noticed it was missing the other day," she whispered, indicating the toy Highlander. "I searched everywhere but under the bed because my knee was too sore to bend down. When Isobel told me you'd found him..." Her voice broke, and she couldn't continue.

She'd reached them by now and stared at Ewan sleeping on Gavin's shoulder. She raised a hand and gently sifted Ewan's hair with her fingers. "Och, my sweet lad. You canna know how happy I am to see you." She raised wet, joyful eyes to Gavin. "I would know him anywhere. He's the spitting image of you at that age."

"Aye, and full of mischief and daring."

"We'll see about that," she said lovingly as she reached up. Gavin passed him over.

Annag laid Ewan on her shoulder too, swaying back and forth and humming a low, calming lullaby.

When his eyes fluttered open, she rubbed his back in soothing circles, and he closed them again with a sigh. "He's well?" she whispered.

"Aye. We found him in a keep on MacIntyre land—happy and well cared for."

"They stole him?"

His mouth tightened, but he found himself not wanting to speak ill of Deirdre. "I doona know what transpired when he was taken, but I believe the woman he lived with is innocent in this regard. She's treated him like a son, and he calls her mother."

"Thanks be for that." She pressed her lips to Ewan's hair and squeezed him a little closer. "The angels kept him safe."

An angel named Deirdre.

He scowled at the thought. He couldn't help it.

"You canna be bitter, Gavin," she said. "It's over. Ewan is back and unhurt. And Cristel is gone."

"He's the only pure and true thing she ever gave me."

"And he makes all she put you through—the lies, the manipulations, the deceptions—worthwhile. For him, you would do it all over again."

Aye, he would bear any pain for his son. Even the pain of losing him if he had to.

It wasn't lost on him that the heartache he'd finally released would soon find a home in Deirdre.

Deirdre sat on the finely carved and embroidered chair, shivering in front of the roaring fire. Kerr had wrapped his extra plaid around her, muttering something under his breath—prefaced by "bloody," no doubt—then asked Isobel, who'd been staring at her, wide-eyed and pale-faced, to bring Deirdre another. Isobel had jumped, looking guilt-stricken, and scurried from the room.

It didn't matter. The only thing that could warm Deirdre now was her son in her arms. Gavin MacKinnon had taken him into the keep and up the stairs, and he had no intention of returning him. No matter what Kerr MacAlister said.

He's a good man. He willna hurt Ewan or you. He just needs time, Deirdre. No matter what happens, I willna allow him to separate the two of you. Well, she couldn't *allow* herself to believe that.

Isobel ran back over the rushes, carrying an armful of blankets. Her cheeks were wet, and when she saw Deirdre's gaze on her, she quickly wiped them dry.

Deirdre lowered her eyes. "I'm sorry to bring such trouble into your home." Her voice scraped past her raw throat, barely above a whisper.

Isobel dropped the blankets on a chair. "You haven't brought trouble; you brought Ewan. Kerr told me what you did for him, how you nurtured him. Loved him. And Gavin said he is grateful for the care you gave him." She picked up a blanket and doubled it over before placing it on Deirdre's lap. "I doona know what the future holds, Deirdre, but I know that my brother is not a cruel man. I canna believe that he would willingly cause you such pain."

"Aye," Kerr said from behind her, hands squeezing her shoulders. "Losing Ewan was a blow to him—to us all. As you more than anyone can imagine. One day Ewan was just gone, and we had no idea what had happened to him. Gavin was convinced Ewan was alive, and he ne'er gave up, but our search kept pointing us in false directions. Two and a half years of worry that he was hurt, sick, hungry, scared, lonely. It ate at all of us, but it ate at Gavin most of all."

Deirdre's stomach heaved at the thought. She would never have survived the agony of not knowing what had become of her son.

"And what of Ewan's mother?" she asked.

"She died of the pestilence," Isobel said. "Gavin had had reports of plague near the gathering place and had told her it wasn't safe, but she ne'er listened. When it became clear she planned to take Ewan with her, he forbade it. She waited until he was gone and then did it anyway."

Deirdre sucked in a sharp breath. The sick feeling of agony in her stomach turned to a burning outrage in her chest. *My sweet boy could have died!*

"I see how you feel," Kerr said. "'Tis how Gavin felt too, but one hundred times worse. The rage—the hate—he felt toward Cristel festered and grew in those two years. I doona wish ill on any living being, but if anyone deserved to be struck down by the pestilence, it was her."

"If she was so awful, why did he marry her?" Deirdre asked. She'd had no choice in her nuptials, but surely a laird as powerful as Gavin MacKinnon could make his own choices.

"Because I didn't know," Gavin said, stepping out from the bottom of the stairwell and crossing toward them. "As far as I knew, we had a joyful, exciting courtship. I thought we would be happy together—but she ne'er once showed me who she truly was or how she really felt about things until after our marriage. She pretended to be someone else to catch my interest, and I fell for every soft look and helpless murmur."

"And that's what you wanted in a wife?" she asked. "Someone soft and helpless?"

He stared at her blankly. "Nay—"

"But you just said—"

"I know what I said!"

Deirdre dropped her eyes. What was she doing, aggravating him? Questioning him? She needed to appeal to that good nature that his sister and Kerr swore he had. But the idea of this Cristel woman taking advantage of him, of him being drawn in by such tactics—or of him failing to understand his own self—scraped down her spine like a dull knife.

She kept her eyes on the blankets next to her, knowing she should say nothing more on the matter, but her mouth opened of its own accord and words spilled out. "'Tis difficult sometimes to see people as they truly are, if they doona wish you to see them. And sometimes 'tis difficult to…be who you truly are for fear of dislike or censure or even…humiliation. And sometimes just because of our circumstances. But sometimes what we are drawn to is an idea of a person, of how they will complete the picture we've created of ourselves and not the real person.

"It may be that she did show you who she truly was, and you didn't want to see it."

Gavin stared at her, a muscle jumping in his jaw, and her heart sank. What was it about this man that made her open her mouth when for years she'd kept it shut? Maybe he felt familiar to her because of Ewan? Or because they both loved him?

Whatever it was, she had to block it from her heart, her mind, and say nothing else that might upset him.

"Ewan will sleep in the nursery from now on," Gavin said stiffly. "He has his nursemaid, Annag, with him, and she will soothe him at night until he no longer wakens."

Deirdre jumped from her chair, her heart squeezing till she couldn't breathe. The blankets that covered her tumbled to the floor. "Nay! You canna! Is your heart truly so cold?"

So much for that vow of silence.

"My heart is warm, Deirdre, and it's bleeding for my son, but—"

"You have no idea what that will do to him."

"He'll cry, possibly even scream because things are different here, and he's not with you. But eventually he'll stop. I doona want him associating his home here with you."

"You think he's just going to forget me? I'm sure you wish it were so, but he will remember."

"Aye, but if he gets used to sleeping with you here, it'll make it that much harder when you..."

"When I what, Gavin? At least have the stones to say it!"

He stepped forward, his face grim, but she didn't retreat or drop her eyes even one inch. "When you leave, Deirdre. And my stones are big enough and hard enough to say anything to anyone when it comes to *my* son. To do what *I* think is right."

"For *you,* maybe. Not for Ewan."

"I'll tell you what *was* right for Ewan—that his own mother had loved him. But that ne'er happened. And that his father had been able to keep him safe, but that ne'er happened either. And that some monster ne'er targeted a child in order to control MacKinnon wealth and land, but the devil take them, that did happen.

"Now I have to choose what's right, what *will* happen, and I'm telling you, Deirdre, you canna stay. Even if I wanted you to. Which I don't. Our clans may soon be at war. And until I know better, you are my prisoner. Your husband, your father, even your brother, may soon be bloody heaps on the battlefield—cleaved in two by my sword!"

She stepped closer to him, one hand pressed against her stomach, the other pressed against his linen shirt—and over his heart. "Please. You think you have all the answers, Gavin MacKinnon, but you doona. Your son is terrified of the dark. He's afraid to be left alone."

"And now he has Annag to help him with those fears."

"Do you think we didn't try for years to help him? The nursemaids chastised me for letting him sleep with me, but I was the only one who could soothe him. The only one who could make him feel safe."

"I will make him feel safe, Deirdre. I am his father."

"So you keep telling me, over and over, and I doona care. We're not a couple of dogs pissing o'er our territory. He's a wee lad that needs both of us. He is happy and well-adjusted in the day, Gavin, but he canna abide being alone in the dark. Think about what might have happened to him when he was taken. Were his needs met? Was he tended to at night?"

Gavin's face clouded over, turned dark and forbidding. He removed her hand from his body, then stepped away.

"Nay, I willna speculate. I'll bring your husband before me, and I'll demand answers."

He whistled abruptly, then called out, "Clyde!" The big, tough-looking man who'd ridden with them from her keep came forward. Other than Gavin and Kerr, he was the one the others had turned to for instruction. She hadn't noticed he'd been keeping guard near the door. She scanned the great hall and saw others on guard—one by each stairwell entrance and more up on the balcony.

Kerr stepped forward and raised a hand to waylay Clyde. "Send your men away, Gavin. Send them all away. We need to talk—as family."

"Nay. He'll accompany Deirdre to her room. Isobel, too, if she so desires. But I'll keep a guard on her. My keep, my decision."

Isobel pushed between her brother and Kerr MacAlister, a hand on each man's chest, trying to hold them apart. "Kerr, let Clyde show her upstairs. As much as I would like to accompany Deirdre to her room, I would stay for this family *talk*. Gavin is right. It *is* his decision, and Deirdre isna family."

"She is to me," Kerr said.

Gavin threw his hands up in the air. He no longer looked like a heartless, indomitable laird but a man who just wanted to kick his brother's arse. "God's blood! You're so full of shite. You've known the lass for only two days."

"I claim her, Gavin. She is blood to me, and I claim

her. If you hurt her, you not only hurt me, but the rest of the lads and Gregor too."

"And just how do my actions against Deirdre affect Darach, Lachlan, Callum, and Gregor?"

"The same way it would if I did something to hurt Isobel."

Gavin pressed close, and Isobel seemed in danger of being squashed between them. "Isobel is my sister—I was there when she was born. And you want to marry her for Christ's sake." He flung a hand in Deirdre's direction. "She's just a cousin who is…what, four times removed? You ne'er even knew she existed."

"It doesn't matter."

"Aye. It. Does! You should be on my side in this!"

"I am on your side!"

Deirdre's heart pounded like a tree knocking against the keep's wall in a gale. She watched the men—foster brothers, friends—at the edge of a precipice. At any moment, one might draw his sword and a life would be taken. If not one of theirs, then maybe Isobel's, who stood so bravely between them.

Surely this was the end of their friendship, their alliance! And all because of her.

"Please, stop! I will go with Clyde," Deirdre said into the sudden silence. "You canna come to blows o'er this."

"Aye, they can," Isobel said, "and maybe they should."

"Nay! 'Tis bad enough what is happening with Ewan. I willna have a death on my hands too!" She grasped Isobel's arm and pulled her away from the men, who had since straightened and were looking at her a little bemusedly. "Come with me now, before you get hurt."

Isobel's brow furrowed, and she gently stopped her. "Doona worry, Deirdre. This isn't the first time they've fought, and it willna be the last. 'Tis how it is in our family. You'll see that as the days go by." She looked up at her brother. "Isn't that right, Gavin?"

He scowled at her and moved to a side table by the hearth to pour a cup of mead for himself. "I'm not planning to keep her locked up, if that's what you're asking."

He tipped back his head and took a long swig, and Deirdre found herself watching the muscles move in his throat. She was fighting a strange urge to bite down on that hard-looking bump—whether in desire or anger, she couldn't tell—when an ear-splitting scream sounded from upstairs.

Six

GAVIN SPEWED THE LAST SWALLOW OF MEAD BACK into his cup, hurriedly dropped it on the tray and raced toward the stairs. Kerr and Isobel trailed after him, concern etched on their faces.

Ewan!

Deirdre arrived at the stairs before him, her skirts hiked up and looking ready to sprint upward, despite not knowing where the nursery was located. He wrapped his hand around her upper arm, making sure his fingers didn't dig into her soft flesh.

"No!" he said.

She turned frantic eyes to him. "But it's Ewan!"

"I know who it is, and Annag is up there with him. She'll calm him and get him back to bed."

"You doona understand. It's too much for him!"

Ewan wailed again, and Deirdre looked like she might burst from her skin in her desperation to get to him. "Maybe if he knew her beforehand, it would work, or if the room, the keep, wasn't new to him," she continued. "But the last thing he'll remember is being on your horse in my arms, riding through the forest. That's too much change for a bairn, too quickly."

"I'll go," Gavin said. He signaled Clyde, who rushed forward surprisingly quickly for such a burly man. Gavin handed Deirdre over to him.

"I'll come too," Kerr said. "He likes me. I can make him laugh."

"And me," Isobel said.

"Nay, just Kerr. Isobel, go with Deirdre and Clyde, please. Help get her settled. I doona want any more new faces."

"But maybe he'll remember me?" Isobel lifted her chin stubbornly. "We used to play together all the time. I was like a mother to him, when Cristel was so distant."

"He didn't remember *me*, Isobel. He was too young when he was taken to remember any of us." Gavin grasped her shoulders, directing her toward the other staircase at the opposite end of the hall.

Clyde followed her, leading Deirdre. She resisted, and he wrapped his arm around her shoulders to keep her moving. The man was built like a mountain. She had to go with him or she'd be flattened.

She looked over her shoulder at Gavin, her eyes pleading. "He'll think I've abandoned him!"

"Nay, I'll explain that you're sleeping in your chamber. He's four years old. He'll settle down eventually, like he did when you were at the gathering."

Gavin couldn't bear to look at her desperate, heartbroken face anymore. He stepped through the stairwell entrance and quickly climbed upward, Kerr on his heels. Ewan's sobs increased in volume as they neared the nursery.

His son sat on his bed, no longer in his plaid but still wearing his long, travel-stained linen shirt, with his back in the corner and his knees pulled up. A candle burned on the bedside table, and the fire still crackled in the hearth. Annag sat beside him with the same carved warrior in her hand that she'd held earlier.

Aye, his lad was kicking up a storm—scared and upset but angry too. And desperate, same as Deirdre. When Annag tried to give him the toy warrior, he kicked it away. "Where's my mother?"

"Ewan, stop yelling," Gavin said from the doorway. "Deirdre is downstairs in her bedchamber, sleeping. She's verra tired. You'll wake her up."

The boy's face crumpled, and he started sobbing as soon as he saw Gavin. Annag turned her head to him, relief evident in her face. "'Tis good you're here. I canna settle him."

Ewan crawled over the bed and ran toward Gavin. Heart swelling, Gavin leaned down to swoop his son into his arms, to love him and comfort him, but Ewan dodged past him and out the door.

"Ewan!" he said sternly.

"Whoa! What do I have here?" Kerr's voice boomed behind him. Gavin turned to see his foster brother picking up a squirming Ewan.

Kerr sniffed loudly, then said, "Is it a rabbit? I hope so. I'm terribly hungry."

He gnawed on Ewan's arm, but instead of laughing, the boy yelled, "Put me down!"

Kerr ignored him. "Well, it canna be a rabbit. Rabbits canna talk." He lifted Ewan higher in the air and sniffed his tummy. "Are you a badger, then? Badgers can talk."

"No, they canna!" Ewan began to giggle. "I'm a boy."

"A boy? Lads canna talk! Only lasses."

"They can too. Even better than lasses."

"Gooder," Kerr corrected him.

Ewan scrunched up his face in confusion. "What?"

"Boys talk even gooder than lasses."

Gavin rolled his eyes in exasperation. Just what he needed—Deirdre getting after him for ruining Ewan's grammar on top of everything else. He reached for Ewan, and Kerr handed him over.

"Boys doona talk better than lasses," Gavin said, "but they definitely talk better than uncles. And bears."

"Bears canna talk either," Ewan said.

"I know several bears who can talk. Beginning with the bear behind you."

Ewan looked over his shoulder as Gavin walked with him back to bed. When he giggled, Gavin could only assume Kerr had done something funny.

"Ewan, I'm sorry I wasn't here when you woke. It must have been frightening to be in a place you didn't know, with no one you remembered." He stopped in front of Annag, who'd risen from the bed and faced them with a smile on her face. "This is Annag. She used to take care of you before you lived with Deirdre. She also took care of me and Aunt Isobel when we were bairns."

"Who is Aunt Isobel?"

"She's my sister. You'll meet her in the morning. You used to play with her all the time when you lived here before."

"How come I canna remember her?"

"You were a wee bairn when you left. You hadn't yet turned two."

Ewan looked around the room, his eyes lighting on the carved, toy warriors with interest. "Did I play with those?"

"Aye, you did. They were your favorite."

"I have some at home that Old Mungo made for me. Mama and I take them outside, and we play with them in the woods. Did Ma and I play with these ones too when we were here?"

Gavin took a moment to answer. "Nay. Deirdre ne'er played with them. She...didn't live with you when you used to live here."

"Where did she live?"

"At her keep...you didn't know her then."

Ewan quieted, his eyes growing troubled. "But she's my mother."

Gavin sat on the bed with him, then laid him down. "This is your home, Ewan. We've been waiting for you to come back. And we're all so happy to see you again. Your mother...your real mother..." He searched for the words, but they wouldn't come. How could he tell this little boy, his son, that his mother wasn't actually his mother? He'd be confused and even more anxious.

Ewan rolled away from him, onto his side, working the quilt between his fingers. The embroidered dragon moved back and forth like it was roaring—something he'd done as a bairn too.

Maybe he did remember. Maybe he'll slip into his old life and be happy—without Deirdre.

Ewan sat up and looked at the low table with his set of toy warriors on it, then crawled across the bed toward it. Gavin turned to watch him but stayed sitting, wanting him to explore the room on his own without any pressure. Kerr moved away from the door, toward the window, and opened the shutter to let in some cool night air.

Ewan picked up the smallest Highland warrior, which had always been his favorite, and jumped it across the table, making crashing sounds with his mouth every time the warrior landed. Annag came over to him and picked up another warrior.

"Are we fighting someone then, laddie?" she asked.

He looked up at her. "Aye. We're fighting the MacKinnons. My dragon's going to slay their laird."

Quiet descended on the room, other than the crackling fire—a quiet that was as noisy as the middle of a real battlefield. Annag straightened and caught Gavin's eye, her gaze filled with concern and pity. The pressure built again, his chest too tight for all the emotions that careened through him.

Ewan continued to walk around the table, jumping and crashing his smaller warrior into the other warriors, knocking them over. He stopped and looked over his shoulder at Gavin. "Mama's sleeping," he said, then without warning, he bolted for the open door, his wee legs flying under his loose linen shirt.

"Ewan!" Gavin shouted as he jumped from the bed to catch him. But at the same time Annag stepped between him and the door, her back to Gavin, and he almost knocked her over. He steadied her, then darted around just as Kerr passed him, and they smashed shoulders.

"God's blood!"

"Bloody thorns!"

They yelled at the same time.

"Doona curse in front of the bairn!" Annag shook her long finger at them.

"The bairn isna here," Kerr said. "By now he's halfway back to Deirdre's keep!"

"Mama!" Ewan cried out in the distance.

Gavin cursed again—this time under his breath—as he ran out the door. He just saw Ewan's white shirt disappear down the stairs at the other end of the hall. Fear propelled him now. What if the lad fell?

Deirdre would give him that look again—the same one she gave him when Ewan tumbled off his horse and Thor almost stepped on him. *Why weren't you watching him?*

Ewan yelled again as Gavin ducked his head and ran down the stairs. He could hear Kerr—even bigger than him—bringing up the rear. His size made it difficult to move quickly in the confined space.

"Mama!"

And this time he heard a desperate-sounding Deirdre yell back, "Ewan!"

Devil be damned. She knows.

"Ewan, I'm here, sweetling!"

He reached the next landing and looked down the lit passageway. Ewan tore along the hall toward a surprised-looking Clyde. He stood guard outside one of the rooms, his legs spread for better balance, one arm anchored across the opening, like he was trying to keep someone inside. The door was open, and Gavin could see Deirdre—her long, black hair loose and flowing over her shoulders, her fair skin glowing in the candlelight—peeking around Clyde's huge shoulder.

"Ewan!" she yelled again when she saw the lad.

"Mama!" His son darted straight at the big warrior, who looked as concerned as Gavin had ever seen him, and Gavin almost laughed. Clyde could face down a trained warrior with a huge battle-ax or a wild, rampaging boar single-handed, but send a four-year-old in a nightshirt running at him, and he looked like he'd seen the hounds of hell.

Gavin slowed, waiting for Clyde to scoop up Ewan or to hold him in place. But Ewan feinted left, then right, darted between Clyde's legs, and disappeared into Deirdre's room.

"Where'd he go?" Clyde asked, whipping his head around.

Gavin sighed. "Through your legs."

"Nay! I'd have..." He looked behind him and shook his head. "My daughters ne'er moved so fast at that age."

Gavin stood in front of him and signaled for him to step aside. When Clyde moved, Gavin walked through the doorway and found his son in Deirdre's arms, his legs wrapped around her waist and his arms around her neck. She'd retreated to the farthest corner in the room and stared at Gavin with pleading, yet also defiant, eyes.

"They told me you were sleeping. But you're still dressed," Ewan said to her.

"Aye, laddie. I was just about to get ready for bed. Gavin—your da—knew that I was sleepy."

"Why is he my da? I thought that Da was my da."

"So did I, sweetling. But you ne'er saw your other da much, and he didn't play with you like Gavin does. And Gavin also has Thor."

"Aye, and he said I can get my own horse too!"

"It'll be a grand place to live, doona you think?"

Gavin had moved slowly toward them and stopped in the middle of the chamber, waiting for his son's answer. Praying he'd say yes.

"Aye. But I want to sleep with you. I doona like it upstairs."

Deirdre's gaze clashed with his. She'd said encouraging things to Ewan about Gavin and his new home—and even called him "da," for which he was grateful—but in this she stayed quiet.

He would have to tear his son from Deirdre's arms.

~

Deirdre's eyes drifted open, her lids heavy and body leaden. A sunlit bedchamber came into view—the carved wooden door across from her, a beautiful standing wardrobe in the corner, and a wooden chest beside it. She lay on a canopied bed under a heavy quilt, still wearing her long, white linen shift from the last few days, dirty and wrinkled from the road. The air was cool, the fire having gone out sometime after she'd handed a sleeping Ewan to Gavin last night. When he'd returned her son to the nursery in the wee hours of the morning—for the third time.

Nay, that wasn't right. Ewan had come down a fourth time, and she and Gavin had sat quietly with him in front of the fire as they waited for him to fall asleep, in a strange kind of...camaraderie.

Ewan had wanted to sleep with her in her bed, of course, and had whined and cried to do so, but she'd seen the stubborn no in Gavin's eyes. Sitting in the chair had seemed like a reasonable compromise. Next time maybe she would walk Ewan back up to the nursery herself. If there was a next time.

She looked toward the chairs grouped in front of the cold fire and realized she had no memory of handing her son to Gavin that last time. Or crawling into the bed.

Was I too tired to remember? Or did...did...Gavin lift me up, just like he did Ewan, and lay me down here?

A shiver ran over her, and she sat up. "Ewan!"

A creaking sound startled her as more light poured into the room. She turned her head, expecting to find her son on a chair playing with the shutters. Isobel stood there instead, tall and willowy, her long, blond hair hanging in soft curls to her hips. She'd just opened the wooden coverings over the window.

She turned to face Deirdre, her skirts swishing and a smile lighting up her face.

Deirdre couldn't help staring. She was by far the most beautiful woman Deirdre had ever seen—even more so than Deirdre's mother and sisters—and her eyes were the same startling blue-green as Ewan's and Gavin's.

How did I miss that last night?

In comparison, Deirdre hadn't even washed off the dirt of the trail or the smell of Thor. Embarrassment crashed over her.

"He's well," Isobel said. "He broke his fast with Gavin and Kerr, and now they're outside in the bailey, kicking around a ball. That was a favorite sport of Gavin's when he was younger."

Isobel moved to a side table and poured some mead from a pitcher into a cup. "Gavin had all kinds of toys made for Ewan when he first disappeared, thinking he'd find him right away. But then winter came upon us, making travel more difficult, and all our leads turned out to be false. 'Twas a desperate, worrying time."

"I'm sure it was," Deirdre said faintly. Isobel placed the filled cup on a tray beside a steaming bowl of oats and an apple and carried it toward her. Deirdre pulled the quilt up higher, trying to hide behind it. Isobel would surely take one look at her dirty face, smell the horse on her, then pinch her nose, make a face, and leave.

"Gavin lost himself in whisky for a while, but fortunately, with the help of Gregor and his foster brothers, he stopped drinking so much. Kerr especially stayed close, keeping an eye on him, which was both a blessing and a curse." She sat down on the side of the bed beside Deirdre. "I know he's your cousin, but he's a most annoying man."

Deirdre scooted a little farther away and tried to smooth her tangled hair with her fingers. "He is annoying—he took my hairbrush. And I only just met him, cousin or not."

"He took it?" Isobel asked indignantly.

"Aye, he pulled it from my bag and tossed it on the steps of my keep. He said I could have it only if I told him what was running through my mind."

"Well, I hope you told him in great, colorful detail!" A frown marred Isobel's beautiful face.

"Nay! I didn't want to aggravate him."

"Och! That one likes to be aggravated. The louder

he gets the happier he is. 'Tis when he's quiet that you have to worry."

"He wasn't quiet last night, and he and Gavin almost came to blows. And you right in the middle of them! I was worried they would strike you."

"Strike me? Nay. Although they'd yell at me, no doubt. And they've both threatened to lock me in my bedchamber from time to time, but the consequences for *that* would be to the heavens and back."

"Consequences? You mean…from you?" Deirdre asked.

"Aye. Who did you think I meant?"

"I don't know. But…"

"But?"

"Well, surely they're bigger than you. And stronger."

"Aye, but I'm meaner." Isobel grinned wickedly. "I'd strike when they'd least expect it, and I'm verra creative. No one wants to be on *my* bad side."

Deirdre gazed at her, unable to comprehend exactly what Isobel was saying. "So you would take your revenge—deliberately hurt them or bother them in some way—and they would…allow it?"

Confusion replaced Isobel's grin, a feeling Deirdre could understand. "Well, yes, except…what do *you* mean 'allow it'?"

Heat prickled Deirdre's chest and rose up her cheeks. She had to force the words out. "I canna imagine that they wouldnae beat you for…disobeying them."

Isobel's eyes grew wide. She clasped Deirdre's hand—the only part of her body that had been thoroughly washed since she'd left her keep days ago. "Is that what happened to you? Did your husband beat you to keep you in line?"

Deirdre's brows shot up. "Nay! Lewis would ne'er hurt a fly. He's a kind, gentle soul. And I thank the saints every day that I was sent to him."

"His father, then? I've heard he's a cruel man."

Deirdre squirmed, wishing she'd never started this inane conversation, especially as she hardly knew Isobel. "I met his father when we were married, but not since then." She tugged her hand free of Isobel's grasp, grabbed her food tray, and began spooning the oatmeal into her mouth—without tasting it, without thought—something she hadn't done for years.

Her mother's voice sounded sharply in her head. *Shove the food in a little faster, Deirdre. It'll go to your chest and your hips that much quicker.*

She closed her eyes and forced the spoon down. When she opened them, she saw realization had dawned on Isobel's face. "'Twas your family, then. I'm so sor—"

"Doona be sorry for me. I haven't seen my family in seven years. Other than my brother, when he came to visit, but Lewis said something or did something, and Boyd left the next day. I was glad to see the back of him. He's a degenerate." Deirdre slowly put the bowl back on the tray and took a deep breath.

Isobel stared at her, her mouth opening and closing several times, obviously wanting to talk about it. Finally, she said, "It's a lovely day, maybe we could take Ewan to the loch for a picnic later on. He used to love going there when he was younger. I used to toddle in the water with him, and Gavin would put him on his shoulders and cross right to the island that lies a little way out."

"Aye, that sounds lovely." Deirdre sounded stilted, even to her own ears. "Ewan loves getting wet—and getting me wet along with him."

"How long have you had him, then?" Isobel asked, looking her right in the eye.

Deirdre wanted to look away, to claim that she was Ewan's birth mother, but Isobel didn't even blink, and the weight of her expectations held Deirdre in place. Tears gathered and slowly ran down her face. Aye, there was to be a reckoning. She couldn't protect anyone anymore, let alone herself or her son.

"Two years last fall," she whispered.

"Did Lewis bring him home to you?"

"Aye."

"And what did he say?"

Her throat had tightened, and the muscles in her face jerked in response to her grief, knowing that with this one conversation she was relinquishing her son. The corners of her mouth pulled downward, and her chin quivered. "That Ewan was his bastard, and I was to raise him as my own."

"And he told you the bairn's name was Ewan? You didn't give him that name yourself?"

"Nay, he came to me as Ewan."

"Do you remember exactly when that was?"

She nodded jerkily. "The fifteenth day of September. I didn't know his exact age or day of birth, and neither did Lewis, so I decided his birthday would be the day he was given to me. He's four now, isn't he?"

"Aye. And his birthday is November first—All

Saints' Day. You didn't find it odd that your husband knew not the day of his son's birth?"

"He said he wasn't there when Ewan was born and that Ewan's mother had recently died. I was to be his mother now, so it was my decision." She covered her mouth with her hand to hold back the sobs that erupted from deep within her. But she'd been holding in so much for so long, and the pain of it curled her over. "And I was just so happy to have a bairn. To love and be loved. He curled right into my arms, and he's been there e'er since."

Isobel wrapped her arm around Deirdre's back and pulled her close. "Och, love. Doona cry. Something will be arranged. I doona know what exactly, but none of us will take Ewan away from you."

Deirdre sat up, both hands now pressed tight against her mouth. She tried to slow her breathing, to swallow her sobs. Finally, she lowered her hands. Isobel's cheeks were wet too, and it somehow made it easier to know someone else felt her pain. That had never happened to her before.

"You're a kind woman, Isobel, and I thank you for your help. And for Kerr's as well, no matter how annoying he might be. But 'tis Gavin's decision, and he'll do what he thinks best for Ewan, as is his right."

"Aye. But doona despair, Deirdre. You've only just arrived. And soon, Gregor and the rest of Gavin's foster brothers will be here, and none of them will want to see you separated from Ewan either."

She nodded and forced a smile, but her hope waned with every passing moment.

Isobel brushed a strand of hair back from Deirdre's

cheek and tucked it behind her ear. "That's the smile. None of my brother's foster family will be able to resist that, whether they're married or not. So tragic and beautiful."

Deirdre's eyes jumped to Isobel's, expecting to see mockery and scorn, but Isobel's face held none of that. If anything, she looked a little…envious? Nay, that couldn't be right. She had nothing to be envious of.

Deirdre didn't even have her son.

She heard a laugh outside and recognized it immediately. Ewan. And then she heard someone else laugh—a man. She didn't know who it was, but when she turned to Isobel, a beaming smile had lit up her face.

"That's Gavin," Isobel said. "I haven't heard him laugh like that since Ewan was taken."

She hugged Deirdre tightly, and Deirdre could do nothing to shield herself; she had nowhere to hide her soft, rounded body.

"Thank God for you, Deirdre MacIntyre. You've brought my nephew *and* my brother back to me." Isobel jumped up with a grin and strode to the door. "I'm sure you'll be wanting a bath—and a hairbrush. I'll send some of the lasses up with a tub and some steaming hot water. You deserve it after all you've been through. And I'll see what I can do about getting some new shifts and dresses for you. I'd give you some of mine, but unfortunately, I doona have your curves. God must have thought it a grand jest to bless me with the body of a fourteen-year-old lad. A jest on my future husband too."

She stopped at the door and looked back at Deirdre, who felt like her eyes might pop out of their sockets. How could Isobel say that? Deirdre would kill to be as long and lean as she was—and as Deirdre's mother and sisters were.

"'Tis a shame you're already married," Isobel continued. "I canna imagine my brother would be able to resist you for long otherwise. 'Tis a heady combination."

Deirdre scrunched up her brow, confused. "Surely, you're a daft lass, Isobel MacKinnon. I doona understand a word you just said. What combination are you talking about?"

Isobel laughed and shook her head. "You havenae any idea, do you?"

"About what?" Now she was just annoyed. She threw back the covers and rose from the bed, frowning at the blond beauty.

"About you, sweetling. Look at you—the face of an angel, the body of a siren, and the heart of a saint—with a wee bit of the devil thrown in too, I think. And you love my brother's son to the ends of the earth and back. How could any man resist that? Gavin may kill your thieving husband for taking Ewan, but in a corner of his heart, he may also kill him for you."

Seven

"Did you sleep last night?" Kerr asked.

Gavin glanced up from where he leaned, his forearms on the top rail of the corral that penned in the five baby goats—and one baby Ewan. The mother had sickened when the kids were too young to care for themselves, and they'd been brought into the stable to keep warm and safe. Now they were thriving—just like his son. Aye, the similarities weren't lost on Gavin.

"Not much. I returned Ewan to the nursery four times."

Kerr's brows raised. "He escaped that often?"

"Nay, I didn't try to stop him from leaving after the first time. He'd wake, sometimes we'd talk for a while, even play for a bit, but then he'd always run for Deirdre."

"And what did she do?"

He shrugged. "She was waiting for him when he came down, and she held him by the fire until he fell asleep. I suppose she couldnae sleep either."

"She didn't break her fast this morning, so she must have slept eventually."

Gavin rolled his neck on his shoulders. He didn't want to talk about this with Kerr. "The last time Ewan came down, she fell asleep holding him."

"In the chair? That couldnae have been comfortable."

"I...transferred her to the bed after I put Ewan down. 'Twas naught. She weighs no more than a lass."

Kerr slowly turned his head to look at him. Gavin refused to look back. After a moment, Kerr returned his attention to Ewan playing with the baby goats, but his fingers tapped on the wooden post. Gavin knew it was only a matter of time before Kerr brought it up again.

And he didn't want to share that time spent with Deirdre—in front of the fire as she held his son—with anyone. The castle had been quiet, everyone but the guards asleep, and the time with her had been intimate. Peaceful.

And that had bothered him.

Deirdre's life was anything but peaceful right now. He'd come into her keep during the dark of night and shredded her existence to pieces—and it would only get worse once he'd sent her away and gone to war with her clans. She'd have no one. No husband, no child, no means of support if the MacIntyres cut her off or the MacColls refused to take her back.

He'd do his best to take care of her physical needs, and Kerr too, by the sounds of it, but she would lose all the wealth and status she'd had as the next lady of Clan MacIntyre.

And he knew how important that was to a woman like her, a woman bred to be a laird's wife, with few other skills.

Isobel would deny it, but it was no different with

her. Gavin hadn't even thought about it until meeting his foster brothers' wives. Until he'd seen how Amber and Maggie in particular had bucked tradition and could take care of themselves. Caitlin too, with her knowledge of animals and farming.

He sighed. "Do you think we should teach Isobel how to fight?"

Kerr's mouth flattened. "Nay."

"I'm not talking about daggers or a bow like Maggie wields, but if she had some skill in self-defense, like Amber, she would be safer."

"Why are we talking about Isobel when you're thinking about Deirdre?"

Now it was Gavin's turn to flatten his mouth. "I am not thinking of Deirdre."

"Aye, you are. And how could you not? She's a lovely lass, and you have the power to break her or save her. That's about as basic as it gets for a man."

Gavin huffed in exasperation. "You've been in the sun for too long. Your brain has been cooked like a steaming pile of oats—mushy and stuck together like glue."

"Nay, I just doona romanticize things the way you do."

"My feelings for her are not romantic."

"In that we agree. They're mostly angry, but deep down you feel the pull toward her—whether she's married or not."

"The only pull I feel is the need to get her out of Ewan's life. You weren't there at the gathering, Kerr. You didn't see the fear and panic in her eyes. She knew what I'd lost and still couldn't get away fast enough to go back and hide Ewan from me."

"Aye, Gavin. Fear and panic. Listen to your own words. You said that you were rude to her, and you behaved aggressively."

"I did not!"

"You used crude, cruel words, by your own admission, and I can only assume that your tone was the same. She had the right to protect her son."

"Not from me she didn't. And he's *my* son."

"And how was she to know that?"

"She only had to look at my face, in my eyes, and she would know."

"Nay, I meant how was she to know that she didn't need to protect Ewan from you? You were harsh and unkind. What kind of mother would she be if she let that kind of man anywhere near her son?"

"Are you saying I'm unfit to be Ewan's father?"

"I'm saying that you have a well of rage within you—and you have e'er since you married Cristel—that you haven't let go. Unless you can accept what happened and move on, your son will either be corrupted by it, as you have been, or he will grow to hate you for it, as I did my father. Let it go, Gavin, and find a way to keep Deirdre in his life instead of punishing her. Punishing them both."

"I am nothing like your father!"

"Nay, you're not. But you're also not like your old self either. Or *your* father. Or Gregor."

The blood pounded in Gavin's veins. That tight, hot feeling invaded his chest, throbbed in his temples, and burned his ears. He'd spent all last night and this morning taking care of his son, playing with him. And then Kerr gives him a lecture about being a better man?

"She took my son. She ran from me."

"Someone else took your son. She loved and protected him—from others as well as from you."

Gavin's lips pulled back from his teeth in an angry grimace as he turned on Kerr…just as Ewan called out, "Mama!" and ran toward him. His son reached his arms up for him, wanting to get out of the pen. Schooling his expression, Gavin lifted Ewan from the enclosure. The lad immediately squirmed to get down, but Gavin held him tight as he turned around to see Deirdre and Isobel descending the stairs from the keep.

Kerr let out a low whistle, then moved forward. Isobel saw him coming and glowered. He held his hands out to the sides and continued walking. "Keep frowning, dearling. It just makes it that much sweeter when I finally make you smile."

Deirdre's lips tipped up proportionately to how much Isobel's brow furrowed. They were opposite in every way—small and curved versus tall and slender; dark and fair-skinned versus blond and tanned; soft, gray eyes that drew you in versus sea-green eyes that startled you with their vividness.

Gavin understood why his sister was a renowned beauty, but it was Deirdre's long, dark locks and fair skin that he couldn't stop wanting to touch—and the rest of her, despite his seething anger at her actions. Aye, his fingers itched to caress the lush curves of her body. His hands wanted to palm that rounded arse as he—

"I want Mama!" Ewan screamed in his ear, shattering not only Gavin's fantasy, but quite possibly his eardrum as well, and he realized how tightly he'd been squeezing his son.

"Aye, lad, so do I," he said gruffly.

He put him on the ground, and his son ran across the bailey to Deirdre, but it wasn't the happy, excited yells of a lad who'd had a fun morning with his da and uncle. No—Ewan was sobbing and crying out for her.

Deirdre reached down and swept him into her embrace, coming to his rescue once again. Ewan wrapped her up tight, arms around her shoulders, legs around her waist, and tucked his face into the crook of her neck. Gavin looked back at the goats, trying to determine what the trouble might have been. Had one of the goats butted or bitten him? Or maybe some hay had lodged in his eye—he'd noticed Ewan had been rubbing them for quite some time.

He looked back at the four of them. Kerr and Isobel had gathered around Deirdre to help soothe Ewan. Gavin stood apart, his feet rooted to the spot, feeling like an outsider in his own castle—in his own family. No matter what he did, how much time he spent with his son, Ewan kept returning to Deirdre for comfort.

He shoved his fingers through his spiky hair, a bit longer than usual by now, and this time when he fisted his hand and yanked upward, he got just enough purchase on the strands to feel a bite of pain.

It felt good.

He turned on his heel and started walking, not sure where he was going. He ended up in the stable in front of Thor's stall. The stallion huffed and tossed his head, sensing Gavin's mood, but then he dropped his muzzle and snuffled his rider's shoulder. Gavin leaned into Thor's soft cheek for just a moment before he opened the stall, readied the horse, and swung into the saddle.

He pressed his heels into Thor's flanks and leaned forward. The horse sprang into a run. Groomsmen jumped back as he exited the stables and crossed the bailey toward the portcullis.

"Gavin!" Kerr yelled from behind him.

He didn't answer, and he heard Kerr whistle to send men after him. Gavin crossed under the iron gate and wheeled around on the other side of the castle wall. Thor raised up on two legs, front hooves slashing the air, a reflection of his master's agitation.

"Close the portcullis," Gavin ordered the guard stationed there. "And tell Clyde not to open it until he canna see Thor's backside—no matter what Laird MacAlister threatens!"

"Aye, Laird!" the man said just before the portcullis dropped down with a rattle and a bang.

Gavin turned Thor and raced across the open fields toward the tree line in the distance.

Gavin spent all day evading "capture" by Kerr and his men. He'd ridden long and hard along creek beds and game trails, even leading Thor by the reins up the side of a rocky mountain. He'd allowed them to get close on several occasions and hid silently as he watched them go by.

One of those times, Kerr had stopped and looked around, surely recognizing it was a good place for Gavin to stay close yet unseen. He'd gone to the spot Gavin had originally chosen and looked under the brush, but Gavin had moved somewhere else that was harder to access. He held his breath as Kerr looked right at him—or rather, at his current hiding spot.

His foster brother rubbed the back of his neck in exasperation. "Come on out, ye wee shite, and quit being a bloody *ablach*! The lad was just tired from being up most of the night. Bairns need their mothers when they're exhausted."

Gavin set his jaw at that and remained hidden. *She is not his mother!*

Kerr and his men left, and when Gavin was sure they'd moved on, he came out, brushed himself off, then pulled Thor from his hiding spot. "You're a good lad," he said, rubbing the soft fur on his nose up and down. He wandered aimlessly for a while, then stopped on a sloping meadow. Letting go of the reins, he flopped down onto the grass, his arms and legs spreading out as he stared up at the blue sky.

The sun was warm above him, but the grass was cool—opposites, just like his conflicting emotions. He was grateful for Deirdre, yet he was angry with her as well. He felt protective toward her, but he also wanted to tear Ewan out of her arms. He wanted her gone, yet he *wanted* her.

Aye, at least I've finally admitted that *to myself.*

A soft whistle sounded in the trees. One of his men, checking on him.

He whistled back. *I'm well.*

It was a lie. He sat up, his arms on his knees, and looked out across his land. He knew he was being an idiot, running and hiding from Kerr, but he'd needed to escape, needed the physical exertion and exhilaration of staying one step ahead of his foster brother to calm the chaos in his body and his mind.

It was the next best thing to fighting Kerr—fighting anyone—and beat escaping into the bottom of whisky-filled cups.

He'd thought that when he got Ewan back, life would be perfect. That having his son in his arms would magically make everything good again.

But here Gavin was, feeling like the hole inside him had grown so big that even Ewan couldn't fill it. And most of the time, Ewan didn't care to. No, he had Deirdre now, leaving Gavin feeling upended, and… enraged. At Cristel who had tricked him, at the people who had kidnapped his son, at Deirdre for stealing the lad's affection away from him.

She was an imposter who'd taken Gavin's place in Ewan's life for two and a half years. Time Gavin could never get back.

She'd replaced him.

Nay. I willna have it! I am the boy's family. Not her!

"Laird MacKinnon."

Gavin stiffened, even though he recognized Finn's voice immediately. The fact that someone had been able to sneak up on him unawares—especially his own man, who wouldn't have been trying to keep his presence hidden—increased Gavin's agitation.

Finn could have put a knife in his back and he wouldn't have noticed a thing until too late.

He turned, and the tall, skinny lad smiled at him uncertainly. "I whistled, but you ne'er whistled back. Someone's here."

"Who?" Gavin asked, rising to his feet.

"A messenger from Lewis MacIntyre."

"Where is he?"

"At the border by McGilly Creek. We knew you were out here and came to fetch you rather than escorting him to the castle. 'Twill not take us long to get there."

Gavin whistled for Thor, who was grazing at the edge of the clearing. The stallion lifted his head, ears pricked forward, and trotted swiftly toward him. "Does my foster brother know he's here? Or my sister?"

"Nay, but we can send a runner to find Laird MacAlister and alert the castle."

"'Twill not be necessary," Gavin said quickly. Thor arrived at his side, and Gavin mounted the stallion. "'Tis a MacKinnon matter. I doona want anyone else to know."

Finn's brows rose in surprise. "Aye, Laird. I'll spread the word."

Gavin urged Thor onto the path toward the border, anticipation thrumming in his veins. He hadn't thought the MacIntyres would respond this fast. Although Finn had said it was a message from Lewis MacIntyre, and not his father...someone who had followed behind them from Deirdre's keep, perhaps?

When he reached the border crossing by McGilly's Creek, he saw a lean lad around Finn's age standing beside an old horse that looked ready to drop. The mare's sides heaved, and her head drooped nearly to the ground.

The lad rubbed her neck, but he hadn't led her to the creek. Too nervous to move, perhaps. The three MacKinnon warriors who guarded him weren't menacing, but they looked battle-hardened and ready to fight.

Gavin whistled as he dismounted, and when one of his men ran forward, he said, "Take the mare for a drink and bring water for me and the lad. He looks ready to fall down. And take Thor too. The mare will feel better if he's there."

"Aye, Laird."

They approached the lad, who looked even more nervous than before. When the guard reached for the mare's reins, the lad shook his head. "Nay, I'll keep her."

"She's done in, lad," Gavin said. "He's just going to water the horses at the creek. And Thor is good with the females, no matter their age. He calms them."

He reluctantly gave up the reins, and Gavin indicated for them to move under the shade of a sprawling tree. "I'm Gavin MacKinnon, Laird of Clan MacKinnon. You have a message from MacIntyre?"

"I'm Tomaidh, Laird. The message is from the son, Lewis, not from Laird MacIntyre. Master Lewis has asked to speak to you privately. His father isna here yet, but once he is, the opportunity will be lost. And Master Lewis asks you to bring along his wife, Lady MacIntyre. He said she is innocent, and he wishes for her safe return."

"What about my son? He ne'er mentioned Ewan?"

The lad blanched and swallowed. "He said naught about the lad. Only that he wanted to talk with you before his father arrived. He's at a shepherd's hut on Campbell land. I can take you and Lady MacIntyre there as soon as you're ready."

Gavin peered at him and determined the lad was

not attempting to deceive him. The question was whether Lewis MacIntyre told the truth or not. "Were you at the keep, Tomaidh, when I arrived with my men to take back Ewan?"

"Aye, Laird." His voice shook, and Gavin almost felt sorry for the lad.

"You made good time. Did you leave right after we did to find Lewis?"

"Maybe an hour after. Master MacIntyre was at a…place along the way, so we didn't lose any time coming here."

"A place?" What was Lewis MacIntyre doing when he wasn't with his wife?

The lad nodded but didn't add anything further, and Gavin didn't intend to force him. "Were there any other men there? Guards?" he asked.

The lad shook his head this time. "Nay, but we stopped and picked up Old Ailig and Colla MacIntyre on the way."

"So, if what you say is true, Lewis MacIntyre is waiting to speak to me—a man who kidnapped his wife and a lad he claimed was his child—with only two other men to help him should he need it. Is this something you'll swear to?"

The lad rubbed a shaking hand across his brow. "'Twas how it was when I left, Laird. I doona think Master MacIntyre intends to deceive you. He's just concerned for his wife and wants her back. Our keep has naught to do with Laird MacIntyre and the castle folk. And whate'er happened with your son, Lady MacIntyre is as innocent of any wrongdoing as her husband says. She's a kind, generous woman."

Gavin nodded and clapped a hand on the lad's shoulder to reassure him. "I believe you, Tomaidh. And you have naught to worry about. Rest here until I return."

"Thank you, Laird."

Gavin passed the approaching guard on his way back to Thor. He took the water the warrior held out and drank thirstily. When he was done, he wiped his arm across his mouth. "It looks like we'll have another beautiful day tomorrow. A good day for traveling."

"Are you going somewhere, Laird?"

"Maybe." He handed back the cup. "Take care of the lad and put him at ease. The mare too. They'll need to be well rested for tomorrow…just in case. And keep some of your men here tonight."

Gavin's mind drifted back to last fall and the attack on Callum's land by an unknown force of twenty men. Seasoned warriors, but not good enough to take down Callum, Gavin, and four of their men.

Still, it was only due to good fortune that Callum's wife, Maggie, hadn't been killed.

"And gather at least ten men, including a marks-man…just in case."

"Aye, Laird. I'll gather our best. Just in case."

Gavin pushed Thor hard on the way home. He wanted to beat Kerr back to the castle so he wouldn't have to ride with him and answer any questions or talk about his "rage." Aye, maybe he wasn't like his old self anymore, but too much had happened for him to remain the same. And as far as he knew, his father had never gone through anything like Gavin had suffered with Cristel and Ewan.

But even more importantly, he didn't want to talk to Kerr about Lewis MacIntyre's request for a meeting—or Deirdre's return.

At least not until he knew what he planned to do. He was fair certain, if he did choose to return Deirdre, he'd have to do it behind his foster brother's back. Isobel's too.

He shoved a hand through his hair and tugged, welcoming the sharp pain.

He was a third of the way into the clearing around Castle MacKinnon when thundering hooves sounded behind him. He didn't turn around. He knew who it was, and he sighed.

"You have leaves in your hair," Kerr said as he reined in his big black stallion.

"From hiding in the brush and watching you stomping through the forest, looking for me like a wee lad of ten. Not that I was worried. You couldnae find your arse with a… Oh, wait, of course you could. 'Tis the size of a—"

"I knew you were there. I was just giving you time to run off *your* wee sulk," Kerr threw back at him.

"I wasn't running. I was evading."

"Oh, aye. Well, evade this." Kerr's fist punched Gavin's shoulder just as Gavin kicked his foot into the back of Kerr's thigh.

They both fought to keep seated in their saddles, and when Gavin urged Thor into a gallop, Kerr accelerated right beside him. They raced neck and neck toward the portcullis, their bodies bent low over their mounts, their hands and feet trying to push the other rider off course.

At the last moment, Gavin took advantage of a rise in the path on his side and directed Thor to leap forward and land just far enough in front of Kerr to knock his stallion sideways, so Gavin crossed under the portcullis first.

His men and some of the castle folk had been watching the race and cheered his triumph. He laughed, his blood pumping though his veins, exhilaration pouring through his body, and he did a little victory lap around the bailey. "Clan MacKinnon!" he yelled, and his men returned the cry: "Clan MacKinnon!"

When he neared the keep, he caught sight of Isobel sitting on the top stair, laughing. Deirdre and Ewan stood on the grass below. Deirdre held the round, leather bag that Gavin and Ewan had been kicking around the bailey earlier. Deirdre's other hand crossed over Ewan's body and held him tight against her legs, even though the lad struggled to get free.

To get to his da!

Anger burned through Gavin, turning his exhilaration to ash. He hadn't told her not to play with the ball, but still it infuriated him—that was his and Ewan's game—and then to top it off, she kept his son by her side.

Kerr reined in beside him. "She's just holding the lad back from the horses. You doona want him running under their hooves again, do you?"

Gavin clenched his jaw and then forced himself to release the tight muscles, to smile. "Nay, of course not." He turned Thor toward the stables, and Kerr fell in beside him. "I was thinking perhaps tomorrow we could have a family outing at the loch. Spend all day there. You and Isobel could go ahead with Ewan—'twill be good for you to have some time alone with her. And it will give me time to talk to Deirdre without everyone around. 'Tis time we cleared the air, and for me to take her needs into consideration, so I have a better understanding how to move forward from here."

Kerr glanced at him, his brows raised. "Aye, a family excursion would be nice. And I always welcome time alone with Isobel."

Gavin nodded and looked up at the sky, but his mind was elsewhere, making plans. And he repeated the words he'd said earlier after speaking to Lewis MacIntyre's messenger. "It looks like we'll have another beautiful day tomorrow. A good day for… the loch."

Eight

DEIRDRE WOKE THE NEXT MORNING WITH DREAD twisting her stomach. Gavin MacKinnon had let Ewan sleep with her last night.

Why?

He'd been gone all day yesterday and then disappeared into his solar as soon as he'd returned home. He didn't even appear for the evening meal, nor when Ewan ran down to her room in the middle of the night.

She'd sat up with her son at first, waiting for Gavin to appear and take him back up to the nursery. In a strange way, she'd missed him—missed the intimacy that had been woven between them the night before as they'd sat together in front of the fire, waiting for Ewan to fall asleep. And before that, when she'd sat all day cushioned against his body on top of Thor, his arms encircling her and Ewan, keeping them safe.

She pulled her son close to her body under the covers and pressed her nose to his hair, inhaling deeply. He smelled like Ewan, like her wee lad, and tears sprang to her eyes.

Is this the last time I'll hold him in my arms? Is that why Gavin didn't come for him last night?

Ewan squirmed, and she realized she was squeezing him too tight. She kissed his head and whispered, "I'm sorry." Her voice sounded thick and broken.

"S'all right, Mama," Ewan slurred sleepily. He wrapped his arms around her neck and pressed his soft, rounded cheek to hers.

"I love you, sweetling. So much," she said into his ear, her voice hitching. The tears flowed freely now. "No matter what happens, ne'er forget that. I am your mother, and you'll be mine to the edges of the earth and back. Hold on to that forever."

"Aye, Mama. I love you too."

Ewan snuggled into her, and she turned her face into the pillow to muffle the sounds of her sobs. A soft knock at the door broke the quiet.

This is it.

Ewan sat up, rubbing his eyes. "Someone's here."

The door opened quietly, and Annag pushed her gray head around the edge. When she saw Ewan watching her, she smiled brightly and came in. Deirdre sat up too, pulling the covers up over her linen shift and letting her hair fall forward to hide her wet face.

"It's time to get ready, lad," the nursemaid said. "You have a busy day today!"

Ewan had played toy warriors with Annag before bed last night and had fallen under her spell, just like everyone had reassured Deirdre that he would.

"What are we doing?" he asked, as he pushed back the quilt and crawled out of the bed.

"We're all going to the loch. We'll be able to play

in the water and even have our midday meal there! We can take your warriors too, if you like, and set them up on the rocks and in the forest."

Ewan let out an exuberant *whoop* as he jumped up and down in his white linen shirt, his bare feet dancing and his blond hair flopping over his brow. A smile split his face, making those blue-green eyes sparkle like the afternoon sunlight shining on the sea. Deirdre would remember him looking like this forever.

"Is Mama coming too?" he asked.

"Nay," Gavin's deeper voice intoned from the doorway.

Deirdre gasped in surprise as Gavin pushed her bedroom door open wide. She pulled the covers up to her chin and couldn't help searching his face—for what, she didn't know. For some sign of compassion and pity, perhaps? Or regret?

But he gave nothing away.

"Just Aunt Isobel and Uncle Kerr. And Annag, of course," he continued as he stepped inside. "And I wouldnae be surprised if some of the lads from the village will be there on a lovely day like today."

Ewan looked at Gavin, then over to her, then back to Gavin, trying to decide what to do. She could see his conflict—he really wanted to go, but he also wanted to stay with Deirdre—and she hated that he'd been put in this position. Finally, he walked around to Deirdre's side of the bed. "What will you do when I'm gone?" he asked.

She reached under his arms and lifted him into her lap, using her hair to screen them in again. "I doona know. But I want you to promise me that you'll do your very best to have fun today. And you must promise me one other thing. Can you guess what it is?"

"Nay."

"Promise that you'll always remember how much I love you. No matter what happens or what anyone else says, you are loved. By me, by your da, by Annag, Aunt Isobel, and Uncle Kerr. By all the people who knew you before you came to our wee keep and by all the people there who knew you, me most of all. You are a bright, shining star, Ewan. A gift to me and everyone else who's ever known you."

She held him tight, her voice muffled in his hair. "You bring love and laughter wherever you go, dearling. Thank you for that."

"I like it when you laugh," he said.

"I like it when you laugh too." She pressed her face to his hair, trying to wipe away her tears, then lifted him off her lap and guided him toward the door. "Go now. Have a fun day playing in the water. Just doona go in too far, and doona forget to tell the adults you're going in."

"Aye, Mama." He walked toward Gavin, then stopped halfway and turned around. His bottom lip trembled. "Mama, can I get a dog?"

A laugh puffed out from her lips despite the pain that threatened to break her in two. Her son had been asking her for a dog every week for the last year. She'd always said maybe, knowing the housekeeper would quite possibly lose her mind if a dog came to live with them in the keep. Now she looked him straight in the eye and said, "Yes, Ewan, you can have a dog. Your da will get a puppy for you from the first available litter." She raised her chin and looked Gavin straight in the eye. "Isn't that right, Laird MacKinnon? You will give your son a puppy as soon as possible. The pup will bring Ewan great comfort and distraction in the days to come."

He stared back at her, looking so grim she almost shivered. The shadows around his eyes had grown even darker, as if he hadn't slept at all last night, and the planes of his face were hard and unforgiving. And yet he was still a braw man. She'd been rendered breathless by it at times when she'd seen him laugh—like yesterday when he'd raced into the bailey on his horse.

Aye, she could imagine that he'd once been as braw as Isobel was bonnie—before his marriage and before he was filled with disillusionment. Before Ewan was taken and before he was ravaged by despair.

"Aye, Deirdre," he said, then looked at Ewan. "My son will have a pup as soon as the litter at the miller's is ready to be sold. Two males, I think, to keep you safe."

Ewan *whooped* again. Louder this time and with even more exuberance. "Can I really? You're not just saying that, like when Mama always says 'maybe'?"

"Aye. You have my word."

"Not two males," she said forcefully. "A male *and* a female. Boys need a woman's love to feel safe too."

Gavin swung his eyes back to Deirdre. She didn't dare blink, refused to blink, and for the first time, *he* dropped his eyes from hers. As he should. As much as he was hurting her by taking her son away, in taking Ewan's mother away, he was damaging his son for years to come.

Shame on you.

He looked up, almost as if he'd heard her words, and she finally saw the guilt etched on his face. So that was it then. He *was* taking her away.

"Go," she said, knowing she couldn't hold in her despair for much longer, and the last thing she wanted was a traumatic scene in front of Ewan. If she thought giving in to her emotions in front of him would do any good—for him and for her—she would yell and scream despite what had been drilled into her when she was growing up.

But she could see Gavin's mind was made up. Her leaving, her separation from her son, was inevitable, and she needed to make the transition as easy as possible for him.

Annag grasped Ewan's hand and led him toward the door. He stopped at the doorway and looked back at her, an adoring smile on his face. "I love you, Mama."

She smiled back tremulously. "I love you too, Ewan. I'll see you again as soon as I can." He left with a skip and a hop, no doubt thinking about puppies and fun times at the loch.

Gavin stood just inside her room, his arms hanging stiffly by his side. "I realize this must come as a shock to y—"

Deirdre threw back the covers and marched toward him, no longer hiding her agony or concerned about her state of undress.

His eyes widened as she planted her hands on his chest. She shoved him backward until he stepped across the threshold to her room into the passageway. "You're a monster," she said, then closed the door in his face and slid the bar across.

❧

The sun was warm on Deirdre's bent head. She'd been back on the saddle in front of Gavin now for about three hours and surrounded by fifteen of his men, including Tomaidh, a stable hand from her keep, and the three other warriors that she'd traveled with before—Clyde, Lorne, and Sheamais. She didn't know exactly where they were going, but they'd met up with the warriors near a creek, and Tomaidh told her they were on their way to meet Lewis—a half-day's ride away on Campbell land.

She'd only been able to nod in response and give him a forced smile, her cheeks wet and eyes red. Tomaidh had reached up and squeezed her hand in comfort, but Gavin had urged Thor forward, breaking the connection between them.

He canna even allow me that small bit of solace.

She'd held herself stiffly in the saddle the entire way, refusing to lean back against the man who had taken her son without any apology or thought of compromise. He didn't want to accept that things had changed, and he refused to consider how to make things work among the three of them, to find a way to keep Deirdre in Ewan's life.

He wanted to go back to the way things were, not how it was now. He was set on doing what was best for him, not Ewan—and in doing so, he was hurting his son.

And killing her.

"Deirdre," he said, his voice devoid of emotion.

She couldn't answer. Her throat was too tight, her sorrow too thick.

"I know you probably doona want to talk to me—"

She emphatically shook her head.

"If there was some way—"

"Doona lie to yourself," she croaked. "If you wanted what was best for your son, you would have tried to find a way."

"He needs to look to me. It's confusing for him to have us both there."

"You had two fathers. You doona seem confused by it."

"It's different, he's younger, and you're a laird's daughter."

"I'm his mother."

"Nay, you're not. Deirdre, I think—"

"I doona care what you think. Stop talking to me."

Gavin's arms stiffened around her. Well, what had he expected? Did he want her forgiveness or understanding? She wouldn't give it to him.

He was a selfish blackheart, the newest addition to the list of too many people who had hurt her.

She didn't care what he felt. Nay, she didn't care about anything at all anymore. A black cloud had descended upon her, leaving her feeling empty and almost numb to the pain that had eviscerated her earlier. She knew she cried, because her cheeks were wet, but the agony of loss no longer sliced through her.

When she'd lost Ewan, she'd lost hope. She'd lost feeling. She'd lost the will to live.

Her survival no longer concerned her nor did appeasing Gavin, because she was dead inside.

Time passed in a blur. Seconds became minutes; minutes became hours.

"Laird MacKinnon," she heard Tomaidh say, and she glanced up slowly to see the lad had moved his horse closer. "Is there a reason we're going so slow? If it's because of my mare, I assure you the rest yesterday did her a world of good, and she can go faster. At this rate, we willna arrive to meet Lewis until after dark. Not that it matters to him, he'll wait, but you'll end up returning in the night."

The fog cutting Deirdre off from reality lifted a little, and she realized they *were* moving slowly. Not nearly as fast as when they'd left. Maybe Thor was injured? Nay, he didn't seem to be limping, and he tossed his head a few times as if in protest to being restrained.

It must be Gavin then. She looked down and saw the muscles in his arms bulging and the reins held taut.

"'Tis not because of your mare, Tomaidh," he said, his voice rough. He brought Thor to a stop, and everyone fell into defensive positions.

Deirdre slowly glanced around the glade, wondering if…if… Were they turning back? She whipped her head around and looked at Gavin over her shoulder, hope bursting like a shard of light through the darkness that had enshrouded her.

Gavin's face was stony, his jaw rock hard. A tiny muscle twitched above his eye. "'Tis only a rest," he said.

Disappointment crashed through her, and a sob broke from her lips. She had to get down. To get away. She wouldn't travel one step farther from Ewan.

She threw herself off Thor, and Gavin barely grabbed her arm in time to stop her from falling. As soon as her feet touched the ground, she yanked her arm free of his grasp.

"Deirdre, wait," he commanded, but she didn't turn around. She just put one foot in front of the other. She couldn't quite see where she was going through the haze of tears and the curtain of her hair swooping forward across her cheeks, but she had a general sense of direction. Anywhere away from him. She blinked, clearing her vision for a moment, and followed a trail leading into the tree line.

A whistle sounded, but she paid little attention to it—her concentration was fixed on steadying her legs and not falling down. The ground veered sharply upward once she was in the trees, and she kept going, her breath wheezing in and out of her tight lungs and throat.

She grew light-headed from lack of air, and black dots danced in front of her eyes, but she kept pushing herself forward.

Her foot caught in a root, and she tumbled to the ground, her hand landing on a sharp rock and cutting her palm. The pain, real physical pain, felt good, and she smashed her hand down on the rock again just to feel more.

A loud sob burst from her throat. She stood, lifted her skirts—her old skirts from her old home—and ran.

She'd made up her mind that morning. If she couldn't keep Ewan, she wouldn't keep *anything* to remind her of Clan MacKinnon. Nothing but the toy horse Ewan had given to her when she went to the gathering, so she wouldn't be so lonely.

How many days ago was that? It seemed like a hundred. But it had been only a week at the most.

Just when she thought she might drop to the ground, her legs trembling and knees weak, the path became level once more. She found herself in another small clearing, a cliff rising on her right and curving around in front of her, and a rocky drop-off on her left. She crept toward the edge, her breath still laboring in her chest, her face wet, and blood trickling down her fingers.

She stopped and looked down into a deep, sheer gorge. The only way to go from there was back along the trail she'd just climbed up.

Nay, she wouldn't return that way. Back to Gavin and the looming despair and emptiness he'd brought upon her? Back to being unloved, alone, and childless?

She placed her toes right on the very edge, her skirts blowing in the breeze that swept up the cliff. Pebbles loosed from where she stood and fell silently down to the bottom. She waited to hear the tiny pings as the pebbles hit, but the sound never came.

She needed something bigger and heavier to throw over the edge. Something that would crash and break loud enough that she could feel it. She thought of the sharp rock she'd fallen on during her climb—how good the physical pain had felt to her aching soul.

How good it might feel right now.

She leaned forward and curled her toes over the edge.

Gavin dropped Thor's reins at the edge of the clearing and stepped into the trees. He needed privacy. His head and heart were chaotic, confused messes, and there was no way he could lead his men right now. His hands shook, his breath whooshed noisily in and out of his lungs, and that muscle twitched over his left eye again.

What was wrong with him? He'd kept it together better than this after his son had been kidnapped. And now that he had Ewan back and Deirdre leaving his life, he was coming apart—the last five years crashing in on him all at once.

Every fiber of his being was yelling at him to turn around, to return Deirdre to Ewan, to keep her safe—for the sake of his son, but in some confusing way, for him too.

He'd stopped the ride because he couldn't continue forward. To see Lewis…to see *her husband*. He didn't want to give her up. But he also didn't want to keep her.

Did he?

He shuddered, and a wave of longing mixed with confusion surged from his chest, making him gasp—long and pain filled. Mindlessly, he slammed his fist against a tree. Once. And again. The skin on his knuckles tore open, but the sting was minimal compared to the discomfort of the teeth-breaking clench of his jaw and the tightening pressure in his head. He slumped against the scratchy bark, breathed deeply, regularly, forced his heart to slow and his muscles to relax.

Kerr was right. I am broken.

Instead of focusing on the joy of getting Ewan back, of moving into the future with his son, he'd refused to let go of the past—and the anger and pain were tearing him apart. He felt like he was suffocating from the inside out.

A monster, Deirdre had called him, and she was also right. She'd saved Ewan, and now Gavin was taking him away. Taking *her* from his son.

Cristel wasn't Ewan's mother. She'd given birth to him and then shown no interest in him thereafter. He'd thought at first it had to do with the sadness some women felt after giving birth, but she'd been happy and relieved. She'd done her duty, she'd said. He had an heir. She would not abide him in her bed, nor Ewan at her breast. Whereas Deirdre was devastated by the separation. She was losing *her son.* A child of her heart.

Aye, no matter who gave birth to him, Deirdre was Ewan's mother.

Finally, Ewan had a ma.

An involuntary sigh—one of acceptance and relief—released from his chest, and the pressure eased. He peered in the direction he'd seen her and her guards disappear into the woods.

Urgency struck him like a fist. *Find her. Tell her. Beg for her forgiveness.*

He strode forward quickly, parallel to the edge of the clearing. The ground began to rise about the time he came across his man Lorne.

"Laird," the warrior said, acknowledging him.

"Tell Clyde to pick two men to continue on with Tomaidh," Gavin said. "The rest of us are heading back." He searched the woods but didn't see Deirdre. "Where is Lady MacIntyre?"

"She followed the trail up. Sheamais is farther ahead. He knows this land well. He says the trail leads to a cliff, and there is no other way for her to come down. We gave her some privacy to calm herself. She's…upset."

Dread began as a whisper in Gavin's gut, then

rapidly escalated. He found himself sprinting up the trail, his heart racing even faster than before, his ears straining for any sound—sobs, a scream, or, God forbid, a sickening thud.

Her name pulsed on his tongue like a living thing. He wanted to yell out—*Deirdre!*—but what if he startled her and she panicked and she…

God…please…let her still be there.

Sheamais must have heard him coming and had raised his weapon just in case. He lowered it as Gavin tore past. "Laird?"

"Stay here!" Gavin yelled as he crested the rise. Moments later, he burst into the clearing. He scanned the top of the cliff, but it was empty. No one was there. He raced forward. "Deirdre! Oh, dear God. Nay!"

He reached the edge, dropped to his knees, and peered into the gorge, looking for her broken body. Despair burned his guts and scraped at his chest like a poison inside of him. "Deir-dre!"

He'd done this. He'd as good as pushed her over—cut out her heart and left her with nothing to live for.

Then, from across the clearing, "Gavin."

He whipped his head around so fast that his hand slipped off the edge of the cliff. Pebbles dropped down and pinged on the rocks below. He righted himself as Deirdre gasped and raced toward him.

Pushing up, he tried to stand, but his knees wobbled, and he stumbled.

"Get back from the edge!" She grabbed his arm and tugged him away from the precipice.

She's afraid. For me. After all I've done.

When she stopped and finally looked at him, he

stared at her face. Her eyes were dark pools of anguish, so ravaged by her despair and grief. Pain he'd caused… yet she was afraid *he'd* be hurt. This woman, whom he'd just eviscerated, had wanted to save him.

He tried to speak but could only manage a whispered croak. He swallowed and tried again. "I thought…"

Her eyes widened, and she shook her head. "I would ne'er do that when Ewan is alive. Aye, it crossed my mind, but not for more than a moment. What if he needed me and I was gone? As long as he is in this world, I will be too."

"Even though you thought you might ne'er see him again?" His chest and throat tightened again at the sacrifice she'd made for his son.

Her face crumpled, and she stepped away from him. He moved toward her, wanting to comfort her, to tell her all would be well, that he would do his best to keep her and Ewan together.

"Deirdre—"

She held a hand out to him and took a deep breath to steady herself. "Nay, listen. Please." She lifted her skirts and knelt on the grass in front of him in supplication. "Laird MacKinnon—"

"It's Gavin," he said hoarsely. "You've used my name before." He stood there dumbly. He knew he was the one who should be on his knees asking forgiveness from her.

She quickly raised her eyes to his, then dropped them again. "Gavin. I ask you—no, I beg you—doona separate me from Ewan." She spoke in a rush now. "You're right. I'm not his mother, but he loves me like I am.

And I love him like a son. If you care about him, and I know you do, you'll want him to be happy and feel safe. If I just disappear from his life, he'll feel abandoned and unloved, and that will stay with him forever."

He grasped her hands and tried to lift her up, but she pulled down.

"Nay, I'm not done. I know you said it was impossible for me to stay because of who I am—a laird's daughter, another laird's daughter-in-law—but none of that matters to me. I doona have to be Deirdre MacIntyre. I can take another name, be anyone you want me to be. You can tell Lewis and my family that I died. Tell them I jumped here today. That I was unstable, and I almost took you with me when you attempted to save me."

He tried to lift her again, wanting to comfort her in his arms, but she misunderstood and panicked, talking faster and louder, almost fighting him in her desperation. "Please! I'm smart and educated. I can continue teaching Ewan. Or I can be another nursemaid for him. I can help Annag. We'll say I'm her niece or goddaughter or something."

"Deirdre, hush. You doona have to do any of that. I canna tell everyone you died. And I doona—"

"Yes, you can! I doona mind—I want you to! If you're worried people will recognize me, set me up on a farm or in another village. Just bring Ewan to visit me. Please! Even once a month. I canna bear for him to think I've left him behind," she wailed.

Gavin bent to clasp her upper arms and lift her up to standing this time. He wrapped his arms around her and tucked her tightly to him as she sobbed into his chest.

"Doona take him away. Please, doona take him away!"

"I promise, Deirdre," he said. "We're turning around. You'll be back with him tonight. I willna take him away from you again. But you will stay with him as Deirdre MacIntyre, his mother. Not his tutor or his nursemaid. I'll keep you with him as long as I can and for as long as you want to stay. It will not be my choice to separate the two of you."

She'd stopped talking, looked up at him, and listened—eyes searching his face for signs that he spoke truthfully. "Verily?" she whispered.

"Aye, do you remember what I told you when we left your keep?"

She shook her head, and he didn't blame her. How could she remember anything when she'd been consumed with fear that her son would be taken away from her? "I said I would ne'er lie to you. That you wouldnae always like what I had to say, but I would always be truthful."

Her lips trembled, and his eyes were drawn down to them, lush, red, and wet from her tears. His arms tightened around her, and he was suddenly aware of how she felt against him. Soft and curved, her flesh yielded against the hard planes and bulges of his muscles.

She stepped back, and he almost groaned at the loss of her warmth. If she had been his, he would want her against him always.

"So, we can leave now, then? You'll take me back to Ewan?"

He could see she couldn't quite believe it, believe *him*, and he clasped her hand and squeezed. "Aye."

She smiled, those red lips trembling, her eyes filled with relief and joy. "Thank you, Laird MacKinnon. Thank you."

"Gavin," he said, insisting again, then he lifted her hand and bestowed a brief, chaste kiss to the soft spot between her thumb and first finger. "And I doona deserve your thanks. 'Tis me who is grateful. Thank you, Deirdre, for loving my son—our son. And for saving him. I ne'er should have separated you. I'm sorry. I promise to do better from now on, to be a better man—a better father to Ewan and a better... friend to you. Please, forgive me."

She nodded jerkily, and a sob broke free. She pressed her lips together. He longed to press his there too, to kiss the tears that ran down her face, to feel her mouth tremble against his.

Turning away before he did something he'd regret, Gavin led her across the clearing toward the trailhead. He whistled to let Sheamais know they were coming.

They were going home.

When they reached the bottom of the trail and entered the clearing, his men had already mounted their horses and were waiting for them, Clyde at his usual place in the front. Tomaidh hurried toward them, tugging his mare behind him. "Laird, the men told me you're heading back?"

"Aye, Tomaidh. I'll send two of my men with you, but I need to return Lady Deirdre to our son immediately. Tell Master Lewis I have complete faith in my men. He's to tell them everything he would have told me—especially how he came to have Ewan."

"But Master Lewis—"

Deirdre tugged her hand free from his and grasped Tomaidh's arm. "Nay, Tomaidh. I doona want to go back. Ewan is staying with the MacKinnons, and I want to stay with him. Lewis gave him to me, saying he was my son and I was to raise him. He'll understand why I choose to remain with him now."

"But...he's your husband!"

"Aye, and he'll also understand when I say, I know he willna miss me. I've enjoyed our games of chess and his companionship on many long nights. He's a good man, but that will ne'er replace my son's love."

Tomaidh continued to look concerned and confused. "You're certain?"

She nodded. "Tell him he has my eternal gratitude for taking such good care of the young lass who came into his keeping seven years ago and for giving Ewan MacKinnon to me. I doona know what happened, but I know in my heart he would ne'er have stolen him, and I thank him for my son's life. I hope to see him again someday soon."

Tomaidh dipped his head in acknowledgment. "Be well, my lady."

"And you, Tomaidh."

The lad turned the mare in the direction they'd been heading originally, followed by two of Gavin's warriors. Another man brought Thor over, and Gavin took the reins. "Are you ready, lass?"

She nodded. "Will we be home before dark? I would like to tuck my son in."

"Yes. And I'll tuck him in with you. 'Tis good for him to know we are on the same side." He looked at the sun in the sky. "We'll be home in just a few hours."

"Surely it took longer than that to get here? Will we take a different route back?"

"Nay. But…in my heart I didn't want to take you to Lewis, no matter what my head said was the right choice, so our pace slowed as we drew closer. Now that we're on our way back to Ewan and I've decided to keep you with us, my head and heart are aligned. We may run the entire way back."

Her brow raised. "I love my son, and I'm overjoyed you've changed your mind, but when it comes to running all the way home, my heart and my backside are *not* aligned. 'Tis all right if we put Ewan to bed a wee bit later, so that I can still walk up the stairs when we get there."

He grinned, and he felt the joy of it all the way down to his toes. When she grinned back, he couldn't help the laugh that burst from the very center of him. It wasn't just his heart and head that had finally aligned. Deirdre had set his soul free too.

Nine

The castle came into view in the dimming light. Elation pushed up from Gavin's chest, causing him to suck in a loud, rough breath of air. He was home. Deirdre was home. Their son was waiting for them.

It felt like they were almost a family.

She turned her head and looked at him over her shoulder from her seat in the saddle. "Are you well?"

"Aye, lass. Verra well." He felt awash in happiness, and even the prospect of facing down Kerr didn't daunt him. It was a penalty he'd gladly pay for lying to his foster brother and Isobel, and for trying to separate Deirdre from his son. It's not like Kerr would kill him.

Not on purpose anyway.

Deirdre turned her head forward again and leaned against him. He wanted to wrap his arms around her middle and rest his cheek on her hair—inhale her scent—but he couldn't do that to her. Or to himself.

He was drawn to her in so many ways, but he couldn't act on his feelings. She'd chosen *their* son over her husband, but she was still married to Lewis—who she claimed was a good man. As did Kerr.

For her sake, he would withhold judgment until he knew the truth about Ewan's kidnapping.

Not only would it besmirch his honor to make advances of that nature toward a married woman, but she might feel unsafe. In her eyes, her position in the castle was dependent on his goodwill. She might worry that if she didn't reciprocate his amorous feelings, he'd separate her from Ewan again.

He was in a powerful position over her. He must never forget that.

They passed the half-built cathedral, and Deirdre's eyes stayed on it as they rode by. He liked that she was interested in so many different things—architecture and mathematics, as well as other topics he'd heard her talking to Ewan about. As she'd said earlier, she was smart and educated.

"What sort of subjects did you study?" he asked.

She paused before answering, and he imagined that wee furrow forming in her brow as she tried to understand his meaning. It made him smile.

"You mean when I was a lass?"

"Aye. I know you studied mathematics, but what else?"

"Language, music, history, art. And geometry. That was my favorite. My tutor gifted me with his geometry set when I left my clan to marry Lewis. I used it to teach Ewan. I'm sad I left it behind."

"We'll get you another one, lass."

"Thank you."

"'Tis similar to my education," he said. "But we also learned about war, of course, and politics. And how to manage our lands and resources for the good of the clan."

"And from everything I hear, you've done well."

"Aye, we've been prosperous. My father did not have a head for trade or commerce, but he listened well to those who did. Men he trusted, including Gregor MacLeod. I understand more than he did, but I still listen."

"'Tis the sign of a good leader." Her voice picked up. "My tutor read much of Thucydides's *History of the Peloponnesian War* to me. I was fascinated by Thucydides's account of the conflict between the Spartans and the Athenians."

"We studied it as well. He did a fair job recording the battle, for sure."

"A fair job? But it was wonderful—and from both sides!"

Her enthusiasm and indignation amused him. "Aye, I only meant…he's an Athenian; he will be biased in his account, aye? 'Tis human nature."

"I doona think so. He writes from an objective point of view. His descriptions are detached from emotion and judgment."

"And still you loved it. Do you speak Greek, then?"

"Nay, only Latin, English, and French. And Gaelic, of course. Verily, I doona have an ear for language. I could learn the grammatical rules and the words, but I always had a hard time comprehending what my tutor was saying."

"We had to learn all those and more. And Gregor made sure we understood. If we didn't and made a strategic mistake in our war games because of it, we got a dunking in the loch. Then we had to run around the castle wall several times." He smiled just thinking about it.

She gasped. "That sounds awful."

"Aye, it was. Especially if I brought my fellow warriors down with me. They ne'er let me forget it. Kerr still brings up a mistake I made once on the coldest day of the year. That dip in the loch was the worst ever. We were all shivering and blue when we got home."

"But you could have died!"

"Nay, Gregor kept a keen eye on us, and we watched out for each other. It made us stronger and faster, and 'twas a better punishment than cleaning out the chamber pots, which we were also forced to do on several occasions. But *those* transgressions usually involved Gregor's *uisge-beatha*. He kept the good whisky locked up tight." He grinned in remembrance. "We found the key."

Deirdre looked over her shoulder again and laughed. The sound made him catch his breath—the way her face lit up made him lose it all over again. The sooner they arrived at the keep the better, before she suspected that the hard lump pressing into her arse was anything more than just his sporran.

"Will Ewan be fostered with Gregor, then?"

"Aye, I hope so, but not for several years. And my foster brothers doona have children yet, although Darach's wife, Caitlin, is pregnant, and Lachlan and Callum are both recently married. But Gregor may have other lads in mind for fosters, other alliances he wants formed."

"Did you e'er see your family once you went to live there?" She sounded worried, and he had to smile—a mother already missing her son.

"Aye, we went home during the harvest to help, and our families were welcome to visit anytime. We still gather together regularly. You will see Ewan grow up, Deirdre. Doona worry."

They'd reached the portcullis, and the horses trotted under it just as the sun was setting. He peered toward the stairs of the keep, looking for Kerr and Isobel. Sure enough, the door at the top of the stairs flew open and Isobel ran out. She stopped halfway down, her long, blond hair still visible in the dying sun, her hands clenching her skirts anxiously.

Regret washed through him like a storm. Aye, he'd hurt more people than just Deirdre today.

It was tempting to go to the stables first, to delay the inevitable, but he directed Thor straight toward the stairs. The door at the top opened again, and Kerr came out. His face was shuttered, his fists clenched, and his mouth shut.

Aye, there was to be a reckoning.

He sighed. "Promise me something."

"Anything," Deirdre said.

"When we dismount, you will take Isobel with you up to the nursery, and you will shut the door. Kerr and I need to…discuss what happened. He's upset."

"But he looks so calm."

"That's the problem. If he were yelling at me, I would tell you not to worry."

"So you're saying I should be worried?"

"Nay, I just meant…Kerr willna hurt me, Deirdre. Not much, anyway. And God's truth, I deserve it. But I doona want Isobel in the way. Kerr and I have to work it out or it will drive a wedge between us. Understand?"

"And you canna work it out with words?"

"Nay."

"But you're all so educated!"

"What does that have to do with anything? Educated men canna fight? Thucydides was a historian and a general. We're warriors, Deirdre. Nothing will clear the air better than a hard-fought tussle."

She made an exasperated sound, and he suspected she also rolled her eyes. It made him want to nip her ear. Then lick it. See if she was still rolling her eyes after that.

He whistled, and a stable hand ran to meet them at the bottom of the stairs. Gavin dismounted and handed over the reins, then reached behind him and unstrapped his sword, which he also gave to the young groom. "When you're done with Thor, deliver the sword to my bedchamber."

The lad's eyes grew round, and he sagged under the weight as he took the heavy broadsword. "Aye, Laird. Would you have me take it to the blacksmith and sharpen it first?"

"Nay, that willna be necessary."

He reached up to help Deirdre dismount, and she slid easily into his arms. Her trust warmed him and gave him more strength to face Kerr's wrath and Isobel's condemnation. When Thor was led away, he kept his arm around Deirdre, not letting go until Isobel lifted her skirts and ran the rest of the way down the stairs.

She'd been crying, her eyes red.

He released Deirdre, thinking his sister intended to hug her new friend, but instead she sprang into Gavin's arms and squeezed tight. He barely caught her in time to steady her.

"You're back," she whispered into his ear, and he knew she meant the old Gavin had returned. "You would ne'er have come home with her unless you felt *her* heart breaking, unless you opened your heart again and chose to share Ewan with her."

He slowly returned her embrace, then squeezed even harder as emotion filled him. "Aye, Izzy. I'm back." His throat tightened, and his voice came out sounding rough and raw. "And I'm sorry I've put you through such hell the last few years. E'er since Ewan was taken—"

"Nay, e'er since you married Cristel. But that doesn't matter anymore." She lifted her head from where she'd tucked it against his neck and smiled. "We're whole again." Then she reached across and grasped Deirdre's hand, drew her closer. "Thanks to you."

"Aye, Deirdre, thank you," he said. "And remember your promise."

"What promise?" Isobel asked.

"That I'd tuck Ewan in before he fell asleep," Deirdre said. "Will you come with me, Isobel?"

"I'd like to, but Kerr has turned quiet. I'm afraid he'll kill Gavin."

"He willna," Deirdre said. "I'll make him promise me, and then we'll leave them to *talk*. They're educated, civilized men. They doona need to resort to violence."

She marched toward Kerr, her gaze focused on him. Isobel's eyes widened, then she hurried to catch up. Gavin saw Kerr's gaze shift to Deirdre, then back to him, then quickly back to Deirdre when she stopped right in front of him. Kerr's lips barely moved as he responded to whatever she said.

Gavin wanted to hear, and he mounted the stairs. Could it be that Kerr MacAlister had finally met his match in his cousin? This small, soft bundle of goodness whom no one wanted to disappoint?

He edged closer, and when Kerr's eyes shifted to his again, Gavin's brow rose. His foster brother, who was easily twice Deirdre's size, looked unnerved. Kerr never looked unnerved by anyone. Finally, he heard him say, "I promise not to kill him, Cousin. And I willna yell at him either. And aye, he is a delicate flower."

"What?" Gavin said, his ire rising, and Kerr smirked.

Isobel tugged Deirdre past Kerr and into the keep. Gavin kept climbing the stairs, glaring at Kerr, who dropped his smirk and glared back.

"I am laird here," Gavin said. "'Tis my land, my castle, my keep, and my son. You doona get to tell me what to do. The only one I need apologize to is Deirdre. Which. I've. Done."

He smacked shoulders with Kerr as he walked past and whistled sharply to his men as soon as he entered the keep, ordering them to leave. God alone knew what he and Kerr had just started. And Deirdre may think she'd averted a fight by getting Kerr to promise not to yell, but the reality was just the opposite.

Kerr shouting was the least of his worries.

The men all scrambled to get out, knowing what was brewing. Gavin moved toward the small hearth, Kerr hot on his heels.

"Where's your sword?" Kerr demanded.

Gavin rounded on him. "Not here. So you canna draw yours. You get one punch because I lied to you. After that, I punch back."

"Two punches. You lied to me and to Isobel. You made her cry."

"Nay, looking at your ugly-arse face made her cry. And she's forgiven me, so you canna use her."

"Your son has been sick with worry. I lost count of how many times I had to pretend to be a bear to distract him."

Gavin huffed out a surprised laugh, then forced a frown. "You're so full of shite. You liked it. Being a bear is as natural to you as breathing."

Kerr started to yell, but Gavin pointed his finger to the ceiling. Kerr glanced at the stairs to make sure the women weren't coming down. When he swung his head back, he also swung his big, meaty fist and caught Gavin by surprise, smashing into his chin.

Gavin stumbled back and tripped over a stool in front of the fire, landing hard on his arse and his elbows. Kerr jumped and landed hard on *him*. He shoved him down, and Gavin's head smashed against the rushes on the stone floor, which cushioned the blow. Another blow hit his shoulder, which made two punches, and Gavin started to fight back. He grabbed a handful of twigs from the kindling pile beside the fire and shoved the scratchy ends into Kerr's face. His foster brother reared up and spat out some of the offending pieces that jammed into his mouth. Gavin took advantage and smashed his forehead into Kerr's nose.

"God's blood!" Kerr yelled, rising and stumbling backward, his hand over his nose. "That hurt, you donkey-loving blackheart."

Gavin fell back to the rushes, one hand rubbing his jaw. "I said one punch. You took two." He pointed to the blood running through Kerr's fingers that held his nose. "That's on you."

Kerr sat down heavily on one of the chairs and tilted his head back. "Well, get your arse over here and fix it."

Gavin pushed up from the floor, wincing as he put weight on his shoulder. He crossed to Kerr and on the way saw the young stable hand from earlier frozen in place at the door, watching them. He had Gavin's broadsword in his hands.

Gavin sighed and held out his hand for it. "Thank you, lad," he said as the boy rushed over and gave the sword to him. "'Tis just a wee dustup between brothers, aye? You can tell everyone that I won."

"He did not!" Kerr bellowed.

"Hush, or you'll have the women down on us." Then Gavin looked at the lad and mouthed, *I won*, as he pointed to his chest.

The lad grinned and ran to the door, letting it slam behind him.

Gavin laid the sword and scabbard across a chair and leaned over Kerr. Kerr dropped his hands, his fists clenched by his sides.

"Do it," Kerr said. "I doona want it to heal broken."

Gavin gently explored the bridge of Kerr's nose with his fingers and felt where the cartilage needed to be aligned.

"A dirty fight," Kerr grumbled. "First you shove twigs in my mouth, and then you head-butt me."

"And who swung first without any warning? 'Twas you."

"What's the point of fighting if you warn someone

firs—aaagggrrrhh!" Kerr yelled as Gavin squeezed hard and adjusted the cartilage back into place.

"There you go. No warning. Just how you like it." Gavin wiped his fingers on his plaid, moved his sword, and slumped in the chair beside Kerr. "I would ne'er have gone for your face, except you went for mine first."

Kerr grunted, then sighed. He would be a frightening sight to those who didn't know him, his long, dark hair hanging loose around his massive shoulders, several days growth on his square jaw, and blood smeared under his nose.

"So, tell me what happened after you lied to Isobel and me and had us take Ewan to the loch. Where were you going?"

"To meet Lewis."

Kerr whipped his head toward him. "God's blood, the MacIntyres are here already?"

"Nay, just Lewis. He sent a messenger and asked to meet before his father and Deirdre's brother arrived."

"I canna believe you didn't tell me."

It was Gavin's turn to sigh. "Me neither. I was just so..."

"Angry."

"Aye."

"Out of control."

"Aye."

"Foolish and idiotic."

Gavin ground his jaw, forgetting the hit he'd taken to his face, and then winced at the pain. "Lewis was waiting for us on Campbell land. He asked that I return Deirdre. He said she was innocent of stealing Ewan."

"You talked to him?"

"Nay. I sent two of my men instead. I doona know if he'll speak to them."

He lifted his hand to rub his chest, trying to ease the tightness. "I couldnae go through with it. I couldnae separate Deirdre from Ewan—from our son." His heart began to pound as he remembered his desperate run up the trail. "She…she went off on her own when we stopped. I'd already decided to turn around, but I hadn't told her yet. She was devastated, grieving, and the guards hung back to give her some privacy, but they left her in a clearing with a cliff on one side. I thought…"

Kerr's eyes widened. "Did she—"

"Nay! But when I first got there and glanced around the glade, I didn't see her. I was peering over the edge, looking for her body on the rocks below, when she called my name. She'd been on the other side of the clearing. I couldnae believe it, I was so happy to see her. While I was trying to find words to speak, she began begging to stay with Ewan. She offered to sacrifice everything for him—her name, her position as lady and as his mother, just to stay near him."

"You didn't agree to that."

He shook his head. "She will live with us as Deirdre MacIntyre and raise Ewan as long as I can keep them together—a lifetime, hopefully." He clenched his hand in a fist and struck the middle of his chest, shame washing through him in waves. "While I was wallowing in my anger and need for vengeance, she was planning to give up everything. I almost destroyed the person my son loves most in the world because I refused to let go of past hurts."

Kerr reached across and squeezed his shoulder. "But you've done so now."

"Aye. Ewan is our son. We'll raise him together as his mother and father. And hopefully, she'll teach me how to be a better man in the process."

"You already know that, Gavin. You've just forgotten."

He let out a long puff of air. "I hope so. And in the meantime, we'll continue to prepare for war. I still need the truth as to why Ewan was taken in the first place and by whom. It could be as simple as a small boy wandering off at the wrong time, but if there's more to it than that, we need to know."

"Gregor and the lads will be here soon. They may have more information from their spies in other keeps. Do you remember any mention of the MacIntyres or MacColls in the information we already have?"

Gavin knew Kerr referred to the parchments Callum's wife, Maggie, had given them at the end of summer last year—detailed notes that she'd taken through several months of spying on her cousin Irvin Sinclair. They all believed a conspiracy existed, targeting their six clans, but they didn't know who was leading it. "Nay, there's no mention of them. I reread the papers last night. But if Ewan was targeted to keep me doing someone's bidding, we need to make sure all our loved ones are kept safe."

"Aye." Kerr tapped his fingers against his leg. "What I doona understand is why they put Ewan in Lewis's keep where we could easily find him. It doesn't make sense. Maybe we should head out to speak to Lewis in the morning anyway. He may have some answers."

"Nay, he will have moved on, and we doona have his messenger to show us the route. All I know is he was holed up in a shepherd's hut on Campbell land half a day's ride away. That could be anywhere. We'll wait for my men to return and then decide what to do."

Kerr rose, wincing at the movement, making Gavin wish he'd avoided his face after all. "Aye, you're right. And we doona want to be caught out with too few men when war is upon us."

"Agreed," Gavin said. He watched as his brother yawned and then winced again. "Are you heading to bed?"

"Eventually. I want to check on Isobel and Deirdre first. You should try and sleep too. You may have an easier time of it now that you've made the right decision about Deirdre."

He was halfway to the stairs when Gavin stopped him. "Kerr."

His foster brother turned. "Aye."

Gavin had to clear his throat before speaking. "Thank you. You ne'er once doubted me these past few years when I insisted Ewan was alive. And you stood by me when I drank too much and cursed the world and everyone in it. When I was…cruel…and ne'er smiled for months on end. You have my gratitude and my love. As a friend and a brother."

"You make me sound like a bloody saint! Saint Kerr. Tell your sister that and insist she marry me right away. I think she'll dry up and blow away all alone just to spite us both."

Deirdre lay on her bed, her mind whirling over the events of the day. She still couldn't believe that they'd turned around and Gavin had brought her back to Ewan—to stay at Clan MacKinnon as long as she wanted.

She'd raced to the nursery upon their return, hoping her son might still be awake, but he was fast asleep. Isobel had hung back by the door and Annag had quietly retreated to give Deirdre time alone with him.

Crawling up on the bed, she'd covered his face with kisses and whispered words of love to him. She'd tried to stay strong, to swallow her sobs, but they'd shuddered past her lips anyway. Ewan had turned sleepily toward her, wrapping his arms around her neck.

She would never go back. Even if her family, and her husband's family, demanded her return, she and Ewan were safe here.

Gavin had promised.

She turned over on her own bed and dragged the covers across her shoulder. Relief and gratitude poured through her, but guilt rose as well. The idea that she'd be the cause of a war among the clans left her stomach in knots, although the fight with the MacIntyres was most likely inevitable whether she was involved or not. Not that she thought Lewis was guilty of abducting Ewan, but his father was a controlling, frightening man. Deirdre would not be at all surprised to find out he'd been part of the kidnapping.

When she thought about what might have happened to Ewan during that ordeal—how closely he'd come to dying from the plague or the mistreatment he might have received from his kidnappers—she couldn't help shuddering. She remembered how dirty he'd been when Lewis had first brought him to her, how thin his body, and how terrifying his nightmares.

It put his fear of the dark and being left alone at night into a whole new perspective. What had made him so afraid?

It was all too much for her to think about when she couldn't change any of it. All she could do now was concentrate on caring for her son and healing him with love and hugs. And maybe healing his father too? Aye, she found herself wanting to take care of Gavin no matter what had gone on before between them. What woman wouldn't want to? He was a braw man—a strong, fair leader, with a powerful body and handsome face. He might look hard and unforgiving at times, but she'd also seen him laughing with Kerr and overcome with emotion to see his son alive.

To see *her* alive.

That thought also sent a shudder through her. For a few seconds before she'd called out his name, Gavin had believed she'd jumped from the cliff—and he'd been devastated. She had mattered to him.

Then on the ride back to the keep, he'd pulled her tight against his body and between his legs. She'd felt the occasional tremor running through his muscles, the pounding of his heart against her back as if he relived those moments when he'd thought she'd died.

It was a wondrous realization that after all they'd been through, he cared about what happened to her.

She turned over on her other side and fluffed up the pillow. She should have been asleep by now. She was exhausted, but she was also wound up, feeling restless and needy. Alone.

Even though she was back with her son, had been loudly claimed as cousin by Kerr, had a new friend in Isobel—who made her laugh despite being a wee bit batty—and had been accepted by Gavin…despite her newfound family, she still wanted something…more. Something she couldn't quite name.

Her body pulsed, a deep ache in the center of her belly that she knew well—

Desire. But also loneliness.

She'd felt it as a girl, ignored and unloved by her parents and siblings, then as a young woman mostly forgotten by her husband and left childless.

Until Ewan.

Until he'd swept like a whirlwind into her days and sprawled across her bed like a growing weed at night.

But some nights, like tonight, the ache couldn't be assuaged. She wanted more than just her son in her arms—she also wanted his father.

She huffed out a frustrated breath and threw back the quilt. The heat poured off her body despite the coolness of the room, the fires long since burned down to embers. It was usually around now that Ewan woke up and ran into her chamber.

She closed her eyes and counted down, waiting for him to call out for her, waiting to see if Gavin would stop him along the way and take him back to the nursery. And would it be such a bad thing if he did? She was sure other fathers got up in the night and comforted their children so their mothers could sleep, although those parents were probably sleeping in the same bed. Naked, maybe, from loving each other earlier in the night. Or a bairn between them suckling at its mother's breast.

She sighed this time and let an image develop in her mind: she and Gavin under the quilts, facing each other as she nursed their child. Her breasts would be even bigger than they were now. Ripe and full. Would he like how they looked? How they felt?

She pulled the quilt back up to her shoulders to cover herself and ran her hands over her breasts, cupping them through her linen shift. She felt the weight of them, heavy in her palms, felt their warmth and softness.

The urge rose to touch herself further, but she resisted at first. That twinge of guilt always accompanied her need for release, for self-care and love. She breathed deeply, trying to move past the craving, but it didn't help.

With a breathy moan, she gave in and unfastened the tie at her neck, loosening her chemise. Closing her eyes, she slipped her hands under the soft material. Her nipples had hardened into protruding nubs. She trailed her fingers over them, imagining they were Gavin's fingers, gentle but rough at the same time, causing heat to bloom in her belly...and lower.

She stroked her breasts rhythmically, squeezing and pinching, pretending Gavin had moved their sleeping bairn to its cradle and returned to their bed. He stretched out over her body and wedged his hips between her welcoming legs, a slow burn in his eyes, a tender smile on his lips. The weight of his body pressed down on the apex of her thighs where she needed it most.

Smothering her groan, she pulled her knees up and spread them. Slipping one hand down her quivering belly, she parted the damp curls that guarded her sex and stroked her fingers through the slick folds. If only they were his fingers circling and gliding, his mouth on her breasts, sucking and licking, even biting the soft, sensitive undersides.

She neared release faster than ever before, picturing him rising over her body, lifting her hips with one big hand and pushing inside her. Her breath quickened, the image in her head so real—the two of them twined together, their breath mingling, their bodies undulating—that she would swear she felt his mouth crushing hers, his hands kneading her breasts, his hips rocking against her mound.

Maybe making another bairn for her to love.

Her hips jerked up to the rhythm of her fingers as her other hand strummed her nipples. Faster. Harder. She bit her lip and turned her head into the pillow to muffle her moans. She'd never reached the pinnacle this quickly and almost regretted how soon the waves swamped her, wanting to stay lost in her fantasy for a while longer.

Instead, she floated back down to earth, her body languid, her lids heavy as her breathing eased.

And just in time.

"Mama!" she heard Ewan call. She sat up and listened for a heavy tread in the hallway or the door to Gavin's solar opening and closing. Isobel had let her know that Gavin rarely slept more than a few hours a night. Maybe now that Ewan was safe, and he could see that their son was happy, he would be able to sleep through the night.

"Mama!" Ewan cried again, closer this time. Rising from her bed she quickly moved to her washstand, dipped her hands in the water-filled basin, dried them, and then hurried to the door.

She peeked her head out, looking for Gavin, but all she saw was Ewan barreling down the dim passageway toward her. With his white nightshirt glowing in the candlelight, he resembled a wee ghost.

"I'm here, sweetling," she said, stepping out and scooping him up when he reached her. He curled into her immediately and went limp.

She peered into the shadows again, searching for Gavin. When he didn't appear, she retreated, shut the door, and leaned against it.

Is he leaning on his door, thinking about me the same way I'm thinking about him? About Ewan? Does he miss us?

Maybe he used to hold Ewan at night and he'd like to do it again? It didn't seem fair that she got all the nighttime cuddles.

If they were truly parenting him together, then shouldn't he get this time with their son too? At the moment, Ewan wanted only her, but that could change.

It should change.

Gavin waited for a moment in the dark at the top of the stairs, his eyes glued to Deirdre's closed door. He took several long, deep breaths as he tried to calm his racing heart and slow the pounding of his blood through his veins.

By all that was holy, he had never, in his life, seen anything more arousing than what he'd just witnessed—Deirdre stepping into the hallway in the candlelight, wearing her linen shift, her cheeks flushed and her eyelids heavy like she'd been asleep, her long hair tousled and hanging free. The tie at the top of her chemise hung loose, exposing the valley between her breasts, the outline of them—high and full—revealed by the soft light behind her. And if that wasn't stirring enough, her nipples had pressed hard and erect against the soft material, causing his mouth to water just thinking about them.

How would they taste? How would they feel on my tongue?

And then she'd turned away from him, toward their son who was running along the passageway from the opposite direction. She'd reached down for him, and Gavin had had to clench his teeth to hold back a groan at the feast that had been laid out in front of him—the thin material clinging to her arse, dipping into her cleft and molding against the rounded globes; her small waist, usually hidden by the folds of her plaid over her arisaid, indented like an hourglass; the curve of hips he could hold on to with his hands. For a moment, he'd even imagined he'd seen the outline of her sex, swollen and damp, against the flimsy chemise. She'd been backlit when she straightened, and he'd almost felt like he was gazing at her naked.

God's blood! Why couldn't he lay her down and…

Nay, he could not! Not ever. She was married and under his protection. She'd saved the life of his son!

So he'd covered his eyes, but not before she'd turned and peered into the shadows, looking right at him for a moment, his son in her arms and her lips gently pressed to his hair.

The virgin, the mother, and the siren all rolled into one…and he couldn't ever let on that he thought of her in such a way. This was her home now. He never wanted her to leave it.

She'd turned and retreated into her room, and he'd sagged with disappointment and relief against the cool, stone wall.

He'd been sitting in front of the hearth in the great hall when he'd first heard Ewan call for her. He'd moved up the stairs quickly and quietly, ready to help if Deirdre didn't appear. But she'd stuck her head out the door after Ewan's second yell, making sure the hall was empty before she stepped out. Making him a pervert in the shadows.

But by then it was too late.

Who else might have been watching from the shadows? Who might have seen her? A surge of protectiveness washed through him, and he marched to the other end of the passageway just to be safe.

No one was there.

When he passed her door on the way back to his chamber, he slowed, listening for any sound. He leaned his forehead on the wood and imagined that she was just on the other side, listening for him.

No thump or rustle emerged to give him a hint.

Sighing, he straightened and walked to his own door. It opened and closed with a creak that he usually didn't notice but now sounded as loud as clashing swords.

He wondered if tonight would be the night he would sleep, as Kerr had suggested. Probably not. Tiredness shrouded him like a cloak, but he was also edgy and restless. And so damn aroused that every step he took hurt, as his engorged cock bounced and swayed behind his sporran.

He'd definitely have to take care of that to have any hope of sleeping.

He reached behind him to unstrap his broadsword and realized he'd left it downstairs. He couldn't remember the last time he'd done that. No matter. He'd just go get it in case Ewan found it there in the morning. His son had a penchant for knives, and most likely Gavin's broadsword would be the biggest and sharpest knife he'd ever seen—or remembered seeing.

Gavin opened the door and glanced down to adjust his sporran over his jutting plaid—just in case anyone was downstairs. He stepped toward the hall and looked up in the same motion, stopping abruptly. Deirdre stood just inches away, holding a sleeping Ewan. Her clenched hand was raised in front of her as if she was preparing to knock.

She gasped, those soft-gray eyes widening and her cheeks flushing, and she was so damned lovely that everything inside of him stilled for a moment to take her in. She'd wrapped a plaid around her shoulders and over Ewan, but he stood so close that he could feel the heat of her body radiating into his skin. She took an awkward step backward, and he quickly grasped her arms to steady her.

Ewan protested sleepily and she raised a finger to her lips, then indicated that she wanted to come in.

He raised a brow—and other parts of his body too. She wanted into his bedchamber?

He stepped back into the room without thinking,

and she walked past him. "Are you going to bed?" she whispered.

He had to swallow before answering. Still, he could manage only a grunt and a nod.

"Do you want to sleep with Ewan?" she asked. "'Tis not fair that I always get to hold him at night. By the time he wakes, it will be light, and at that point, he should be more curious than afraid that you're beside him instead of me. I think it will work."

Again, she'd put her own needs and desires aside for someone else. He reached for his son, suddenly wanting to do exactly as Deirdre suggested. He'd often slept with Ewan when he was a bairn and in need of comfort, his soft, warm body a wee lump on Gavin's bare chest.

His eyes began stinging, and he blinked to clear his vision, lifting his sleeping son onto his shoulder and closing his eyes. He opened them when he heard Deirdre move and saw she'd stepped away from him and back toward the door.

Her hair gleamed in the candlelight, a swathe of silky black all the way down to her wool-covered arse. But now he knew what was under that blanket and couldn't look away.

She turned at the door, and he glanced up to meet her gaze, which was a wee bit forlorn—and made him feel guilty. He considered returning Ewan to her based on that alone, but she must have read his intention, and she crossed her arms firmly over her chest, her mouth setting mulishly.

He stopped, squeezing Ewan a little tighter. "Thank you. It means a lot to me."

She nodded and stepped over the threshold into the passageway. "I'll keep bringing him to you until he's used to it. He should adjust to sleeping with you in no time. Until we can break him of the habit, of course, and he stays in the nursery."

Gavin smiled. There was no chance she actually desired to break their son of the habit entirely. Neither did he. Not yet. "Of course."

He wanted to pull her back inside. He even shifted Ewan in his arms without thinking, so he could reach out for her.

He grasped the door instead. "Good night, Deirdre." Then, because he didn't trust himself, he shut it and dragged the heavy bar through the loops and secured it. Best for Ewan that way too.

But it felt wrong. Almost as if he was locking Ewan in with him and Deirdre out. And God knew he loved his son, but what he truly wanted was to have Deirdre in beside them.

Which could be a problem, when your son's mother was married to someone else.

Ten

"Stop going so fast!" Deirdre yelled.

Gavin looked up at her sitting on Thor's back and grinned. He kept striding around the bailey, tugging the stallion's lead to make him go faster.

Every time she yelled at him, Gavin's cock hardened a little more. Sweet, angelic Deirdre, losing her temper and showing all the fire she had buried deep inside was a sight to behold. Frightened, timid Deirdre, gaining her confidence and feeling safe enough to express how she really felt was a sight to hold close to his heart.

She hadn't averted her gaze from his once since she'd started hollering.

Deciding to wake Deirdre up early the next morning and teach her how to ride had been an impulsive idea, but it was good for Ewan too. Gavin looked over at his son, laughing and squirming excitedly on the back of Kerr's stallion, which Kerr led in much the same way Gavin was leading Thor. The lad had no fear of being on the back of a horse and was a natural rider.

His mother, however…

"Ewan, sit still!" Deirdre shouted at him.

"I canna. I want him to go faster. *Ruith!*" the boy said, leaning forward and repeating the word he'd heard Gavin say to make Thor gallop. The horse ignored him, of course. He was trained to respond to Kerr's commands alone—just like Thor would respond only to Gavin.

Kerr, however, could follow orders. He picked up the pace, making Gavin grin and Ewan whoop with delight. A couple of prime Highland lairds and warriors, leading highly trained warhorses around the bailey, with naught but a bairn and a frightened woman on their backs. Gregor would love every minute of it.

"Gavin, stop him. Now!" Deirdre shouted.

More blood pooled in his groin, and he grinned. "Aye, sweetling. Whate'er you want." He broke into a jog across the bailey, making Thor increase his speed as they headed toward Kerr and Ewan. Deirdre shrieked and grabbed on to Thor's mane. If she fell, Gavin would be there to catch her—and squeeze all those soft curves against his body.

Lusty images from last night played in his head—Deirdre in her flimsy, white chemise, picking up Ewan in the passageway, the candles backlighting the dips and swells of her body. But in his mind's eye, when she looked into the shadows this time, she saw him and beckoned him forward with a sultry smile, her breasts swaying against her linen shift, her eyes promising a night filled with—

"Gavin!" she screeched.

His fantasy shattered, and he saw she was leaning too far to the left, her eyes wide and her breath coming in panicked gasps. One of her feet had come out of the stirrup. How had that happened? And why hadn't she put it back in?

He slowed Thor and anchored a hand on her waist to push her upright again. His fingers just brushed the underside of her breast, and when she was properly seated, he let go only reluctantly. God's blood, he didn't want to. He wanted to touch her in the same way Darach and Lachlan touched their wives, the same way Callum had touched Maggie when he was courting her. Aye, Callum had always had his hands on Maggie even before they'd been married. They'd even slept together every night.

The difference being, of course, that Maggie had been Callum's betrothed, and Deirdre was already married to someone else.

Anger and denial clamped down like a vise in Gavin's chest. He scrubbed a hand over his jaw, scraping his fingers across the bristles. She. Was. Not. His.

He grabbed her foot and placed it firmly in the stirrup. "Doona take your foot out again. What did I tell you?"

She glowered at him, and that lush, kissable mouth flattened into a straight line.

"Deirdre?" he commanded.

"If I take my feet out of the stirrups, I lose control." She repeated his words begrudgingly.

"Aye. And what just happened?"

She threw her hand in the air and gesticulated wildly. "You started running across the bailey, that's what happened!"

She started to slip again, and he pushed her back

upright. "So you thought taking your foot out of the stirrup would make it better?"

"Nay. I doona know what happened. Suddenly my feet were just out."

"Feet?" He looked around Thor and saw her other foot dangling free. "God's blood! Well, why haven't you put it back in?"

"Doona yell at me, Gavin MacKinnon!"

"I'm not the one who's yelling!"

"Mama?" Ewan asked, sounding concerned. He had that uncertain look on his face that always gutted Gavin.

Deirdre paused, then forced a smile on her face and lightened her tone. "I'm well, dearling. Just becoming acquainted with this…sweet…horse."

"Then why are you yelling at Da?"

The tightness in Gavin's chest loosened, and he suddenly felt like his heart had expanded too much for his chest to contain it.

For the first time ever, Ewan had called him Da.

Even this morning when he'd woken up beside Gavin and they'd ended up wrestling on the bed, Ewan had never addressed him. And as a young lad toddling around the bailey before he'd been taken, Ewan had been slow to speak and had communicated mostly by pointing and grunting. He'd said *An* mostly, short for Annag. And *up*. Never *Da*, and he'd certainly never called Cristel *Mama*, like when he called for Deirdre.

Gavin walked Thor over to Ewan, dropped the reins, and reached for his son.

"Nay, Da. I want to keep riding," Ewan protested.

Gavin pulled him down and squeezed him tight. "You will, but you'll ride Thor instead. And your mother's only yelling because she's frightened. She needs you with her on Thor to feel safe." He placed Ewan in front of an alarmed-looking Deirdre, then looped the reins over Thor's head and handed them to his son. Thor would follow Gavin's direction no matter who held the reins.

"Gavin," Deirdre protested, "I doona think—"

"Just keep your feet in the stirrups, Deirdre, clench with your thighs, and stay seated. Otherwise you'll fall and bring our son down with you."

"I canna do it!"

"Aye, you can. You'll do anything to keep Ewan safe."

Kerr snorted, and Gavin flashed him a grin. 'Twas genius to manipulate Deirdre this way—for all the right reasons, of course. She would find a way to keep her balance if it meant saving her son.

He whistled for his customary guard and strode toward the portcullis. Thor's breath puffed on his shoulder as he followed obediently. Ewan leaned forward, shook the reins, and said, "*Ruith!*" Deirdre let out a distressed moan and mumbled something under her breath. Before he'd gotten to know her better, Gavin would have assumed she was praying for assistance. Now he knew she was probably cursing him in multiple languages.

That also made him hard.

"Where are you going?" Kerr asked.

"I want to go to the forest. *Ruith! Ruith!*" Ewan chanted again.

"We're not going anywhere," Deirdre said. "One more time around the bailey and that's it. Turn around, Gavin!"

Gavin didn't turn around. "Down to the cathedral," he told Kerr. "Do you want to come?"

"Not bloody likely," Kerr said.

"Not bloody likely," Ewan repeated.

"Ewan!" Deirdre said. "We doona speak like foul-mouthed dogs."

"But Uncle Kerr did."

"And he will ne'er do so again, or Aunt Isobel will find a way to correct his behavior, and I'm assured he wouldnae like that."

Kerr clamped his hand over his heart. "Och! Doona tell Isobel. I'll be a good dog." Then he barked twice and panted with his tongue hanging out of his mouth. Ewan burst into laughter, shaking the saddle.

"Sit still," Deirdre shrieked.

Kerr barked some more, then veered off toward the stables. "I'm going to go find Isobel and beg for a treat."

"'Twill be good practice for you, Cousin," Deirdre shot back. "But doona expect more than a pat on the head."

Gavin snorted as he led Thor under the portcullis, six of his men, including Clyde, waiting in the field beyond to group loosely around them. He liked this Deirdre who wasn't afraid to best a man as big and powerful as Kerr. As smart as she was, she could probably best Gavin too—and maybe even Callum, the smartest of all his foster brothers.

Aye, the thought of that, Deirdre besting every single one of them, hardened him even further. Which made the walk across the field toward the cathedral, situated halfway between castle and the village, more than a little trying.

Ewan chattered the whole way there, and Deirdre muttered under her breath and gasped as Ewan flung himself this way and that. She shrieked once when her foot came out of the stirrup and then nearly fell trying to get it back in. Her muttering increased in volume and intensity after that, as did the glares she shot at Gavin.

He was focusing on Ewan, who looked like he was trying to climb up Thor's neck, when Deirdre gasped again—and not from fright this time, but from wonder.

He looked back to see her staring wide-eyed at the cathedral. It just looked like a half-finished stone church to him, albeit on a much grander scale.

"Who's the master builder?" she asked, her tone almost reverent.

"A mason by the name of Cinead O'Rourke—an Irishman. Our old mason, Archi, was retired and living in Edinburgh when my mother convinced him to come work for us. He died at the end of last summer after falling from one of the scaffolds."

Deirdre's eyes widened. "Archibald Cameron?"

"Aye. Did you know him?"

"I knew of him." She sighed. "Unfortunately, a fall like that isna uncommon for a master builder. And if they doona die from the impact, they may lose the use of their legs. Had he been with the cathedral since the beginning?"

"Aye. After he died, Master O'Rourke came to visit—not knowing, of course, about the accident. He's an old apprentice of Archi's, and he was saddened to see his mentor's work unfinished and languishing."

"So you gave him the job."

"Not at first. But after I read some of the letters

between him and Archi, I knew it's what Archi would have wanted. And I doona know when I would have had time to search out a new master builder."

They came to a stop in front of three steps that led to a door under an archway. His men spread out around the entrance.

"Ewan, look," Deirdre said excitedly, pointing up to where the MacKinnon family crest was carved on the middle stone of the archway. "That's called the capstone. It's the very last stone to be placed when you build an arch of any size, and when it goes in, it locks all the other stones in place, so they stay up on their own. If the capstone comes loose, the whole structure will collapse." She hugged Ewan, her fear of being in the saddle apparently forgotten in her excitement over the cathedral. "Can you imagine how loud that would be? A great, big crash!"

She made a crashing noise, and Ewan copied her. And she didn't even protest when he shook his arms and body. Instead, her eyes scanned the rest of the building—stone walls halfway built on one side, a vaulted roof towering upward at the far end. "I know it doesn't look like much because this arch here is small, but some arches in the great cathedrals soar as high as the tallest trees you've ever seen—even taller. And all because of this wee stone at the top."

"Higher than a mountain?" Ewan asked.

"Higher than some mountains, for certain. Think about the blocks you build castles with in your chamber, and how hard it would be to get them to stay up in an arch like this."

Ewan squinted at the doorway in front of him

and then farther up to the arch towering six or seven stories at the end of the building. "I could do it."

Gavin huffed out a pleased laugh.

"Aye, you could with the right tools, that's for certain," Deirdre said. "You'd need a compass, a set-square, a plumb line—"

"What's a plumb line?"

"It's a ruler with a string attached that has a weight tied to the bottom. When the ruler is level, the string hangs down in a straight line. The mason uses it to measure if the rocks are in alignment. Maybe someday your da will take you to some of the cathedrals we have here in Scotland."

"Maybe we can take your mother as well," Gavin said.

Her eyes jumped to his, filled with…hope? Aye, she looked hopeful and pleased. Suddenly, his first priority was to take both of them to see the cathedrals as soon as Ewan was old enough. Maybe someday they'd even cross to the mainland to see the great churches of Europe.

"And do you know how they build cathedrals, Ewan?" Deirdre asked.

"With stone. I can see it right there." He pointed to the wall.

"Aye, but they use geometry and arithmetic to know where to place the stones and how big and what shape each stone should be—just like you do with me when we draw triangles and rectangles. All the measurements are verra precise or the building willna stay up."

He made the crashing sound again. Gavin suspected

that was the only part of this lecture his son would remember.

"Aye," she said with a smile, her eyes still scanning the arched dome at the far end of the building.

"Can we go inside?" Ewan asked, already scrambling down on his own.

Gavin reached for him just as Deirdre realized her son was sliding off. She tensed, but Gavin wrapped his hands around the lad on his way down. "I've got him." He put Ewan on the grass, then reached for her. She leaned on Gavin heavily, almost falling into him, and he had to step back to brace himself. He held her close for a moment, savoring the feel of her against him before he set her down. She swayed and then winced.

"Are you well?" he asked.

"A bit sore. 'Twas a difficult ride." She shot him a sideways look, bordering on condemnation, and he grinned.

"Not at the end. You seemed to forget you were on top of a horse when you had something else to occupy your mind."

She grunted in acknowledgment and moved up the steps toward the door. "It's so quiet here. I imagined the work on a cathedral would be loud and energetic. Rocks being dumped and chiseled, cranes and pulleys winding up and down, men shouting to one another."

"And crashes," Ewan said.

"Aye. Maybe they're having a rest?"

She was right—something here was wrong. The hairs on the back of Gavin's neck rose as he pulled her behind him. When was the last time he'd been down here to check on how things were progressing?

In the New Year, maybe, and only a few times before that. Had he sensed any problems then? Nay, but the cathedral had held little interest for him. He hadn't wanted to stay long, especially with the darkness that had overtaken him during the winter months. It had been difficult to search for Ewan then, and he hadn't had his foster brothers and Gregor to distract him like he had last summer.

The cathedral had been his mother's project, and then Archi's. Now…now maybe Deirdre would take it over.

He was just about to draw his sword when the door opened inward. A partially bald, middle-aged man, his shoulders straight and broad and his chest muscular, stood in the opening. His ginger-colored beard was scraggly, and he wore a dirty, saffron-colored léine over leather trews. Beads of sweat dotted his upper lip, and his eyes darted between Gavin and his men behind him.

"Laird MacKinnon!" he said with a hint of an Irish accent.

"Master O'Rourke," Gavin replied. "We came for a visit, but we didn't hear any activity."

"The men are upstairs having their midday meal. Otherwise, the rock dust gets in their food. They'll be down shortly."

"'Tis a beautiful day. I would have thought you'd be outside?" Deirdre said. She sounded shy yet excited, and looked at O'Rourke with a sweet, expectant smile on her face.

Gavin felt a kick in his heart; she looked so lovely. He expected to see an enamored look on O'Rourke's face, but the man's mouth was slightly pinched, almost like he was annoyed.

"Not today," he said.

Gavin frowned when Deirdre lost her smile and dropped her eyes from the master builder's. That would not do.

"This is Deirdre MacIntyre," he said, his tone silk over steel. "She is my son, Ewan's, mother. She will be living at the castle with us from now on, and I'm hoping to persuade her to be your contact there. She knows more about cathedrals and their construction than I ever will."

Deirdre gasped in surprise as O'Rourke's eyes widened.

"Gavin, I will do whatever I can to help you, but are you sure?" she asked. "Isn't there anyone else with more experience?"

"I agree, Laird," O'Rourke said. "I doona think—"

"Nay. I want Deirdre to do it. I canna think of anyone else who is better qualified. She has a quick mind, a head for math, and a heart for cathedrals. You're fortunate to have her. She'll also be much more inclined to listen to you than I will."

Several heavy footsteps descended a staircase inside, likely the men returning to work, but O'Rourke still hadn't retreated to let them in. Gavin stepped directly toward the man, their eyes locking. After an almost imperceptible hesitation, O'Rourke backed away and dropped his gaze.

Gavin reached out his hand for Ewan. "Take my hand, Son. 'Tis not safe to run or play in here."

"Aye, Da." Ewan's small hand curled into his, and Gavin's heart squeezed at the feel of it. He looked up, taking a moment to breathe through the tightness in his chest. Deirdre met his gaze, and she smiled. She had to know exactly what he was feeling.

They moved together into the half-built cathedral. Other than Master O'Rourke, Gavin didn't recognize any of the laborers, but then he hadn't paid attention before either. Several men were working at wooden benches, chipping at stones with chisels and other tools. Another man stirred a vat of mortar, then carried it to a far wall with a pile of stones haphazardly dumped beside it. Several wheelbarrows were filled with bigger rocks that were waiting to be sized.

"I didn't see any oxen outside, or carts," Deirdre said. "How are you transporting the rock from the quarry? And I would have thought to see much more rock piled up after the fall and winter months."

"They're in the walls," O'Rourke said, his shoulders tense and his mouth pulling down at the corners. He did not look at Deirdre. "Did you think we'd waste six months just sitting here? Laird MacKinnon is paying us for our time. I wouldnae squander it."

"Oh, well, of course. I'm sorry. I didn't mean to imply otherwise. I just thought..."

"Thought what, Deirdre?" Gavin encouraged.

"That the fall and winter months were used to stockpile more rocks while the mortar set and the stones settled from the spring and summer's work."

Gavin looked over at O'Rourke. Had he made a mistake hiring the man?

O'Rourke sighed. "Aye, she's...right. I didn't want to say it, because Archibald Cameron was my mentor, but when I inspected his work after I arrived, I was surprised to see he'd made little progress the previous year. The rocks in the wall had already settled, and the mortar was dry. We worked hard over the winter to try and catch up."

"Was he ill?" Gavin asked. It was possible. Gavin certainly hadn't been focused on much over the past two and a half years other than helping his brothers and getting his son back.

"I doona know for certain, but I think so," O'Rourke said. "Very few of his laymen were still here when I arrived. A few said he'd stopped making much sense when he spoke and had taken to doing strange and dangerous things."

Deirdre pressed her hand to her mouth, her eyes filled with sadness. "He shouldnae have been climbing the scaffolds any longer." She looked at the wooden supports that stretched up the walls, holding up the rocks in the ceiling that had yet to be locked in place with a capstone. "'Tis dangerous enough for a younger man with a healthy mind and body. I canna imagine what it must have been like for him."

"He died doing what he loved," the mason said.

"Why didn't you tell me this before?" Gavin asked.

"You were occupied elsewhere, Laird." O'Rourke's eyes fell on Ewan, and the man smiled. "Now that your search has ended happily, you'll have more time."

"Even so, I would have liked a report. Send one immediately if anything else happens."

"Aye, Laird." O'Rourke dipped his head respectfully.

Ewan had been leaning against Gavin's leg, watching the master builder, when suddenly he asked, "Where's your plumb line?"

O'Rourke stared at the lad blankly, then looked up at Gavin, his brows raised in question. He noticed the mason rarely looked at Deirdre. One of those men who thought women were of lower status than the oxen in the field, perhaps. It would do him good to have to work with Deirdre, so he could see how smart she was—and how capable. And if he refused, Gavin would find another mason. This time with Deirdre's help.

"He asked about your plumb line," she said. "We were talking about the tools a master builder used to build cathedrals—rulers, compasses, plumb lines..."

O'Rourke nodded stiffly. "It's upstairs with my other tools. I doona like to leave it lying around."

Gavin nodded. "I can understand that. In fact, I doona think I ever saw Master Archibald without his tools in his hands or hanging from his belt." He looked at O'Rourke's empty hands and empty belt. "In the whole ten years that I knew him."

O'Rourke raised his gaze and looked Gavin in the eye. "We're an unusual breed, master builders. Every one of us is different. The good thing is I am strong and healthy, and I can easily go upstairs to get my tools—where I left them beside my midday meal before I became aware you were here. Would you like me to bring my plumb line down for the lad to see?"

Gavin was about to say yes just to irk the man, who was getting on his bad side, when Deirdre spoke instead. "Nay, that willna be necessary. Instead, why doona you give us a tour of the building, and Ewan can see all the different ways geometry has been used to build this cathedral?"

Deirdre sat in front of her bedside table, having removed everything from the top of it and piling it on her bed. She'd then dragged over the chair that had been beside the fire, to begin using the table as a desk.

The steward had brought her parchments, ink, and a quill earlier, after Ewan had fallen asleep. Deirdre had been working ever since, despite the sputtering of her candle as the wax melted slowly into a puddle.

She'd added more logs to the fire not long ago, but now the room was too hot. Braiding up her hair and wrapping it on top of her head helped, as did untying the neck of her chemise and pulling the material up over her knees. She was tempted to strip it right off, but just the idea made her nervous. What if someone caught her? And was it possible she wanted to be caught…by Gavin?

That thought flustered and aroused her, and she had to go back and rework several minutes' worth of calculations because her mind kept wandering.

With a sigh, she glanced at her candle. She was running out of time, and she wasn't even close to figuring out what was wrong with the cathedral. All she knew for certain was that something didn't seem right. It was obvious Master O'Rourke wouldn't help her. The only reason he'd even answered her questions was because Gavin was there.

She sighed and wished she had her old geometry set with her…along with exact measurements from the cathedral. She could only guess at the dimensions of the building right now, since Master O'Rourke had said he didn't have the exact numbers and would have to look for them. That was something she'd found very odd. She'd imagined the master builder would have all those measurements in his head. Maybe it was different because he hadn't been the original builder.

He'd said he would find the measurements and send them to the castle, but he hadn't done so yet.

Obviously, he didn't like her. Whether that was because she was stepping on his toes or because she was stepping on his toes *and* she was a woman, she didn't know.

She wished she didn't care, but she did. Too many unhappy memories from her childhood. Too many fears making her feel insecure and unlovable.

Then she heard her son, yelling for her from down the hallway—"Mama!"—and she smiled. Ewan made her feel secure in his love.

She laid down her quill and crossed the room, chemise dropping back down around her legs and her smile still on her face. Aye, she couldn't wait to hold her son.

Just as she opened the door, it occurred to her Gavin might also be waiting for Ewan. She swiveled her head toward his chamber, located next to hers, and found him standing in the doorway, his shirt loosened and his hair mussed, looking right at her.

She gasped, warmth flooding through her.

"Mama!" Ewan yelled as he barreled into her from the other direction, wrapping his arms around her legs.

"Careful," she said, as she turned to Ewan and bent over to pick him up.

Gavin made an odd sound, almost as if he was in pain, and she swung toward him as she settled their son against her body. He'd propped one arm against the doorjamb and leaned heavily against it, his face flushed in the candlelight, his eyes glittering under weighted lids.

She froze. The only part of her moving was her racing heart. She tried to speak, but all that came out was a breathless squawk. She swallowed and tried again. "Do you want him to sleep with you?" she finally asked.

He switched his gaze to Ewan and straightened from the doorjamb, then shifted his sporran over the front of his plaid. Was he nervous?

"Nay, you can have him tonight," he said, his voice rough. He rubbed his hand over his cheek, drawing her eyes to his hard jaw and strong-looking face. His beard looked in need of a good trim though.

Ewan lifted his head from her shoulder and stretched his arms and body out toward Gavin. "I want to sleep with Da." He almost fell, and Gavin moved closer as she tried to balance Ewan again. "Please, Mama."

Gavin stroked his hand over Ewan's head. "Your mother wants—"

"I doona mind. He can sleep with you if he prefers." She shifted Ewan to pass him over, but before she could move him away from her body, Gavin slid his hands around his son's chest. The backs of his fingers and his knuckles brushed against her breasts, right across the straining, sensitive tips. A ripple of need crashed through her body, causing her stomach to clench, her breath to catch, and the muscles on the inside of her thighs to quiver. She pressed them together before she fell and lifted her eyes to his.

He had stilled, almost like *he* was now frozen in place, and she could see the hectic, almost wild need in those blue-green eyes—the color even richer, almost magical. Was that…for her? Did Gavin MacKinnon want *her*?

He cleared his throat. "I'm sorry. I didn't mean to take liberties." He pulled Ewan the rest of the way into his arms and stepped back. "Have a good sleep, Deirdre." Then he disappeared into his room with her son. A moment later, she heard the bar slide across the door. She released the air that she'd been holding in a loud whoosh and sagged against the jamb.

Did he actually say, *Have a good sleep?*

She almost laughed. *No way in hell will I be able to fall asleep now.*

Eleven

"Mama," Ewan whispered into her ear.

Deirdre opened her eyes slowly and stared into Ewan's bright, blue-green gaze. She smiled and reached to pull her son into her embrace, his head on the pillow beside her as he snuggled in.

She'd kicked off the covers in her sleep, and her shift had rucked up to her thighs. The room had finally cooled down after the fire she'd built last night, the breeze from the open window nice against her skin.

If only it had been like this after she'd given Ewan to Gavin.

When she'd come back into her room, the heat had been sweltering. She'd been tempted to strip and lay with her arms and legs spread on the bed, burning on the inside as well as out from the way Gavin had looked at her. She hadn't, because she hadn't wanted to bar the door in case Ewan wanted to come in during the night.

Anyone else could have come in too. And maybe she'd been hoping someone would.

She heard a sound and shifted her gaze to see her

bedchamber door closing. Her heart jumped, and she sat up quickly, pulling the covers over Ewan and herself.

"Who was that?" she asked.

"Da. He telled me not to come in here, but I knew you'd be awake. I telled him you ne'er barred your door. He didn't believe me."

Deirdre flushed hot again. So he'd seen her then, sleeping without covers, with her shift pulled up and the tie loosened at the top. She almost ran to bar the door now, but what was the point? She'd already been exposed. She wiped at her mouth, worried suddenly that she'd been drooling. How much of her body had he seen? She'd been on her side, so her breasts would have been squashed together and pushed out of her top.

Embarrassment invaded every inch of her. She felt fleshy and ungainly. It was one thing to be completely covered by her shift in the hallway, another to be seen lying awkwardly on the bed.

Doona run, Deirdre. Everything jiggles. Her brother's jest reverberated in her head, alongside her sisters' laughter. She'd been twelve when they'd taunted her that time, and she'd wanted to hide under the bed, hating everything about her awkward body. No one in her family looked like her. Her older sisters were all shaped like their mother—tall and slender. They'd made her try on their silk dresses in the European style just so they could laugh when she tried to squeeze herself into the confining material.

Her tutor and nursemaids said to pay them no mind. That they were being cruel only because they were jealous.

A year later, her brother hadn't been laughing

anymore. Her stomach sickened just thinking about him. If there was anyone in this world she would happily wish dead, it was Boyd.

A knock sounded at the door, and Isobel stuck her head in, then pushed all the way in when she saw they were awake. "Gavin's headed to the stables already, but I'm starving, and Bonni said she'll make a feast. Come eat with me." Then she whispered, "And I doona want to sit there alone with Kerr. He's been more annoying than usual. I swear, everything he says is intended to irritate me."

"What's annoying mean?" Ewan asked her.

"It's when a wasp keeps buzzing around your head, but when you try to swat it away, it keeps coming back," Isobel explained.

Deirdre bit her lip to stop from smiling. She had the feeling that would come back to haunt Isobel someday. Ewan had started jumping on the bed, and she grasped his arm to stop him. "Go with Aunt Isobel. I'll be down as soon as I've washed up."

Ewan leapt to the ground, making the same crashing sound as yesterday when he landed. His new favorite sound, obviously. Then he stuck out his arms and ran for the door. "Aunt Isobel, I'm a wasp! Try to swat me!"

Isobel held the door open wide for him so he could run through. "Hurry," she said to Deirdre, before she closed the door behind her. Deirdre could hear her chasing Ewan down the passageway.

She would wager Isobel's body didn't jiggle as she ran. Nay, she was even slimmer than Deirdre's sisters and mother.

But…a few days ago she'd spoken enviously about Deirdre's curves and disparagingly about her own lack of them. Maybe…maybe neither she nor Isobel were correct?

Didn't she try to teach Ewan that there was beauty in all the different shapes in Nature?

She'd challenged many of the other false beliefs her family had instilled in her. Maybe it was time she challenged this one too.

Deirdre threw back the covers and rose from the bed, moving to stand where she had some space. Closing her eyes, she raised her arms out to the sides and tried to feel her body around her bones—not with her hands, just her mind, sinking down inside and *feeling* it. The muscles that moved her and allowed her to run with Ewan. The heart that let her love, and the mind that enabled her to think.

She put her hands on her shoulders and was about to run her palms down the shape of her body—and try not to hate everything about it—when the door clicked.

She let out a little shriek and opened her eyes.

"What are you doing?" Isobel asked. "I knew you'd be dawdling." She looked closely at Deirdre. "You look guilty. Were you exercising?"

"Why would I feel guilty about exercising?"

"Because I told you to hurry." Isobel stepped closer, interest growing in her eyes. "Is this what you do every morning? Your secret for"—she waved her hand in a circular motion toward Deirdre—"all that?"

"Nay. And I'm not exercising, I'm…I'm…" She didn't know how to put into words what she'd been doing, and a blush stole up her cheeks.

Isobel stared at her, fascinated, and then her eyes grew round, and she turned a fiery red. "Lord have mercy," she said, and she ran to shut the door and slide the bar across. "Doona you know to always bar the door before you do *that*?!"

"I wasn't *doing that*!" Deirdre's warm cheeks suddenly burned as hot as Isobel's face was red. "I was…I was…trying to love my body."

Her friend's eyebrows rose. "'Tis the same thing, is it not?"

"I doona think so. But you should try it."

"I should?"

"Aye." Deirdre felt her words bubble out as her excitement begin to rise. "I was told terrible things about my body by my mother and siblings when I was younger, cruel things that were meant to wound, that have ne'er gone away.

"And then *you* said that I was shaped like a siren. And even though that's a horrible thing to say—I would ne'er want to drown some poor, unsuspecting sailor—you meant it as a compliment. You, who are everything I've always wanted to be—tall and slender and fair. And yet you speak about my shape with envy."

She rushed forward, took Isobel's hand and pulled her into the middle of the room where Deirdre had stood alone just a moment before. "And what is even more incredible to me is that you doona like your shape any more than I like mine. We envy each other, and how pointless is that?"

"About as pointless as us standing in the middle of the room talking about it?"

"Aye, so let's do something about it."

"Is this where we switch bodies?" Isobel asked. "Because I'm fairly certain that willna work."

"Nay. This is where we love ourselves. Together. Close your eyes." Deirdre did as she'd directed Isobel and then thought about what to do next. "We should run our hands o'er our bodies, and while we do it, think about how much we love them."

"We're to touch our own bodies and not each other's, correct?"

"Of course!" Her eyes flew open, and she could see Isobel's teasing grin as she made gentle fun. Deirdre couldn't help grinning back at her. She closed her eyes again. "On the count of three, then. One…two…"

"Um, Deirdre?"

"Aye?"

"I'll be at my feet before you even get o'er your breasts."

Deirdre snorted, tried to contain her amusement, but couldn't hold back the puff of laughter that burst from her chest. Her very large chest. "If only those poor sailors had known my breasts would float."

Isobel burst into laughter and Deirdre followed right behind. She tried to catch her breath, but the more Isobel laughed the more she laughed too. When Isobel leaned on the corner post of Deirdre's bed then turned and collapsed backward on the mattress, her belly heaving, Deirdre did the same.

"Your own God-given raft," Isobel said. "Did you know I canna swim? Nay—I start sinking right way and I panic. I'm so skinny, I canna keep myself up."

"Have you tried moving your arms and legs?"

"Oh, is that how it's done? How did I e'er survive without you?"

"By not going in the water, apparently."

"Well, I will now that I know you can jump right in and save me." She pointed to Deirdre's breasts, and they laughed again.

It was a few minutes before they managed to calm down, but then one of them would snicker or giggle and set the other one off again. When a loud pounding at the door interrupted their hilarity, they quieted down to the occasional snort.

"What's going on in there?" Kerr demanded through the door. "God's blood, I can hear you all the way to the end of the passageway. Poor Ewan is the only one downstairs eating, and he's eyeing those bloody knives again."

"We're having a glorious time in here without you—"

"The knives?!" Deirdre shrieked, cutting off whatever else Isobel had been about to say to annoy Kerr. As much as Kerr was guilty of saying things to irritate Isobel, Isobel was just as guilty of the same thing.

She supposed that's what happened when two people who should be together weren't. If they couldn't love each other, then they would passionately fight each other.

Deirdre jumped up and dragged Isobel to the door. When she opened it, she stayed hidden behind it so Kerr wouldn't see her state of undress. He glanced inside curiously.

"Go!" she said to Isobel as she pushed her through the opening. "And look after Ewan while I dress."

"Aye. But make sure you actually get dressed this time!" Isobel shook her finger in Deirdre's face, who glared at the offending digit.

"Do you know what I do to tall, skinny lasses who shake their finger in my face?" she asked.

"Toss them in the loch?"

"Aye. And I doona jump in after them."

"You're both bloody batty this morning! What are you talking about?" Kerr asked, his face creased in confusion.

"About sirens," Isobel said. "And drowning sailors." She turned and headed toward the stairs. "Doona get involved, Kerr. Or she'll drag you in there too and have you touching yourself in no time."

"What?" he roared.

Deirdre burst out laughing and quickly shut and barred the door. 'Twas Isobel's problem now. Exactly how she wanted it, no matter what she might have said.

Deirdre held her hand over her forehead, shading her eyes from the midmorning sun, and peered toward the village. She, Gavin, Ewan, and their guard had just passed the cathedral, and she was hoping the settlement would be closer than she remembered.

When it came into view, she sighed. They were only about halfway there.

It wasn't that she didn't want to visit the center of Clan MacKinnon, it's just that she didn't want to ride there on the back of a horse, especially by herself.

Her mount was a small, sedate mare this time, not

nearly as tall as Gavin's ride, but the beast could still decide to take off at a gallop—with her on it—no matter that Gavin had assured her the female would stay close to Thor.

Ewan was on a pony, which was good, as he'd already fallen off—twice. She'd wanted to get mad at Gavin for it, but their son had jumped up unhurt both times and climbed back onto his ride, who'd just stood there munching grass. Ewan had named him Horsey, and the placid pony didn't even twitch his ears when the lad jabbed a foot here, an elbow there, or generally bounced around, pretending a wave of warriors were attacking them.

"Are you afraid Ewan's horse will run off?" she asked, noting the long lead between Horsey and Thor. It was the first time she'd spoken since they'd left the castle, other than to make embarrassing squawking sounds every time her mare adjusted her gait or even moved her head. The mare also snorted a lot, which scared Deirdre, but less than it used to—thanks to her long days traveling on Thor.

"First of all, he's a pony, not a horse," Gavin said, "despite what our son decided to name him." She couldn't see his face, but from his tone of voice, she suspected he'd rolled his eyes. "And second of all, the fear was not that he'd run off but that he wouldn't move at all if we didn't make him."

Alarm raced through her. "So you're forcing him? Will he get mad and try to bite Ewan?"

This time it wasn't her horse that snorted. It was Gavin. "Aye, we're forcing him. He's fat and lazy and likes to graze all day. And nay, he willna bite, even if

Ewan sticks his hand in his mouth. Which I wouldnae be surprised to see him do."

Deirdre's eyes widened, then she shouted, "Ewan, doona put your hands in Horsey's mouth!"

Gavin did roll his eyes this time. "Well, if he hadn't thought of doing it before, he will now."

Deirdre bit her lip. He was right. So did she tell Ewan again, to make it clear, or hope that—as was often the case—he hadn't really been listening to her?

"Gah!" she said, undecided, then yelped when her mare tossed her head and sped up a wee bit to get closer to Thor.

Gavin looked over at her a little bemusedly. "I canna believe that, for such a smart lass, you are so uneducated about horses."

His criticism stung. Hurt whirled through her, stronger than the powerful urge to defend herself. Her jaw tightened, and she dropped her eyes instead.

"Och, lass. I'm sorry," Gavin said. "Doona do that. Please. 'Twas a thoughtless thing for me to say."

"Do what?" she asked, curiosity bringing her gaze up.

"Lower your eyes. I'd prefer you to yell at me and tell me I'm an insensitive ass than lose confidence in yourself."

Her cheeks bloomed with warmth. And now she wanted to drop her eyes again, but this time out of embarrassment. She did—for a moment—but then she looked directly at him and said, "You're an ass."

And he smiled. It was his first real smile this morning, and her heart kicked.

"I know," he said.

"And just so you know, I'm not uneducated about horses. I've read books about them."

His eyes twinkled, and she knew he was laughing at her, but now it didn't feel like a slap in the face. "Just so *you* know, sweetling, reading about horses does not mean you know anything about them. The only way you learn about horses is to ride them, care for them, and train them yourself."

"Is that why you have Ewan riding his own horse already?"

"It's a pony, not a horse. Which you should have learned from at least one of your many books."

"So…a pony's not just a baby horse?" Deirdre asked innocently.

She already knew the answer, but it was worth asking just to see the disbelieving look on his face. "Nay! A pony is not a baby horse. A foal is a baby horse. A pony is a pony. Just like a donkey is a donkey and a dog is a dog."

When she snickered, his eyes jumped to hers. He grinned and nodded his head. "Well, at least your education taught you something."

They continued in silence for a few more minutes before he said, "And why weren't you taught how to ride? Did your father not believe it was a suitable pastime for a lady?"

Her stomach clenched, and this time when she dropped her eyes, she couldn't raise them for anything. This wound went too deep to be dismissed so easily, and she knew her face would show her pain, her humiliation—and reveal how young and scared and vulnerable she'd once been.

How much she still was.

"Nay. My mother rode. And my sisters."

She didn't say anything else, hoping he'd just drop it. But he wouldn't be Gavin if he didn't keep on pushing her to her limit. She hadn't even noticed that he'd leaned across their horses until his fingers nudged up her chin.

"I willna judge you, Deirdre. You can tell me what happened."

She briefly shook her head and dislodged his fingers. He sat back with a concerned sigh. "Aye, lass. Another time. 'Tis important I speak to you about something else anyway."

She jumped her gaze to his as alarm rang through her body. "What is it?"

"Naught to do with Ewan. Well, not in that way."

"Something I've done, then? If it has to do with Kerr, Isobel and I were only teasing."

He glanced sideways at her. "What did the two of you do?"

It would sound ridiculous and lewd—and most uncouth—if she told him about this morning. "I canna explain, and it was Isobel who said it anyway. You can ask her."

He grunted and then ran his palm over his jaw. "This is about…when Ewan calls for you at night. I think it would be better if…"

Her brow creased in confusion. She had never seen Gavin so lost for words. Or so flustered. "You doona want Ewan to sleep with me at night anymore? Is that it?" She would miss her son, and it would be a struggle, for sure, but if this was something Gavin insisted on, she could make it work. He'd made so many adjustments for her, she could do this for him. Especially now, as Ewan was settled in his new home and could sleep with Gavin or Annag if he needed a nighttime cuddle.

"Nay, that's not it. When he calls for you at night, I doona want you coming into the hall. 'Tis not safe. Stay in your room, open the door wide enough to let him in and no further, and then bar it behind you both. I willna always be there to protect you should something happen. I'll be on patrol some nights or even away for months at a time. What if..."

Her eyes widened. "What if what?"

"Castle MacKinnon is large, Deirdre, and I want to think it's safe. But I've seen too many instances in my brothers' keeps where their wives were put in danger because of treacherous or deluded men...and women. Barring your door and staying inside your chamber at night is the best way to keep safe."

She wanted to say, *but I'm not your wife.* Just to be able to say the words *your wife*—and to look in his eyes as she said them. Instead, she said, "Well, what about Ewan when he comes to my chamber at night?"

Her imagination began to run wild as she thought about who might be lurking in the shadows.

"I've thought about that, and I'm going to put some guards in the upper stories. Which is why you should also stay in your room when you're not...covered."

"Oh. You mean in my shift. I'm sorry, it willna happen again. I didn't mean to offend anyone."

"Deirdre, I wasn't offended. Not in the least, believe me."

There was something in his tone, a nuance she

didn't understand. He was saying something more than just the words.

He turned forward and clenched his jaw. "I wouldnae want anyone else in the hallway—a guard, a guest, or someone more sinister—to see you and think 'twas their right to take advantage. If that e'er happened, there would be blood to pay."

A chill shivered up her spine at the same time as warmth bloomed in her chest. Is this what it felt like to have a man care for you? Protect you? Her husband certainly wasn't that man. She'd hardly ever seen him draw a sword, let alone use one. And her father barely seemed to know his youngest daughter existed.

As for her brother—well, he was another story entirely.

She decided that she liked it—the feeling of someone caring enough about her to protect her, someone strong enough to take down her enemies.

It proved that she had value. If not to her family, then at least to Gavin MacKinnon.

"Does that shock you?" he asked. "That at my heart I'm a primitive man. Maybe even part beast?"

"Ne'er a beast, Gavin MacKinnon. A man who dispenses justice."

"And how will you feel, Deirdre, when the justice I dispense is a sword in the belly of your father, or your brother. Maybe even your husband?"

She didn't answer right away, choosing her words carefully. "All I ask is that you doona kill anyone without proof or provocation. For their sake, but also for yours. I shall make it clear to my family that I willna leave Ewan's side, and Ewan is staying here. If they come for me or for our son, I pray you'll protect us both."

Twelve

Deirdre tried to quell her panic as the villagers swarmed around their horses. Surely someone would bump the mare or step on her hoof or something, and she would take off like a startled rabbit across the town square—with Deirdre still on top.

Gavin sat astride his mount, gathering the lead attached to Horsey, who was resisting being dragged closer. "Stay calm, Deirdre," he said, sounding unconcerned, "and keep your feet in the stirrups. The mare willna run unless Thor does, and I am in control of Thor."

Gavin wasn't even looking at her, but it was like he could see what was happening. She jammed her feet back in the bloody stirrups.

"I canna see Ewan!" She strained to look around Thor.

"I have him." Gavin lifted a smiling Ewan into his arms. "Say hello to your mother, Son."

"Mama!" Ewan shouted excitedly to her over Gavin's shoulder. "Did you see me? I rided Horsey all the way here."

"Aye, you *rode* well, Ewan. Such a brave, strong lad. And you only fell off twice."

"I didn't fall. The first time I was knocked off by a huge warrior with a sword just like Da's. But Horsey kicked him and knocked the blackheart down, so I could stick my sword in him."

He looked at her expectantly, his smile huge and eyes excited. Deirdre swallowed and forced herself to smile back. "And the second time? What happened then?"

"There was a giant, and he lifted a tree and throwed it at me."

She liked this story much better. Her smile turned into a grin. "He *threw* it at you? What did you do next?"

"He ran at me. And I was scared, but then Horsey got in front of him and tripped him. And then when he was down on the ground I sticked my sword in him." Ewan lifted his hand and made stabbing motions and sounds with his imaginary sword.

Her smile drooped. She caught Gavin's gaze and could see he'd bit his lip to keep from laughing.

"Stuck, Ewan," he said. "You stuck your sword in him."

Ewan did the stabbing motion again. "I stuck my sword in him again and again."

Deirdre nodded, feeling a wee bit faint. It had been a trying ride from the castle, and learning her son had spent the entire time imagining himself and Horsey stabbing other living things—multiple times, no less—hadn't made her feel any better.

The mare lurched forward without warning as Thor began to move, and Deirdre let out a wee shriek.

"Put your feet in the stirrups, Mama!" Ewan yelled.

Bloody hell! How had they gotten out? She jabbed with her feet but kept missing, and when the mare nickered and tossed her head, Deirdre froze and began to tip sideways.

"She's falling!" Ewan yelled again.

The horse stopped suddenly, and Gavin's hand reached out to steady her, but she was done. She'd had about as much of this as she could take. She was getting down.

Grasping his arm with both hands, Deirdre slid from the mare. But now that she was on the ground, pressed between the big bodies of the two huge horses, she wished she was on top again. Fear tightened her throat until she could barely breathe.

"God almighty!" Gavin exclaimed. He shifted Thor away from her, but the mare sidestepped to get closer to the stallion again, almost knocking Deirdre over. The only thing that kept her upright was Gavin's hand wrapped around her forearm. She looked up and saw him straining to keep her from falling while keeping himself and Ewan seated on Thor.

What if Ewan falls down here?

"Let me go!" she said, eyes wide with fright.

"Nay. You're not going anywhere, Deirdre." He whistled, and a huge MacKinnon warrior that she recognized from before was suddenly beside her. He slapped the mare on the rump, and she skittered away. "Artair, lift her up," Gavin said to him, "but stay down there in case she slides off again."

"Aye, Laird."

"Nay," Deirdre said. "I doona want to come up.

I'm happy down here now that I'm not being crushed to death."

Gavin sighed. He swung his leg over the saddle and easily jumped down beside her. Ewan whooped with delight when Gavin lifted him off the horse and sat Ewan on his shoulders.

"*Ruith! Ruith!*" he commanded his new mount.

Gavin ignored him and handed the reins to Artair. The other warrior took both horses and the pony and led them away.

"Where are they going?" Ewan asked.

"To have a drink. Something I think your mother could use right about now as well." He held Ewan's feet in one hand and grasped Deirdre's hand in the other—and didn't let go as the growing crowd surged around them.

"Laird!" people called out. And, "Look, there's Ewan!"

Happy, excited faces smiled and pointed at her son, who looked excited but also confused—and more than a wee bit overwhelmed.

Aye, she understood that feeling.

Gavin shook hands and kissed cheeks and even kneeled in front of one ten-year-old lass who sobbed while she stared up at Ewan. Another huge man with a bushy beard stood behind her, his cheeks wet and his hands on her shoulders. From his muscular chest and arms and the leather apron he wore, Deirdre guessed he was the MacKinnon blacksmith.

Gavin gently wiped the girl's tears. "'Tis alright, Rhona. Ewan is back safe and sound. And look how big he's gotten. He can talk now and ride a pony. The two of you will be up to mischief in no time."

Rhona reached her arms up to her friend, still crying, and Ewan leaned forward into her embrace. He patted her back. "'Tis alright," he said, repeating Gavin's words. "You'll be better in no time. 'Tis alright. I'm right here." He obviously didn't understand what was going on or why the girl was crying, so he continued with the words Deirdre usually said to soothe him when he was hurt or upset.

She felt her own tears well up—in empathy for the young lass who must have been an older playmate before Ewan was taken, but also pride in her son who'd responded so lovingly to the girl's need for comfort.

The lass stepped back after a few moments, and Gavin rose and walked toward a wagon at the side of the square. He lifted Ewan in first, helped Deirdre up, then climbed up beside them and faced the crowd. Many of them had raised their arms in the air and were cheering. Some were singing a song that sounded like one she'd heard growing up, but some of the words were different.

A song of victory.

She suddenly felt awkward standing on display beside their laird. It wasn't like she was a MacKinnon. Nay, she was a MacIntyre, and a MacColl before that, two clans who might have been involved in Ewan's kidnapping. And if they had been, if it was her father or her husband who had done such a thing, she would never speak to them again. Ewan could have been killed!

Cutting all ties with her father wouldn't be a hardship. She hadn't spoken to him since the day he sent her away to marry Laird MacIntyre's son—and hardly ever before that. He hadn't even come to the wedding.

Her husband, however, was another matter entirely. Lewis MacIntyre was a companion and a friend, but he certainly didn't feel, or act, like a husband. He hadn't known what to do with a fifteen-year-old bride and had thankfully been patient, thoughtful, and gentle with her. Unfortunately, Lewis had also been gone more than he was there, and their marriage had never had a chance to bloom into anything past friendship.

She'd dreamed of passion and listened in on some of the other young lasses talking about it at her keep, but until she'd met Gavin—felt the heat of his gaze on her and the quickening of her blood—she'd never once experienced desire for another person.

And now, here she was. By his side and raising his son. And still married to Lewis.

Gavin lifted his arm and the crowd quieted. Ewan must have felt discomfited as well and he clung to her legs, his face buried in her skirts, his arms wrapped around her thighs. She idly ran her hand over his hair in soothing strokes, letting her own hair fall forward like a shield. A reflex for her, she realized. A way to hide, hoping no one would see her.

Nay, she was here to stay. She was Ewan's mother, and Gavin's clan had to accept that. They had to accept her.

Raising her chin, she let her hair fall back. Gavin glanced sideways and met her eyes. He smiled encouragingly before he turned back to his clan.

"We have been blessed this past week to have a member of our family returned to us," he said. "My son, Ewan Ailbeart Gregor MacKinnon—named after my father, our late laird, Ailbeart MacKinnon, and my foster father, the great Laird Gregor MacLeod—has finally come home. After two and a half years, my worries for his safety and his well-being have been put to rest."

The crowd cheered again, and Ewan buried his head deeper to cover his ears.

"I canna tell you how happy I am to hold my young lad again, to play with him, and even watch him sleep—aye, I've been doing a lot of that." The crowd laughed quietly with understanding. "And I'm even happier that he is a loving, carefree, and fearless lad." They laughed louder at that as Ewan had yet to take his face out of Deirdre's skirts. She rubbed her hand over his hair again, and he stuck his tongue out quickly at the crowd before hiding again. That had them hooting with laughter.

"I owe my son's happiness and well-being to this woman—Deirdre MacIntyre, youngest daughter of Laird MacColl." Gavin rested his hand on her back between her shoulder blades. "She is Ewan's mother."

The crowd quieted and then started buzzing as people began whispering to one another.

Gavin raised his other hand. "Listen. Please. Two and a half years ago, Deirdre was given my son not knowing who he was. All she was told was that the boy's mother had died, and she was to be his new mother. I doona know what would have happened to him if this had not occurred, where he would have ended up, or how he would have been treated otherwise. Ewan survived his kidnapping as a happy, well-loved lad because of her, and she has my eternal gratitude. I hope she has the clan's gratitude too. I have offered her a home here, and she will continue to raise Ewan and be a good friend to me, to Isobel, and to all of you."

"And she's my cousin!" Kerr shouted out from the back of the crowd.

Deirdre scanned the throng of people and found the huge, dark-haired man leaning against the doorway to the baker's establishment, a wide grin on his face and a bun in his hand. He raised his other hand in greeting when their eyes met, and she smiled. "Look, Ewan," she said. "There's Uncle Kerr."

Ewan looked out. When his gaze found Kerr's, the man made a face at him, which Ewan copied. When Kerr danced a wee jig, Ewan did too—much to the crowd's amusement—before he hid his face in Deirdre's skirts again.

"Is she married?" Someone—it sounded like a young man—shouted from the crowd. "A lovely lass," someone else said, and Deirdre felt her cheeks flame. She held on tighter to Ewan, her life buoy now. Gavin kept his hand on her back, his thumb rubbing soothingly on her neck under her hair, but she also sensed tension in him.

Gavin raised his other hand again, and the voices quieted. "Deirdre *is* married, to Lewis MacIntyre, son of Laird MacIntyre, but she's chosen to stay with her son—the child of her heart. There is much we doona know about Ewan's kidnapping that we're hoping to uncover in the coming days and weeks. Much we need to understand before we act."

He crouched beside Ewan and held his hand out to him. Ewan went willingly, and Gavin straightened with his son in his arms. "What we do know is that Deirdre is Ewan's mother now. She's staying at Clan MacKinnon and will help raise him. When we know who kidnapped Ewan and why, we will be going to war with them with all the might of our allies behind us. Those who dared attack us—by attacking my son—will live to regret it."

Deirdre's cheeks hurt from smiling. Everyone had been so lovely to her, from the miller, his wife, and their three sons, to the tanner, his wife, and their three daughters. The blacksmith named Bruce, who was a widower, and Rhona, his only child. The weaver named Ailig, who'd been married thrice and had borne no children at all. All the farmers, tinkers, tanners, bakers, warriors, and weavers thanked her, squeezed her hand or her cheeks, or pulled her into an embrace.

Everyone, that is, except O'Rourke, the master builder. She'd spotted him three times. Once when she was atop the wagon and he'd directed a most sour look at her, and then once when she'd been amongst the crowd.

The third time, she'd chased him down as soon as she could, lifting her chin. She was determined to get those measurements and better understand the problems she'd seen with the cathedral. "Master O'Rourke! Good day, sir. Such a fine morning. Are you well?"

She placed her hand lightly on his arm so he would turn to face her. He did. Slowly.

"Aye, Lady MacIntyre. I'm well. Busy as always.

The cathedral is such a large project to be away from for long."

She smiled at him, pleased he'd brought up the subject. "It is a large project. I was wondering if we could find a time to talk about it. I noticed that—"

He turned away from her sharply, and when he faced her again, his hand gripped another man's arm. "Lady MacIntyre, have you met the clan's teacher? Master Royce MacKinnon. I understand he's recently returned from Edinburgh. He visited the great cathedral there and the one in Glasgow too."

Her eyebrows rose as excitement filled her. "Good day, Master Royce. Maybe someday you'll teach my son, and you can tell him all about Saint Giles' and Saint Mungo's. I canna imagine how grand they must be in person. I've seen them in drawings, but I've ne'er—"

In the few moments her attention had been centered on the teacher, the master builder slipped back into the crowd. All she saw was his shoulder disappearing behind two large men who looked like laborers.

"Master O'Rourke!" she called after him.

"A strange fellow, that one," the teacher said. "This is the first time he's expressed any interest in my time spent exploring the great cathedrals. I was hoping to sit down with him and have a good discussion about the mechanics of the construction."

"Aye, me too. And that is odd. I thought perhaps he didn't want to speak to me because I was a woman, but it appears that is not the case."

"Nay, Lady Deirdre. 'Tis not the case at all."

She found O'Rourke again after much searching

and called his name, but he hurried away in the opposite direction as if he hadn't heard her.

Obviously, he was avoiding her, which was both frustrating and worrying. Gavin had made her his liaison for the cathedral, and she wanted those proper measurements. Hard to get if O'Rourke refused to help! She scowled to herself.

"'Twill all work out, love, doona you worry about a thing." Deirdre looked across at the old woman who had spoken. Her spine was horribly twisted and bent over, and she used two canes to walk in an awkward, labored fashion. Deirdre hurt just looking at her.

Lifting one of her canes, she tapped her temple with a finger. "I have the sight, aye? When our laird decided to keep you by him, everything changed. It will look dire for a while, but your son and our laird will live to rule Clan MacKinnon for many years to come.

"Always choose love, Deirdre MacKinnon, and you will ne'er be steered wrong."

"Oh, but I'm not a MacKinnon," Deirdre said, shivers prickling up her spine.

The old woman nodded. Then she pinched Deirdre's cheek with shaky fingers, like so many others had done before, and slowly disappeared into the crowd.

Deirdre stared after her, her hand raised to her tingling cheek. She hoped to catch another glimpse of the poor wretch, but it was like she'd been swallowed up and vanished.

"Strange words," someone said beside her.

She looked over to see a man standing sideways to her, only his profile visible. He wasn't much older than Gavin, with brown hair that hung straight to his shoulders and a hard-looking face and body. One of Gavin's warriors, perhaps? She found it strange that he ne'er turned toward her.

"Aye. And fanciful. Do you know her?"

"Nay. I'm not a MacKinnon either."

She faced him fully now, hoping for a better glimpse, but he angled himself away from her.

"Who are you?" she asked.

"I'm someone who can help you leave, if you want to."

Cold invaded her body. "I doona want to! I'm staying with my son, and he's staying here. He's a MacKinnon."

"Doona get upset Lady MacIntyre. No one's taking you anywhere against your will. I'm just offering assistance should you need it."

She lowered her voice. "Are you a MacIntyre or a MacColl, then? I doona recognize you."

"I'm neither, but I'm here on their behalf. Both those clans are concerned for your well-being. You doona belong here."

"I belong wherever Ewan is. Now leave, before I start yelling and bring Gavin and all his men down on you."

The man didn't respond. He just stepped behind her and melted into the crowd. She spun to keep him within sight, but amazingly, he too was hidden from view within seconds. She kept scanning the multitude of faces, thinking she might get a glimpse of him so she could identify him later if she needed to, but he'd completely disappeared.

A chill crept up her spine. What if they intended to

take Ewan again? Panic engulfed her, and she looked around wildly for Gavin.

"Deirdre. Are you alright, lass?"

She turned, saw Kerr, and hurried toward him. "There was someone here—just a minute ago—he offered to help me leave. What if he takes Ewan?"

Kerr put down the cup of mead he was drinking and whistled sharply. "Did you recognize him?"

"Nay, and I didn't get a good look either. He stayed turned away from me. His hair was brown, cut to his shoulders, and he looked like a warrior."

"Was there anything unique about his plaid?"

"I didn't notice. But when I asked him if he was a MacIntyre or a MacColl he said neither." She looked around again. "Where are Gavin and Ewan? What if he means them harm?"

Kerr wrapped his arm around Deirdre's shoulder, comforting her even as he used hand signals to communicate with other warriors in the crowd and on the perimeter. "Ewan is already back at the castle with his friend Rhona, the young lass who was so upset. Annag is with them, as well as Rhona's father, Bruce—whom you met—and several guards. Do you remember Artair? The huge warrior who helped you earlier when you were being crushed between the horses? He's Rhona's uncle as well as Gavin's trusted man. Believe me, no one will get past them to harm the children."

"And Gavin?" she asked.

"Gavin's a highly trained warrior, and he'll have at least two men guarding his back. Trust me, he can take care of himself. 'Tis hard to imagine, but even I have a hard time beating him in a fight." He pointed to his swollen nose. "And he fights dirty when he canna win the honorable way."

Deirdre raised a brow. "He fights dirty—you mean like a Highlander?"

Kerr roared with laughter. "Aye, Cousin. He fights like a Highlander."

Gavin tucked the wee, wooden watermill in his sporran, a present he'd bought for Ewan to play with the next time they were by a stream. It was an exact miniature of the real thing, and Gavin couldn't wait to see how it worked—and to show Ewan, of course.

He'd been looking for something to buy Deirdre as well, but nothing he'd seen so far had been right. For some reason, he'd found himself hemming and hawing over what she might like. Everything he'd been shown seemed either too personal or not personal enough. He'd considered jewelry, but gems were often a gift given to a wife on their wedding day. Like the ones he'd given to Cristel—and then tossed beside her burned body after she'd died from plague.

The others had been easier. He'd looked through the weaver's hut and bought a beautiful plaid for Isobel, but it seemed presumptuous to give Deirdre a MacKinnon-woven plaid at this early date. She might want to retain some independence from the MacKinnons or appreciate a design more common in her old clan. He'd then looked for a book, but no one had any for sale. Aye, the written word was difficult to find in the Highlands.

He'd glanced up at the cathedral, thinking about what she loved about it, and the perfect idea came to him. He just hoped it was still available.

A few minutes later, he stood in front of a tidy cottage next to an empty chair and some wildflowers growing in pots. He knocked on the door, smiling in anticipation of seeing his old tutor. Shuffling steps sounded within the cottage before the door creaked open. An elderly man stood there, stooped and gnarled, and after squinting up at Gavin for a moment, a smile lit up his face. He grasped Gavin's hand.

"Laird MacKinnon! I heard you were back and that you had found your son. I canna tell you how happy that makes me." The man's voice wavered with joy, his eyes watering, and he rubbed a shaking hand over his cheeks to wipe the wetness away.

Gavin's throat tightened, and he took a moment to settle the emotion before speaking. "Aye, Master Chisholm. I found him. He's as happy as a rabbit in a field of clover and as bright as the sun. He has a new mother now too, who has loved him as her own the entire time he was gone."

"A new mother? Did she take him?"

"Nay. She doesn't know what happened to him before he came to her. But he's her only child, and she's chosen to come live with us rather than be separated from him. You'll like her. She's well educated and has a love of learning. I wish to buy her a gift, but nothing I saw in the village seemed right for her. And I thought maybe..."

"You thought maybe I would have something for a lass with a love of learning." He turned and gestured for Gavin to follow him inside. "If you were looking for a book, you willna find one for sale so easily around here. If someone does come through with one, they always know to bring it to me first. I canna read the print anymore, but I still canna resist buying them." He tapped his head. "I'm turning barmy in my old age."

Gavin snorted. "Barmy as an old fox, is my guess. By the time you're done telling them you canna read anymore, they've probably lowered the price by half."

His old tutor nodded his head and chuckled. "You may be right." He led Gavin toward a shelf in the sitting room. "Take your pick. And I'd like to give her one too, my own thanks for the care she took of your lad. Maybe someday she can come by and read it to me."

"Thank you, Master Chisholm. She's a kind lass. I'm sure she will come for a visit. And I'll bring Ewan by to see you too. He'll like the pictures in your book of weapons over the ages. Much to his mother's chagrin, he has a love of warfare—in the way only the young can have, of course."

"Aye. Before their first battle."

Gavin nodded, his eyes scanning the books on the shelf. He pulled one out that looked new, and he suspected Master Chisholm hadn't read it yet. Or rather, couldn't read it. It would be a kindness to both Master Chisolm and Deirdre if this was the book he chose for her to read to him.

"This one here. She would be happy to receive this from you," Gavin said.

His old tutor took the book and looked at it closely, then smiled. "Aye. I'd be happy for her to have it. And which book do you want to give her?"

"Not a book, Master Chisholm. I want to give her something mathematical. Ewan's mother has a love of geometry."

Master Chisholm's brow rose, and his eyes lit up. "Och! I have just the thing!"

Gavin nodded, a satisfied smile tipping up the corners of his lips. "I knew you would."

A soft knock sounded at the door. "'Twill be for you," Master Chisholm said. He indicated for Gavin to answer it while he shuffled toward his desk and rummaged through the papers on top.

Gavin strode to the door. Something must have happened—his men knew he wasn't to be disturbed when he visited here. Clyde stood on the other side, one hand resting on the pommel of his sword that was strapped to his hip.

"What is it?" Gavin asked, worry for Ewan, and for Deirdre, shooting through him as Clyde entered.

"Everyone is well, Laird, but we're conducting a search for a man who approached Lady Deirdre."

An icy wind rushed through him, and even though Clyde had said she was well, he still needed to ask. "She wasn't hurt?"

"Nay, not at all. She's with Laird MacAlister on the way back to the castle. But..."

"But what?" He thought he detected a glimmer of amusement in Clyde's eyes. A rare occurrence.

"She refused to get back on the mare or to ride with Laird MacAlister. And Laird MacAlister refused to get her a wagon."

"So, what then? They're just standing there?" He was beginning to sense that a deep well of stubbornness resided within Deirdre. Or "Lady Deirdre," as he'd heard several of the men call her now. He was happy the clan had taken to her. They could be a closed bunch.

"The Lady Deirdre is riding *the bloody pony*, as Laird MacAlister called it. But then Lady Deirdre corrected him and said *the pony was named Horsey*. So Laird MacAlister started calling it *the bloody Horse pony*! To which Lady Deirdre said, *Doona you know anything about horses, Cousin? A pony is a pony, and a horse is a horse. As much as you may wish it, there is no such thing as a bloody horse pony.*

"And they were still arguing about it when they left the square," he added.

Gavin grinned. "I think I will put my coin on Lady Deirdre." Then his smile faded, and he scowled. "This man you're looking for, was he a MacKinnon? What did he say to her? Something inappropriate?"

Clyde's eyelid twitched, the only sign of his perturbation. "Nay, Laird. 'Twas more serious than that. He was a spy. He offered to help our lady escape."

"But…she's not a prisoner."

"Aye, but I suppose our enemies doona know that."

Gavin sighed. He knew spies likely existed at Clan MacKinnon, just like the MacKinnons had spies in other clans. And it had been confirmed last year that someone was conspiring against Gregor's clan and those of his foster sons. Still, for some reason it came as a surprise. A deadly surprise.

"And no sign of him?" he asked.

Clyde shook his head. "'Twas no more than a minute or two from when he spoke to the Lady

Deirdre to us beginning a standard search. We should have had him, but he just disappeared."

"'Tis worrying. Keep me informed," Gavin said. "Anything else?"

"Aye. The men returned from their trip to see Lewis MacIntyre. He would not speak to them. They said he packed up immediately and left."

Gavin huffed out a frustrated breath. "No surprise there. I should have gone myself."

"'Tis naught you can do about it now. I'm sure it willna be long before his father, Laird MacIntyre, and maybe even the Lady Deirdre's brother descend upon us. I've been told they're on the move. Two or three days at most, I would think."

"Do they have men with them?" Gavin asked. The information came from their spies and could be trusted.

"Not enough to worry us, especially with our allies here. MacIntyre would be addlepated to think he could attack all six of you at once and win. It would take much planning and a traitor in our midst to succeed."

Gavin grunted. "That's what I'm afraid of."

Clyde nodded and left the cottage. Gavin shut the door and then turned to face his old tutor, who hovered in the background, waiting. "Have you something to show me, Master Chisholm?"

"Aye, Laird." He shuffled forward and handed Gavin a package, his eyes alight.

Gavin opened the tin box and looked inside—and smiled. "This is perfect. Exactly what I was hoping for."

He could hardly wait to give it to her.

Thirteen

DEIRDRE TRIED TO SINK GRACEFULLY INTO THE CHAIR beside Ewan's bed, but she ended up falling onto the seat like a drunk. She barely repressed a groan as her thighs and back protested. That *bloody horse pony*, as Kerr had called it, had been an even more disagreeable ride than the mare. Deirdre might have been closer to the ground, but she'd had no stirrups, and she'd had to hold her toes up or they would have dragged through the grass.

She would have gotten off and walked, but she'd refused to let Kerr win. She'd insisted on the pony, and she wouldn't give in. Who knew she would have missed those bloody stirrups so much?

She scowled. Her cousin's cursing was rubbing off on her. But she had to admit it felt good.

"Mama, why are you frowning?" Ewan had pulled the covers up all the way to his chin and lay back against the pillows.

"Was I? I didn't realize."

"Were you thinking about Uncle Kerr? Aunt Isobel said he was annoying like a wasp and she wanted to swat him. And I know you doona like wasps."

Deirdre barely held in a laugh. "Nay, I was thinking about the stirrups on the horse."

"Are they annoying too?" Ewan asked.

"Aye." *Bloody annoying!*

"But they also give you a place to rest your feet and stop you from falling off. Isn't that right, Deirdre?" Gavin's voice came from the doorway, and she glanced over…and had to take a moment to catch her breath.

He'd shaved. And trimmed his hair. And he looked so…braw and bonnie. Aye. Laird Gavin MacKinnon, properly cleaned up, was breathtaking. If Isobel was the beauty of the Highlands, Gavin would be her male equivalent. A Highland Adonis.

"You're muttering again," he said to her. "What are you saying?"

Heat flooded her cheeks as alarm raced through her. "Naught of consequence!"

"She said *a Highland add on his*," Ewan told him.

"A Highland add on what?" he asked.

Ewan shrugged. And yawned.

Deirdre snorted. Just one of many ridiculous conversations she was sure to have with Ewan and his da…almost like they were a family.

And she supposed they were, in a way. Certainly, they were that to Ewan—his mama and da. And it was…comforting to share Ewan's care with someone. No longer having to worry about their home falling apart around them or if they were safe in their ramshackle keep. Obviously, they hadn't been, seeing how easily Gavin, Kerr, and their men had broken in. And even if Lewis had been home, he couldn't have protected them.

More than that, it was nice to have someone with whom she could share the funny things Ewan said or did. Someone who cared about her son as much as she did. Not to mention the other people she adored who were now part of her life. No matter how batty Isobel might be or how annoying Kerr definitely was, they both made her laugh and groan and scoff and think about things differently. All the while making her feel welcome. And wanted.

Aye, she felt wanted here.

Gavin walked forward quietly, looking at Ewan, and she turned to see that her son's eyes had closed. One arm rested above his head on the pillow and his lips were slightly parted. If he wasn't asleep yet, he would be in minutes.

Gavin stopped beside her, and she glanced up to find him watching her. Their eyes locked and held for a moment, and everything within her stilled.

He lowered himself to the edge of the bed, facing her, and from behind his back, he produced a box. It was wrapped in a soft, yellow cloth and tied with a blue ribbon. "This is for you," he said quietly, handing it to her.

She stared down at the box, wondering. What could it be? And why was he giving it to her?

"It's so pretty," she said. "Is it for Ewan?"

"Nay, Deirdre. I said it was something for you. Open it."

Her heart began to race, and her chest squeezed. "You mean…like a…a…"

"A gift," he interjected. "Have you ne'er received a present before?" He said it as a jest, a small laugh puffing past his lips before he realized she wasn't smiling. "Deirdre?" he asked.

She could hear the incredulity in his voice. She raised her eyes to his, feeling like she might cry. "Nay, I've ne'er received a gift just for me before. Other than Ewan, of course. But he wasn't Lewis's child to give."

"He's my child to give, and I freely gave him to you. Although I doona like the idea of 'owning' Ewan. And I think he chose you as much as you chose him."

Now the tears did fall, silent streams down her face. "Thank you," she whispered. She looked at the present in her hands. It was relatively flat and covered her lap. It had some weight to it and felt like the box might be tin. She grasped the end of the ribbon. "Do I just..." And she pulled a little.

He wrapped his hand over hers, the heat and strength of it engulfing hers, and helped her tug. The ribbon came loose, and the cloth fell away over her skirts, revealing a metal tin, as she'd suspected.

She lifted it up, and something slid around inside. Her eyes rose to his.

"Open it," he encouraged. She could see he was excited to give it to her—something he'd chosen that he'd thought she would like. That he wanted her to like.

And *that* was the gift he was giving her. It didn't matter what was inside. Despite his conflicted feelings about her relationship with Ewan when they first met, this man, who had already given her the greatest gift possible, had looked for and bought something for her. Only for her.

Something to please her.

She didn't think. She just leaned forward, cupped his cheek with her hand, and pressed her lips to his.

It didn't last long, just a moment or two. But when she pulled back, she could still feel the warmth and softness of him pressed against her mouth, his smooth skin against her palm and fingertips.

A puff of air escaped from his lungs and blew across her face as she retreated.

"It's perfect," she said, her eyes glued to his face.

"You haven't opened it yet." His voice croaked as if he was having a hard time speaking.

"It doesn't matter. Whatever is inside, I love it."

He took the tin box from her, lifted the lid, and held it out. "Look," he whispered.

She slowly lowered her eyes, almost not wanting to see what was there, not wanting this gift of his to be diminished in any way. Her gaze fell on the mostly wooden objects inside, and at first, she didn't understand what she was seeing. Then she gasped and reached for them, lifting out pieces of the geometry set: several sizes of rulers, a compass for drawing perfect circles, and a right-angled triangle.

"Oh, Gavin," she breathed. "They're perfect. Thank you." Once she received the information about the cathedral, these would help her work on the problem.

"You're welcome. They belonged to my old tutor, who lives in the village. He also asked me to give you this—a gift from him." He handed a book to her. She held it almost reverently, her eyes wide. "He's hoping you'll come visit him. Perhaps read to him. His eyesight is failing."

"I'd be happy to." She glanced through the book, scanning the handwritten text and hand-drawn images inside. "Gavin, this is all so much. It must have cost a fortune."

"'Tis naught." He put the book and the geometry set aside and squeezed her hands. "Deirdre, how could you ne'er have received a gift before today? Surely your husband at least gifted you something on your wedding day. Or during Yuletide?"

Shame welled within her, that awful reminder of how separate she had been from her family. How forgotten by her husband.

Unwanted.

"My family was not like yours. I was found…wanting…from a young age. I never fit in with my siblings or my parents, and I was happiest with my nursemaids and my tutor. Time spent with my family was…trying. I doona have any happy memories with them. Certainly, none of the kind that I've strived to give Ewan."

He leaned forward and kissed her forehead, much more chastely than her kiss. "And your husband?" he asked. "You have affection for him. 'Tis customary to give one's bride a gift when you are married."

"He may have given me a gift. I was young, Gavin, only fifteen, and very frightened. I remember so little of my wedding or…afterward. But Lewis was kind to me, and his keep was free from strife. We played a lot of chess together when he was home. I was happier there than I ever was at my clan. Especially after Ewan arrived." She stroked her hand through her sleeping son's hair and smiled at him. "He opened up everyone's hearts."

"Aye. A child's love can do that."

"He isn't just a gift, Gavin. He's a blessing. He taught me I was worthy of love and that I had value. I will cherish him for the rest of my days."

"As your family should have cherished you, Deirdre. Being treated poorly by your family wasn't your failing, love. It was theirs. Ask Kerr about it someday. He killed his father after his father tried to kill him. And then he took on his uncles and cousins and won. He wasn't at fault. They were."

She nodded, unable to talk as a flood of pain and realization overtook her. *It wasn't my failing.* It was her mother's and father's fault. Her siblings' fault. Gavin didn't find anything wrong with her, nothing to ridicule or criticize. And neither did Kerr or Isobel. Nor Ewan. Nay. They just accepted her.

And if they did bring up her failings, it was said with love and humor. They teased her in a different way than her siblings had teased her. Never to hurt. Nay, they teased her in a way that made her feel a part of them, like over her inability to keep her feet in the stirrups.

Her throat tightened. Her mouth trembled, jerking down uncontrollably at the corners, and she raised a hand to cover it.

She belonged.

Gavin said something under his breath, then he rose, took the gifts from her hands, and put them up on a shelf where Ewan couldn't reach. He returned to her and grasped her hand.

"Come on. I have another gift for you."

Gavin held tightly to Deirdre's hand as he led her higher and higher up the circular stone staircase, heading up to the highest turret on his castle, to a place he'd often retreated when Ewan was missing.

He liked the feel of her hand in his. Smaller and warm, but also somehow familiar, like he'd been holding it his entire life. He hesitated, then laced their fingers, clasping their palms intimately together.

Aye. Much better.

In his other hand he held a candle, so they could see, although the light didn't reach far. "Almost there," he said.

"Where are we going?" she asked. Her breath was labored, and he slowed.

"You'll see."

One last turn and they reached the small landing at the very top. He placed the candle holder in a wall sconce, released her hand, and unbarred the door that led outside. It squeaked heavily when he pushed it open and then placed a heavy stone against the wood to hold the door open. The wind, which was a constant force up here, whipped at the short strands of his hair and plaid.

He turned to her, blocking the wind with his body. "Do you have a ribbon for your hair? That blue one, maybe, that I used to wrap your present?"

She reached into her plaid and pulled it out.

"Here, let me." He didn't want her to tie a fancy bow and have the wind blow it out at the first big gust.

"All right." She handed him the ribbon and turned around. "Are you planning to braid it too? Add some curl at the front so it looks pretty?"

She teased him, and he liked it. “You doona need any curls to look pretty.”

If he hadn’t had his hands on her shoulders, he wouldn’t have noticed her reaction—her body stilled, then she inhaled a breath of air and didn’t release it.

He caressed her silky tresses with his fingers, the candlelight making the dark swathe gleam. “Breathe, Deirdre.”

She let out the breath she held in a gust, and the candle flame flickered.

“Has no one e’er told you that before either?” he asked quietly as he tied her hair back at the nape of her neck. What was wrong with her family? With Lewis? She spoke highly of Lewis in one breath, but then in the next breath she said her husband had ne’er given her a gift nor told her she was pretty. Not that those were necessary requirements for a loving union, but they were part of making someone feel loved and desired. There was more to being a husband than being kind and playing chess—a different type of intimacy that appeared to be lacking in their marriage.

“Isobel told me. It was kind of her.”

He spun her around to face him, hands on her shoulders, and she gasped. She deserved to know that she was more than just a kindness to people. “I didn’t say you were beautiful to be kind, and I’m quite sure Isobel didn’t either. I said it because it’s true. Because every time I look at you, my heart stops. I see you across the room and you steal my breath. I feel your body close to mine, touch your hand, and I wish with every inch of my soul that you weren’t married. Not a kindness, Deirdre. Never that.”

She stared up at him, her eyes wide, the light blue-gray irises now a midnight blue. Her lips had parted, and he dropped his gaze, focused on them. What had he compared them to when he'd first met her? The inner petals of a young rose. Aye. An apt description.

He could just see the tip of her tongue through the parting of her lips, and he wanted to capture it with his own. Suck on it. Gently, at first, then with more force, his hands cupping the sides of her head and holding her in place.

His breath rushed from his lungs in a short, jagged spurt, and he released her. Turning back to the door, he braced himself for the onslaught of the wind. Welcomed it.

I ne'er should have said that.

Stepping outside, he waited until she joined him, then removed the rock and let the door bang shut. Four paces, and he was across the stone floor, resting his hands on the battlements.

The sun was setting; the sky was colored with ever-changing shades of orange, pink, and purple. In the distance, he could see the cathedral and past the sprawling MacKinnon village and the forest beyond, where the quarry was located. To his right stretched the loch, a long, blue line that snaked for miles, all the way to the Great Western Ocean.

"It's beautiful," Deirdre said as she leaned on the battlements beside him, one hand pushing back a strand of black hair that the wind had plastered across her face. "But windy. I can see why you tied the ribbon so tight. I'm surprised. I didn't think the wind had picked up so much from earlier."

"It didn't. The wind blows like this up here most days. It's what makes it so ideal."

"Ideal for what?" That little furrow he'd come to recognize had formed between her brows again. He wanted to smooth it with his thumb.

He turned to face her, a wicked grin transforming his face. "For screaming." Then he looked back out, opened his mouth, and let out a howl at the top of his lungs—long and hard enough that she took a frightened step backward, but not enough for her to run to the door.

The scream was surprisingly more feral and filled with emotion than he thought it would be, frustration and anger shoving up from the very center of him. At Deirdre? He thought he'd let go of his anger toward her.

Nay, it was something else—something more primitive—and he felt a twisting inside of himself like a tiger springing toward another male. A beast fighting for his female.

For his mate.

He finished on an angry growl. Deirdre took another step back, her eyes jumping to the door. He laid his hand over hers and stopped her from running as he caught his breath.

"Your turn," he said when he could speak. His voice sounded shredded, like that tiger he'd been imagining had reached up and scratched his throat.

She stared at him, shock and alarm skittering over her face, her mouth slightly open. His eyes dropped to the lush shape, and for a moment, all he could focus on was her lips—what he wanted to do with them, how he would take her over one kiss at a time, until she was screaming to the wind just like he'd been. Screaming his name.

Stop looking at her mouth!

"What do you mean, it's my turn?" she asked.

He lifted his eyes to hers. "No one can hear you from up here, Deirdre. The stone walls and heavy door block the sound from traveling inside, and outside, the wind whips your screams away and throws them to the sky. When Ewan was gone and the days passed with no sign of him, I would come up here and rage to the wind. I hollered out all my despair, fear, and frustration at the top of my lungs. It didn't take away the pain, because Ewan was still gone, but it lessened the ferocity of my feelings, so I could… function."

"But…I doona have anything to scream about."

His brow rose. "You ne'er received a gift until today. Your family excluded you—from riding horses, if naught else—and at fifteen you were married off to a man you ne'er knew. I'd say you have a lifetime's worth of things to scream about."

She looked out over the view again, splotches of red stealing up her cheeks and her eyes shining with emotions. And not happy ones. When she tucked her chin down and swung her head around in an unconscious movement, he realized she was trying to hide behind her hair, but he'd tied it back too tightly.

She looked miserable…and ashamed.

He moved behind her and wrapped her in his embrace. "Deirdre. You're a mother now. You know that a good parent loves and supports their child. How they accept their child's differences and encourage their interests, even if they're not their own. Did your parents do this for you?"

She shook her head.

"And was that their failure?"

She nodded jerkily.

"Then why are you blaming yourself for their mistakes? You were once as small as Ewan. Imagine if he was made to feel as you did."

She let out a sharp, involuntary sound, like a rabbit or mouse would make if they were hurt.

"Would you want him to take on the shame of his parents' indifference, or would you want him to know that *they* were wrong? Cristel ne'er loved Ewan. She didn't want to marry me, and she didn't want children. Duty and greed motivated her, not love and caring. Had she still been living, Ewan might have felt the same way you did—unloved and unwanted by her."

He wove his fingers through hers and held her arms out to the side. "Scream, Deirdre."

"I canna."

"Aye, you can. Scream!"

She let out a short yell.

"That's not good enough. Louder!" he demanded.

She screamed again, a more powerful burst with more suffering behind it. But he *knew* there was so much more, that she hadn't scraped through the sludge at the bottom of her heart that weighed her down or dredged the dark pool of pain in her guts that muddied everything she thought about herself. Getting to that would be like loosing a winter tempest.

He wrapped his arms around her middle, pressed them into her stomach. "Scream from here!"

With that, she let loose a heartbreaking roar that was part rage, part devastation, part fear, part anguish—and she kept going. Scream after scream, howl after howl—getting louder, fiercer, deeper; raw and visceral.

Sobs came up, tears streamed down, her face contorting into a mask of pain.

She hammered the battlements with her fists, kicked with her feet, scraped her fingers along the stone, breaking nails and leaving behind bloody smears. She thrashed her head side to side against his chest, then smashed it back hard enough to knock him back a step.

"Deirdre," he cried in alarm, his arms coming around her—soothing her, protecting her, but also restraining her from hurting herself in her anguish.

"Hush, love. That's enough. I've got you," he crooned in her ear.

She fought him still, flailing and yelling, disjointed words cut off by an angry shriek or teeth-clenched growl. She got a hand free and banged it into her own forehead.

He quickly dragged her arm back down and turned her around so she rested against his chest. He pressed every inch of her into his body, trying to absorb her pain, to give her an anchor in the storm, something to hold on to.

A place to come back to.

"Deirdre, you're done. Let it go, sweetling."

She pressed into him. Her arms circled his body, and she squeezed as tightly as she could—and she held him for so long that her muscles began to shake. When she released her grip, she inhaled a great, shuddering gulp of air. And exhaled. Then another one.

A moment passed. She sighed, her fists clenched in Gavin's shirt, then she rose on her tiptoes and pressed her face into the exposed skin of his throat. Gavin stopped breathing. Her hands stroked upward up on either side of his spine and over his shoulders, making his heart race.

He tried to control his breathing, tried to regulate the inhale and exhale so she wouldn't know how affected he was. How much he wanted her.

Then her lips opened on his collarbone, and every puff of air she released felt like a brand on his skin, marking him, scorching a trail of fire all the way down to his groin. He dropped his head into the crook of her neck and smelled her—honey, lavender, and the fresh smell of the wind.

Her lips were on his neck now, and he felt the soft pressure of her tongue, touching him, tasting him. He didn't know if it was intentional, but he could barely contain the groan that rumbled up from his chest.

She bit down, teeth on either side of his Adam's apple, and laved the sting with her tongue.

His blood surged, hot and fast, filling his already swollen cock, and he gasped. He rocked his hips uncontrollably against her pelvis. One hand stroked over the curve of her arse and squeezed the rounded flesh.

"Oh," she moaned, drawing out the vibration from deep within her throat and dropping her head back.

Ne'er in his life had he heard a more arousing sound.

"Touch me, Gavin. Put your hands on me. All over me."

Until he heard that.

Every thought fled his head—that he should stop, that she was vulnerable, that he was taking advantage of his son's mother.

That she was married.

And she couldn't ever truly be his.

None of that mattered as he lowered his other hand to her arse and lifted her against him. "Wrap your legs around my waist, Deirdre."

She did as he requested, linking her ankles at the small of his back and her hands around his neck. He turned, walked them to the wall beside the door and pushed her against it.

They groaned together as the hardened length of him pressed into her mound, her thighs spread for him, wanting him, her nipples stiff points that brushed against his chest. She opened her eyes to half-mast and met his gaze. He was glad the gloaming was still upon them and he could see how her eyes had darkened with her heightened need, how the passion he could feel pounding through her veins had tinged her skin pink.

"God's blood," he murmured, his voice so thick with desire it was almost unrecognizable. She would be pink and flushed everywhere, a darker, glistening pink at the center of her. He couldn't help grinding himself against that spot as he thought of it, imagined how it would look. How it would taste. He thrust once, long and slow, and even though the material of their plaids still bunched between them, his knees shook.

"What do yo—ohhhh." Her voice hitched halfway through her question as he hit the nub at the top of her sex. Her eyes fluttered shut and she arched her throat.

He slid his hands from below her arse and stroked

up her belly and rib cage. When he reached her breasts and cupped them, they filled his palms and overflowed onto his fingers.

Gavin groaned. They both did.

He'd already seen the size and shape of her breasts when the candlelight had shone through her shift, but the feel of them—soft and full, the tips dragging across his fingertips—almost had him losing his seed against his plaid like a boy of fourteen.

"The way you feel," he whispered, leaning down to kiss her temple. "How you smell. Your heat and softness." He kissed down her cheek to the corner of her mouth, his big palms sliding over her breasts and up her neck to cup the side of her head. "Your mouth. I've been dreaming about your mouth since the first moment I saw you."

"Then stop talking and kiss it."

A laugh huffed past his lips. "Aye, Deirdre. I'll kiss your lips."

He lowered his head, but then hovered just above her mouth—the rose-petal temptation of her just inches away.

What am I doing?

His moment of laughter had cleared away the haze of lust and desire just long enough for guilt to hit him like a punch to the side of his head. Cold wind gusted across his neck and down his back, making him shiver, but he was shivering also from the realization of what he was so close to doing. What he couldn't take back.

He was taking advantage of a fragile and vulnerable woman. In this moment, after the emotional upheaval she'd just gone through—that he had encouraged—she did not have the ability to make a rational decision. She'd knocked down all her protective barriers, and her body and heart were wide open. She was vulnerable and exposed. How could she say yes or no when she was in such a state?

Not only that, but she was under his protection. And as Ewan's mother, she might fear he'd take Ewan away from her if she didn't agree. Or she might agree and then later regret it, and her home here might not feel comforting or safe for her any longer.

He dropped his forehead to hers and rested it there as he tried to rein in his need.

She pressed closer. Slid her hands into his hair and tried to pull his mouth down to hers. He resisted. As much as he wanted to kiss her, even just a chaste press of lips like she'd already bestowed upon him in Ewan's bedchamber, he didn't trust himself not to get caught up again. To lose himself in everything *Deirdre*.

"I canna," he said, regret like a wet blanket weighing him down. He lowered his hands to her thighs and pushed them down from his waist. When she was solidly on the ground again, he stepped back—close enough to stay connected and read the emotions in her body and face, but far enough apart that they weren't touching.

She blinked—slowly, like she was just waking up. She raised her hand to her face and rubbed it over her forehead where he'd kissed her, then brought it down to her lips.

"Did I do something wrong?" she asked, sounding lost and confused.

"Nay, Deirdre. I did something wrong. I should

ne'er have done what I did. You were emotional and vulnerable. I took advantage of you."

That crease formed in her brow again. The one he wanted to rub away with his thumb.

She nodded, but he knew it wasn't in understanding, more just a placeholder. Something to do while she tried to comprehend what had just happened.

God's Blood! Why didn't I just take her back to her room!

"Oh. I…I'm sorry."

His brows shot up. "You're sorry? Deirdre, you have naught to be sorry for. 'Tis my fault. All of it. Thank God, I was able to stop before we…"

She raised her eyes to his, and he couldn't read what was in them. Usually she was so open. She dropped her gaze and nodded. "Aye."

Pushing away from the wall, she turned toward the door, and her shoulder hit his chest. She stumbled and he caught her. She sucked in a breath. "Nay, please. Doona touch me. You're right. I don't feel well. I need to lie down." She pulled on the door, but it was too heavy for her.

"Let me," he said.

She leaned on the wall while he opened the door. He stepped inside and reached for the candle, holding it away from the wind.

"Come inside, Deirdre." He wanted to help her, to grasp her hand and steady her, but she was obviously still feeling the effects of what they'd done.

What I did. Bloody, inconsiderate arse!

"Put your hand on my arm." She used him for support as she came inside and then he went down the stairs first. "Lean on me from behind if you need to."

"Aye, thank you."

It felt like the stairwell circled down forever. When they reached the level where their bedchambers were located, he breathed a sigh of relief.

He'd just entered the passageway and intended to walk her to her door, but her hand on his arm stopped him. "I can go the rest of the way by myself."

She squeezed past him, her head down, and he grasped the tips of her fingers. She stopped, her arm outstretched behind her, but she didn't look back.

"This is your home, Deirdre, and you're under my protection. I doona think either one of us expected what happened up there to…happen. That's not to say I didn't want it to happen—I did. But we canna jeopardize your place here—for your sake or for Ewan's."

She turned her head. Met his gaze…and nodded.

He squeezed her hand. "You're married, love. I canna see any way past that. Otherwise…"

Otherwise, what? He'd marry her? His eyes drifted over her, remembering her shape, how she felt. The fullness of her breasts and the small, flat expanse of her belly.

Was she barren? Had she and Lewis tried for children and she'd failed to conceive? Maybe if she was barren… Nay, there was no *maybe.* If they went ahead and she conceived, his child would be born out of wedlock.

It surprised him how much that thought appealed to him. Her conceiving his child. Carrying their bairn in her belly for nine months, suckling their baby at her breast.

Loving their child.

It would be nothing like when Cristel had conceived. He'd ne'er been allowed to touch his wife after that. She'd encouraged him to find a lover—to have as many bastard children as he liked. She didn't care, for either of them.

But that didn't matter anymore, because Deirdre loved Ewan. Would she love Gavin too if they were married? What would it be like to have her adoring eyes turned on him?

He filled up with contentment and bliss just thinking about it.

"Gavin."

He raised his eyes. Her gaze wasn't adoring now. It was frustrated and a little bewildered. And she tugged on her fingers, which he hadn't released.

Idiot.

He did so and watched as she made her way along the passageway, her hair still tied back in a ribbon—*his* ribbon, tied by *his* hands—her hips swaying from side to side under her skirts.

He sighed and scraped his hand over the bristles on his jaw only to be met with smooth skin. He'd forgotten he'd shaved. He'd trimmed his hair too—or rather, someone else had done it for him. All so he could look nice when he gave Deirdre her gift. Which said what about him, exactly?

After he'd married Cristel, she would let him into her bed only if he was freshly shaved. His hair, of course, had been past his shoulders then. Was that what he'd intended all along with Deirdre? Without realizing it?

A married woman under his protection. His son's mother.

He was worse than an idiot; he was a blackheart.

Gavin waited until she disappeared inside her room before heading to his solar. Sleep was a long way away—if he slept at all tonight. And not because he worried about his son, this time, but because he wanted something he couldn't have.

Kerr was sitting at the desk when Gavin entered his solar—a desk that had been in Gavin's family for generations. Made of pine, it was solidly built with drawers on both sides and built-in wells for both ink and sand. The MacKinnons had ruled this land and this castle for centuries.

Gavin stood at the door, watching his foster brother write with a quill on a parchment. The fire burned brightly; the wooden shutters stood open so the chamber didn't overheat. Two candles burned on the desk and several more in wall sconces.

Gavin crossed the wool rug on the floor and sat in one of the chairs facing the desk. Kerr glanced up briefly, then returned to his letter. "You've shaved. I haven't seen you without your whiskers since before Ewan was born. And you've trimmed your hair."

A niggle of guilt squirmed in Gavin's gut. "Are you my style advisor now?"

"Nay. Just an observer. And cousin to your son's married mother."

It was no secret what Kerr was implying.

"I haven't lost sight of that fact," Gavin replied, his jaw tight, knowing full well that he had lost sight of it many times. The most recent time almost leading to a mistake he wouldn't have been able to rectify.

Kerr huffed in disbelief. When he finished writing,

he sprinkled his letter with sand to absorb the excess ink, then blew it away. He folded the parchment, took off his ring, and sealed it with hot wax from one of the candles.

Kerr sat back in his chair and leveled his gaze on him. "Have you considered killing Lewis so you can marry her?"

Gavin's brows rose. "I've considered killing him but for the abduction of my son, assuming he was involved. And I've considered killing Deirdre's father too."

"For Ewan, then. Not for Deirdre."

Gavin scrubbed his hand through his hair. The urge was there to yank on it, to feel the pain of the strands coming out, but his hair was too short for that now. "It would be unjust to kill a man simply to marry his wife."

"'Tis nothing simple about it if you're in love with her. I would kill any man who stood between me and Isobel."

"Anyone stupid enough to do that would deserve to die," Gavin said dryly. "But the only one standing between you and Isobel is Isobel."

Kerr grunted and tucked the letter he'd just written into his plaid. "And your mother, making you promise on her death bed to let Isobel choose her husband. She ne'er liked me."

Gavin smiled. They both knew that wasn't true. His mother had adored Kerr and taken him under her wing like a mother hen. She'd wanted Kerr to come live with them to keep him safe from his father, but both Gregor and her husband had explained repeatedly why Kerr had to stay with his clan if he was to someday lead the MacAlisters.

"Who's the letter to?" Gavin asked.

"My man in charge at home. I want them on high alert, and I want extra men on the border with the Campbells. All of you have been attacked now except me and Gregor. And fortunately, so far, you've all prevailed now that you've found Ewan alive."

Kerr rose and moved to close the shutters. The wind had picked up and was blowing inside in cool gusts. "Whether the attacks were part of the same conspiracy, I doona know," he continued. "But I do know that other forces are involved. And that we doona know what clans are supporting them. The man who approached Deirdre today with the offer to help said he was neither a MacIntyre nor a MacColl."

"And the group who attacked Callum and Maggie weren't MacDonnells or Sinclairs."

"Aye. So, who's leading the charge? If we're going to defeat this conspiracy against us, we need to cut off the head of the snake."

"Is it even a Highlander? Could it be a Lowlander?"

"I doona think so. Highlanders are a closed, stubborn bunch." Kerr crossed to the other chair beside Gavin and sat down. "If the conspiracy is as big as it appears to be, another Highlander would have to be pulling the strings."

"Someone smart enough to stay hidden, then. And to know that if he wanted to rule the Highlands, he'd have to go through the six of us first."

They fell silent for a moment, then Gavin reached across his desk for some opened parchments and began rifling through them. "We've had news that Laird MacIntyre and Boyd MacColl are on the move, heading in our direction. A few days at most until they're here. What have you heard from your spies?"

"Not much that we didn't know already. The relationship between Lewis and his father is strained. Laird MacIntyre has gone through several wives in the past decade, trying for a son."

"Several wives?"

"Three to be exact. They keep conveniently dying. He has one daughter who lives with her mother's family. Lewis visits her on occasion. Her father does not."

"And what of Lewis? What do we know of him?"

Kerr sighed. "I doona know what to make of it."

Gavin put down the parchments he'd been scanning and stared at Kerr, his heart beginning to pound. "Tell me."

"By all accounts he's a good man, but he doesn't spend much time at home with Deirdre. He has many excuses for his departures, saying he's going to his father's keep or on a journey for the clan or to a gathering somewhere, but no one believes him. And those who do know what he's up to are tight-lipped about it."

"Another lover?" Gavin asked. His jaw hurt from clenching his teeth. As much as he wanted Deirdre for himself, the idea of her being hurt or betrayed by someone *she* loved was enough to send him into a rage.

"Possibly. Whatever it is, 'tis good we have her safely here." Kerr tapped his fingers on his knee. "There was some mention of the lack of funds for the keep's maintenance and for the care of Lewis and his family. His father sends gold regularly, more than enough to sustain them, but the steward sees little of it. You saw the state of the keep when we arrived."

"Aye, and no guards to speak of. So Lewis is a *good* man who visits his sister, plays chess with his wife, and steals from his father."

Kerr yawned. "'Tis too much for us to figure out tonight. Or too much for me, anyway." He rose and stretched out his arms. "Is Ewan still coming in to sleep with you?"

"For the last two nights."

"And Deirdre doesn't mind?"

"She doesn't seem to, but I'm sure she misses him."

He nodded. "As you would if the situation were reversed. You look more rested. Are you sleeping yet, Gavin? You canna doubt now that Ewan's safe, especially if he's locked in your chamber with you."

"I'm still awake for most of the night, but I'm lying down with Ewan once he comes in. Maybe I'm sleeping more than I realize." He sighed and dropped his head back onto the headrest and looked up at the ceiling. "Something still doesn't seem right. I fall asleep, but I canna stay asleep. I often wake up with my heart racing."

"Maybe you just need time for your body to adjust. Or to have someone other than Ewan to be sleeping beside you—and I doona mean my cousin. How long has it been?"

Guilt hit Gavin like a hammer this time and he straightened in his seat, pretending to turn his attention back to the parchments in his hand. "I haven't slept with a woman since before Ewan disappeared."

"And who was that? Cristel?"

"Not Cristel. Someone else. And only once. I hadn't slept with Cristel since Ewan was conceived."

"I'm sorry, Brother."

"I was too, but if I hadn't had Cristel in my life, I wouldn't have Ewan. So my terrible marriage was worth it in the end."

"And what about Deirdre? If Ewan hadn't been taken, you wouldnae have her in your life either. And Ewan wouldnae have a mother. Does that make Ewan's kidnapping worth it too?"

Gavin frowned. He folded the parchments and tossed them on the desk. Nothing and no one could be worth the two and a half years of worry and pain that he'd gone through after Ewan had been taken.

Could they?

He opened his mouth, tongue pressed behind his top teeth, ready to say nay, but found he couldn't get the word out.

That was surprising.

Kerr grunted and headed to the door. "You doona have to answer. 'Tis something to ponder, that's all.

"But if the answer is aye, start thinking about how to get rid of Lewis. Without killing him."

Deirdre woke in the middle of her bed, the covers pulled up to her chin and her pillow wet beneath her cheek. The fire still burned low in the hearth and the room was warm, but despite being fully dressed in her woolen arisaid and chemise, she was freezing.

She'd come back into her chamber, barred the door, and then climbed straight into bed and sunk into sleep. Her dreams had been chaotic and jumbled, upsetting nightmares about her family and Ewan. Each dream felt like it was swirling her toward a black pit. But every time she neared it, Gavin would appear and pull her to safety—only to disappear again.

Was that why her pillow was wet? Bad dreams?

She felt her neck—perhaps she was getting sick. But it wasn't sore. Her throat, however, felt like she'd shoved a torch down it and burned out her voice box. It didn't hurt so much as it felt…used. And abused. And when she tried to make a noise, it came out almost a whisper.

All that screaming and yelling.

She buried her face in her pillow, feeling the shame of it. What must Gavin have thought of her—the way she'd hit and kicked and scratched, the sounds she'd made like a feral beast, the whole rotten display? All of that from being told to scream into the wind. When he'd done it first, she'd been frightened at the ferocity that had appeared on his face, but he'd still been contained somehow. Though he'd had to catch his breath afterward. And he'd sounded a wee bit gutted.

Maybe that was what was supposed to happen? She'd never heard of yelling like that before—for the sake of releasing old wounds—and wondered if all of Gavin's foster brothers did that. Of course, none of them would have known the heartrending pain of losing a child like Gavin did.

She pulled the covers up higher and shivered. How could she be so cold? She should build up the fire, but she didn't want to crawl out from beneath her quilt.

And how much difference would it really make when the chill seemed to be coming from inside herself?

Cold. Alone.

A sob pushed up from her chest suddenly, and she covered her mouth.

Was that where the chill was coming from? Her loneliness? Gavin had made her yell and scream, and in the process, she'd ripped off the scab of her childhood and her lonely marriage, leaving a painful wound behind.

She sat up and hugged her knees to her body, needing to press something physical into the ache. And she listened—for anyone else out there, any human connection she could make. But the castle was quiet. She rose from her bed and walked toward the stone wall that her room shared with Gavin's chamber. Was he in there? Was Ewan in there with him?

She hadn't heard her son cry, but that didn't mean he hadn't woken and already come down. She stood there, shivering. *What should I do?*

Nay, not *should*. What did she *want* to do?

She heard steps in the passageway, ran to the door, and threw it open. A guard had passed on his rounds, and he whipped around at the noise, drawing his sword. Deirdre let out a little shriek, and a second later, Gavin was standing in front of her, facing the guard.

"Put your weapon away, Finn. You frightened her."

"Och, I'm sorry, Laird. Lady Deirdre, forgive me. I didn't mean you any harm." The young man sheathed his sword. "The passageways are clear, Laird."

"Good. Take your position at the bottom of the stairs."

Finn nodded once and retreated. Gavin faced her. "Are you well, Deirdre?"

She took a moment to answer. "Aye. I woke up, and I was cold." She looked past Gavin, trying to see into his room. "Do you have Ewan in there with you?"

"He's asleep. He came down about an hour ago. I brought him in with me when you ne'er responded."

She stepped around him and into his room, knowing she shouldn't but doing it anyway. Now she was doing what *she* wanted. The chamber was about twice the size of hers, with a bigger hearth and a bigger bed, also covered in quilts. She could just make out Ewan's golden head on the pillow in the dim light, and the need to hold her son beat at her like the wings of a trapped dove.

She didn't look back at Gavin to ask his permission, she just crossed the room, crawled under the quilts with their son. She lay on her side, facing him, and pulled him close. He snuggled into her arms, and his breath puffed warmly on her chest. She closed her eyes, listened to his breathing, and that lost, empty space began to fill up inside.

When the bed jostled a minute later, she opened her eyes to see Gavin, his linen shirt on and the tie open at the neck, crawling under the quilts from the opposite side of the bed. He lay on his side facing her, Ewan in the middle.

Their eyes met, and she marveled at the beauty of him in the firelight. Her hand rested on the pillow next to him, and he slid his hand on top of hers, palm to palm, their fingers entwined. Just like when he'd held her hand on their climb up to the turret.

They stared at each other across the pillows in silent communion. And Deirdre knew that this was where she belonged.

Aye. She'd finally warmed up inside.

Fourteen

Gavin struggled to open his eyes. His lids felt anchored down with weights, and his body felt as heavy as though he'd been cast in lead. He knew he was in his bedchamber, and he was aware the castle had come alive hours ago, but for the life of him he could not throw off the black oblivion that kept dragging him back under.

He managed to move his fingers, feeling the lack of another hand that had held his during the night. He'd been filled with warmth and peace, a level of contentment he hadn't felt since he'd been a lad and his mother had rocked him to sleep in her embrace. Or after his son had been born and Ewan's wee body had rested skin-to-skin against Gavin's thudding heart. Aye, *that* was contentment.

But it was also his past.

Last night, he'd felt that happiness and wholeness deep in his bones—that was his future. If he could just figure out how to keep it with him this time.

He relaxed and the oblivion enveloped him again. With a heavy sigh, he stopped fighting and let himself be pulled under.

The next time Gavin woke, his eyelids were still heavy, but he lifted them without struggle. He lay on his back under his quilts, staring up at the blue canopy over his bed. The shutters were closed, but bright light spilled through the cracks.

He sat up tiredly and scrubbed his hands over his face. What time was it? And where were Deirdre and Ewan? He glanced over at the other side of the empty bed and then toward the window again before tossing back the quilts and rising to his feet.

One thought kept repeating in his mind as he crossed to the window—he'd slept.

And when he pulled the shutters back and stared out at the sun high in the sky and the bailey full of people going about their daily chores, he couldn't believe it.

It was well past noon. Gavin had slept for more than twelve hours!

He moved to a side table, where a jug of watered-down mead and a bowl of cooked oats sat on a tray. The mead was still cool, the oats warm, and he wondered if their delivery had been the cause of his awakening. He wolfed down the food and drink, used the pot, and then stripped down for a wash.

He was almost finished dressing when men's loud laughter and boisterous voices penetrated the stone walls and thick wooden door of his previously quiet bedchamber.

Deirdre stared, round-eyed and nervous, at the five big, brawny men striding across the great hall toward her. She recognized Kerr, of course, which meant the other four had to be Gavin's foster father and his brothers. Ewan clung to her legs and hid behind her skirts when he saw them.

Deirdre wished she had someone to hide behind too.

All of the MacKinnon castle folk were running around under Isobel's direction, setting up a place for the recent arrivals and family to eat their midday meal together. Gavin still slept, much to everyone's amazement, and Isobel had given strict orders not to wake him. Intent on staying out of the way, Deirdre had retreated to a corner with Ewan where he played with his toy soldiers. No one paid them any mind.

Except the five Highland lairds, who were bearing down on them now.

"Doona worry, Ewan, I'll save you from the ugly-arse monsters!" Kerr declared as they neared. He scooped a squealing Ewan high into the air and then flew him past the other men. Their smiles looked like they might break their faces, they were so wide. She even spotted a few tears, which were quickly wiped away.

After a few of the men ducked and weaved around him, making Ewan laugh, Kerr transferred the lad to one massive arm and then drew his sword from its sheath with the other.

Deirdre couldn't believe what she was seeing! Was he mad? She scowled at him so hard that he hesitated, put down the sword, and backed slowly away from it with his hand raised.

"Fight! Fight!" Ewan shouted, his fists swinging in the air.

"Nay, lad. Look," Kerr whispered as he pointed at Deirdre. "We woke the dragon."

She tried not to smile, but it broke through anyway. With an exasperated sigh, she picked up Kerr's sword to put on the mantel, but it was so heavy that she almost dropped it. How had Kerr drawn it from its scabbard with one hand?

An older man with wings of gray in his auburn hair came to her aid. This could only be the great laird Gregor MacLeod. "Where would you like it, lass?" he asked.

He had such a kind look on his face, her shyness evaporated. "Where Ewan canna reach it, please. He has a fascination with anything sharp and pointy."

Gregor smiled and nodded. "I remember. Even when Ewan was barely walking, Gavin had to watch him like a hawk." He placed the sword up high on the mantel, then turned to her and took her hand. "I'm Gregor MacLeod, foster father of these four scoundrels. And Gavin too, of course. Kerr has told us that you're Ewan's adopted mother and that you've chosen to stay with him. It warms my heart."

One of the lairds, a braw man with chestnut-colored hair and brown eyes, joined them. "Aye, lass. You have our thanks. I'm Darach MacKenzie. 'Twas such a joy to hear that Ewan had been found, and then such a relief to know he'd been loved and cared for the entire time he was gone. I canna imagine what might have happened to him if not for you. My wife is with bairn, aye, and it drives home what happened to Ewan, and to Gavin and his family, even more so than before. You have done us all a great service."

Another man joined their group, his shoulder-length light-brown hair secured in a leather tie, and his dark-blue eyes glinting devilishly. "I'm Lachlan MacKay. My thanks to you as well, Deirdre. 'Tis rumored you're an angel in disguise, and I believe it. Kerr has claimed you're his cousin, of course, but we all know better. You're much too dignified to be a MacAlister. Your sweet tone gives it away, if naught else."

"Of course I'm claiming her," Kerr said loudly from behind them. "She's the only decent and kind relative I have! And look at her—she's the spitting image of me! Beauty personified!"

"If by spitting image you mean that you spat on a mirror and then compared the two of you, I agree," the last laird joked. By process of elimination, that had to be Callum MacLean. Everyone laughed again, including Deirdre. Callum squeezed in beside Lachlan and clasped her free hand, his bright-green eyes filled with gratitude. "I'm Callum MacLean, Deirdre. You are indeed beauty personified, both inside—where it counts the most—and out. Thank you for keeping our Ewan safe."

"Aye," the men responded together, like the chorus in the Greek plays she'd studied.

"My Maggie is with bairn as well," he continued. "And as Darach says, it made us feel Ewan's disappearance even more keenly. We canna thank you enough."

His eyes shone with love when he spoke of his wife and growing bairn. Yearning swelled in Deirdre's chest. What would it be like to be loved like that by a man as good as Callum MacLean? By any of these men?

To be loved like that by Gavin?

Now her heart stuttered, and she had to catch her breath before speaking. "My heartfelt congratulations,

Laird MacLean. May your child always be safe, happy, and healthy—and your wife as well."

"'Tis Callum. And yes, their health and happiness are all we wish for."

Another round of "ayes."

A pang of envy and loss shot through Deirdre's breast as she thought about the journey the pregnant women were on. No matter how difficult the births, they were surely excited to bring new life into the world—and their husbands were excited right along with them. But she could understand his worry too. Death during the delivery was all too common an occurrence.

"My Amber will be with both Caitlin and Maggie on their birthing days," Lachlan said. "So doona worry about them, lass. Amber is the best healer in all the Highlands." Lachlan's voice was filled with pride.

"Verily, 'tis a good thing Maggie's pregnant," Darach said. "Otherwise she'd be climbing out of windows to avoid Callum's incessant lectures about her safety."

Callum raised one brow and appeared to think about it for a moment, then sighed. "I canna deny it. 'Tis true." More laughter. "Only the other day she decided a discussion we were having was at an end. And in order to escape me, she threw a rope out of the window and climbed down to the bailey—with me standing right there. What kind of a wife does that?"

He said it with such love and amusement that Maggie's heart squeezed again, although she didn't understand how his wife could climb out of the window. Wasn't she afraid she would fall?

"I doona doubt you're confused, Deirdre," Darach said. "Maggie's our very own warrior woman. All the women in our family are in their own way. Just like you've been a warrior for Ewan."

"Oh, I doona think—"

"Aye, you have been," Callum confirmed. "Maggie is a warrior in the truest sense. There is none better than her with a bow or a dagger, but she has a penchant for escaping castles in dangerous ways."

Deirdre marveled that a woman could be so bold. And then she looked across at Isobel, who was shepherding them all into their seats for their midday meal, and she realized that Isobel might not shoot arrows or slide on ropes out of windows, but she was bold as well. Isobel held her own with these powerful men, and they all respected her for it.

It was humbling to think she was now part of this family—or on the periphery of it, anyway.

Everyone sat but Gregor, who glanced around the great hall. "Did no one tell Gavin we're here? Surely, he can hear us from his solar, especially with Kerr booming like an elephant. What is he doing up there?"

They all looked at Deirdre expectantly like she should know, and a blush stole up her cheeks. "I havenae been upstairs in several hours, but I assume Gavin is still in his bedchamber."

"Da is sleeping!" Ewan said, laughing. "And he isn't even sick. Mama said we were to be verra quiet and move like wee mouses this morning when we woke up, so we didn't jostle him on the bed. He missed breakfast, and now he's going to miss our midday meal as well!"

Almost as one, the men—and Isobel—turned to look at her, their brows raised. Deirdre's slow blush suddenly turned fiery on her cheeks. "It wasn't like that!" she protested, humiliation seemingly coming on fast. None of the men made a peep. "I was fully clothed, and I wasn't feeling well last night." She pointed to Ewan, who was still laughing at the idea of his da sleeping through their meal. "He had Ewan in there with him! He's my son too. I needed to hold him!"

"Ewan or Gavin?" Isobel asked, looking perplexed, and all four of the foster brothers snorted.

Deirdre turned to ice inside, a cold contrast to her burning skin. Were they laughing at her?

Gregor reached out and gently covered her hand with his. "You're a part of our family, Deirdre. A beloved sister to the lads and daughter to me, just like Isobel, Maggie, Amber, and Caitlin. The lads meant no offense. They were just being thoughtless."

He turned a stern eye on the grown men around the table, who squirmed in their seats.

"Sorry, Deirdre."

"Aye, sorry, lass."

"It won't happen again, Cousin."

"Please, forgive us."

"Well, that's all well and good," Isobel said, "but I want to know what Gavin was thinking. Deirdre is married!"

This time Kerr covered Isobel's hand and squeezed gently. "'Tis not always as simple as that, love. Gavin is working on the problem."

Deirdre's brows rose. "What problem?"

Silence fell, and then Gregor spoke again. "How to keep you here permanently, Deirdre. For Ewan, of course. But for all of us as well. None of us want to lose you."

Isobel snorted. "Especially my brother, apparently."

Deirdre narrowed her eyes at Isobel, then turned to Gregor. "Can you make them run around the castle walls a few times? Isobel included. Better yet, put them on chamber pot duty."

"What's a chamber pot doodie?" Ewan asked.

"It's when your aunt Isobel picks up all the pots in the castle and washes them out. And if she doesn't, Mama is going to side with Uncle Kerr on everything he says and does from now on. He is my cousin, after all. I may even give him secret information."

"You wouldnae," Isobel shrieked. "And they say I'm the one with the mean streak!"

Kerr smiled and crossed his arms over his chest. "Blood is thicker than water. I told you she was a MacAlister."

Gavin strode to the window as he fastened his plaid over his léine, wondering if the sound of laughing had drifted in from outside. He looked out but could see no sign of Gregor, Darach, Lachlan, Callum, or Kerr.

Were they here? Already? He crossed to the door, grasped the handle, and stopped. God's blood, if it was them, he wouldn't hear the end of their jests about him sleeping past noon. No matter how happy they might be about it.

Gavin grinned. *'Tis a small price to pay.*

He opened the door and listened—for Deirdre and Ewan, as well as for the others. He knocked on Deirdre's door first, just to make sure she wasn't in there, then made his way to the head of the stairs and hurried down.

He stopped about five steps up from the bottom and surveyed his great hall. It was busy, as it always was during the midday meal, but even more so with the arrival of his family.

A wide, rectangular table had been set up in front of the smaller hearth, and Kerr, Deirdre, Ewan, and Isobel sat eating roast duck and greens with Darach, Lachlan, Callum, and Gregor.

He hadn't seen the other men since Callum's wedding, and he brimmed with joy at their presence, but still his gaze sought Deirdre. He took her in, trying to read everything in her demeanor, her composure, and that mercurial smile of hers—sometimes bashful, sometimes gleeful, sometimes just a wee bit wicked.

She sat between Gregor and Darach, with Callum the next seat over. Gavin sighed with relief. They would take care of her—would sense her shyness and her goodness—and know what she meant to him.

His knees wobbled alarmingly, and he almost dropped his arse onto the stairs. As it was, he had to lean his shoulder against the wall to stay upright.

What she means to me.

Kerr had seen it. And his other brothers and Gregor were sure to see it too. Kerr's words from the night before rang in his head: *Start thinking about how to get rid of Lewis.*

He didn't know how in God's name he could manage it, but he would. He would wait years if he had to. Deirdre wasn't going anywhere as long as Ewan was in the keep, and he hoped she wouldn't want to leave even if Ewan wasn't here. Perhaps they could petition for an annulment—it would be easy enough to cite adultery as the cause on Lewis's behalf if they could prove he had another lover.

Church law moved slowly, and the cost to see the annulment through the courts would be high, but he had plenty of gold, and Gregor had plenty of influence. And if Lewis needed money—if he was taking the coin from his father that was intended for the keep—then maybe more money from Gavin would expedite matters.

Aye, one way or another, they could make it work. They didn't have a choice if they…if they loved each other.

This time he did sit on the stairs. Heavily.

Christ almighty, I'm in love with Deirdre.

He rubbed the heel of his hand over his heart, assuaging the ache that had started there. Was she in love with him too? He had no idea. He'd thought Cristel had loved him—and look how wrong he'd been.

Deirdre is not Cristel.

But how could she love him after the way he'd treated her? She'd saved his son, saved him, and he'd almost sent her away for it. He thought back to that moment when he'd believed she'd jumped from the cliff, and he shuddered.

Aye, she may not have any interest in him after that.

Except…she'd crawled into his bed. She'd held his hand while *they* slept. He still couldn't get over that. Morpheus had claimed him for over twelve hours. It didn't come near to making up for the hundreds of hours he'd missed in the last few years, of course.

He glanced over again at his family, and his heart swelled. For them all, not just Deirdre this time. Kerr and Isobel sat at the far end of the table with Lachlan, and a laughing Ewan sat between Gregor and Kerr.

They had all supported him since Ewan had gone missing, believing him when he'd insisted his son was alive—with little more than a feeling to go on. And they hadn't abandoned him when he'd changed, become hardened and cruel, imbibed too much and raged at the world.

He owed them all a debt of gratitude, this perfectly imperfect family of his.

He rose and stared down at them, filled with love and happiness. Then he roared, "Who let the dogs into my keep?"

Gavin continued down the steps and toward them as everyone looked up. Then the men began to bark and howl like dogs. Ewan laughed excitedly and began to jump around on his seat, pretending at being a dog too. Gavin saw Deirdre and Isobel look at each other and roll their eyes in tandem, making him laugh. Aye, he liked that his sister and his…and his…his wife-to-be—aye, that sounded right—had become such good friends.

His knees weakened again, and he grabbed on to a passing soldier to steady himself.

"Laird?" the man asked.

Gavin patted the fellow's shoulder where he'd grabbed on. "'Tis naught, lad. Just pleased to see you." He threw his arms wide and laughed. "Pleased to see all of you."

Deirdre glanced over and he caught her gaze. Held it. A blush stole up her cheeks, and he was reminded of her flushed cheeks last night before she fell asleep.

"Da, you're up!" Ewan yelled and ran around the

table to reach him. Gavin caught his son under his arms and threw him high into the air. The world was a bright, beautiful place when you weren't weighed down by grief, fury, and fatigue.

He tucked Ewan against his side and faced his family, his smile wide and filled with joy. "Have you all met my son—again?"

A cheer went up, and the men gathered around to pull him into bear hug after bear hug, with much backslapping and ribbing.

He looked over at Deirdre again and saw she was smiling at them, her eyes awash with emotion. He couldn't take his gaze off her.

The lads and Gregor sat back down at the table. He followed them. "Shove down," he said to Darach, wanting to sit next to Deirdre.

Darach didn't move. "Say please, ye wee *ablach*."

"Shove down *please*, ye wee *ablach*."

Deirdre got a pinched look on her face, like she wanted to reprimand him, but Darach grinned and slid around the corner. He took his trencher of food with him, bumping Callum farther down the bench. Gavin sat next to Deirdre, close enough that he could rest the length of his leg against hers. Ewan was still in his arms and he leaned across to kiss his mother on the cheek, who kissed him back.

Gavin wanted to do the same thing and was contemplating precisely where he would kiss her when Kerr said, "Gavin, I assume you've thought long and hard about what to do since our discussion last night. Do you have a plan?"

He glanced at Kerr, who stared back at him from

the end of the table, his eyes narrowed. "Aye. It may take a while to implement, but I have one."

"A plan for what?" Isobel asked. Deirdre looked at him curiously too.

"A plan to keep Deirdre here, of course." He slipped an arm around her shoulder, deciding that kiss could come later when they were alone, and pulled her even closer. "Has Kerr told you all that Deirdre is Ewan's mother and she will be living here from now on?"

"Of course I did," Kerr said. "And that she's my cousin as well. In case anyone forgot about that." He looked sternly at Gavin. "Anyone."

Gavin grinned. "Did he also tell you that she's an angel? She saved Ewan and she saved me. And she's staying here from now on."

"Aye, lad. You just said that," Gregor said. "No one's arguing with you. We'll support whatever the two of you decide to do, as long as no innocents are hurt. But keep in mind it may not be as simple as you think."

"It is simple. Deirdre stays here."

"What is this big plan you're all talking about?" Isobel huffed in exasperation. "And doona tell me it's just about keeping Deirdre here because…ohhhhhh." The frustration cleared from her face, and she looked from Gavin to Deirdre, then back again.

Deirdre's brow puckered. "Because…what? What am I missing?"

Isobel's cheeks flushed pink, and Gavin sighed inwardly. Why couldn't Kerr have waited to speak to him until they were alone? He and Deirdre needed more time together. More time to talk and laugh together. More hand-holding and stolen kisses. He needed time to make her fall in love with him.

And now it looked like Isobel was going to spill the beans about Gavin's plans to marry her.

"I canna believe I've been here for almost a quarter hour, and no one has said anything about me sleeping past noon." That should change the subject right quick. He braced himself for an onslaught of jests. When nothing came, he raised a brow at them all.

"Da, you missed breakfast and the midday meal!" Ewan thought this was very funny. "You must be so hungry!"

"Aye, so hungry I'll have to eat your meal." He reached toward Ewan's trencher, filled with food the lad had barely touched, grabbed a bannock, and pretended to eat it.

Ewan laughingly fought Gavin for it, who conveniently lost the fight just as one of the servers came by with a full trencher for his laird. Ewan hopped down with his food and ran back to his original spot between Gregor and Kerr.

"So that's it? My son is the only one with an opinion on the matter?"

"What matter?" Lachlan asked. "If you mean that you slept late, well, I think everyone here is happy about it. If it turns you into an agreeable idiot rather than a miserable bastard, crushing the spirits of nymphs and fairies everywhere, you can bloody well sleep late every day."

"What fairies?" Ewan asked, his smile drooping. "Da stomped on the wee folk?"

"Nay, Ewan," Lachlan continued without missing

a beat. "These were big fairies, bigger than any giant I've ever seen. And they had fangs." He put his fingers to his mouth and made a scary face, then jumped his hand across the table to Ewan, who screamed and then laughed when Lachlan tickled him.

"Giant fairies with fangs?" Ewan asked. "I fighted a giant yesterday when I was on Horsey."

"You *fought* a giant yesterday?" Deirdre asked, correcting Ewan's grammar in the nicest possible way.

"Aye! But then…but then…it turned into a giant Fairy Giant and tried to bite Horsey."

Kerr made a disgruntled sound. "That bloody horse pony."

"What's a horse pony?" Callum asked.

"Not a horse pony. A pony named Horsey. You're going to be a father soon," Gavin said. "You have to learn these things."

Callum pulled a piece of parchment from his sporran and pretended to write on it. "A pony named Horsey. Got it."

"But then…" Ewan continued.

"There's more?" Darach asked.

"Aye. Horsey turned into a dragon. Just like Mama."

Everyone at the table burst into laughter, including Deirdre.

"What did the dragon do next?" Deirdre asked.

Ewan looked at her, then at Gavin, then back to her. "She married my da."

Fifteen

Deirdre sat beside Isobel on the hay bale near the stables and watched Ewan running around with a long twig for a sword, pretending he was fighting the giant Fairy Giant with fangs. If he had nightmares tonight, Deirdre was waking up Lachlan to sit with him.

Her cheeks still felt hot from the multitude of embarrassing moments she'd experienced during the meal with Gavin's family, culminating in Ewan's comment about Deirdre the Dragon marrying his da. She'd wanted to become the mythical dragon right then, spreading her wings and flying far, far away.

Everyone had fallen silent and then Gavin had pulled her even closer, kissed the top of her head, and said, "I doona think a dragon can marry a human. 'Twill work better if your da is a dragon too, so the two dragons can fly together and have lots more dragon bairns."

To which Ewan had said, "Oh," then had a bite of his bannock.

Beside her on the hay bale, Isobel sighed. "I can see you're still thinking about it. Your cheeks keep turning red, then white, then red again. Truthfully, 'tis verra pretty. Reminds me of my favorite pastry cook makes during Yuletide, with all the dried red berries in it. I may have to eat you."

Deirdre huffed out a laugh and lightly smacked her friend with the back of her hand. "Might I remind you that I'm the dragon here? If there's any eating going on, it'll be me gulping you down in one bite."

"I'm afraid I doona taste good. Verra bland." She pressed her blond hair against her skin. "See? All the same color."

Deirdre snorted. "Doona make me laugh. I'm not done wallowing in my mortification."

"You have naught to be mortified about. 'Twas Ewan who said it, not you. And I thought Gavin handled it quite well with talk of making him a dragon too."

"And having dragon bairns!" she added, her cheeks flushing all over again.

Isobel linked their arms together and squeezed. "Isn't that something you'd like? To have another one? I know I've been thinking about bairns more and more since Ewan returned."

Deirdre paused, closing her eyes for a moment to calm the grief, frustration, and desire that had exploded within her at Isobel's words—and at the pain that accompanied them. "I doona know how that would be possible when my husband isn't here," she said carefully.

Isobel glanced at her from the corner of her eye. "But you *can* have bairn? I wondered because I know you've been married for many years."

"I doona know for sure. Only God can truly

know," she said evasively, hating that her cheeks had flushed again.

"Well…I just think it's unfair that the woman is always to blame when it comes to being barren. Why canna it be him instead? Look at your father-in-law. How many wives has he had over the years as he tried for another son?"

"Four wives and two children, including Lewis. And for all we know, the children may not be his. I know Lewis is nothing like him, and I've heard his sister is a sweet girl. And Laird MacIntyre's wives have not fared well."

"Aye, I've heard he's a cruel man. You were lucky not to have much to do with him."

She nodded, hoping Isobel would drop the subject, but her friend had more to say.

"It would be good to be intimate with a man again, though, wouldnae it? I mean, the way I hear it from the maids and from some of the warriors—conversations they certainly didn't know I was privy to—lovemaking can be highly pleasurable. If it wasn't, we wouldnae end up having bairn."

"I suppose so," Deirdre agreed.

"You suppose so? You doona know? Well…maybe Lewis wasn't very good at it, then. I heard Kerr and Gavin talking once about Cristel. They were discussing…*you know.* Gavin was upset, otherwise I'm sure he wouldnae have been so indiscreet, and he said Cristel did not want to participate in the marital act."

Deirdre gasped and her eyes flew to Isobel's. "Why not? How could she not have liked it? He's so strong, he can just lift you up and put you down anywhere, and he's big all over, yet his hands were so gentle, and then they weren't, and—"

She stopped abruptly at the crafty smile on Isobel's face, and she realized what she'd said. And just how much she'd given away.

"I knew it," Isobel said. "You and Gavin."

"There is no me and Gavin. 'Twas one time, that's all, and we didn't do what you think we did."

"Well, what *did* you do, then?"

"I canna tell you!"

"Aye, you can."

Deirdre faced front, crossed her arms over her chest, and set her mouth mulishly. Ewan ran past them, still swinging his twig.

As soon as he was far enough away, Isobel said, "I doona doubt he had his hands all over you." She looked at Deirdre's chest. "Does it feel better because they're bigger?"

"I doona know," she said, exasperated, dropping her arms so her breasts weren't pushed up and out so much. "I have naught to compare it to. Why doona you ask Kerr to touch you and discover how it feels? I've seen how you look at him when you think no one's watching. He's a big, braw man. I'm sure you've thought about how his body would feel on top of yours. Or with your legs wrapped around his waist as he pushes you against a wall." Her voice grew weak at the end as she described what Gavin had done to her, but Isobel was too busy blushing this time to notice.

"Deirdre!"

"What? You started this conversation."

"It doesn't matter anyway, because neither of us will be finding out anytime soon. At least you have Ewan."

"What does *that* mean?"

"It means you've chosen Ewan over your husband, so you willna be able to have any more children or to experience the pleasure of coupling with a man unless you choose to do so outside of wedlock. And the only man I can choose is Kerr, because every other man is afraid to even glance my way and anger him. And I doona want to marry Kerr. So I'll also ne'er know a man's touch and end up childless."

Deirdre's heart sank. She hadn't thought of Kerr's interest in Isobel that way, but it was true—Isobel wouldn't be allowed to choose another, despite her mother's dying wish.

She grasped her friend's hands. "You have my support in this, Isobel. I will speak to my cousin and to Gavin about it. 'Tis your choice, and yours alone. You willna be forced to marry Kerr for any reason… But I am curious, why doona you want to marry him? He's strong, smart, protective, and braw. He'll treat you well, and he's verra amusing. And he'd be a wonderful father." Her brow furrowed in bemusement. "When you're together, 'tis like someone puts a candle to kindling and the flames blaze."

Isobel sighed noisily. "Because."

"That's no answer."

She ticked off on her fingers. "He's annoying, he deliberately baits me, he likes to tell me what to do, he doesn't listen to what I say, he's here too often, he chases off any man that might be interested in me, he scares me sometimes, he—"

"He scares you?"

"When he goes quiet. Usually, he's nattering in my ear or being noisy and boisterous like he is with Ewan. But then something might happen—something serious—and suddenly he's like a poised snake ready to strike. It's scary. You should have seen him when Gavin took you to meet Lewis. One minute we're having a lovely time with Ewan at the beach, the next, his focus is pinpointed on one thing—Gavin and what he's doing. I swear, if my brother hadn't come back with you, Kerr might have killed him."

Deirdre's eyes widened with shock. "I doona believe it. Besides, they did fight, and Kerr told me Gavin broke his nose."

Isobel huffed. "Well, it would have come close. My point is—"

"You have a point?"

"My point is that it's not fair that men can tup outside of wedlock but women canna. Did you even think twice about Lewis having a bastard when he brought Ewan home to you?"

"Nay. I was just so grateful to have a child to love."

"Exactly. And if someone does get the blame, it's ne'er the man, it's the poor lass who carries the bairn. And she's left to raise the child herself if she doesn't die during childbirth."

Deirdre squeezed her friend's hand. "What a sad tale you've just told. Isobel, are you thinking of…?" She couldn't say the words, almost as if saying them would give permission to Isobel—and to herself—to do exactly that, consequences be damned.

She left it up to Isobel to understand her meaning.

Isobel's eyes went wide. "Nay. 'Tis as I said before, no man would dare come near me because of Kerr. But my point is still valid."

"And what would Gavin do if you fell pregnant out of wedlock?" Deirdre's breath locked in her throat as she waited for the answer.

"He would bluster, of course, and demand I tell him the father's name. He'd probably insist I marry the poor man, and then at the last minute take it all back and tell me it's my choice. So I'd ne'er tell him in the first place."

"And would he allow you to raise your child here? His sister's bastard growing up beside his heir?"

"Aye. I have no doubt he would love my child the same way he loves me, legitimate or otherwise."

Deirdre's eyes misted over suddenly, and she reached across to hug this woman with whom she felt so close. "As would I," she said.

They broke apart when one of the village girls came running up to them, the breath huffing past her lips. She bobbed a quick, respectful curtsy to both before she turned to Isobel.

"Lady Isobel, Ophelia has gone into labor. My father is asking for you."

"Thank you, Pip. It's about time. I'll be there as soon as I can. Go in and see Bonni for some milk and food if you like and take some back for your brothers and sisters. Have one of the men help you carry it."

The lass bobbed another curtsy. "I will, m'lady. Thank you."

Deirdre's brows rose. "And here we were just talking about childbirth. That's a coincidence if ever I've seen one. Maybe even a sign from above?"

Isobel let out a wee snicker. "Ophelia has about seven bairns in her, I wager. So, seven signs?"

"Seven? She's a dog?"

"A pig. A favorite of mine for several years. I made farmer Busby swear to never butcher the dear thing. He made me swear to come to every birthing then and help out." Her smile faded and sadness filled her eyes. "His wife died last year—from fever, not childbirth. 'Twas an awful time. She left five bairns behind, and the littlest one was only Ewan's age."

Deirdre pressed her hand to her heart. It hurt just thinking about it.

Isobel sighed and rose to her feet. "You can come with me, if you like, but it'll require a ride to the village. Although I suppose we could ask them to prepare a wagon for you."

"Nay, thank you. Another time."

"Maybe I'll take Ewan with me?"

"Are you sure? He can be a handful."

"I'm sure. He can play with the other children if he loses interest." Isobel whistled to get his attention. "Ewan, do you want to go to a farm with me? My favorite sow is giving birth."

Ewan's face lit up, and he dropped his twig. "Aye! I do, I do!"

"Enjoy yourselves!" Deirdre yelled as they headed into the stable, followed, as always, by their guard. Gavin wasn't taking any chances with their safety. He'd even put a guard on her, which made her feel protected and cherished.

Suddenly at loose ends for the first time since she'd left her keep, she looked out toward the bailey, watching all the people go about their day. A few young lads and lasses ran around waiting for their parents, a groomsman led several mares toward the corral, the laundress and two of her helpers carried big baskets of clean clothes toward the keep, the blacksmith, still wearing his heavy, leather apron, chatted with the housekeeper, and in the distance, several groups of warriors drilled with their weapons, overseen by Clyde.

She spotted one of the serving girls holding a tray and an empty pitcher, laughing and flirting with a stable hand. Another couple walked by, their fingers twined together the same way Gavin had twined his fingers with hers. The couple reached the kitchens and shared a kiss before they parted ways.

Longing wound through Deirdre. All those people out there, free to follow wherever their hearts led. Free to make connections and love each other. And all she could think about was how unfair it all was. She married Lewis when she was fifteen, had no say in the matter, and now she was supposed to spend the rest of her life alone? And if not for Ewan, childless?

Lewis didn't want her—he'd been staying away longer and longer each time he left—and yet she wasn't allowed to be with a man who might want to spend time with her. Want to make love to her.

And it wasn't as though she'd even chosen Lewis. Aye, he was a good man, and living with him had been better than living with her family, but it seemed unjust that she couldn't now move on.

Isobel was right. It wasn't fair that men could tup outside of marriage, but women could not. Would it be so bad to crawl into bed beside Gavin again? And often? The next time without Ewan between them? She wanted desperately to be touched by him. To be joined with him.

And if a child came of their coupling, she knew he would take responsibility for the bairn. For her as well. It was in his nature.

Conversely, if Gavin didn't want to be with her, he would make sure she never crossed his bedchamber threshold again. Aye, he wasn't one to mince words. What had he said to her as they'd left her keep, so many days ago? He would always be truthful with her, even if she didn't like what he had to say.

Was she willing to find out his true feelings now? Ewan had called her a dragon earlier, and then Gavin had asked to be turned into one too. So that he could fly with her and have bairns with her. That had to mean something. Didn't it?

She pressed her hands over her belly, thinking of her empty womb and of a bairn she might someday grow within it. Gavin's bairn. She pushed her hands lower and squeezed them between her knees, thinking of his body wedged there instead, giving her pleasure.

He'd rebuffed her up on the turret for a host of good reasons, but not before he'd groaned with pure carnality at the feel of her.

Aye. Gavin MacKinnon, her son's father, desired her. And his bedchamber was right next to hers.

Now the question was what to do about it. Could she be a lion? Or was she still a mouse?

She settled her hands just below her breasts, where her stomach had started to churn at just the thought of what she might do. She sighed. Being a lion was much harder than being a mouse.

She'd returned to idly watching the castle folk in the bailey when O'Rourke, the master builder, appeared, heading toward the keep. Deirdre jumped up from the hay bale and almost called his name before she stopped herself. If she got his attention, would he run again? Or was he here looking for her? Maybe he had the numbers ready for her?

Aye, that must be it—although she was surprised he wouldn't just send the measurements to the castle with one of his men.

Maybe he wanted to make amends for his rude behavior?

She hurried to catch him…and then he did something odd. He stopped at the side of the stairs to the keep and bent down to adjust his hose. Well, that wasn't too odd, she supposed. Except he glanced around the bailey like he was looking for someone—or maybe avoiding someone—before he climbed the stairs.

She gasped. Was he looking for her? Making sure she wasn't there? Gaze narrowing and jaw setting, her lion settled into her heart and peered through her eyes. Finally.

She did not like this man.

Hurrying forward, she ran up the steps, passing one of the guards she hadn't seen before. "Lady Deirdre," he said. She raised her eyes to his in greeting but was shocked to see his gaze wasn't on her face. He was staring at her breasts, and not in a discreet way. Nay, he was almost insolent about it.

She crossed her arm over her chest protectively, and he finally met her gaze—with no apology whatsoever in his face. Nay, she'd swear he was smirking inside. She walked past him stiffly, determined to report him. Or she'd take a page from Isobel's book and get back at him in another way. Arrogant *ablach*.

Deirdre crossed into the great hall and looked for Master O'Rourke. There he was, at the far end of the hall over by the entrance that led to the kitchens. He disappeared down the passageway, and she raced after him. She was about to turn into the kitchens when she heard footsteps in the circular staircase beside her.

Was this the same staircase she and Gavin had taken up to the turret? Aye, it was. They just hadn't taken it all the way down. She hesitated, then decided to climb upward. She spotted a candle flickering in a wall sconce just a few steps away and picked it up.

After a brief hesitation, she squared her shoulders and ascended the stairs rather than going for help. Her guard had stayed outside, and the other guard who'd stared so rudely at her was not an option.

Maybe O'Rourke was meeting someone and would exit the staircase before he reached the turret. At every new rotation of the stairwell, she listened for him—in the passageway toward the chambers and farther up.

Then she heard echoed cursing, and the door at the top scraped open. He'd gone all the way. What could he possibly be doing up there?

She hesitated again and almost went back down. That warrior at the main door to the keep had left her feeling vulnerable, and she would never trust being alone with him. But the master builder had never threatened her in any way. She might not like him, but she didn't fear for her safety. Lifting her chin, she quietly continued upward.

The door at the top was propped open with a heavy rock. Deirdre crept forward and peered out…and then frowned in confusion. The master builder was alone, and he had an object in his hands that Deirdre couldn't identify. Something that he was holding in the direction of the cathedral—or out toward the forest? The wind whipped his hair and plaid in all different directions.

He mumbled under his breath and then turned far enough for her to see that he held a circular magnifying glass, about the circumference of his spread hand. What on earth was he using *that* for?

She put down the candle and stepped through the doorway, curiosity driving her. Immediately, the wind grabbed her hair and blew it around her face. She gathered it into her fist. "Master O'Rourke."

The master builder jumped and yelped with fright, almost dropping the magnifying glass. He turned to her, a scowl on his face, and Deirdre took a nervous step backward.

"What are you doing sneaking up on me? Look what you almost made me do!" He gingerly laid the glass on top of one of the merlons.

Guilt washed through her and her insecurities rose again. The mouse overtook the lion. "I'm sorry. I didn't mean to frighten you. Pray forgive me, sir." She dropped her gaze and then realized what she'd done and forced her chin back into place.

Now he looked offended. "I wasn't frightened. You startled me, is all."

She almost rolled her eyes. What a touchy man he was. Her dislike simmered, and she held on to it, gaining some strength from the whisper of anger that threaded through her. "Of course not. I didn't mean to imply otherwise." She looked from him, out to the cathedral, and then back again. "What are you doing up here?"

He puffed up with indignation. "Not that it's any of your concern, but I'm...examining the winds on the castle this high up. Seeing how the structure is withstanding the extra force."

She raised a brow and looked around at the rock-solid walls. "I doona think you have much to worry about. The structure has been *withstanding* the wind for several centuries."

"To your uneducated eyes, perhaps. But as master builder, I see things differently. And what I find will help determine how I proceed with the cathedral dome."

Now it was her turn to be offended. "I am not uneducated, sir. I've read extensively about cathedrals and their construction, and I have a head for mathematics, geometry in particular. Laird MacKinnon has put his trust in me, and I doona intend to let him down. I've asked you before for the exact dimensions of the cathedral, and I expect to receive them tonight. I noticed several irregularities in the construction so far that you need to address before you move forward."

She fought to hold his gaze, and for the first time, she felt a niggle of fear. Perhaps she'd miscalculated. His eyes had narrowed on her, and she could feel his enmity.

"As you wish, Lady Deirdre, but I'll need longer

than half a day. Will tomorrow be soon enough for you? And if there's any further delay, I'll be sure to inform you of it right away."

Her breath released from her lungs in relief. Fortunately, the wind whipped the sound away, so he didn't hear it. "Aye, master builder. Tomorrow will be soon enough."

He nodded once, then stepped past her toward the door.

"Master O'Rourke," she said, and he paused with one foot over the threshold. "Thank you. I'd like us to work together on this. I truly am an admirer of your profession."

He opened his mouth as if to speak, then changed his mind and closed it. After another nod, he disappeared into the castle. Deirdre listened to make sure he'd left, then moved to the castle wall and looked at it closely. She didn't see any wear and tear on the stone, other than what would be considered normal erosion, and there weren't any obvious signs of stress or undue fatigue.

Had he been lying to her?

She looked out toward the cathedral once more and noticed the magnifying glass laying on the merlon. She hurried over and gently picked it up. She'd never seen one this big before, or this heavy, and wondered where he'd gotten it.

She lifted it to eye level and looked out into the distance—first to the cathedral and past that to the village and the forest beyond, where Gavin had told her the quarry was located. The image in the glass jumped significantly closer. She focused it on the cathedral.

What else would the master builder have been looking at?

The walls looked stable and straight. They must have been built when the first master builder was still there. She looked higher, at the dome, inspecting it, and gasped. Aye, that is what O'Rourke must have been looking at. She could see cracks and depressions where the mortar and stone weren't holding up properly—whether because the mortar hadn't dried all the way through before the support was taken away, or because the size of the stones hadn't been correctly calculated, and the capstone couldn't distribute the weight of the ceiling outward rather than down.

Stunned, she lowered the glass. The master builder must be sick with worry over this—it was at least a year's worth of work lost. No wonder he'd made up the story about the wind and the castle walls! He was probably still reeling from the shock.

She felt for the man, but ultimately, the matter had to be corrected and, in all likelihood, a new master builder found. Unless the problems were left over from when the old master builder was here. But how would they know?

Either way, she had to tell Gavin. But first she'd talk to O'Rourke when he brought the building dimensions up to her tomorrow—if he came.

She shook her head, her stomach curdling with disappointment. It was almost as if the man didn't know what he was doing.

Sixteen

Deirdre sat on the bench in the great hall, tapping her fingers and toes to the music. A bagpiper and fiddler had arrived after the evening meal, and an impromptu celebration had broken out. More people streamed into the castle as day turned to dusk, and more and more ale and honey mead was consumed.

She hadn't heard music like this since before she'd left home to marry Lewis. Her marriage had been a dull event, and since then, there had never been any money for a musician. And none had wandered off the beaten track to find them in her small keep anyway.

But this was heavenly! Although it was much too rambunctious a rhythm for the angels. Nay, this was music for the sprites and pixies.

Ewan was out there running around with some of the other children, and Isobel was dancing a lively Highland reel with Gregor, Gavin, and some other castle folk. Kerr stood at the edge of the dancers, talking to Father Lundie, the priest who had arrived earlier. He'd been at Callum's keep when word was received that Ewan had been found, and he had followed

Callum and the other lairds in the wagon with the supplies. Deirdre had had a lovely time meeting him earlier when the caravan had arrived, and she'd found him to be a kind man with a sincere desire to help people. He was a favorite of all the lairds and had officiated at three of the lairds' weddings only last year.

Darach, Lachlan, and Callum, the lairds in question, sat drinking and laughing together at a table back from the music but still in front of her.

As always, Clyde stood guard by the door, his expression stony and his eyes alert.

She knew the moment Gavin noticed her sitting by herself on one of the benches pushed back against the wall. She'd made her excuses earlier and gone upstairs to her bedchamber as soon as the music looked like it was about to begin. But she'd listened to it, her door open a crack, her hips swaying, and humming under her breath.

She'd felt thirteen again, longing to partake in the fun but almost sick to her stomach at the thought. Sometimes she'd been forced to participate in events like this back home, and that was even worse than being excluded. Her mother had always made a special point of telling Deirdre not to embarrass them. But what she was really saying was *you're such an embarrassment.*

And she would hear the snickers and the mean-spirited comments about her body from her siblings, all the jests about her breasts bouncing and arse flapping as she danced. Those had made her stiffen up and feel awkward and clumsy, when before that, in her rooms, her nursemaids, tutor, and several other servants had practiced all the dances with her and they'd had a wonderful time. Someone would hum or sing the tune, and someone else would drum out the beat, all while Deirdre whirled around the room, quickly memorizing the steps and instinctively feeling the music.

What a wonderful, freeing experience that had been for her…but it was never the same when her family was there.

Which of course made her realize, as she tapped her toes, listening to the music and longing to be a part of the revelry downstairs with Gavin and the others, that her family wasn't actually here. She'd allowed them in only by believing what they'd said about her.

So Deirdre'd crept back downstairs, sitting first on the top stair, then halfway down, then finally making it all the way into the great hall and sitting on the bench nearest to the stairwell.

And she'd been enjoying herself until Gavin came bearing down on her. Now her stomach dipped and her heart beat madly in her chest. She would have darted back upstairs but she felt frozen in place, almost as if he held her there with his eyes, ordering her to stay still and not move a muscle.

She wanted to melt into the stone wall and disappear, and she found herself slumping down as though to make herself invisible. He stopped in front of her, eyes intent on her face. Then he held his hand out to her, palm up. She looked at it like he held a swarming wasp nest and shook her head emphatically. No.

He didn't step back, he didn't put his hand down; he just continued to stare at her and wait.

"I canna dance," she blurted out. "I willna dance, and you canna make me." When he didn't move, she said, "Oh, Gavin, please. Just go away."

"I'll help you," he said. "You can lean against me like you did on Thor, and I'll lead you through the dance."

"I'll step on you, or I'll fall down."

"Your feet are tiny, and I'll catch you. Trust me, Deirdre."

"Nay," she wailed, but she put her fingers in his grasp anyway and allowed him to pull her up into his arms. She rested there for a moment, her body pressed to his, trying to absorb some of his strength.

"What are you afraid of, love?" he asked.

She stared at the hollow in his throat, her thoughts chaotic, her emotions running wild—like they'd been doing every day since he'd captured her. It was overwhelming. She didn't want to have to face down one more thing.

"Am I your captive?" she asked.

"Nay, of course not." He tilted her chin up, his brow furrowed with concern. "What made you ask that?"

"Sometimes I think it would be easier if I were. Then I wouldnae have to think about all the things I could or couldnae do, all the *choices*. I'd just do as you wanted. It was easy with Ewan, locked away in my own little castle." Her arms slipped around his waist. "This is hard," she whispered.

He raised his hand, brushed his fingers down the side of her face. "Dance with me, Deirdre. I willna let you fall. Ever."

"I'm scared."

"Aye, love. So am I."

They weren't talking about a Highland reel anymore. "I doona want to dance down here. I doona want people to see me." She leaned the side of her face into his palm and closed her eyes. "Come upstairs with me?"

He stilled, like a great hunting cat. Several moments passed, and he pressed her cheek to his chest. She could hear his heart pounding, feel the quick rise and fall of his lungs. She turned her head and kissed him through his linen léine.

"Ewan..." he said, his breath gusting past his lips.

"Has Annag to take care of him." She kissed him again. "Capture me, Gavin."

She knew the moment he decided. His arm tightened around her, his hand pressed more firmly against the side of her head. Not hurting her, just...making a decision for the both of them.

She sighed, became softer, more malleable. And everything about him hardened even further, which didn't seem possible. She knew he would take her tonight. Because she was his.

Gavin MacKinnon had captured her.

He turned her toward the stairs, his arm stealing all the way around her shoulders. They'd just mounted the first step when a voice stopped them.

"Gavin," Kerr said, his voice firm.

Gavin stiffened, and his arm tightened around her. He turned his face toward her and looked over his shoulder at his foster brother. She ne'er looked back. She didn't want to see the condemnation in her cousin's eyes.

"What is it?" he asked.

"You may want to rethink your plans for the evening. Laird MacIntyre, Lewis, and Deirdre's brother, Boyd, are here earlier than expected. Boyd isn't Laird

MacColl yet, but he will be shortly. We expect them within the hour."

Deirdre gasped, and when Gavin turned all the way toward Kerr, she did so too. "Does that mean my father is dying?"

Kerr's face softened and Gavin pulled her in closer, as if to shield her from the news. "Aye, lass. For quite a while. You didn't know?"

"Nay. I haven't seen him since I left his keep. He ne'er came to my wedding nor visited me once o'er the past seven years. My mother either." Her mouth firmed. "Boyd came though. I was glad when he left."

"You doona have to see them," Gavin said. "In fact, I donna want you to. Take Ewan and stay with him in the nursery. I'll come and get you when it's over." He glanced at Kerr. "Isobel too. For all we know, Laird MacIntyre will decide he wants her for his next wife."

"Agreed. You tell Isobel though. She'll defy me just to be obstinate."

The music stopped. Deirdre slipped out from beneath Gavin's arm and hurried through the dispersing crowd to where she'd last seen her son with the other children. When she couldn't spot him anywhere, she began to panic. Why had she left him alone?

"What is it, lass? How can I help?" Gregor laid a comforting hand on her shoulder.

"I canna find Ewan." She looked around frantically. "Ewan!" she called.

"I'm here, Mama!" Ewan appeared, holding his friend Rhona's hand.

The older girl smiled sweetly. "I've been watching him, Lady Deirdre."

Deirdre rushed forward and lifted her son into her arms, then kissed the top of Rhona's head. "Thank you, lass. And what about you? Is your da nearby?"

"He's chatting to my uncle Artair over by the hearth. He willna be long. Is it time for Ewan to go to bed?"

"Aye, lass. The celebration is over."

In front of them, Isobel allowed Callum to help her up onto a bench and clapped her hands to get the crowd's attention. "Thank you for coming, everyone! A lovely night cut short, unfortunately, but we have unexpected visitors, and the lairds need to see to business. The first of which is your safety. Please return to your homes. We doona expect any trouble, but 'tis best to be safe!"

Callum helped her down, and then Isobel hurried toward her. "My brother has asked that you and I stay out of sight until the meeting is over. Apparently seeing the Beauty of the Highlands and the Siren of the Seas together will send the MacIntyres and MacColls into uncontrollable fits of desire."

Deirdre's eyes widened. She clamped one hand over Rhona's ear and pulled her head against her body, so the other ear was covered too. "Isobel! Doona speak so in front of the lass. She's too young for such talk."

Guilt covered Isobel's face. "Och, I'm sorry. You're right." She pulled Deirdre's hand away from Rhona's ears. "I'm sorry, lass. You didn't really understand what I was saying, did you? I was spouting off nonsense to make Lady Deirdre laugh."

"'Twasn't amusing?" the girl asked.

"Nay, not amusing at all." But Isobel's lips twitched as she said it.

Deirdre sighed. "Maybe a wee bit amusing, but that's all."

She spotted the blacksmith, weaving through the crowd toward them. "There's your da now. Have a good night, lass."

Ewan leaned over to hug her, then Rhona bobbed a curtsy to the ladies and ran to her da.

Isobel grasped Deirdre's arm and tugged her toward the stairs. "Come on. I sent Annag up already. I have a plan. We'll tuck Ewan in, then find a place to listen. This is about you as well as Ewan, and you have every right to hear what's going on."

Any signs of the recent revelry had been cleared from the great hall, and the benches and tables were stacked in the far corner against the wall. A dais had been set up in front of the large hearth, and Gavin sat on the center of it in his father's chair, the intricately carved arms, legs, and back telling the story of the MacKinnons all the way back to their Norse ancestors. Behind him in a row stood his foster brothers, with Gregor directly behind him in the middle.

The MacKinnon banner had been pinned above the hearth. Also raised on the wall were the standards of the six clans—a show of unified strength.

Gavin's anger simmered just beneath the surface, ready to explode. He suspected the MacIntyres and MacColls had conspired against him to kidnap his son and had treated Deirdre in a way intended to diminish her, if not worse. The only one who might be forgiven on that account was Lewis, so long as Gavin could get over the fact that he wanted to beat the man senseless for touching Deirdre, husband or not. He clenched the chair's arms just thinking about it.

Gregor's hand landed on his shoulder. "Clear your head, Gavin, and your heart. Ewan and Deirdre are here with us now, and they're not going anywhere. We'll kill our enemies when we know their plans. Not before."

"It's bold of them to come here together," Callum said. "I'm surprised they didn't just send Boyd."

"Or even Boyd and Lewis, since Laird MacIntyre is not enamored with his son," Lachlan added.

Darach nodded. "'Tis arrogance on MacIntyre's part. They think they have an edge over us."

"Or they know something important that we doona," Callum added. He could practically hear his brother's mind whirring.

"A fighting force?" Kerr asked.

"Perhaps. Undeclared allies, if naught else," Gavin said.

"Aye. Must be. They havenae a chance against us alone." Lachlan scowled. "They struck against Gavin the first time when they stole Ewan, and now they're planning a second attack."

Stole Ewan.

Gavin fought the urge to race upstairs and check on his son one more time. He'd done so twice already, panicking the first time when Deirdre hadn't been with their son. He'd found her in Isobel's bedchamber.

"What I doona understand is why they didn't use Ewan against you. Or against us when they first had him." Callum was an expert at puzzles. If anyone could figure it out, it was him. "Maybe they thought he had sickened and died. They weren't expecting pestilence to hit the gathering."

"And then Lewis gave him to Deirdre without telling his father," Darach said.

"He intervened." Gregor spoke with quiet authority.

Gavin clenched his jaw and then released it. "If that's what happened then…aye. The timing fits, and Kerr and Deirdre say he's a good man. For that act alone, he may live."

They heard the portcullis being raised. It banged shut a few moments later, exactly as Gavin had ordered.

"Remember to watch," Gregor said. "I want eyes on each man at all times. Read their reactions, their postures, and their faces as much as what they say. I want to know the state of the relationships between the men and when each one of them is lying—both to us and to one another."

"Aye," the others said in unison.

It didn't take long for the two MacIntyres and Boyd MacColl to arrive, and boots could be heard stomping up the steps toward the main door.

"We're getting closer, lads," Gregor said quietly. "I doona think Laird MacIntyre is the chief conspirator against us, but I'll wager he knows who it is."

"Canna we just take him now and make him tell us?" Kerr asked.

"Nay, not until we know what he has planned. I wouldnae want to risk setting something in motion by killing him. Not until I know what it is."

The door opened.

Clyde strode through followed by several other

MacKinnons, the guarded men between them. The burly warrior walked directly to Gavin and stood on the floor to the right of his laird. Artair, the huge warrior and brother of the MacKinnon blacksmith, stood opposite him on Gavin's left.

Laird MacIntyre approached them first, a big, tough-looking man with sharp eyes and a cruel mouth. He had a large broadsword sheathed between his shoulder blades, and Gavin suspected he knew how to use it.

"So all six of you are here," the laird sneered. "Running like bairns to each others side for a simple domestic dispute."

Gavin leaned forward in his chair, the heat washing up his cheeks in anger. "The abduction of my son is not a domestic dispute. It's a cause for war between our clans."

"I know naught of your son. I do know that you invaded my land, my keep, and abducted *my* daughter-in-law. *That* is an act of war."

"Good," Gavin said grimly. "We're in agreement, then."

The laird held his gaze for a long moment before he shrugged. "We'll see what her family has to say."

From behind Laird MacIntyre, Boyd MacColl, Deirdre's older brother, glowered at him. Gavin wanted to gut this man, more than any of the others, for the cruel things he'd said to Deirdre when she was growing up.

The age difference between them was about the same as between him and Isobel. Gavin had cherished his sister, considered her a gift. Boyd should have done the same.

He narrowed his eyes at the man, trying to see the resemblance to his sister. It was there—not in his coloring, for he was as fair as Isobel—but in the shape of his face and eyes, which were the same light gray-blue as Deirdre's.

But that was where the similarity ended. Boyd was pale and his face puffy, even though he was tall and slight of body—the sign of a man who drank too much. Dark circles rimmed his eyes, making him look shifty and somehow unwholesome. Nay, that wasn't right. It wasn't the dark circles that made him look shifty, but the way his gaze darted around the room, filled with avarice. But for what? The MacKinnons didn't display their wealth and prosperity on the walls of the keep. His home was comfortable and well appointed, but the emphasis was on practicality and strength, not gold.

And then it hit him, and rage boiled up from the pit of his stomach. Boyd was looking for Deirdre.

"Where's my sister?" the man demanded, as if on cue.

Gregor's hand pressed into Gavin's shoulder, and he did his best to tamp down his anger. When Gavin spoke, his tone was frigid. "She willna be making an appearance."

"I demand to see her. You canna keep her here."

"She doesn't want to see you, and she's *choosing* to stay here to raise my son."

"She canna. She's married! If she doesn't return to the MacIntyres, she's coming home with me." Boyd sounded almost peeved, like a child being denied what he wanted.

Gavin stared at him—hard—until the man lost his

bravado and dropped his gaze, reduced to muttering under his breath.

Then he turned his attention to Lewis MacIntyre. Lewis stood behind his father, an unassuming-looking man with light-brown hair and eyes. Apprehension and worry had filled his gaze and pinched his brow.

When Gavin's eyes landed on him, Lewis asked, "Deirdre, is she well?" His voice was low and tight, and Gavin nodded. A pit formed in his stomach. This man…Deirdre's husband…he cared for her.

Did she care for him too? Was there more to their relationship than Gavin realized? More than just kindness and games of chess?

"Aye. Both she and my son are in good health and spirits."

Relief filled Lewis's eyes, as well as resolve—but for what?

The man turned his gaze to Kerr, standing opposite him on the dais. He nodded. "Well met, Kerr MacAlister. 'Tis good to see you again, although I wish it were on better terms."

"Well met to you too, Lewis MacIntyre." Kerr nodded back at him. "What can you tell us about Laird MacKinnon's son, Ewan? Your wife tells us that you gave Ewan to her to raise. Right around the time the lad disappeared."

Lewis's jaw tightened for an instant. "She speaks the truth. I swear to you that it was not an act of malice. I found the lad in the forest near the MacIntyre border. When I saw him, he was alone. I had no idea he was Laird MacKinnon's son. I thought at the time I was saving an abandoned bairn. I gave him to Deirdre to raise because she is a loving and kind woman and had room in her heart for him."

"There you have it," Laird MacIntyre said. "My son found and cared for the lad. You should be thankful."

Gavin's anger surged. "If it was simple chance, then why did you name him Ewan when my son ne'er spoke? Am I to believe that was happenstance?"

Lewis tensed and turned his gaze to Gavin. His pulse beat rapidly in the hollow of his throat. "Nay, Laird MacKinnon, 'twas not a coincidence. I searched the lad when I found him. The name Ewan was on a piece of parchment. I chose to use the name for him, but I was not certain it was his until the recent revelation that Ewan was your son."

"A parchment? Do you still have it, Lewis?" Kerr asked.

Lewis turned back to his boyhood friend, relief lessening the tightness around his eyes. He was mistaken if he thought Kerr was any less dangerous than Gavin. Or prone to forgiveness because of their history.

"I do… 'Tis tucked away somewhere safe. I'll search for it when I return home. Perhaps you can retrieve it when all this is over. It would please me to repay your hospitality from our youth. You will find the quail is even more plentiful around my keep than it was around yours."

Kerr hesitated, his lashes flickering—an almost imperceptible giveaway to anyone but his family. "Aye, perhaps," he said. "I remember well our time together. I have fond memories of us swimming together in the loch and trapping rabbits for our dinner. And quail too, as you say."

"Aye, a feast for kings." Lewis smiled, but it didn't reach his eyes. "'Twas a relief to get away from the castle and our fathers' watchful gazes. We got up to much mischief over the visit, most of which we kept hidden."

Kerr returned the smile, but his was insincere too. Had something happened when the two were lads? Or was something else at play?

"Maybe now is the time to finally come clean, then. My father is dead, of course. But we could certainly confess all of our adventures to *your* father." Kerr pointed to Laird MacIntyre as he spoke.

"Ah, that may take all night, and we have more important things to discuss right now. I think it would be best to reminisce later. And perhaps you and I had best get our stories straight first, aye?"

He laughed and Kerr laughed with him. "Aye. Later then, old friend."

Laird MacIntyre made a disgruntled sound. Had he noticed that something had just passed between Kerr and Lewis? He still looked as though he'd been carved from stone, the same as when he entered.

"I remember that visit as well, Kerr MacAlister," the laird said. "I also had an entertaining time with your father. I was much aggrieved to hear that you'd murdered him a few years later."

"What you call murder, Laird MacIntyre, I call self-defense. But I didn't just kill my father, if you recall. I also killed three of his men and one of my uncles. A few days later, I killed two more of my uncles. They arrived to murder me and left without their heads. You'd do best to remember I'm not a man to take the protection of myself or my family lightly—as my one remaining uncle well knows."

The laird nodded. "Aye. I'm sure your uncle, the other Laird MacAlister, remembers those events as clearly as if they happened yesterday."

Was that a giveaway? Or a plant? Did MacIntyre want them to believe Kerr's uncle would hold a grudge all these years?

The laird turned to Gavin. "As much as the lass may want to stay with your lad, she canna. She is married to my son. We have a marriage contract in place."

Gavin shrugged as if he didn't care, but inside he'd turned cold with anger. He took a moment to breathe through it, tapping his fingers on his chair as if he mulled over the problem. Finally, he said, "A marriage contract can be broken when one party does not fulfill their obligations. Seven years and no issue from the marital bed. Could be Deirdre's barren and has no value to you as a wife. Could be your son is seldom there to sow the MacIntyre seed."

"Either way, we will decide, not you. Deirdre will return with me to my castle."

"Nay," Lewis said. Laird MacIntyre's eyes widened slightly, indicating his surprise. "She is my responsibility, Father. She'll remain with me."

"She'll return to the care of her family home. Her mother and I will care for her." Boyd sounded like a boy among the men, with no power at all. No one even bothered to respond.

"'Tis a moot point," Gavin said. "Deirdre is staying. She's my son's mother. He canna be without her."

"And my son canna be without her. If you willna

return her, we will consider it an act of war. 'Tis willful abduction."

Gavin nodded and smiled grimly. "'Tis an acceptable assumption on your part. I am much aggrieved by this situation, as are my allies. I doona believe the disappearance of my son is as simple a story as what Lewis has told us. Ewan's name wasn't changed, and someone knew who to look for at the gathering." He leaned forward and stared at Laird MacIntyre. "I think the outbreak took everyone by surprise. I think whoever snatched Ewan died from the plague. And now here we are, and the only thing stopping me from putting my sword in your belly is my foster father, who counsels caution. You have one hour to get off my land. The MacIntyres and the MacColls will ne'er cross it alive again."

Lewis's eyes widened, and his gaze jumped to Kerr's. Aye, so the man wanted to come back. To speak to them.

Gavin rose from his chair and jumped down. He headed straight for Laird MacIntyre, flanked by Clyde and Artair. The MacIntyre laird drew his broadsword at the same time Gavin did. They swung at each other, swords clashing and sparks flying. Gavin pushed forward until he was nose to nose with MacIntyre. Behind him, Kerr and Darach restrained Lewis, while Lachlan and Callum restrained Boyd.

"I'll see you dead for what you did to my son, MacIntyre. You almost succeeded, but almost isn't good enough. I have my son back, and I have your daughter-in-law. I win. You lose.

"Go back to your empty keep and tup your

young, fertile wife until your stones burst. From what I hear it willna matter. There's naught but dust inside them anyway."

"You have nothing I canna take back," MacIntyre said before shoving himself away from Gavin and striding toward the door, Boyd and Lewis falling in behind them. Clyde, Artair, and the other MacKinnon warriors surrounded the enemy to escort them off their land.

Gavin was so angry he shook, and he was tempted to take the laird's head despite what Gregor had said.

"You have one hour," he shouted instead. "Ride hard or you're all dead."

Seventeen

No one spoke, not until the door closed behind the MacIntyres and Boyd MacColl, and their footsteps retreated down the stairs.

Gavin swung around to Kerr, re-sheathing his broadsword between his shoulder blades. "What did he say?" Gavin asked.

But Gregor whistled sharply and pointed upward. Obviously, he was worried they might be overheard. The group moved quickly and quietly toward the stairs, in the way they'd been trained. Gavin took the lead, bounding up three steps at a time. When they hit the landing and turned, he came to an abrupt halt, the others crowding in behind him.

"What are you two doing here?" he asked his sister and Deirdre. They looked like they'd just jumped up from sitting on one of the steps, probably in the process of running back to their rooms.

"What does it look like we're doing?" Isobel said, hands planted defiantly on her hips. "We're listening."

"Nay, sweetling, that's not called listening. It's called eavesdropping," Kerr boomed from behind him.

"It's my keep," Isobel retorted. "I can *listen* as much as I want to."

"We heard swords clashing," Deirdre said worriedly. "Is Lewis all right?"

Jealousy roared through Gavin's body. "He's fine," he said stiffly, wishing he had his beard back so he could scrape his nails through it. Instead, he shoved his hands into his hair. "'Twas not your husband I clashed with. It was his father. I think 'tis as you say. Lewis is innocent. I doona think he's been included in this conspiracy."

Gregor made a shushing sound. "Move it. All of you."

Gavin grasped Deirdre's hand and helped her up the last few steps. He stepped to the side with her, and the others strode past them toward the laird's solar at the end of the passageway. "I'm sorry, but you canna come in with us for this discussion. We are officially at war with Clan MacIntyre and Clan MacColl. We will be discussing strategy and the various clans' strengths and weaknesses. The others willna want that information shared. I'll tell you what I can, but I canna betray their confidences. I also doona want to put you at risk by having too much information."

"I understand," she said. She looked toward Isobel, who stood at the solar door, arguing with Kerr to let her in. "I doona think she truly wants in; she just wants to defy Kerr."

Gavin nodded. "Aye, 'tis something Callum also said. Kerr may have to accept that she will never be his."

"'Tis true, although I doona think she'd know what to do with herself if he stopped trying."

He turned to her, kissed the back of her fingers,

and then dropped her hand. "And what about you, Deirdre? You asked me earlier to take you upstairs, but I see now that your husband cares for you and you him. When this is over, you may regret your decision. To many people, marriage vows are sacred. I wouldnae want us to do anything you might come to regret."

She dropped her gaze, and this time he didn't raise her chin. "You are Ewan's mother," he continued, "and you'll always have a cherished place here. But you should look to the future. Our time together has been verra emotional, both highs and lows. You may feel differently toward me in three months. If Lewis survives this conflict, and it is safe for you to do so, you can go for a visit…or for longer. We need to take a step back."

Deirdre shook her head emphatically, but she still didn't look at him. "If you'll have me, this is my home. I do care for Lewis. He's been nothing but kind and considerate toward me for the last seven years, but I've ne'er been happier than the last few days I've spent here. Even when I was riding that bloody horse pony." She glanced up at him—finally—a smile on her face, even though he could see her distress beneath it.

He cupped the side of her head. "Aye, well. 'Tis not a decision we have to rush, no matter how much it might feel like it at times. You willna be able to go back, Deirdre. You must be certain you want to go forward—with me—and know the cost. Your marriage to Lewis will be over…but it won't. Do you understand? An annulment, if Rome will grant you one, can take years." He sighed. "'Tis fortunate we were interrupted, I think. We will speak on this again later, aye?"

"Aye," she whispered and dropped her eyes again.

He pulled her toward him and kissed her forehead "Get some rest. I'll wake you if anything else happens tonight. And can you check on Ewan, please? I canna stop worrying even though I know he's safe. Call for me immediately if you think something's wrong."

She nodded just as Callum called his name. "Gavin!"

"I have to go." He turned away and headed toward the solar, passing Isobel on the way. "Izzy."

"Aye?"

"Can you stay with Deirdre tonight? At least until Ewan comes down to see her. I doona want her to be hurting and alone."

"Of course, but…be careful, Brother. I doona want you to get hurt either."

He knew she meant his feelings for Deirdre, and he gave her a quick, one-armed hug. "I'm afraid 'tis too late for that."

He entered his solar and strode to his desk. The room was a good size, but with six large, muscular men taking up space alongside the chairs they'd added for everyone that afternoon, it suddenly seemed cramped.

He sat and looked at Gregor, who sat opposite him. "You think MacIntyre has spies nearby? Within the keep?"

"I think that he has absolute belief in his success, which probably means he has spies close to you. Maybe even several of them, waiting to strike. We know they kidnap loved ones. You should check on the family members of your most trusted men and the folks in the castle."

"Aye, and randomly double or triple the guards, so

if one strikes, the other two they're matched with can fight back," Darach said from his spot beside Gregor.

"Be blunt with Clyde about it too. Gauge his reaction." Callum stood beside the closed shutters. Every once in a while, he opened one slightly and peered out. "Maybe even set traps and see if Clyde or anyone else bites. God knows, if I'd been warier of the people in my keep, Maggie wouldnae have been in so much danger."

Lachlan stood with one arm resting on the mantel above the hearth. "Speaking of people in your keep, maybe you should—"

"Nay." Gavin glowered at him.

"You doona even know what I was going to say," he protested.

"You were about to accuse Deirdre of being a spy."

"She's my cousin," Kerr said indignantly from in front of the closed door.

"What does that have to do with anything?" Lachlan glanced at Callum. "Tell them I'm right."

"He's right," Callum said. "Everyone should be a suspect..."

"See!" Lachlan said.

"But I doona think she is." Callum crossed to a chair beside the fire and sat down. "I've been watching her closely since we arrived, and there's no artifice or malice in her that I can see. She cares about Gavin and Isobel as well as Ewan."

"And me!" Kerr added.

"Aye, she gets exasperated with Kerr—but in a loving way."

Kerr beamed. "I'm verra loveable. And brawny and braw."

Gavin snorted. "And humble."

"Aye. The humblest of us all."

"But it's how she looks at Gavin that convinced me," Callum continued.

Gavin whipped his head toward Callum. He had to clear his throat before speaking. "And how is that?"

Callum grinned. "Like a woman in love."

The men all sighed. And then Kerr said, "I think I may just cry a little."

Gavin picked up a coin from the desk and hurled it at Kerr's head, but he caught it and held it up triumphantly. "Not only humble, but I have the best reflexes too—ow, that hurt, ye wee shite. That too. Jealous blackhearts, all of you. Ow." Everyone had grabbed something round and hard to throw at Kerr.

"Watch yourselves, lads," Darach whispered. "You doona want to set him off. He may go quiet."

"I'll go quiet on your arse," Kerr replied, "and I'll tell sweet Caitlin you hurt my feelings. Imagine the disappointment in her eyes when she finds out her husband was mean to her favorite brother-in-law."

"Your brains are addled," Lachlan said. "Everyone knows I'm her favorite."

Gregor held up one finger, and they all quieted. "I am most definitely sweet Caitlin's favorite." Then he turned to Kerr, who was now rubbing at several red spots on his forehead. "What did Lewis tell you? That was some kind of code he sent you, aye?"

"Aye. We ne'er hunted quail. While Gavin was facing off with his father, Lewis said he'd come back as soon as he could. He asked for passage for himself and several women and children."

"Women and children?" Gavin asked, then caught the coin that Kerr threw back at him.

"Aye. Took me by surprise too."

"Who are they?" he asked.

"I doona know. Maybe it has to do with the money he's been skimming from the funds his father sends. Ask Deirdre. She might know."

"Nay. I doona want her to know Lewis might be coming in case something happens. She…cares for him."

"He cares for her too," Gregor said, "but once he was assured of her safety, he didn't seem too concerned about her return."

Gavin made an angry, dismissive sound in his throat. Lewis was her husband. He should have done everything in his power to get her back.

Callum pointed at him. "And that is the look of a man in love. Lewis and Deirdre love each other, but they're not *in love*. I'd say it's more like a brother and sister, except her brother doesn't seem to care for her either."

"Nay, he's a nasty piece of shite, isn't he?" Lachlan asked.

"Aye," they all agreed.

Gavin fisted his hand around the coin. "She said he came to visit her once, and Lewis did something to make him leave the next day. She was grateful."

"Let's hope Boyd dares to step on the battlefield when the time arrives. 'Tis always good to rid the Highlands of rats," Gregor said.

"Aye, let's hope." Gavin leaned back in his chair and sighed. He was tired suddenly and felt the need to sleep beside Deirdre. "If she stays here, I'll petition Rome to annul their marriage. If we can prove adultery, we'll have a good case. But it will still take years."

"If she stays? I thought that was settled," Kerr said.

"She says she wants to stay. But…"

"But?"

"She cares for her husband—Gah, I hate that word! She may decide to stay with him once everything settles down. They took a vow."

"She would ne'er leave Ewan," Kerr said.

"Nay, but she may still want to stay with Lewis. Visit him on occasion. Or go back to live with him when Ewan is fostered to one of you. We haven't known each other long, although it feels like I've known her forever."

The men all nodded, as if they could relate—even Kerr. Thinking of Isobel, no doubt, although he had known her for most of her life.

"I can relate. Somewhat," Darach said. "Of course, I found out Caitlin was married at the same time the marriage was declared invalid. And I married her the next day."

"Deirdre and Lewis have been married seven years, and he's not a bad man. She speaks fondly of him."

Silence fell. His brothers and Gregor felt his pain, but there was naught they could do to help him.

"Have faith, Son," Gregor finally said. "It's what holds me to this life—that someday I will see my sweet Kellie and our bairns again." He rose from his chair and stretched, then reached into his bag beside him. "I brought a bottle of my father's *uisge-beatha*. I think we all deserve some of the good stuff after today. Let's toast Deirdre and Gavin and pray for a quick resolution to their difficulties."

They found enough cups for all of them—from the desk, the mantel, and a side table—and soon raised their drinks in the air.

"May true love find a way," Gregor said simply.

Eighteen

Deirdre woke with a start, sitting up to find Gavin sitting on the bed next to her.

"Shhh," he whispered. "Doona wake Ewan." He'd placed a candle on her bedside table, and she could see he still wore his plaid from earlier. She glanced at the shutters, but no light yet seeped around the edges. At least their meeting hadn't run until morning.

"Do you want to come sleep with us?" she asked.

His eyes jumped to hers. "Always, Deirdre." He raised his hand and tucked her hair behind her ear. She waited, breathless. Was he going to kiss her? His fingers trailed along her jaw toward her chin, and his gaze dropped to her lips.

A soft knock sounded at the door. He sighed and rested his forehead against hers. "But not now. Things are afoot. I need you to get dressed and come downstairs. I'm going to carry Ewan back to the nursery, and Annag will stay with him."

Cold invaded her body, chasing away the heat his touch had kindled. "What is it? Are you leaving for war already?"

"Nay, Deirdre. Not yet. We received word that Lewis is on his way back. He wishes to speak with us without Laird MacIntyre or Boyd present. He has further information about his father's plans and Ewan's kidnapping, I believe. And he's asked to see you before he leaves."

Her eyes widened. "Where's he going?"

"I doona know, but our messenger said he has two women and several children with him. And he left a packed cart on the road. Deirdre, it looks like he's running."

"Running? But where would he run to?"

"I doona know." He paused. "He may ask you to go with him."

"Nay! I willna leave. This is my home now. You said so."

"Of course, it is." He gave her a tight hug. "And I doona want you to go." She wrapped her arms around his waist and squeezed back.

"Do you know who the other people with him might be?" he asked.

"I have no idea. Unless he brought one of the families from the keep with him."

"Maybe. He should be here soon. We can ask him." He pulled back and kissed her quickly on the lips. She fancied that it was almost as if he couldn't help himself and hoped he felt the same as her—that if the kiss was any longer, he wouldn't be able to stop it.

He rose and strode quietly around to Ewan's side. "Get dressed but wait for me here. We'll go down together."

She nodded, threw back the covers, and rose from

the bed as he picked up Ewan. When he straightened, his gaze dropped from her face and drifted down her body. His eyes darkened as he looked at her. Her pulse began to race, and she glanced down at her white linen shift. The tie was fastened, and the material billowed away from her body. What could he possibly see of her, especially with only the candle behind her for light?

He made a strangled sound, and her eyes widened with concern.

"Are you alright?" she whispered.

His lips tweaked at the corners. "Nay, you'll be the death of me. Get dressed, love. I'll return shortly."

He left with Ewan, and she quickly moved to a stand with a basin of water on top. After splashing her face to wake herself fully, she rinsed out her mouth and brushed her hair. Then she had a quick wash with the wet cloth and lavender-pressed soap.

She was just pinning her arisaid in place over a fresh chemise when he knocked. "I'm coming," she said.

She grabbed her shoes and ran for the door. He'd already opened it and waited for her there. His eyes fell on the shoes in her hands before his gaze raised to hers once more. "Not so long ago, I waited for you to get your shoes before we left your keep. You were verra afraid, and I was verra angry. I'm so sorry I put you through that, lass." He took her shoes from her. "Here. Let me."

He kneeled in front of her, and she felt the prick of tears in her eyes as he slipped first one shoe, then the other onto her feet. He rose, grasped her hand, and led her down to the great hall. Isobel hurried toward them as they reached the bottom step. "I heard the noise and followed everyone down. I ne'er went back to sleep after I returned to my own chamber. What's going on?"

"Gavin said that Lewis is coming here, and he wants to speak to me."

"Your husband, Lewis?"

Gavin stiffened beside her, and she squeezed his hand. "Aye, that Lewis." She avoided calling him "husband" to spare Gavin's feelings. He squeezed back, then released her and strode toward his brothers, standing in a group talking to a young MacKinnon warrior whom she thought was named Finn.

"What does he want?" Isobel asked.

"I doona know." Deirdre sat on the edge of the dais and waited, Isobel sitting down beside her.

"Are you mad at him?" Isobel asked.

"Lewis?"

"Aye, Lewis. For not being there to protect you when Gavin and Kerr stormed your keep. For not demanding your return earlier."

Deirdre thought about it and felt a surprising niggle of resentment in her breast. Had that always been there? "I'm sure he had his reasons. He did ask about me."

"Aye, and then he reminisced with Kerr about their hunting adventures together as lads."

"Well, by then he knew I was safe. And if he'd been at the keep when Gavin arrived, he could have been killed."

"Where was he? Do you know?"

Deirdre shrugged, feeling the usual tinge of embarrassment when she thought about that side of her marriage. And something more too. It shocked her to realize she *was* angry.

The last time she'd seen Lewis had been at the gathering where she'd first met Gavin. Before that, she hadn't seen a trace of him for over two months. He'd even missed Yuletide. "He did try to get me back before his father arrived. Thank goodness Gavin changed his mind about handing me over."

Isobel glowered at her brother, who was now pacing across the stone floor. "Handing you over—like you were livestock rather than a person. When all this is o'er, I'm going to plan an unpleasant surprise for my dear brother."

Deirdre's eyes widened. "Verily?"

"Aye. I'm good at revenge. *And* at holding a grudge."

Deirdre didn't know whether to be more amused or appalled by Isobel's declaration. "But I was his prisoner."

Isobel made a dismissive sound in the back of her throat. "I'd take revenge on your father and brother too if I could. I didn't like your brother's tone when he spoke about you, or the demands he made. And your husband too, even though you say he saved you. There's more to the story than you've told me, I'm sure."

Deirdre stared at her friend, a lump growing in her throat. Aye. She *had* been treated unfairly, been hurt by people who were supposed to have had her best interests at heart—her brother, her father, her husband. Her mother and sisters too. And she'd just pushed the feelings aside, just accepted their behavior as normal.

Now someone was telling her it was *not* normal,

that she'd been mistreated. That *they* were in the wrong and deserved to be punished for it.

She pressed a hand to her mouth as anger bubbled up. *I'm not a pawn on a chessboard to be pushed around! Not anymore.*

"Furthermore," Isobel continued, oblivious to the effect her words were having on Deirdre, "'tis not just the way you've been treated since you were a lass—tossed from clan to clan, your feelings, your *personhood*, ne'er taken into consideration. But now that you plan to be with my brother—and I can see in your eyes that you do—you will face judgment. You'll finally stand up for yourself and take something that you want, and some arsehole people will condemn you for it."

"Isobel!"

"What? Are you offended that I've compared them to arseholes? You're right. 'Tis not fair to the arsehole."

"God's blood, I doona know whether to embrace you or…or…" Deirdre sighed. "There is no alternative, is there?" She pulled Isobel into a tight hug and whispered into her ear, "Thank you."

"Thank me after I've exacted our revenge. Although I think Gavin will have his revenge first. It may be that he'll be the only survivor around for me to punish." She spotted her brother. "Gavin!" she called across the great hall.

He looked over from where he was talking to Clyde, who looked even more grim than usual. "Aye?"

"Fair warning, Brother. You're on my bad side."

His brow rose. "What did I do?"

"'Tis for when you sent Kerr and me to the loch with Ewan and almost took Deirdre back to Lewis!"

Kerr whistled his approval.

"I brought her back," Gavin said. "And I apologized."

"I'll take that into consideration when I make my plans. I've let things slide since Ewan was taken. Doona expect leniency anymore."

He scowled at her. "You do realize we're about to go to war?"

She shrugged. "When you return, then. Just so you know it's coming. You willna know when or where or how, but it's coming."

"And you know that if anyone gets hurt or something gets broken because of your actions, there will be consequences."

Deirdre's gaze jumped back and forth between them, as did everyone else's in the room. She couldn't believe what she was seeing and hearing. Isobel had flat-out told her brother to expect trouble from her, and no one had batted an eye. Not one of them yelled or threatened or raised a hand to frighten her.

The queen had spoken—for Isobel was a queen, and not a pawn like Deirdre—and they'd all heard her and planned accordingly.

The door opened without warning, and two MacKinnon warriors walked in. One of the men held the door open, and Lewis entered behind him, holding a year-old bairn in his arms. He was followed by two lasses who were maybe six and eight years of age, and a lad who looked to be about twelve years old. Two exhausted and worried-looking women brought up the rear, the youngest one somewhere around Lewis's age. The older one resembled her, and Deirdre guessed her to be the younger woman's mother.

Deirdre rose slowly from where she'd been sitting on the dais, her gaze trained on her husband and the child he held. Lewis walked forward, nodding to the lairds, but his eyes scanned the great hall until they landed on her.

He stopped, and the women and children caught up behind him. The youngest lass leaned against Lewis's legs, her thumb slipping between her lips. Lewis glanced down and gently removed the offending digit from the child's mouth. The other lass stayed back, wrapping her arm around the younger of the two women, who hugged her back as if she needed the support. The lad stood tall and straight, staring at Gavin and the other lairds, his eyes wide and filled with awe.

Deirdre walked forward, her chest burning and her heart pounding. Her jaw felt tight yet loose at the same time, as if she didn't know whether to scream in rage or sob in betrayal. Or hug the bairn—Lewis's bairn?—close to her chest.

"Deirdre, stay here," Gavin said, his hand lightly grasping her arm as she moved past him toward Lewis.

"Nay." She was a queen, not a pawn. A lion, not a mouse. She kept going, and he released her, moving into step behind her instead. From the corner of her eye, she saw the other lairds forming a tight-knit arc to their rear.

She stopped in front of Lewis and the two bairns. "You're well?" she asked him.

"Aye. Deirdre, I—"

"May I hold him?" she interrupted, reaching her hands out for the bairn.

Lewis nodded and handed over the child. The

younger woman let out a soft moan as Deirdre settled the wee one against her chest and shoulder. She closed her eyes and gently squeezed the sleeping bairn, loving the weight and warmth of him in her arms, the distinctive baby scent.

She opened her eyes, and her gaze landed on the young lass. The girl stared up at Deirdre, her thumb back in her mouth. Deirdre smiled and ran her fingers over the girl's cheek. "You must be the princess," she said.

The girl stopped sucking and took her thumb out of her mouth. "Nay, I'm Aili."

"Ah, it's a secret, then. Princess Aili." She whispered the name at the end.

Moving toward the older women, Deirdre kissed the bairn's cheek and passed him over to the younger of the two adults. The woman took him gratefully, and their eyes met. "You have a lovely family," Deirdre said. Then she smiled at the older lass who stood beside her mother. "A queen *and* a princess." Her gaze drifted to the young man who looked so much like Lewis. "And a fine Highland warrior."

The boy blushed and looked down, but Gavin said from behind her, "Chin up, lad. You canna see your enemy approaching if you're looking at the ground."

The boy snapped his chin up, his gaze on Gavin. "Aye, Laird."

"And doona slouch. Keep your feet slightly apart and your weight centered, so you're ready for an attack."

The lad nodded, his eyes shining, and he adjusted his stance.

Deirdre turned at last to the older woman among

the group. She looked pale and anxious, and Deirdre squeezed her hand. "You have naught to fear. Your daughter and her family are safe here, and you as well."

The woman's eyes filled with sudden tears, and her mouth trembled. She grasped Deirdre's arms, her grip tight. "Lewis said you were a kind woman, that you would ne'er harm an innocent. My daughter is innocent. My grandbairns are innocent."

Gregor stepped forward and wrapped his arm around the older woman's shoulders. "Aye, they are. Come with me now. Bring the children. We'll go to the kitchen and have something to eat while Lewis and the lairds talk."

The woman nodded and gathered up the children and their mother, but the younger woman resisted. "I'm staying."

"Geneen, please," Lewis begged.

"Nay," Deirdre said. "This is about her too. Her family. Let her stay."

Geneen handed the bairn to her mother and then crossed her arms over her chest and stuck out her chin. Gregor led the children and grandmother out, signaling for Isobel to follow him. She did so grudgingly.

Lewis caught Deirdre's gaze. "I doona want Geneen hurt."

"How could she possibly be hurt? You've spent seven years playing chess with me and naught else." Anger burned at the edge of her voice.

Behind her, Gavin sucked in a startled breath.

"Did you ever intend to tell me, Lewis? Or did you just expect me to stay untouched and childless my entire life, thinking there was something wrong with me? Believing that it was my fault my husband stayed away, why he rejected every shy, awkward advance I made?" Gavin wrapped one arm protectively across Deirdre's chest. She grabbed on to it for support. "Did you know what it cost me every time I tried to invite you to my bed?"

"I'm sorry, Deirdre," he said. "It was hard for me too."

"Hard for you? How could it have been hard for you? You were able to go home to your family while I stayed alone and lonely in your drafty, old keep. Is that why you gave me Ewan? Did you know he was Gavin's son?"

"Nay! I swear I didn't know he was Laird MacKinnon's son. But I suspected foul play and I thought my father might be involved."

"Please, he's speaking the truth," Geneen said. "I was there. We were on one of the back roads—one we traveled often, so we wouldnae be seen." She glanced apologetically at Deirdre. "We came across two men, recently dead from sickness. We carried on, and that's when we heard the bairn crying. He'd wandered off, and he didn't seem ill. I was pregnant at the time—a difficult pregnancy—and we eventually lost the bairn. I couldnae take on another child at the time. When Lewis suggested giving him to you, it seemed like the perfect solution to everyone's problems."

Deirdre released a pent-up breath. She leaned back against Gavin and closed her eyes. "It was," she said. "I'll always be grateful that you brought me Ewan and that you saved him. And for being kind and considerate of me. I'm sorry I snapped at you."

"You have naught to be sorry for," Gavin said.

"Aye. You should be yelling and screaming. I'm the one who's sorry," Lewis admitted.

"You said you thought foul play was at work. Why?" Gavin asked him.

"'Twas unusual that the lad had no one with him to care for him. And he was verra dirty and unkempt. A loving parent wouldnae have allowed him to be so neglected. The men looked rough, like warriors. 'Twas hard to tell because of the sickness, but I thought I recognized one of them from my father's personal guard." He reached into his sporran and ripped out a lining that hid something behind it. He pulled out two torn pieces of plaid and a parchment, and passed them all to Gavin. The others gathered closer. "The plaids are from the men. The greenish one is a MacIntyre weave. I doona recognize the other one."

Gavin passed the plaids around to his foster brothers before he opened the parchment. "Where did you get this?" he asked after he read it, his voice tight with anger.

Deirdre brought his hand down so she could read what was written on the parchment: a description of Ewan, highlighting his unusual eye color and blond hair, as well as his first name.

"This was to help them find him," she said, her voice rising. "To know which boy to take."

"Aye." Gavin spoke through gritted teeth.

"'Twas on the body of one of the men," Lewis said. "The man with the plaid I didn't recognize."

"You searched them thoroughly?" Gavin asked.

Geneen moved closer to him, in defense of her man. "As well as he could. The bodies were diseased."

Gavin nodded. "I imagine that would have been difficult. Thank you for putting yourself at risk and for bringing it to me. What can you tell me about your father? You're obviously leaving, so you must be renouncing the lairdship. Does he know about Geneen and the children?"

"He knows about my eldest son, Leith, and that I was in love with Geneen as a young man, but he doesn't know the extent of it. Nor that we have other children together." He met Deirdre's eyes, then dropped his gaze. "He doesn't know that we're still together. That we've created a happy home and life together."

Deirdre stared at him, bemused but also deeply hurt. She was his wife, yet he hadn't wanted any of those things with her? "I doona understand why you married me, then. You would have had your two eldest at least by the time I came to you."

"I had no choice, Deirdre. My father commanded it, and I was afraid that if I said nay, he would find out about Geneen and the children and kill them."

Deirdre gasped. "Surely he wouldnae have committed such a monstrous crime? Your daughter would have been little more than a babe!"

"Nay, *he* wouldnae have done it," Lewis said bitterly. "He would have ordered someone else to do it. They would have slaughtered Leith, Leslie, and Geneen, who was pregnant with Aili at the time, and most likely murdered her mother too. I would have lost everyone I cared about." He scrubbed a hand over his face, his fingers digging into his jaw. Geneen gently squeezed his arm.

He sighed. "And then I met you, Deirdre, and you

were so young and scared and…beaten down. Another victim of my father and of your own father. Not to mention your piece of shite brother." He turned to Gavin suddenly, looked him directly in the eye. "Under no circumstances are you to release her into her brother's care. He's a degenerate of the worst kind. His feelings toward Deirdre are unnatural. I almost killed him when he was at our keep, and I am not a man of violence."

Deirdre gasped, shock and horror crashing through her, but also shame, all those confusing feelings from so long ago twisting her stomach.

Gavin tightened his arm around her. "We will take care of him. Boyd MacColl will ne'er lay a hand on another lass."

Lewis exhaled heavily, sounding relieved. "I am glad to know you care for Deirdre. And I can see she cares for you too." He looked at the door. "When the priest gets here—"

"Priest?" Gavin interrupted. "You mean Father Lundie?"

"Aye. I've met him several times over the years. When I heard he was here, I beseeched one of your men to bring him to me."

"What is it, Lewis?" Deirdre asked, her voice filled with concern.

He glanced at the door again, looking nervous.

Geneen squeezed his hand, and he held on to it like a life raft. "When the priest is here," she said, raising her chin.

They fell into an awkward silence. After a moment, Lewis blurted out, "I'm sorry I canna help further. My father and I were, for all intents and purposes, estranged. He did not include me in his plans, so I canna give you much information, but I do know you canna trust him. He's here because it suits him, not because of Deirdre or Ewan. I fear he has an attack planned against you, and he will strike sooner rather than later. He mentioned other men—and that you wouldnae know what hit you."

Silence fell as everyone took in his words.

"Would you be willing to spy for us?" Callum asked.

"Nay!" both Geneen and Deirdre said together.

"It's too dangerous," Deirdre added.

"If I thought it would do some good, I would consider it. But my father willna share any information with me. I've already been sent back to my keep in disgrace. I suspect he's planning to kill me soon whether he has another male heir or not."

"We can help you," Kerr said. "You're welcome to come live at Clan MacAlister."

Lewis smiled and nodded. "Thank you, old friend, but we've made plans. We've been working on them for years."

"You've been stealing the money intended for the keep?" Kerr said.

"Aye," Lewis answered. "Whate'er I thought could be spared."

"Where are you planning to go?" Gavin asked.

"Geneen's mother has family in Cambria. It's far enough away that my father willna find us. But..." Lewis looked at Deirdre.

"But what?" she asked. Gavin tensed behind her and made a soft huffing sound next to her ear. She looked at him and saw his expression had turned to ice.

"I was worried about you...*we* were worried about you. It doesn't look like you'll be in need of us now, but Geneen and I planned to speak to you about coming with us."

"To Cambria?"

"Aye."

"No!" She practically yelled the word, and Gavin relaxed behind her. "That is to say, no thank you. I appreciate you thinking of me, but my home is here. I finally feel like I have a place where I belong."

Lewis smiled at Deirdre, his happiness for her shining through his eyes. "I'm glad, lass. Verra glad. But there's more you need to know. Both of you." He looked at Geneen, who nodded at him encouragingly. Lewis visibly swallowed then looked back at the door again—which suddenly opened.

Father Lundie stepped through, escorted by one of Gavin's men. His hair was sticking up at the back of his head and his robe was creased, as if he'd fallen asleep wearing it. Deirdre imagined he must have been too tired to undress after several days of travel.

In his hands he carried a small wooden case and a Bible. "Is someone in need of assistance?" he asked, hurrying forward.

Lewis turned around and stretched out his hand to greet the priest. "I am, Father Lundie. 'Tis good to see you again."

"Ah, Master Lewis. I didn't know you were here. Good evening to you, sir." He scanned the group. "I pray you're all hale and hearty?"

"Aye, Father, 'tis another matter on which we must speak." Lewis reached into his sporran and brought out a second piece of parchment. This one looked crisp and fresh, other than the crease where he'd folded it. He passed it to Father Lundie, who glanced down and started reading the script.

"I must speak of my misdeeds," Lewis continued, "and I wanted an official from the church here as witness. It gladdens my heart that it's you, even though what I have to say is a devastating breach of trust to Deirdre, the Church, and to our two clans. I pray everyone involved will find their way to forgive me."

Father Lundie's eyes widened as he continued to read. He muttered under his breath a few times and even gasped and crossed himself at a certain point. Deirdre's pulse pounded as she watched him. What on earth could it be? What further humiliation could her husband bestow upon her in front of everyone gathered there?

"Tell us," Gavin said sternly. He had both arms around her now, and she leaned fully against him, her knees weak and legs trembling.

Father Lundie looked up at Lewis. "Shall I tell her?"

"Nay," Lewis said. "'Twas my decision. I'll be the one." He stepped toward Deirdre but stopped when she defensively hugged Gavin's arms. If Gavin hadn't been pressed up against her, she would have taken a step back.

Geneen rested her hand lightly on Lewis's back in support, and he continued. "Deirdre, you have to understand. When my father came to me, demanding I marry you, I felt I had no choice but to go through with the ceremony. My father knew better than to threaten me. Instead, he threatened the lives of Geneen and Leith, my oldest son. He didn't yet know of the others."

"You said that already," she croaked.

"Aye, but it's important for you to understand the gravity of the situation."

"I'm not a bairn, Lewis. You doona need to emphasize the heinousness of murdering children."

He sighed and scrubbed his fingers through his hair, then reached back for Geneen's hand to bring her to his side. "I've known Geneen my entire life. She was the daughter of the stable master at my father's castle. I doona remember a time when she wasn't my best friend. We were young when we fell in love, but it was forbidden. My father sent me away, and I returned for Geneen without his knowledge."

He cleared his throat before continuing. She could see the pounding of his pulse at his throat and the slight tremor in his hands. "Deirdre, Geneen is my wife. We handfasted each other when we were seventeen." A collective gasp went up in the room. Deirdre's knees buckled, but Gavin held her up.

"I married you in bad faith, and our marriage is not valid—on too many grounds to count, the most important one being that I was already married. You are not legally or spiritually my wife, and I am neither legally nor spiritually your husband. I'm sorry to have used you in such a manner, but the lives of my children and my wife were at stake."

He stepped forward, and this time he did touch her, running his knuckles along upper arm. "If Geneen had not been in my life, if I hadn't been in love with her, I would have proudly claimed you. Not at the beginning, certainly—you were far too young. But you grew into a thoughtful, beautiful young woman, filled with grace and possessing a kind heart. You have so much to give." He looked pointedly at Gavin. "Any man would be an *ablach* to not know the gem he had in his possession."

Then he raised her hand and kissed it. "Your loyalty, good nature, and love is a gift, Deirdre. And I wish you naught but happiness."

Deirdre looked at the top of his head. She felt as though she were spinning, her world turned upside down. His pretty words meant naught to her. The one thing in her life that she'd had no doubt about, that she'd known she could count on, was that she was Lewis's wife. Seven years she'd been a MacIntyre, passed over from the MacColls like livestock, just as Isobel had said. And was she now to be passed back? Nay, she would ne'er go back to her father's house. So who was she then, and where did she belong? Deirdre MacColl? Deirdre MacIntyre? Lady Deirdre? Ewan's mother?

Stepping back, Lewis looked around at the five lairds and Father Lundie. "You are all witness to my account. I have a written account as well. I'd like everyone to sign it, including Deirdre and Geneen, so there's no doubt of its veracity."

"Over here," Gregor said from where he stood next to the dais. "I have a quill and ink in my sporran."

So he'd heard too. Who else knew of her disgrace?

The other lairds, Lewis, Geneen, and Father Lundie headed toward the dais, as Gregor pulled out a leather case.

Gavin stayed with her and turned her in his arms. She swayed and he caught her. "Steady. I've got you. Just lean on me and catch your breath."

She closed her eyes, rested her cheek on his

chest, and let him take her weight while she carefully inhaled and then exhaled several times. Nausea swamped her, and she focused on Gavin's heart beating beneath her ear instead of the giant hole that had opened beneath her feet.

Doona look down, Deirdre.

Down right now was the heartbreaking betrayal of her affection and trust. Of the sickening feeling of being used. She might feel differently once the shock had passed, but for now it felt like Lewis had punched a giant-sized hole in her belly.

"Gavin," Kerr called out. "Bring Deirdre over."

"Can you walk?" Gavin asked her. "I can carry you to the chair and have you sign there."

"Nay," she croaked, her voice little more than a whisper. "I can do it." She concentrated on putting one foot in front of the other, keeping her eyes trained on the floor—mostly so she'd stay upright, but also so she wouldn't have to look at any of the others.

Glancing to the side, she saw the children waiting at the entrance to the kitchen with Isobel and their grandmother. If her marriage had been real, would her children have looked like that?

She dropped her gaze again and swung her hair forward to hide her face.

"Nay," Gavin said softly, as he brushed her hair behind her shoulder. "You have naught to be ashamed of. Doona hide, Deirdre." He put the quill in her hand as she reached the dais.

A spurt of anger ignited in her breast, and she almost broke the quill in two. She swung her hair forward again—defiantly this time.

She looked at the letters on the parchment, at her betrayal laid out in ink for everyone to see. The sad, pathetic story that was her life. Words jumped out at her: handfasted, children, adultery, threats and betrayal, nonconsummation of marriage.

Pressing the quill's tip to the parchment, she signed it, ending what had never started.

Callum picked up the parchment, and she heard him blowing on it to dry the ink.

People shuffled around her, talking softly as if…as if what? She might break? That spurt of anger in her chest turned into a flame, and she ground her teeth together.

"Lewis and his family are leaving," Gavin said.

She looked up to see the seven of them heading toward the door. Father Lundie was with them. Maybe he would officially marry Lewis and Geneen now. Not that they needed the church's seal of approval—handfasting was binding.

She clenched her jaw to stop from screaming.

Why was she so upset? She didn't want to go with them. She wanted to stay here with Ewan, Gavin, Isobel, and even Kerr. She wanted to get to know Gregor and all the other lairds better and someday meet their wives. So why did she want to open her mouth and yell out in anger, resentment, hurt, and betrayal? Just like she had from the turret with Gavin a few days ago?

Why did she want to turn around and yell at Gavin too, for everything he'd done to her when they'd first met? He'd threatened her life, dragged her around like a cow on a lead, almost taken her son from her.

Lewis turned at the door with the youngest bairn

in his arms, the bairn who could have been her bairn, and lifted his hand in farewell. Deirdre raised hers automatically, the pressure building in her throat, the flame in her chest turning into a fire. When the door banged shut behind them, her hand dropped to her side—now curling into a fist, her nails digging into her palm.

Silence fell, and she took a step away from the dais, then another one, her back to the remaining people in the room. The guards were gone, the priest was gone, Lewis and his family—*his family*—were gone.

She could feel their eyes on her back, sensed their rising tension as she took another step away from them. How far would she get if she ran for the door? Not that she wanted to chase after Lewis, but she wanted…she wanted… Nay, she *needed* to do something physical. Something pounding and fierce and ferocious. She felt raw on the inside. Savage.

Used. Lied to. Mistreated. Derided. Abused. Torn away from her son like a bloodsucking leech from a slew. God's blood, did she have no value to anyone?

She took two more steps, three more. And then she heard Gavin coming up behind her.

"Deirdre, love. We couldnae have asked for a better outcome. What wonderful news. You're not married!"

And the fire in her chest erupted, became an inferno. It burst from every pore of her body, heating her skin, tunneling her vision. She turned on Gavin, burning hot with outrage. "It's wonderful that I've been lied to for seven years? Manipulated and used for someone else's gain? Cast to Clan MacIntyre by my father because of my *brother's* bad behavior, then dragged to Clan MacKinnon to pay for someone else's bad behavior? Like…like…"

"Cattle," Isobel said.

"Aye! Like a bloody ox for use in the field!"

"Calm down, Deirdre. I only meant—"

"Calm down?" she yelled. "I will not calm down. What if one day he'd just left with his family and ne'er returned? I would have been sitting in his keep for the rest of my life, waiting and worrying, wondering what I'd done wrong—what was so repugnant, so *untouchable* about me that even my husband didn't want me. He gave me Ewan because he wouldnae give anything of himself. I was as good as barren!"

Gavin's face fell. "You want him then? You love him?"

"Nay! I want to *not* have been used and lied to and belittled by everyone in my life who was supposed to care about me."

"I have ne'er lied to you or used you."

"You just invaded my keep, abducted me, and ripped me away from my son instead! Threatened me with losing the only person in my life who truly loved me. The only one who valued me."

"That's not true, Deirdre. I value you. I care about you a great deal. Sweetling, I lo—"

"Hit him, Deirdre," Isobel yelled from the sidelines. "You'll feel better."

She looked at Isobel, her emotions still so savage and raw. She looked at Kerr, saw his big sword poking up from behind his shoulder—the sword she could barely even lift. She marched toward him now, determined to get her hands on it.

His eyes widened as he saw her coming. "Cousin, why are you coming for me? I ne'er treated you poorly. Not once."

"You threw my hairbrush on the stairs."

"Aye, lass, I did. I'm sorry. I'll get you a new one."

"I doona want a new one. I want your sword." She stopped in front of Kerr and held out her hand.

"My sword? But you can barely lift—"

"Give it to me!"

He quickly drew the sword with one hand and handed her the hilt. She yanked it from his grasp, and the tip dropped with a clang to the stone floor. "The blade! Deirdre, doona let it drag on the—"

Isobel smacked his stomach with the back of her hand, and he let out an "ooof," then he groaned as Deirdre scraped the sword tip—previously honed to a razor-sharp edge—all the way back to Gavin on the rough floor. Gavin stood still and stared at her, not knowing what to do. His gaze rose to his brothers and Gregor behind her.

She couldnae yet place the voices with the men.

"Let her hit you with it, Brother."

"But doona let her stab you."

"She canna lift it to stab him. It weighs too much."

"Not anymore. Not with all the chips coming out."

"My sword!" That voice she recognized as Kerr's.

"It's not a wee bairn, you great big *ablach*. It's a bloody weapon. You can get a new one or just sharpen the blade." That was definitely Isobel. "Give him hell, Deirdre!"

Deirdre lifted the sword with a groan and swung at Gavin. He blocked it with the metal cuff on his forearm. "Deirdre, love, give me the sword. Please."

She heaved it again. "You stole Ewan from me. You made me ride that bloody mare."

"Language!" Kerr said, and then she heard a thump, and he made the same "ooof" sound as before.

Deirdre swung again. Gavin deflected the weapon with a single, soft touch, so the blade turned, and the flat side hit his plaid.

"Please, love. Give me the blade."

"Nay! I almost jumped off that bloody cliff!"

He blanched, and this time when she lifted the sword and swung again, he caught the blade in his palm. He gripped harder, and the blade dug in. Blood dripped down the edge and over his wrist.

"Gavin," she yelled and tried to pull it away, but he held on.

He kneeled and put the blade to his neck. "I would die for you, Deirdre. If I could take back what I did, I would. I am so sorry I wronged you, that I failed to see you for the angel you are. You have been my son's savior and my own. You are right. I treated you with less respect than I would show an ox. I will ne'er forgive myself for that, for driving you to the edge of that cliff. Forgive me."

Tears welled in her eyes and streamed down her face. "I will if you release the sword."

He let go but left the blade on his shoulder, almost touching his neck. "I swear to you, Deirdre, I am yours. For now and forever. I am not happy that Lewis lied to you, that he used you and left you. But I am overjoyed that you are not married, because I canna imagine any greater blessing than you becoming *my* wife. Please, Deirdre. Will you marry me?"

She stared down at him—his blood staining the blade, his eyes, those amazing blue-green eyes shining up at her with hope, but also with uncertainty. And she realized that this man, this laird of a great, prosperous clan, as astonishingly handsome as Adonis and as skilled a warrior as Hercules, was frightened that she'd say nay.

"A real marriage this time?" she asked, her voice breaking, wanting so badly what he held out to her. "With us living together, here with our family? Sharing our lives and our bodies? Because I want more bairn. And I want you. I want it all, Gavin MacKinnon, and if you doona intend to tup me—"

Gavin rose in one quick, smooth movement, and the sword clattered to the floor. His hands tangled in her hair as he held her in place. His lips landed on her mouth, and he kissed her.

He angled his head, his tongue slick and soft against the seam of her lips. She opened for him with a gasp and a shiver. Her arms circled his waist and slid up his back, holding on to this man who had become her everything. The heat and hardness of him thrilled her. His gentleness made her want to cry—and then demand more.

"I intend to tup you, Deirdre. Often. So, say aye, and that you'll marry me. Right now. Please, dearling. I canna wait much longer."

"How often is often?" she asked, breathless and shattered.

"As often as you'll have me."

"Aye, I'll marry you, Gavin MacKinnon, with our son there by our sides."

A happy sigh went up from their onlookers, and she even heard a sniffle or two.

"Now that, lads, is a marriage proposal. Somebody get the priest!" Gregor yelled.

Nineteen

"Are you sure you doona want to put off the ceremony for at least a day?" Isobel asked.

"I'm absolutely sure." Deirdre paced back and forth in front of the church's sanctuary, her footsteps echoing off the vaulted stone ceiling.

They were waiting for Gavin to arrive with Ewan, and Kerr to arrive with Father Lundie. What was taking them so long? Surely it didn't take this much time to wake up their child and escort the priest here?

She looked up at the stained-glass windows that depicted the stages of Christ's life, high on the stone wall above the rows of pews. Had the glass lightened since she'd been waiting? Aye, a little. So dawn was nearly upon them.

"Let's wait until this evening then," Isobel pressed. "Then everyone can get a few more hours sleep while Bonni prepares a special feast and we sort out a beautiful dress for you to wear."

"This one is beautiful—the most beautiful arisaid I've e'er worn. And you gave it to me." Deirdre searched with her fingers under her sleeve and pulled out the blue ribbon that Gavin had used to wrap the gift he'd given her the other day. "Here, help me put Gavin's ribbon in my hair." She passed the ribbon to Isobel, and then finger-combed her dark tresses as best she could. When she was done, Isobel looped the ribbon underneath Deirdre's locks and then tied it at the top.

Isobel squeezed her shoulders. "You do look lovely. But even just a day—half a day to prepare—will make the whole thing better. Deirdre, you're getting married. Let me make it special for you!"

Deirdre grasped Isobel's hands. "It is special. I'll have everyone here I care about. A family—a real family—by my side, loving me, wanting to see me happy and cared for. My sister, my son, a father to give me away, my brothers, and my newfound cousin—no matter how annoying he may be at times."

Isobel huffed out a laugh and nodded. "And Gavin, of course."

"Aye, and Gavin. Always Gavin."

"You can count me as a part of that family too, love." Deirdre looked up to see Annag walking down the aisle toward them, a still-sleeping Ewan in her arms. Her kindly face was creased in a beaming smile, and her eyes shone with pleasure. "A grandmother, I hope. The same way I feel toward Gavin and this little one here."

Deirdre hurried over and embraced her. "Aye, dear Annag. I would be honored to have you as my grandmother."

"I'm so happy for you, lass. Both of you. I couldnae think of a kinder woman to be marrying my Gavin."

"Me neither," Gavin said as he entered the chapel and walked toward them. He'd shaved and changed his clothes, his linen léine fresh and white and his plaid crisply pleated. She'd never seen that one before. The weave and colors were slightly different than his others, the dye brighter.

"Och, you look so brawny and braw," she said. "Maybe we should do as Isobel suggested and wait a day so I can look as nice as you."

"Nay," Gavin said emphatically, reaching for her hands. "You're already exquisite, and I canna wait one more minute to make you my wife. My heart aches to look upon you now. If you do anything else to yourself, it might break."

"Well, in that case, where's the priest?" Then she leaned into him and whispered, "I wouldnae want you dying on me before I experienced at least one night of pleasure."

"I heard that," Isobel said, her face scrunched up and her hands over her ears. "And I can ne'er unhear it!"

"Unhear what?" Kerr boomed from the doorway, leading not only Father Lundie inside, but Gregor, Darach, Lachlan, and Callum as well.

"Deirdre is whispering lewd things to Gavin," Isobel said.

Heat scorched her cheeks. "Isobel!"

"Was it more lewd than what we heard earlier?" Lachlan asked.

"Aye, that was by far the most lusty marriage proposal and acceptance I've e'er heard," Gregor said.

"Did she actually say 'tupping'?" Darach asked.

"Nay, I think it was 'tup.' But she did say 'bodies' and 'bairn,'" Callum added.

Deirdre groaned in embarrassment while Gavin

watched his brothers gather around, a grin on his face.

"Make them stop," she pleaded.

"I canna," he said. "If I tell them to stop, it'll just get worse."

"Welcome to the family, Cousin." Kerr's big hands cupped her face, and he kissed her forehead. "I have no doubt you can slay them with your wit."

Father Lundie moved around to the front of the group and into the sanctuary to prepare for the upcoming mass. He winked at her, a sparkle in his eye. "Good morning, lass. By the sounds of it, I'd better marry you soon."

They all hooted with laughter. Deirdre was sure that if the priest wasn't standing in the sanctuary, wearing his official vestments and carrying the Bible, the men would have slapped him on the back and offered him a mug of ale.

"The sun is coming up," Father Lundie said. "What a perfect time for a wedding. God's promise of a new day, and a new life beginning for the two of you."

Gavin stood on the chapel balcony facing the bailey, the keep looming on the other side. The open, grassy area was filled with all the castle folk, warriors, and people from the village. News had spread fast about their laird's wedding to Lady Deirdre, and many had made it there on time. It hadn't been that long—less than two hours—since Deirdre had said aye, but the story of her betrayal in marriage had circulated like wildfire through the clan, as had Gavin's subsequent proposal, even though the sun had barely risen.

It was a love story for the ages. Or it would be, if Gavin could make Deirdre fall in love with him.

When he'd been younger, he'd been attracted to superficial things and full of hubris about himself and his appeal to the lasses. Back then, he'd never have doubted that Deirdre would fall in love with him. The last six years, however, had scoured all of that out of him. All that and then some.

Now he hoped, with Deirdre's healing touch, that scouring had made him a better man.

It wasn't that he didn't see her physical beauty—how could he not? But it was the way she held his son and laughed with his sister and teased his brothers that made him fill up inside. It was her kindness toward others, her sacrifices for Ewan, her ability to forgive that made her even more beautiful to him.

She was a woman worth loving. And he hoped someday he would be worthy of her love in return.

He heard the door to the balcony open. Turning, he looked past his foster brothers, Isobel, and Annag, grouped behind him on either side, and saw Gregor walk through. He was beaming like a proud father, with Deirdre on his arm and Ewan perched on the other side on his hip.

Gavin's heart, which had already been thumping quickly, began to race. She smiled at him, looking a little dazed and a wee bit teary. Aye, he could understand that. He felt the same.

When Ewan saw him, he shouted, "Da!" and leaned toward him. Gavin reached for his son and then held out his hand for Deirdre. "You're a vision, lass. I couldnae be happier than I am at this moment."

She clasped Gavin's hand and stepped up beside him. "I feel the same. I canna wait to marry you, Gavin. And I'm sorry I hit you with the sword."

Snorts of laughter went up from his family—*their family*—and he grinned. "It was worth it if it got you to marry me."

It was then she looked beyond him and noticed all her new clan gathered in the bailey below. She gasped and raised her hand, and a cheer went up. Aye, they were her family now too.

Father Lundie began the ceremony. When it was time, Gavin passed Ewan over to Isobel and gave Deirdre her wedding gift—a magnificent pearl necklace and brooch that his mother had worn and had been in their family for generations. Harvested from Scotland's rivers, the pearls were a stunning array of colors and shapes, grouped together to form a magnificent pattern of the rounder lilac-colored pearls and cream-colored pearls, separated by spherical gray ones.

Deirdre gasped when she saw them. "Gavin, they're beautiful." She ran her fingertips over the pearls, almost as if she was afraid to handle them. "Are you sure?"

"Aye. They were my mother's. And you will be the only one to have worn them since her." He didn't say the words, but he could see she understood his meaning—he'd never given them to Cristel.

"What about Isobel?" she asked.

"They're yours, Deirdre," Isobel said. "It pleases me beyond words to see you with them."

"Isobel will have her own jewels when the time comes," Kerr said.

Gavin glanced over to see his foster brother had laid

his hand on Isobel's shoulder—and she hadn't pushed it off. Aye, weddings had that effect on people.

Deirdre turned so Gavin could put the necklace around her neck. His fingers were shaking, but he finally got the clasp to fasten. "We'll do the brooch later," he said.

When it came time for their vows, his voice and hand steadied, and he firmly pledged to love and honor her as he slipped the matching pearl ring onto her finger. Her voice wasn't as steady as his, but that had nothing to do with uncertainty and everything to do with the emotion that hitched her breath and caused her chin to tremble.

Finally, they kissed, and a cheer went up from the crowd and their family. Father Lundie beamed, then led them back into the chapel for the wedding mass. It all passed in a blur at that point, anticipation roaring through Gavin as the priest finally ended his last prayer. How many steps to the bailey, then to the keep, then up to their bedchamber? How long would it take to get through the well-wishers? How could he avoid his clan wanting to come up and undress the bride for him without killing anyone?

Gavin clasped Deirdre's hand, and he could feel it trembling. She squeezed his arm close and kissed his shoulder. Aye, she also anticipated their joining.

After his disaster with Cristel, part of him couldn't believe his fortune, to be married to a woman who *wanted* his touch. But another part of him, a small but persistent part, kept whispering that it couldn't be real. What if she didn't like the physical act? Or how he touched her?

Worse, what if she was pretending, like Cristel had, and everything changed as soon as their marriage was consummated?

She stood on her tiptoes and whispered in his ear. "Do we have to do anything else, or can we go straight to bed?"

He huffed out a laugh and then kissed her. Nay. Deirdre was nothing like Cristel.

Gavin scowled at his clan gathered around them. One hour had passed—*one hour*—since they were married, and he and Deirdre were still in the bailey, having just been seated at a table on a dais near the keep. Additional tables and benches had been laid out in the bailey to accommodate as many people as possible, and a breakfast feast was being served.

He couldn't help but be moved by the way his clan—directed by his housekeeper, Isobel, and his cook—had come together on such short notice to throw an impromptu celebration for them, but he also wanted to roar out his frustration. Not that anyone would have heard him over the noisy clamor of his clan and the bagpipes and fiddle being played exuberantly nearby.

His only consolation was that Deirdre sat beside him, tightly gripping his hand and tapping her foot impatiently—even though she smiled. Although he doubted how sincere it was when she said, "How much longer?" through gritted teeth.

He kissed her, and his clan cheered. "We'll break our fast. That's it." He saw the servers moving toward them with their trenchers. "Eat enough to last you the whole day, Deirdre, because we willna be leaving our bedchamber until tomorrow."

She snorted in amusement, and this time her smile lit up her eyes. "Aye, Husband. But if our day is as vigorous as I expect it to be, I'll wager we'll need more nourishment by eventide."

He groaned and kissed her hand. "What exactly are you expecting, Wife? And how much do you know?"

She stared up at him, her eyes darkening, her skin tingeing pink. "I'm expecting all of you, Gavin. You'll hold naught back. And I know enough…although not nearly as much as Isobel, by the sounds of it."

"What?" he croaked. "How does Isobel know anything? Has Kerr been—"

"Nay," she laughed, and kissed his shoulder again. He liked that. "Isobel being Isobel, she has found places to eavesdrop. And you know you canna stop her. She's heard a lot more than my maids told me."

His heart beat a steady, fast rhythm. "If you have any questions, love, or if you're scared—"

"I'm not scared."

"Good. But if you are—"

"I willna be."

He stroked his fingers down her cheek. "I will be."

"Why?" she gasped.

"I want to make it perfect for you."

"Because of Cristel?" she asked, and he knew what she meant. Because Cristel had rejected his touch.

"Aye, but mostly because of you. I want to be worthy of you, love. And I want to pleasure you in every imaginable way possible."

Her lids dropped to half-mast as her gaze turned

fervent, and her lips parted slightly on her slow, deep inhalation. The servers placed their trenchers full of food in front of them.

She kissed his shoulder again. “Then let’s eat, husband. Fast.”

Twenty

Gavin took the steps to the keep two at a time, moving quickly even though he carried Deirdre in his arms. Behind him, the clan cheered them on. He didn't think any of them would follow, but just in case, he'd enlisted his foster brothers' help to guard the stairs. What man or woman in their right mind would go up against Kerr's hulking figure—especially if he had a scowl on his face?

At the top, he turned back toward the bailey and waved. Deirdre did the same. The clan cheered again. Then Gavin carried her over the threshold and into their home.

"Welcome home, Deirdre MacKinnon."

She beamed up at him. "I like how that sounds."

"I do too." He bent his head to kiss her, and she tightened her arms around his neck. Her lips parted with a happy sigh as his mouth touched hers. They pressed gently against each other, moving softly and learning the shape and feel of each other's lips. She shivered, and he pulled back. "Too much?"

"Nay, not enough. Take me upstairs, Gavin." Her

voice had deepened, sounded throaty, and now he was the one who shivered.

He kissed her again and then continued across the empty great hall—not rushing, wanting to draw out this moment. They hadn't really had a courtship, after all, and this felt like part of one. Aye, they'd been drawn to each other, and they'd kissed, but until a few hours ago, the idea that they could be married one day had seemed almost impossible.

He also liked the notion of going slow, of teasing her until her need for him was a physical ache…although he suspected his resolve would wear thin as soon as he closed their bedchamber door. "Even if you hadn't agreed to marry me, this would still be your home for as long as you chose to stay. I hope you know that."

"Thank you, dearling, but know that there was no possibility I would've said no."

He'd reached the top of the stairs now and smiled with just a hint of his old hubris. "Just as long as I agreed to tup you."

She smiled back at him, the devil he'd come to recognize gleaming in her eyes. She unfastened the tie of his shirt and glided her hand inside, rubbing her fingers through his chest hair and scraping her nails across his nipple. "'Twas a hardship for you, I'm sure."

The air left his lungs in a shaky breath, her touch igniting a sizzle of heat straight to his groin. "'Tis hard, all right," he groaned, his stones on fire, and picked up his pace along the hallway.

She stretched upward and opened her mouth over the pulse pounding at the base of his neck, first laving it with her tongue and then sucking at his skin. His knees almost buckled as they reached their bedchamber door, and he leaned against it heavily. "Inside," he rasped, feeling around awkwardly for the latch to open it. It released suddenly, and he staggered in, then leaned his shoulder against the other side to shut it and bolt it closed.

She stared up at him. Her eyes were glassy again and the lids heavy, her mouth red and wet. Never in his life had he seen anything as beautiful. "Did you know that after our first meeting, before I knew you had Ewan, I asked Kerr about you? I said that your lips were like the inner petals of a young rose."

She smiled in a sweet, pleased way. "And what was his response?"

"I canna remember. I was too busy thinking about your lips."

She huffed out a laugh and then squirmed to get down.

He released her legs reluctantly, and she slid to the floor. She stayed pressed to him for a moment before she stepped back and began to wander around his bedchamber. Her eyes landed on the big bed they would now share, then over to his desk, where her geometry set, parchment, and quills had been laid out. She approached the hearth and ran her fingers over the backs of the two chairs sitting in front of it, beautifully carved and with embroidered pillows on the seats and footstools. She moved across to the mantel, where Ewan's toy horse stood watch—the one that she'd brought with them from their old keep.

The fire burned low to keep the stone walls' chill out of the air, and the shutters stood open to the bright, midmorning sunlight. Several tapestries lined the walls, two depicting fields of flowers and the other a hunting scene.

She wandered back to the familiar four-poster bed with the midnight-blue canopy above it and the embroidered blue cover on top. He couldn't wait to see her spread out over the quilt, her fair skin, red lips, and dark hair a gorgeous contrast to the blue. So lush and touchable.

She traced her fingers up and down the wooded bedpost, looking a little uncertain. He waited to see what she would do.

"'Tis an agreeable room," she said.

"Aye."

"And an agreeable bed."

"Aye."

Silence hung between them. She dropped her eyes, then raised them, looking at him through lowered lashes. More heat pooled in his groin.

"Would you like me to undress?" she asked, her voice low and a bit husky.

He had to swallow before answering, and his voice still croaked regardless. "Aye." His cock strained so stiffly toward her under his plaid that it felt like she had him by the tip and was tugging. Hard.

She might be smiling shyly, but the devil was back in her eyes, and he could see her anticipation. As awkward and nervous as she might feel, she wanted him to look upon her unclothed. "I'm not small," she said as if to warn him.

He almost laughed out loud. "Aye, sweetling, you are. You're just rounded through your breasts and hips."

"And my arse."

He groaned. "I havenae forgotten about your arse, believe me." He pushed off from the door and strode a few steps closer…and waited. Let her feel in control—let her take this at her own pace.

She pushed her hair behind her shoulders, then reached up and pulled the ribbon from her dark locks. They tumbled free. He liked that. Her hands found the brooch that he'd gifted her—they'd replaced her old one with it after the mass had ended—and she unfastened it, so her dress loosened. She gave a wee shake that set her breasts in motion, and the dress slipped to the floor. She picked it up and laid it over the back of the chair, along with the brooch, then stood before him in her white linen shift, playing with the tie at her neck.

"Loosen your shift, and then bend over and take off your shoes and hose," he said.

Her eyes rounded, and a delighted smile transformed her face. "You want to see my breasts as I lean over."

"Aye." He grinned back. "Just a peek."

She tugged the linen tie, inch by inch, until it unknotted and fell open at the neck. He could see the tops of the twin mounds and down into the valley between them. Her nipples had hardened into stiff nubs that tented the material. She wrapped her hair over one shoulder and then angled herself toward him, so he'd have a clear view.

"Like this?" she asked with a seductive smile as she slowly bent down, drawing out the anticipation. He found himself holding his breath, his eyes glued to her breasts as they pressed forward into the drooping neckline. One darkened nipple snagged on the edge, and his mouth watered. God's blood, he couldn't wait to taste her, to feel the rounded point on his tongue.

"Aye just like that," he ground out, unhooking his sporran and tossing it to the side, then squeezing his cock through his plaid. It almost hurt he was so engorged, so filled with need for her. He couldn't ever remember wanting a woman this badly or feeling so out of control, but it was so much worse than being sixteen again, because he couldn't just lose himself to pleasure. Nay, he had to make it good for her, so she wanted to be intimate again and again.

Not like Cristel.

She straightened with her hose and shoes in her hands, and her smile slipped. Uncertainty filled those soulful eyes. "Am I doing something wrong, Gavin? Your expression has changed. You look…pensive."

His eyebrows shot up. "Nay. Everything is perfect. Beyond perfect."

She closed the distance between them, the darkened tips of her breasts swaying against the linen, and reached up to smooth her fingers over his puckered forehead. "Then why are there lines here?" She stroked her fingers down his jaw, neck, and shoulders. "And tension here…and here."

He caressed her back and over her hips to knead the rounded softness of her bottom, pressing their bodies together as he did so. His hips thrust against her belly, he couldn't help himself, and the pleasure was so intense that his eyes almost rolled back in his head. "I'm tense because I'm like a lad with my first lover. My blood is so heated I just want to roll you under me and take my pleasure, and I canna do that."

She shivered, and her eyes turned molten. "Why not? Gavin, my blood is heated too. I want your hands and mouth all over me. I ache for you down there." She reached between them and stroked her hand over his cock. He grunted and again thrust into her hand, so desperately out of control. "I want this part of you spreading my flesh and pushing inside. Every inch of me feels hot and heavy and swollen, waiting for you to make me yours."

He blew a forceful breath from his lungs, skimmed his hands back up to the safety of her shoulders. "It canna be so carnal. I want you to like it."

Her brows rose. "Have you not heard a thing I've said?"

He nodded. "Aye, but—"

"Nay. No 'buts.'" She took a step back, frowning. "This is about Cristel, isn't it? I'm not her, Gavin, and I doona want her in our bedchamber with us ever again. Look at me. Want *me*." She backed away from him and gathered up the hem of her shift in her hands. It rose over her bare legs. He held his breath as it reached the V at the top of her thighs, longing to see that most private part of her.

She stilled, hesitating, and when he dragged his gaze to hers, her eyes were filled with that teasing light again.

"Show me," he said, and then cursed himself for sounding so demanding.

"Your plaid first," she said breathlessly.

He wasted no time loosening his plaid and toeing off his boots at the same time, then ripped off his hose. "My shirt too?"

She nodded. With one hand, he reached behind

him and grabbed the loose, white linen shirt that hung halfway down his thighs and yanked it over his head. He stood before her naked, his chest rising and falling in heavy breaths as if he'd just run around the castle wall, his eyes focused on her, his lips slightly parted. His cock was as hard as a bloody tree trunk and felt twice as big. His stones swung heavily down below.

She was a virgin. He'd probably just scared the devil out of her.

Except…her eyes drifted over him, needy and greedy. When they reached his groin, she sucked in a breath of air, and that engorged part of him twitched and swayed.

Her mouth opened, and the tip of her tongue poked out. "Oh my."

She didn't sound virginal. She sounded throaty and lusty.

"Your shift, Deirdre. I need to look on you naked, Wife. Now!" He practically growled the words at her.

"Fast or slow?" she asked.

"Fast."

She lifted the shift higher, no teasing this time. Dark, wet curls appeared, covering her mound, and then the slight dips and swell of her belly. Her hips curved in at the top to a small waist before her breasts flared out again. God's blood. They were perfectly shaped, round, high, and full. Her areolas were colored a darker pink-brown, and in the center of each, a hard nub thrust out.

She pushed her hair behind square shoulders that exactly matched the proportions of her hips and raised her chin. Her pearl necklace circled her neck, glowing against her skin. He'd keep that on during lovemaking.

"Am I…to your liking?" she asked.

She tried to sound bold, but he could hear the tremble in her voice. He walked steadily toward her, feeling a little more in control, which seemed backward now that she was naked in front of him, but hearing her uncertainty—that heartbreaking doubt over her physical appeal—had raised his protectiveness all over again.

"You doona want Cristel in our bedchamber? Well, I doona want your family in here with us either." He lightly grasped her hips and pulled her against him. "You are to my liking, Deirdre. We may ne'er leave our bedchamber again." His cock nestled against her belly, and his stones rested against her curls. "So much so I doona know where to touch you first. You're like a feast laid out for me to devour."

He raised his hands to her face, and she closed her eyes and swayed against him. His fingers trailed over her brow and across her cheeks to her lips. "Should I start here?" he asked as he rubbed his thumb over her mouth. She parted her lips at his touch, and he could see the tip of her tongue peeking over the edge of white teeth. "Aye, right here."

He cupped her face and lowered his head until their lips barely touched, then rubbed his mouth back and forth on hers—lightly, gently, absorbing the petal-soft feel. "Like a young rose," he said before planting his mouth on hers, seeking entrance. Her lips parted and his tongue slid across the welcoming wetness. They danced together, caressed one another, and then withdrew, only to go back in again. Deeper each time, a little rougher, more carnal—teeth scraping, even nibbling.

Gavin pulled back, his breath sawing through his lungs. Her skin was tinged pink, her lips red and glistening, her eyes at half-mast. He caressed his hands down her neck to the tips of her shoulders, then over the top, trailing his fingers lightly down her spine. Her body undulated under his touch, and her breasts swayed, the hard tips pressing against his chest.

"Or maybe I should have started here." He kept one arm wrapped around her waist and slid the palm of his other hand around the front of her body, then upward to capture her breast.

She moaned when he did and dropped her head back, her hands gripping his arms. "Oh, God in heaven, doona stop, Gavin. Aye right there, Husband."

He palmed her, loving the velvet-like feel of her skin, the sight of her breast overflowing into his hand. He brushed his thumb across the tip, the erect nipple branding his skin, and she let out a wee squeal. He grunted, his vision tunneling as he lowered his head and took the nub between his lips.

Sensation burst through his mouth and shot straight to his groin. The smell of her—the sweetness of lavender from her soap mixed with the musky scent of desire—enveloped him. The taste of her—the essence of Deirdre—made him crave more. He opened his mouth wider to suck more of her breast inside, laving her nipple with his tongue in circles and broad strokes, then sucking on it. Finally, he used his teeth, scraping on the soft underside now wet from his mouth, and nipping gently.

She groaned, her hips bucking against him. He bent her farther back over his arm. "Spread your legs," he said, the words so low and guttural they were barely recognizable.

She didn't respond immediately, almost as if it took time for his words to penetrate the haze of desire clouding her mind. Then she widened her stance.

He shifted his weight and wedged his knee between hers before dragging the core of her up against his thigh. He groaned as the heat and wetness there scalded his skin.

"Oh God, Gavin. Oh God," she panted, thrusting her hips against his muscles, sliding her sex along his leg.

He leaned over her and buried his face between her breasts, inhaling and wallowing in the smell of their mixed arousal. It rose as their bodies heated and she readied for his possession.

He kissed up to the tip of her other breast then feasted on that hard nub, sucked as much as he could into his mouth as their movements became more frenzied. His finesse deserted him, and he was left with only a desperate, carnal want and need. He thrust against the soft skin of her belly, both of his hands behind her now, supporting her, squeezing the soft curves of her arse.

Then he grazed his fingers between her cheeks, sliding against her sex from behind. She arched her back with a throaty moan, pushing against his fingers, wanting him to touch her there. He gripped her inner thigh instead, and pulled it up and over his hip. She drew up her other leg at the same time so that she straddled him. Cupping his hands beneath her arse, he lifted her, and her body rose along his, their hips aligning.

"Now?" she gasped.

"I want my mouth on you first."

Three steps and he was beside their bed. She grasped his face between her hands and pulled him to her for another kiss, mouths open, tongues thrusting deep, teeth scraping. He knelt on the bed with her and laid her on the quilt, his body heavy on hers. Her heels met in the small of his back as they rocked together without yet joining. Her center was slick with arousal and he slid along the length of her with ease.

She wrenched her head up and sucked in a shuddering breath. "Now?" she asked again, sounding desperate.

He bit her chin. "Nay, I told you. I want to taste you."

"You did!"

He huffed out a laugh at the insistence in her voice and then kissed along her jaw, sucked on her earlobe until she moaned. He laved over her throat to the delicate bones of her clavicle, and the pearl necklace that lay just below.

"Not your mouth."

She writhed beneath him as he continued down her body, loving every inch of her with his hands, fingers, lips, and tongue. He gently pinched her nipples, licked over every swell and hollow, and ran his fingertips from her knee up her inner thigh. When he nibbled low on her belly, her thighs pressed wide by his broad shoulders, she let out a high-pitched keening sound.

He swirled with his tongue over every love bite, then lifted his gaze, to take her in...and stopped breathing. She was watching him, her eyes almost feral with need, her parted lips red and wet. Her hair tumbled around her shoulders and across the quilt and her breasts quivered with every panting breath she took, reddened with color at the tips from him sucking on them.

She squeezed one of them with her own hand.

He dropped his gaze and looked at her most private area, spread out just for him. Her nether lips flushed a dark, rosy pink, the folds swollen and wet…for him.

For her husband.

Aye, he did this to her. She was excited by his touch, by the idea of him looking at her, taking her over.

This is how it should be between a man and a woman. A husband and wife. He had a real union with Deirdre, and he couldn't be more grateful. Or more in love.

"As much as I love your mouth, sweetling, this is where I want to taste you."

He lowered his head and licked with the flat of his tongue in a broad, slow stroke all the way up her slick skin to the nub at the top. She screamed out her pleasure and jerked her hips so hard she almost dislodged him.

He pushed her knees farther apart, splayed her even wider for him. He held her in place as he licked and sucked and flicked with his tongue, then pushed it inside her body to taste all of her.

Her hands were in his hair now, gripping the short strands as best she could. She held on tight as she found a quick thrusting rhythm, her throat arching as she grunted and groaned, her head thrashing back and forth on the quilt.

She was almost at the brink when he lifted his head and moved along her body with quick kisses. He canted her hips up with one hand as he slid the other one behind her back, curling his fingers over her shoulder. He lay heavily between her thighs, his cock throbbing almost painfully at her entrance.

"Deirdre."

She opened her eyes and gradually focused on him. "Gavin, I need you."

"Aye, love. Me too. Fast or slow?" he asked, just like she'd asked him earlier.

She didn't hesitate. "Fast."

He nodded. "Look at me, sweetling. Watch me." Then he pushed inside her steadily despite her body's resistance and her eyes clouding over with pain. He didn't stop until he was fully seated inside her.

He shuddered at the heat and tightness of her sheath surrounding him, yielding to him, but he didn't withdraw and thrust forward like every muscle was primed to do. He waited for her tensed body to relax, for the breath she'd been holding to finally release from her lungs.

When she looked at him with clear eyes again, he smiled, brushed back the hair from her face, and kissed her. "I love you, Deirdre."

Then he began to move.

Deirdre locked eyes with Gavin as the pain ebbed away, that stunning gaze just inches above her. His body lay heavily on top of hers, fully inside of her, hot skin against hot skin. His scent filled her nose, his taste teased her tongue.

He raised his hand and trailed his fingers down her temple. "I love you, Deirdre."

Tears filled her eyes. No one, other than Ewan, had ever said those words to her. "How—"

She tried to form a complete sentence, but then Gavin rocked within her, and every thought was driven from her head. She arched her back and moaned into his mouth, pleasure consuming her.

Every surface of her body tingled—inside her mouth, where their tongues tangled. Across her breasts and mound where his body rubbed so excitingly. Within her soft, swollen center, where his shaft pushed through her flesh with a pounding rhythm that left her panting. The pressure inside her built as heat and heaviness grew in her loins.

She pulled her knees back and dug her heels into his arse as she lifted her hips to meet his thrusts. "Gavin," she panted. "Gavin. I need…"

"I know what you need, sweetling." He dropped his hand to her hip again, angling her so the hard edge of his pelvis hit that nub nestled just below her curls. She moaned as he ground down on her, so tight and heavy she could barely move.

All she could do was hold on.

She threw her head back on the quilt, dug her nails into his back and shoulders, and brokenly called out his name. "Gavin. Oh God, Gavin."

"Doona hold back," he commanded, his breath shuddering from his lungs as he thrust into her with more force, his rhythm driving them both onward. "I want to hear you, Wife. I want to see you."

She almost laughed. She was in the throes of the most intense feelings of her life and had no ability to hold anything back.

She. Was. Overcome.

And then she was screaming as she came apart—her eyes closed, white stars dancing against her black lids, her hips jerking, her core pulsing around her husband.

He groaned, gripped her tighter, and his even strokes faltered, breaking his rhythm as he shuddered into her. He slammed his mouth down.

Kissed her. Deep. Mindless. Carnal.

Finally, their dance slowed, and they stopped moving, other than for the tremors that shook their bodies. The kiss gentled, and they caught their breath. Deirdre sighed, her legs dropped away from around his waist, and her hands released their nail-biting grip on his back and shoulders.

He dropped his head to the crook of her neck, the ragged puffs of air warm on her skin.

She wanted to stay that way forever, loved and cherished, even though it was hard to breathe with his weight on top of her. But he rolled onto his back and tucked her under his arm, her front along his side.

She sighed and snuggled in, laying her top leg over his. Aye, she felt loved here too.

"Gavin?"

"Aye."

She kissed over his heart. "I love you too."

His breath hitched in his chest, making her smile. He rolled to his side, facing her, stroking her hair behind her ear. "Verily?"

"Aye. And 'tis a good thing we're married, because if we had done *that* last night and not married this morning, I wouldnae have been able to stop myself from coming to you again and again. I would have been with bairn in no time—and no husband to blame for it."

He grinned, and she could see the happiness and relief in his gaze. Relief that she truly was a wanton—for him.

She was about to ask how soon they could tup again, when he said, "You would have stayed with me here, as my wife, and we would have petitioned for a divorce from Lewis. Even if Lewis hadn't been married to Geneen, the divorce would have come through on the grounds of adultery—especially since your marriage wasn't consummated. It just would have taken more time." Then he slid his hand down to her belly. "Maybe you're with bairn already."

A note of happiness echoed in her heart. "Maybe."

He wrapped her tightly in his arms. "Nothing would make me happier than to see my child grow in your womb. But at the same time..." Dread had filled his voice, and he had to exhale heavily before continuing. "Nay. I'll not allow those thoughts into our bed right now. Just know how much I love you, Deirdre, and I would welcome any child that comes of our union."

Deirdre squeezed him back, knowing that his thoughts had gone to Gregor and his lost wife and triplet daughters. "Me too, love."

He rolled onto his spine again, and she settled back into position. Aye, she liked it here.

"Deirdre, can you tell me about your family and Boyd? What happened, sweetling? What exactly did Boyd do?"

She stiffened, and he rolled back onto his side to face her. "If you need more time before you tell me, I'll accept that. But I need to know eventually."

She looked into his eyes, saw his concern for her, his determination to help—but also his need for justice on her behalf.

She stared at his chest, wondering where to begin. Certainly not with Boyd. Nay, she'd have to work up to that. "Before I tell you about my family, please know that I was well loved growing up—just not by the family I was born into.

"My nursemaid was like a mother to me until her passing several years ago, and one of my maids was only a few years older than me. We played together as children, and she came to Clan MacIntyre with me. She married recently, and I felt like I was saying goodbye to a sister when she left for her new home. Ewan and I attended the wedding."

"Aye, 'tis where you were spotted. The person who informed me of Ewan's whereabouts saw you at the wedding."

She stretched up and kissed him on the lips. "Well, now I'm doubly glad I went."

"Me too. Carry on."

She nodded. "My tutor was a wonderful, kind man, and when my…difficulties…with Boyd arose, he spoke to my father about it. My tutor protected me, and he rallied all the castle folk to watch out for me. They were good people. 'Twas only my family who were…off."

That familiar hurt tightened her chest, and she breathed deeply to release it. "I doona remember a time when I felt loved by them or that I belonged with them. I was the forgotten child. I looked different from them, and acted different from them, and seemed to have a different temperament. My mother was cold and critical, and my father was mostly absent. My siblings were all born closely together in years, and they were older than me.

"I was frightened of horses, and when I was six, they dragged me into the stables and put me onto the back of the biggest, scariest stallion in the stable. He threw me into a corner of his stall. Fortunately, I landed on a pile of hay and wasn't injured, but if the stable master hadn't intervened, I could have been seriously hurt."

He pulled her close again. "Or killed. 'Tis no wonder you're afraid of horses. I should ne'er have made you ride."

"Nay, Gavin. 'Tis good for me to learn. I've been working for a few years now to let go of the hurts from my past, to retrain how I think about things. I want to see myself as you and Isobel and Ewan see me, not how my family saw me. Their opinions of me have no place in my life anymore. I'm no longer a mouse to terrorize. Perhaps if they hadn't interfered, I would have grown to love horses. I want to keep learning how to ride."

"And Boyd?" he asked. "Tell me what happened with him. Lewis said he was a degenerate."

She sighed, her stomach twisting like it always did when she thought of him. "'Tis true. I doona remember him much when I was a bairn because he was fostered to another clan, but he returned when I was about ten. For the first few years he was like my sisters, using his words to wound me. When my body began to change, he mocked me in the same way they did—called me fleshy—but as I got older, his attention changed. He was kind at first, brotherly, and I soaked up his attention like a needy puppy."

Gavin growled, and she laid a hand on his chest to calm him. To calm herself. "The first time he touched me in that manner, I was frightened, of course, and embarrassed to tell anyone. But I was also confused. I wanted to spend time with him because I suddenly had a place in the family and a champion against my sisters. I finally belonged. Thankfully, my nursemaid caught me crying the second time it happened and she told my tutor. They made sure I was ne'er within Boyd's reach again. I was sent to marry Lewis not long after that."

"He's a predator, Deirdre. You probably weren't the first girl he abused, and I'm sure he didn't stop when you left. He canna be allowed to terrorize any more lasses. I swore an oath to protect the innocent and bring peace to the Highlands. Boyd willna leave the battlefield alive."

She nodded. If not Gavin, someone else in her new family would dispense justice. That was how it was done in the Highlands.

He kissed her, then rose from their bed and moved to a washbasin on a stand near the window. The celebration was still going strong and would go all day, most likely. That would be good, as then no one would be able to hear her lusty screams.

She crossed her arm over her eyes—mortified. "I was verra loud."

When he didn't respond, she peeked around her arm to see him grinning at her as he washed himself with a small, linen cloth. She was surprised—and intrigued—to see his body was still aroused. Maybe not as much as before, but…enough?

She sat up as he poured fresh water over a new cloth and returned to her. He sat on the bed and pushed her back down. "Aye. I liked your screams." He kissed her and then laid the wet, cold cloth on her mound.

She sucked in a startled breath and clenched his hand, discomfited but also excited. "Gavin!"

"Deirdre!" He began stroking her with the cloth.

"I can do it," she moaned, bringing her thighs together over his arm.

"I *want* to take care of you. Doona be embarrassed. It pleases me to see my seed mixed with your maiden's blood. Not that your virginity would have mattered to me, except that it meant you were unharmed in that way. And you were experiencing everything new with me."

She sighed and lay back, let him stroke her, arouse her. "Not everything."

His hand stilled on the inside of her thigh, and she rolled her hips in protest. "How do you mean?" he asked. His tone was carefully neutral. Too neutral.

She grinned this time and then placed her hands on her body. "I'll show you." She stroked them over her breasts, pinching and rolling her sensitive nipples between her thumbs and fingers before scraping her nails over them.

His breath caught, and she peered through her lashes to see his eyes rapt on her hands. She trailed them lower, slid them down her belly, and pushed her fingers through her curls to play, slowly dipping into her warm, wet crevice.

"Do you…finish?" he asked, his voice cracking

when she bent one knee and let it fall open for better access—and to see his reaction.

"Of course I do. What would be the point otherwise?" Her finger slid all the way down to her opening, her breath catching now, and then back up to circle the hidden nub. And again.

After the third time, his hand pressed on top of hers, stopping her movement, and she could feel it trembling. He raised his gaze to hers, his eyes bright and his skin flushed. The pulse beat frantically at the base of his throat. "Do you think of someone when you do this?"

She smiled, loving the freedom and excitement she was feeling—freedom to say anything she wanted. She reached up with her free hand and wrapped it around his nape, then pulled him down to her. He groaned and came willingly, releasing her other hand as he moved between her spread knees.

She slid her fingers into his hair, playing with the short strands. "Just one time."

"Who was it?" He pushed her breast up, then gently nipped it. "And it better have been me. I want you to tell me exactly what we were doing."

She laughed with a breathy moan and cradled his head to her. "Aye it was you, and you were doing exactly this—except you were tupping me at the same time."

His eyes jumped to hers. "Do you want me to do that? I doona want to hurt you, if you're sore."

"Aye, Gavin. I want you to."

He kissed her again and then skimmed his hand to her hip and positioned her at a better angle. He slid inside her easily this time, closing his eyes and shuddering as he did so.

He huffed out a breath and opened his eyes again when he was all the way in. "Are you alright, love?" he asked, his voice strained.

"Aye, Husband. I'm better than alright." She wrapped her arms around his back and then kissed the front of his bulging shoulder. He was so big everywhere. Strong and powerful, and he'd fight to the death to protect her and their children.

She couldn't get enough of him.

When he began to move inside of her, his strokes long and steady, she kissed and nibbled across to his other shoulder. Instead of a kiss this time though, she bit it and laved his skin with her tongue.

He grunted, cupped her breast in one of his big hands, and suckled it. She dropped her head back and moaned.

He made love to her like that for what seemed like forever, content to play with her breasts and tup her slowly, steadily. The heat spread outward from her center as tension coiled within. When she began to lose control, he slowed down.

"Gavin!" she groaned.

He kissed up her neck to her ear and sucked the lobe into his mouth.

"Oh!" she cried out.

"You're not the only one who's imagined us together, dearling," he whispered in her ear, then traced the inside with his tongue.

"Verily?"

"Aye."

"What were we doing?"

"Some of the times we were doing this." He

continued his controlled rhythm down below while he played with her breasts and kissed and nibbled her mouth.

"And the other times?" she panted.

"It usually depended on what body part of yours I'd just seen. Although after I saw you in your shift, I imagined everything all at once."

"My shift? But you canna see anything!"

"You can when it's dark and the candle's behind you."

"Nay!"

"Aye."

A wolfish grin crossed his face, and he kissed her before withdrawing from her body and rolling her over onto her stomach.

"Oh!" She squirmed.

He stretched out beside her. "*Oh* is right."

She immediately wanted to roll back and cover her arse, but his hand had cupped her backside, and God's blood it felt good.

"I've spent a lot of time thinking about your bottom," he said.

He squeezed, kneaded, and stroked her curves, brushed her hair to one side, and kissed his way down her spine to the dip above her arse. Soon she was arching her back and moaning and panting, just like before. His fingers trailed along her sex from behind and she spread her legs, rocking her hips off the bed, seeking more of his hand and fingers.

"Aye, that's it, love." He rolled her onto her side and fit snugly behind her, pulling her top leg over his thigh. He dropped his head into the crook of her neck, slid his hand down the front of her body, and pushed himself inside.

She screamed louder this time.

Twenty-One

Gavin clasped Deirdre's hand behind him as he led her down the steps to the great hall. Midafternoon light poured through the windows set high in the stone walls, and the room was empty of people—unusual, even if the midday meal was over.

He stopped near the bottom, and Deirdre leaned against him from behind, peering over his shoulder. The feel of her breasts pressed against his back and the scent of her lavender soap from their bath earlier set his body stirring…again. Maybe they should turn around and go back to their bedchamber? They'd been locked in for almost a day and a half. That wasn't nearly enough time with his new wife.

"Where is everyone?" she asked.

"I doona know. They obviously aren't expecting us for another few days. 'Twas madness for us to leave the bedchamber." He turned around and tried to usher her back up the stairs, but she just wrapped her arms around his neck and giggled.

"I want to see Ewan. We can go back afterward." She slid her hand along the front of his plaid and squeezed that part of him that seemed perpetually aroused around her. "Besides. It feels like you need time to recover."

"I can do that just as easily upstairs with you naked beside me."

"Gavin, we need some air! We've been tupping like rabbits in there for the last day and a half."

"And whose fault is that?" he asked.

"Yours," she said, laughing. "Let's go up to the turret. You can press me up against the wall like we did before. That way we can get fresh air, sunlight, *and* exercise at the same time. Ewan's probably napping now anyway."

He slid his hands down to that rounded arse he couldn't get enough of and squeezed. "Mmmm. Or you could brace yourself against the battlements and look at the view as I swive you from behind."

"I doona know whether to be aroused or horrified by that! You could knock me right over the edge."

"Not a chance, Wife." He grasped her hand and stepped around her, leading her back up the stairs.

"We can look through the magnifying glass Master O'Rourke left up there—after you've tupped me, of course. Maybe we'll be able to see Gregor and your foster brothers."

The small hairs on his body stood up, and he came to an abrupt halt. "Master O'Rourke was in the turret?"

Her smile faded at the change in his tone and demeanor. "Aye. I saw him in the bailey the same day your family arrived. I followed him up."

"By yourself?"

She nodded. "Gavin, what's wrong?"

"My men didn't stop him? Or question him?"

"Nay. There was only one guard at the main door, and he let him in without delay. The master builder was in the turret by himself. I thought he was looking at the cathedral. But…"

"But what?"

"I surprised him, and he was angry. He tried to hide it, but I could tell. I thought it was because the cathedral roof was cracked, that he was worried and embarrassed by the work."

Gavin's heart pounded at the danger she might have been in, and he squeezed her close. He could have lost her before she was even his.

"Maybe that's all it was. Let's go up to the turret and see what he was doing." He drew his sword, making her gasp. "Doona worry, love. 'Tis probably nothing. But stay behind me just in case and do whate'er I tell you."

He passed her a candle from a wall sconce and took one in his free hand for himself. The need to hurry rode him hard, but he refused to leave Deirdre behind.

He also needed to know his son was safe. They exited the stairwell on the next floor. Deirdre nudged his back, and he gave in to the urge to race down the hall to the nursery. The door was closed, and he pushed it open without a sound, his heart pounding. Deirdre leaned in beside him. Her breath came in sharp gusts as they peered inside.

Ewan was tucked into bed, fast asleep, a toy warrior clutched in his hand. Beside him, Annag sat in a wooden chair, her sewing forgotten in her lap as she also slept, her head resting against the chair back.

Deirdre let out a relieved sigh, and he wrapped his arm around her shoulder before quietly closing the door.

He squeezed her tight for a moment, then kissed her forehead. "Let's go."

They retraced their steps to the stairwell and continued upward. The door at the top was barred shut, and after placing their candles back in the wall sconces, Gavin cautiously opened it. The only thing that attacked them was the wind, and he sheathed his sword.

"Your hair," he said to her.

She tucked her long locks under her plaid and raised the hood, then followed him onto the turret, holding her plaid tight to her body.

"It's here, Gavin."

She picked up a large magnifying glass from the top of the merlon. It looked heavy, and he took it from her carefully. "Where was he when you first saw him?"

"Right here," she said, "but facing outward."

"In what direction?"

"Toward the cathedral, and he was holding up the glass."

Gavin handed it back to her. "Close your eyes and picture him when you first came through the door. Show me his exact position and exactly how and where he held the glass."

She turned around and closed her eyes. She was still for a minute and then shifted her position and her arms several times.

Finally, she stopped. "Like this."

He moved behind her and then bent his knees, so he was at the master builder's height, and looked out. It was close, but Deirdre wasn't angled toward the cathedral. Nay, she was shifted slightly to the left, facing the forest in the distance, and the glass didn't seem to be at an angle useful for anyone to peer through. Nay, it was held too low to see the cracks in the cathedral roof.

He kissed Deirdre's head as he straightened, then took the glass from her and stepped toward the battlements. A cold fury grew in his chest as he lifted the glass and looked toward the sun. Then he caught the sun's rays on the polished surface and winked them toward the forest.

Deirdre gasped beside him. "You're signaling by reflecting the sun." She looked toward the forest. "Isn't that in the direction of the quarry?"

"Aye," he said, sounding grim. He was coiled in anticipation, expecting a flash of light from the forest to confirm his suspicions—that the master builder was a spy, and he was secretly communicating with someone, maybe even an awaiting army, in the forest near the quarry. Beside him, Deirdre also appeared to be waiting on tenterhooks.

After a few minutes with no response, she sighed. "Maybe he was just looking at the cathedral roof? He could have turned just before I came out."

"Maybe." Gavin changed position and looked at the roof through the glass, easily seeing the cracks Deirdre was referring to. One way or another, it was bad—O'Rourke was either a spy or an incompetent master builder and had to be dealt with. "I need to speak to him now." He put down the magnifying glass.

"I'll come with you," she said, grasping his hand. "I can question him about the roof and simple mathematics and geometry. If he's who he says he is, he should know the answers to my questions."

"Nay, I need you to stay here. If he's volatile or has men with him, you may be in danger. We'll bring him back to the castle and you can speak to him here, aye?"

She nodded, then threw herself into his arms. "Be careful."

"I will, lass. I'll take men with me." He squeezed her close. "In the meantime, I need you to stay up here and keep signaling with the glass toward the forest to see if we get a response. Understand? That will tell us immediately if O'Rourke is a spy and the direction our enemy is most likely hiding."

"Aye."

"If you feel you have to leave, go to our bedchamber or the nursery and bar the door until I come for you. I'll send messages to Gregor and my brothers. I canna imagine they went far. They should be back soon." He cupped her face and kissed her, pressing their lips together for a long moment. "We'll finish what we started up here when I get back, aye?"

She nodded again, and he could see her chin trembling as she tried to smile through her upset. He kissed her again, briefly this time. "I love you, Deirdre. I'll return soon." Then he turned and didn't look back—or he never would have been able to leave.

He drew his sword once he was on the stairs. As he got to the bottom and entered the great hall, several of his men, including Clyde, were entering the keep.

"I need five men," Gavin commanded. "We're going to the cathedral."

"Aye, Laird," Clyde said. He signaled the guards to

take their positions within the keep as he waited for Gavin by the door.

One of the guards eyed Gavin's sword as they passed each other. "'Tis just a precaution," Gavin said. "I doona know yet if anything is amiss."

The man nodded and took his position by the foot of the stairs that led to the upper levels, also drawing his sword.

Gavin skirted the remaining group of guards rather than walking through them as he hurried to the outside door, a habit trained into him by Gregor.

"Did you know the master builder was in the keep?" Gavin asked as he approached Clyde. "Deirdre spoke to him up on the turret a few days ago. I want to know who was on guard that day and why he was the only guard in the keep."

"I'll find out what happened," Clyde said as he opened the door and held it for Gavin. "Are you expecting trouble?"

"Aye. But keep it between us for now." Gavin stepped to the side and waited for Clyde to go down the stairs first—another precaution Gregor had instilled in him. "We have a spy in our midst, maybe several, and I intend to rectify it. My wife and son are in the keep. Naught can happen to them."

"Not to worry, Laird," Clyde said. "We'll make sure they're taken care of."

Deirdre held up the glass and winked the sun's rays off it toward the forest until her arms ached. No one had yet returned the signal. She laid the glass on the merlon before she dropped it and looked toward the cathedral. It pained her to know the cracks were there and to think of how many years of work would be lost when they had to tear down the dome and start again.

Not just time lost, but money too. Although, unlike when she was living at Lewis's keep, money did not seem to be a problem. Aye, the MacKinnons were a wealthy clan, and Gavin was the pinnacle of that.

Not that she cared. He could have been a farmer and she would have been ecstatic to be his wife. The joy and pleasure she'd found in his arms had left her dazed and greedy for more. This feeling between them truly was a gift, and she'd told him so many times since they'd been locked in their bedchamber together—usually when she was in the throes of passion, which had been often.

Any worries she'd had about Gavin finding her unattractive had been alleviated. Aye, the man couldn't keep his hands, mouth, or eyes off her. And any worries *he'd* had about her receptiveness toward him and enjoyment of their physical intimacy had been quashed. Loudly.

Movement below caught her eye, and she looked down to see six men on horses riding from the castle toward the cathedral. Relief rushed through her to see her husband wasn't alone. She picked up the glass and peered through it toward them. Aye, that was him, and it looked like Clyde with him. She would have been happier if Gregor and his brothers were there, but they would return as soon as they received Gavin's message.

Raising the glass, she looked again at the cracks in the cathedral, trying to imagine the corresponding weakness from inside the dome. Where were the stress fractures coming from? Arches were all about even distribution of weight, and if the stones weren't laid in a uniform manner, the whole thing would eventually come tumbling down.

She sighed and lowered the glass to rest her arms again. Gavin's group were over halfway to the cathedral. She'd better go back to her signaling, not that she thought anything was going to come of it. She suspected the master builder was not truly a master builder—and might never have the talent to be one—but she doubted he was a traitor.

Lifting the glass, she pointed it toward the forest and caught the sun's rays again, signaling to all the birds, deer, and wild boar that lived there. She glanced over at Gavin and his men, who were almost at their destination.

She'd just turned her head back to the trees in the distance and decided to rest her shaking arms, when a flash of light sparked at her from the forest. Deirdre's breath stilled in her lungs.

A spy. The master builder was a spy!

"Gavin!" she yelled at the top of her lungs, but the wind whipped her words away. "Gavin, stop! He's a spy! Stop, Gavin!"

It was as if the blustery gusts were laughing at her, howling in glee and eating up her cries. Terrified, helpless tears poured down her face. "Gavin!" she tried again.

The riders were almost there. Deirdre picked up the magnifying glass and turned it on the cathedral so she could see them. She tried to focus on the men below, but she'd pointed it too high, and her arms were shaking.

Something on the roof caught her eye as she was panning toward the door, and a chill ran down her spine. She tilted the glass higher for a closer look and gasped. An archer was crouched on the cathedral roof, an arrow nocked in his bow, pointed at Gavin and his men.

Below, the riders were dismounting.

"Gavin," she sobbed quietly this time, knowing she couldn't do anything to stop the attack. "I love you," she whispered as he entered the cathedral with three of his men. Two of them stayed outside to guard the door.

Moments after it closed, the first guard crumpled to the ground, an arrow in him, followed by the other warrior seconds later.

Deirdre's muscles gave way and she screamed in horror. The heavy magnifying glass slipped from her hands. It hit the stone floor with a crash, chunks of glass scattering everywhere.

The noise and sharp pain of glass bouncing off her leg shocked her into action, and she ran for the door. Gavin was a strong fighter. Maybe he and the others could hold off the enemy until reinforcements came.

She yanked open the door and ran into what felt like a stone wall. Stumbling back, she looked into the face of the guard who had stared so brazenly at her breasts the other day.

The same smirk he'd worn then covered his face now. "Lady Deirdre. Imagine meeting you here. All alone."

Her stomach curdled in the same way it had when she was thirteen and her brother had trapped her in one of the stairwells at their childhood keep. She ignored it. "Please, there's been an attack at the cathedral. I saw it happen from up here. Two of the guards were shot!"

"Good. Just as we'd hoped." His eyes lingered, hot and lewd, on her chest.

She crossed her arms over herself protectively as she'd done before and retreated several steps. This man, this…blackheart, was part of it! He would do nothing to help Gavin.

The traitor stepped onto the turret and shut the door behind him with a sickening smile. "Your brother wants you alive, Lady Deirdre, and I can guess why. He's twisted, that one. We've played together before." The man shoved his hand under his plaid as he talked, his arm jerking.

Deirdre looked around frantically for a way out, but there was only one door, and the ground was a very long way down.

The traitor grinned at her distress. "Good thing is, I've got a partner, aye, and he has a job to do before we leave. So you and I have some time together."

"What is your partner doing?" she whispered, dread twisting through her belly like a snake.

"Laird MacIntyre wants Gavin MacKinnon's son dead. He wanted you dead too, but your brother fought for you. Unfortunately, he didn't fight for Ewan. Pity, really. He's such a bonnie lad. He would have been fun to play with too."

He took his dirty hand out from under his kilt,

which stuck out at a lewd angle. But Deirdre didn't care. Nay, she had only one thought on her mind now. Her son.

The lion inside her roared, and she dropped to her knees.

Twenty-Two

GAVIN GRIPPED HIS SWORD LOOSELY IN HIS HAND AS HE stepped into the cathedral. He'd left two of his men outside to guard the door. Sheamais had gone in first, Gavin next, Lorne and Clyde following to guard his back. It felt appropriate to have these warriors by his side—all three had been with him when he'd taken Lewis's keep and found Deirdre and Ewan. Clyde had been his father's second-in-command before he was Gavin's second-in-command, and the bond between the MacKinnon men was strong.

The cathedral was empty and quiet. Still, every hair on Gavin's body raised in anticipation of an attack. His heart rate picked up pace, but he was calm and in control—and aware of everything around him, from where the stones and tools lay on the floor and against the walls to the layout of the building and the locations of the exits.

"Master O'Rourke," he called out. No one answered. Had O'Rourke already fled? He scanned the empty cathedral again, feeling uneasy. Something was off with the room, but he couldn't put his finger on what.

They spread out in the open area. "Master O'Rourke!" he called again. "It's Laird MacKinnon. I'm here to speak to you."

He moved toward the temporary wooden stairs, gesturing for Sheamais to take the lead and climb in front of him. Clyde and Lorne moved in the opposite direction. He should have brought more men, but not many warriors had been left in the castle since the patrols had been stepped up.

And he hadn't wanted to leave Deirdre and Ewan underprotected.

"Master O'Rourke!" he yelled a third time. Finally, he heard footsteps, and O'Rourke appeared at the top of the stairs.

"I'm up here," he said, sounding sullen.

"Come down," Gavin commanded.

"Nay, you come up."

Sheamais stiffened. "How dare ye speak to—"

Gavin squeezed his shoulder, and the warrior stopped talking.

O'Rourke jumped his gaze from one man to the other, then shrugged. "Come up and I'll show you the cracks in the ceiling. That's why you're here, isn't it? Your wife is concerned about the stability of the arches?"

"That's one of the reasons. Come down, Master Builder."

"Nay. I willna come down just to be dismissed. You come up and I'll show you what's happened and why. 'Tis not all my fault—I inherited the problem from Master Cameron. My problem was I thought I could fix it without tearing everything apart."

"You went into my keep. Up to the tallest turret."

"Aye. So I could see the damage from the outside."

"Why didn't you come to me? Ask me?"

"You were occupied, and your guard let me in. Both times."

The man had been in Gavin's keep, near his son, his wife, and his sister at least twice? "Who was the guard?"

"I doona know his name. I told him what I wanted, and he let me in. If that's a problem, then speak to him about it. Not me."

Gavin gritted his teeth. This man could test the patience of a saint. "Come up to the castle with me. I want you to identify him."

"First you come up here, so I can explain the problem. I want to show you the cracks and then have you look at the diagrams. They're spread out over the tables up here, and I doona want to gather them up and carry them down. No one is here to help me with them—the men have seen the cracks and they've left. 'Tis bad fortune for them to be associated with a crumbling cathedral. I would have left too, but they stole my coin." He turned and retreated into the second level.

"Master O'Rourke! Master Builder!" Gavin yelled, but the damned man didn't answer.

He caught Clyde's eye, and the man shrugged. "It sounds reasonable enough but be cautious. Do you want us to stay down here until the two of you are up the stairs?"

Gavin peered around the room again. Something was not right. "Go check on the men at the door. See if they've seen or heard anything."

Clyde nodded. "Aye, Laird." He moved to the

door, light on his feet for such a large man, sword held at the ready. He stepped outside for a few moments while Gavin, Lorne, and Sheamais held their positions inside.

"Be ready for anything, lads," Gavin said. "I doona trust a word that comes out of that man's mouth."

"He's a sullen *ablach*, that's for sure," Lorne said, crossbow at the ready.

Clyde reentered the cathedral. "They havenae seen nor heard anything. Do you want me to go up first?" he asked.

Gavin shook his head. "Nay. Follow us afterward. Sheamais, go cautiously. I'm right behind you."

"Aye, Laird."

Sheamais started up the long set of stairs. When he was about a third of the way, Gavin began to climb after him. He scanned the area below as he climbed. Clyde and Lorne had taken up defensive positions on the opposite side of the room, and Lorne was in a good spot, but Clyde was not—which was unusual. He was too close to Lorne to be as effective as he could be.

Gavin was about to whistle and signal Clyde to reposition himself when he understood what was strange about the walls. From this angle and height, he could see that the dimensions of the room were off. Was the inside of the cathedral smaller than the outside?

Realization hit, and a pit formed in his belly. God's blood, was it a false wall? Was something or someone behind it? Several someones?

He whistled sharply for everyone to retreat just as he heard an arrow release. "Get down!" he yelled. But he was too late. Sheamais was shot through the throat. "Arrows!" Gavin cried out.

Lorne found cover and released a cross bolt high above into the ceiling. A man fell from a rafter and landed with a sickening crunch on the stone floor.

Gavin whistled again to call the men outside, but they didn't appear. He raced to the bottom of the stairs. When he drew near, a hidden door in the wall swung outward, pushing aside a wooden trestle with a half-empty bucket and tools on top—placed there, no doubt, to hide the door.

How many enemy warriors had been hiding within the cathedral so close to his castle and his family? And for how long?

How did I not see it?

Men poured out of the hidden space behind the false wall as well as through the front door, their weapons raised. Gavin turned and raced up the stairs again.

He was almost at the top when he saw Clyde step in behind Lorne.

And he knew.

"Clyde, nay!" But Clyde raised his sword and stabbed it through Lorne's back in a single, smooth, deadly blow.

Gavin's blood raged. His enemies were approaching him from the top of the stairs now as well. Clyde watched him grimly from behind Lorne, who was in his final death throes.

Gavin had only one choice—to jump. And it was too long a drop.

He stared at Clyde. Four good warriors dead because of this man, a woman about to lose her husband, a son about to lose his father. He sent a silent signal to Clyde with his hand, one that the traitor recognized immediately.

Death. Clyde's death.

Gavin sheathed his sword and jumped.

He did everything he could to soften his landing—loosening his limbs so he collapsed, rolling out of the fall—but still his arm snapped, and his head bashed hard onto the stone.

He pushed himself up to run for the door, but he lurched sideways and crashed back down, unable to balance. Blood poured down his face. He wiped it out of his eyes and tried again, but barely got two steps before he collapsed.

He saw the men coming for him, boots surrounding him. Then Gavin slipped into darkness.

Deirdre knelt on the cold stone floor, her hands touching the ground beside her, her eyes lowered to her assailant's ankles. His hose was dirty, his boots cracked and stained with what looked like dried blood. A piece of broken glass bit into her knee, and she slid her hand beneath her skirt to remove it.

She heard the clink of metal and knew without looking up that the dirty traitor who stood before her had twisted his sword and sporran behind him.

He intended to rape her. She intended to save her son. And her husband, if possible.

She would do whatever it took.

She looked up at him. Let the tears form in her eyes. "Please."

His face shone with excitement. "Aye, you'll please me. And your wee fucking cunt mouth."

She pressed her thumb to the sharp edge of the glass in her hand and focused on the bite of pain as it sliced into her skin, rather than on what was to come.

He stepped closer, lifting his plaid, and the smell of him almost made her gag. She turned her head away. He grabbed her hair, twisted it in his hand and yanked her toward him. She fell forward and braced herself on his thighs as he laughed.

"Open your goddamn mouth!"

He twisted her hair again, and the anger and rage that burst through her gave her the strength she needed. She swung the chunk of glass, sliced hard up high on his inner thigh, cutting as deeply as she could.

He cried out in pain and stumbled backward. His cut leg crumpled beneath him, and he fell to one knee. She jumped up and ran the few steps toward him, swinging the shard of glass again and again, slicing over his neck, face, and chest. Her lion had claws.

He fell to the side, his hands squeezing his throat as blood poured between his fingers. She dropped the glass, raced past him to the door, and yanked it open. She forgot to get her candle as she raced inside, the stairwell darker than Hades. Her hands were slippery on the wall, and she realized she was covered in blood.

The blood of the man she'd killed.

And she'd do it all over again to save her son. To save Gavin. A sob burst through her lips.

God, please, let them live!

She reached the floor the nursery was on, lifted her skirts, and ran faster than she'd ever run in her life toward Ewan's door. What if he and Annag weren't there? What if she couldn't find them? Or if the guard's partner was already in there with them?

She wanted to yell out, scream their names, but she also didn't want anyone to know she was coming—just in case.

The door to the room was closed. She opened it as quietly as she could and squeezed inside. Ewan was asleep on the bed—alive! And Annag too, mending clothes in a chair by the window.

And no one else.

She wanted to break down and cry, hold her son close, but she didn't have time. She quickly shut the door and pushed the bar across. It was thick and heavy, and the bolts that held it in place were secure.

"Deirdre?" Annag called out.

She ignored the nursemaid and pressed her ear against the door, listening for someone on the other side. For footsteps or voices. Or hooves, as far as she was concerned. These men were the devil's helpers, here to murder innocent children.

Annag rose from her chair and shuffled toward her. "Lass, what's the trouble?"

Deirdre turned to her, and Annag let out a startled scream.

"Shhhhhh, Annag."

"You're covered in blood! Where's Gavin?" She patted down Deirdre frantically.

"It's not my blood. Gavin—" Another sob burst from her lips and she covered her mouth, tears streaming down her face. She used her sleeve to wipe them away, and the white linen came away smeared with red. "He went to the cathedral. Archers shot his men. They're coming for Ewan!"

"Child, what are you talking about? Slow down and start from the beginning."

Her mind tumbled around like a sapling caught in a winter storm, and she couldn't think of where to start. "The master builder is a spy, and there are others in the keep. At least two—one was a guard downstairs, a warrior. I killed him, I think, up on the turret. The other one is coming here to kill Ewan on Laird MacIntyre's orders."

Annag paled and leaned against the wall, her mouth drooping, her hands shaking. Deirdre wrapped her arms around the gray-haired woman and led her back to her chair.

"And Gavin? Isobel?" Annag asked, her voice barely above a whisper.

"I doona know where Isobel is—or the other lairds."

"The lairds are on a hunt. They left early this morning."

Deirdre nodded. So they wouldn't be too far away, then. "I watched from the turret as Gavin took men with him to the cathedral. I saw an archer on the roof and I tried to warn him, but he couldn't hear me." Her voice squeaked again, and she had to force the rest of the words out past her tight throat. "The guard arrived as I was leaving to get help. He told me about his accomplice coming here."

"The one you killed?"

"Aye."

"Oh, lass. What did he do to you?" Annag asked, sounding heartbroken.

"He did naught to me before I sliced him with broken glass." She jerked with her hand like she was killing him all over again. Right. Left. Right. Bile rose in her throat, and she forced it down, along with a wave of dizziness. "I have to go to Gavin. He might still be alive. Maybe he and the others are pinned down inside." She jumped up and ran back to the door to listen.

She'd just taken a step toward Annag when the door handle scraped quietly, and someone pushed on the wood. She spun back, her gaze on the barred entrance, her body frozen. When he tried a second time, Deirdre leaned on the door with her hands, even though the heavy bar held him out.

He knocked quietly, and then louder a few moments later. "Lady Deirdre? Annag?" a man called softly through the door.

She backed away as silently as she could. Annag rose from her chair, and the women stood side by side, staring in horror at the door.

"I'm too late," Deirdre whispered, her body shaking with sobs. "I canna get to him now. I canna leave. Gavin will die."

Annag wrapped her arms around her. "Hush, Deirdre," she whispered. "There's another exit."

"Where?"

"A hidden stairwell from the nursery to the laird and lady's chamber. You can leave that way. Gavin would have told you, I'm sure, but you've both been…distracted."

More knocking at the door. A firmer voice. "Annag. Open the door. Your laird wants to speak to you."

Annag clasped Deirdre's hand and drew her toward

the far end of the nursery, behind the screen where a tub and chamber pot sat on the floor. The door was hidden so well behind the tub that Deirdre would never have seen it if Annag hadn't shown her directly.

"Doona forget to wash off the blood and change your clothes before you leave your chamber. And take some of Gavin's weapons with you. Look behind the tapestries secured to the wall."

"Aye." She hugged Annag and then stepped back toward Ewan, but Annag grasped her arm.

"Nay, you'll wake him. The longer he sleeps, the better."

Deirdre hovered on the precipice of doubt. How could she leave her child? But how could she not go to help her husband?

Annag grasped her other arm and looked her in the eye. "Deirdre, go save us. I will take care of Ewan. They'll have to chop down that door with an axe to get in. 'Tis not an easy task, and it will be loud and indiscreet. The only way they'll manage that is if they control the castle, and if that happens, I will hide with Ewan as long as I can in the stairwell. If you canna get to Gavin, get to Gregor or one of the other lairds. They willna allow the castle to be held by their enemy, especially with Ewan inside. Do you understand?"

She nodded. "Doona leave him in the dark by himself. He's frightened of the dark."

"I promise." She turned Deirdre toward the tunnel entrance. "When you get to the bottom, feel for a latch up high on the left. Pull it down and push inward. Go slowly and quietly until you know the room is clear."

"Aye." She refused to look back. If she did, she might not leave. "Tell Ewan how much I love him and how blessed I've been to be his mother."

"*You* will tell him. When you return."

Then Deirdre stepped into darkness.

Gavin woke to a sharp, obliterating pain in his head that made all the other pains in his body seem like scratches from a kitten. That said a lot, because he was pretty sure he'd broken his arm when he'd jumped. Only his training kept him still and quiet instead of shaking or crying out.

Where was he? The floor he was lying on was wood rather than stone. The top level? He tried to focus his eyes, but the light from the holes in the ceiling caused the pain to surge, and he almost vomited.

He heard men talking and tried to make out what they were saying, but it was just murmurs. He looked for them without giving away that he was awake, peering around the room through his eyelashes and keeping his head still.

There. Not too far away. Three men gathered around a table with their backs to him. He could see them gesturing to something laid out on the surface. A map, maybe? Or the layout of a castle? His castle?

He quelled the fear and nausea that rose when he thought about Deirdre and Ewan trapped in that castle. He couldn't think about them now. He had to focus on his present circumstances—something else Gregor had drilled into him.

He recognized two of the three men. Clyde, the

traitorous blackheart, and O'Rourke, the spying master builder who likely wasn't a master builder at all. Gavin should have been paying better attention over the last two years, but he hadn't been able to think about anything other than getting his son back. He'd left too many of his duties to other people without monitoring them.

He'd put his family and clan at risk!

The surge of anger at himself and his enemies made his heart pick up pace, and the blackness threatened to drag him under again. He calmed his breathing and closed his eyes until the wave passed, and then looked back at the third man. He was tall, with long, dark hair that looked like Kerr's, but his build was more like Callum's—long, lean, and strong. He had the stance of a good fighter.

The other men seemed to defer to him. Was that man the leader of the conspiracy against him and his allies?

He watched him, hoping the man would turn around, but he stayed bent over, studying the diagram. Going over his strategy to capture the MacKinnon castle, no doubt.

Gavin couldn't understand what his enemies thought that would accomplish. Gregor, Kerr, and the others would never allow them to keep the castle. They would rout the bastards out and dispense justice, even if it took years.

But their enemies had to know that. Obviously, they must have a plan to take out all the lairds at once. But how?

Gavin gritted his teeth in frustration as the darkness loomed up around him again. He tried to think quickly, to put the pieces together before the oblivion overtook him.

They had Clyde on their side. Gavin's warriors would listen to him—at least initially. They could lay an effective trap in the castle if they got their men in first.

God's blood—is that how they intend to do it?

He heard footsteps moving toward him. He tried to keep his eyes open, to see the face of his enemy, but it was too late.

His body took over, and he slowly sank back into darkness.

Deirdre clutched the mare's reins in her hands. She hid behind a loaded hay wagon near the wall, staring at the open, unmanned portcullis.

She'd watched the guard leave a few minutes ago, and no one had replaced him. And the castle was quiet. So very, very quiet.

What is happening?

Other than the fact that they were overrun with spies, of course.

She'd made it to her bedchamber after leaving Annag and Ewan and had quickly washed away the obvious blood and changed her clothes. When she'd peeked out the door, she'd been devastated to see one of Gavin's warriors at the top of the stairs, whispering with the man who had approached her at the village a few days ago. The one who'd offered to help return her to the MacIntyres.

Another traitor.

When the men had separated moments later, one

heading back down to the great hall and the other to the stairs that led up to the nursery, Deirdre had snuck into the hallway and raced to the stairwell at the opposite end that connected to the kitchens.

From there she'd crept to the empty stables and found the mare she'd ridden a few days ago already saddled—almost as though they had it waiting for her. Well, she hadn't been so easy to kidnap this time.

Now the exit was only a short walk ahead of her, but wouldn't the right thing to do be to raise the alarm? Surely the portcullis shouldn't be left open? They could be invaded!

Aye, that was the point, wasn't it? The portcullis was open and the castle empty so the enemy could come in unhindered. Had all the castle folk been murdered?

She wanted to get to Gavin, but she also wanted to secure the portcullis. She had to keep Ewan and Annag as safe as possible. The more enemy warriors who could penetrate the castle, the sooner he and Annag would be caught. She quickly tied the mare to the hay wagon and crept forward toward the guard station.

"Lady Deirdre!"

She jumped, her heart pounding, and clapped a hand over her mouth to keep from screeching.

"Och! I'm sorry, my lady. I didn't mean to scare you."

Turning, she looked into Father Lundie's concerned face. He'd only just come through the gate, riding into the castle on the back of Ewan's pony. She darted toward him and pulled him off Horsey. He yelped in alarm as she dragged him toward the empty guardhouse.

"I'm sorry, Father," she whispered, "but Laird MacIntyre and my brother have the castle under attack. Everyone is gone—or maybe killed, I doona know—and there are men inside intent on murder."

The priest paled and crossed himself. "Where is your husband, Lady? And the other lairds?"

Her chest cramped, and she scrubbed a hand over her face before answering. "Gavin took some men with him to the cathedral to talk to the master builder—another traitor. I was on the turret and I saw an archer kill the guards Gavin left outside the cathedral door. Another tried to take me and kill Ewan, but I killed the traitor instead. Ewan is safe for now, but I can only imagine that Gavin walked into an ambush."

Father Lundie made a distressed sound.

"I haven't seen the other lairds since yesterday," she continued, "but Annag told me they went hunting." She pointed toward the gate. "Look, Father. It's open and no guard. More men are about to come, I'm certain of it, and if they do, they'll find Ewan. But if I close the portcullis, how will I get out to save Gavin?"

Her voice broke at the end and he squeezed her hands. "Surely the other lairds—"

"Will get here in time? Will not be ambushed and killed once they ride under the gate? This has all been planned, Father. Someone is going to kill the lairds, Gavin, and my son unless we stop them now."

The priest closed his eyes, his lips moving as if in prayer. Deirdre wanted to shake him. This was a time for action, not reflection! She was about to tell him so when he opened his eyes. "What do you want me to do?"

"We need to close the gate. Permanently. Can you jam the portcullis so it stays down? I've read about them, I can show you how it works."

He smiled at her gently. "I understand about mechanical things, my lady. I grew up in a castle near Perth, and my father was a blacksmith. I helped him repair our portcullis on several occasions."

"How fortunate," she said, feeling heartened.

"Nay, not fortunate, Lady Deirdre. The Lord provideth. I'll need to hit the release latch and then jam something into the chain before the grill hits bottom. The timing will be the difficult part."

"You're certain?"

"Aye. And you, Deirdre? Are you certain? You are only one person—a fierce lion at heart, to be sure—but still only one against a cathedral full of enemy warriors. You willna be able to defeat them alone."

"I have to do *something*, Father. What if he's alive? What if I can save him and the others? Save Ewan? As you said, the Lord provideth."

"Aye, lass, that He does." He reached his arms behind his neck and unfastened a chain, then slipped his hands beneath her hair at her nape and refastened it. He lifted the pendant that hung at the bottom of the chain that now sat between her breasts. "'Tis Saint Michael the Archangel. He will give you strength and guide your way in this difficult task. Trust in him."

"Thank you, Father. And may he guide your hand too."

She hurried to the door, peeked out to make sure the way was clear, and then ran to the mare. After untying the horse, she said her first prayer. God knows she'd need every bit of help she could just to make the mare go where she wanted it to.

"Let's go, lass," she said as she put her foot in the stirrup and swung her other leg over the saddle. "I promise you that Thor will be at our destination."

The mare seemed to understand, and she trotted underneath the portcullis without much urging and then toward the cathedral. Deirdre didn't even look up. All she could concentrate on right now was keeping her feet in the stirrups and not falling off.

They were almost halfway toward the falling-down church when she heard the portcullis slam shut. For now, she had foiled the master builder's plan. Surely, Ewan and the other lairds were safer for it.

She and Gavin, however, were another matter.

"Your wife is coming."

No other words could have drawn Gavin out of the black abyss as quickly. They reverberated inside the cavern of his mind like a knock on the door to his consciousness, waking him.

He opened his eyes, then squinted against the bright light that still made his head pound. He let them adjust, and then once the pain had ebbed, he slowly looked in the direction of the voice. A man stood at the window, looking out. The same man from before, with the long, black hair. The one the others had deferred to.

"She's riding here by herself. She really must love you. Although, there's no one left at the castle she can ask to accompany her. I wonder how she made it out?"

Gavin pushed himself into a sitting position with

his good arm. His head swam, nauseating him, and he leaned back against the stone wall for support. He heard movement and cracked his eyelids. The man had turned to face him, but he was backlit by the window, and his face was in shadow.

"Who are you?" Gavin croaked.

"Does it matter? You'll be dead soon, along with your foster brothers and the great Gregor MacLeod." His voice held a note of mockery.

"And my son?" he croaked.

"Him too. I'm sorry for that. I doona like killing children, but Laird MacIntyre insisted. If it'll make you feel better, I intend to kill him as well. When the time is right."

Gavin closed his eyes, swallowing down the bile that had risen in his throat. "It doesn't. But I take pleasure knowing that my son is alive and safe—my wife would ne'er have left the keep otherwise. And he still will be when my brothers and the *Great* Gregor MacLeod take back my castle."

"Maybe. You've all proven to be worthy adversaries—smarter and stronger than I imagined. You thwarted my schemes against your foster brothers' clans, although the fault wasn't in my planning, but that I had to rely on weak men like Laird Fraser, Machar Murray, and Irvin Sinclair. They failed me."

Gavin stayed quiet, hoping the man would continue talking in case Gavin somehow managed to escape.

"I doona like it when things don't go according to plan. Your wife riding here—by herself—was not part of the plan. Her brother claimed she was naught but a frightened mouse."

"Not my Deirdre."

His captor made an approving sound in the back of his throat and turned around to look out of the window again. "I like her spirit. And she's lovely too. I hadn't seen her up close before. Maybe I willna give her to Boyd after all. Do you think if I took her with me, she could grow to love me like she does you? I'll let her keep your son, if he's still alive."

What a master game player this man was. He was like Callum, with his ability to understand people's deepest desires—and fears. Except Callum was a good, just man, and this one liked to get into people's heads and play.

"Naught to say, MacKinnon?" the man asked.

"Nay." He refused to give the conniver what he wanted.

The man shrugged, but Gavin could tell he was disappointed. Aye, he wanted to tie Gavin up in knots, and he'd succeeded.

"She's almost here," he said. "I'll bring her up to you afterward and give you some time together before you die. Maybe I'll make her watch while I kill you. It'll add an extra layer to *our* union—something for me to overcome. I like a challenge."

"You'll enjoy failing to defeat my brothers and Gregor, then. The same as before."

"I doona think so. This time I'm not relying on weak men."

"I wouldnae be so sure. Your plan is already coming apart."

He turned back around to Gavin, who squinted at him, trying to make out the details of his face.

"She's here," he said. "Would you like me to bring her up to watch you die or leave her below for my men?"

Gavin dropped his head back and closed his eyes, let all his emotion—the pain, fear, and devastation that roiled within him—show on his face. He gave the man what he desired. "It doesn't matter what I want. You've already decided." Maybe that would sway him into bringing Deirdre up here. Any additional time he had to heal, to wait for his brothers to come to their assistance, would be welcome.

Then he heard his wife's voice, and he couldn't stop the moan of despair that tore from his throat.

Twenty-Three

"Hello? Master Builder? It's Lady Deirdre! Are you here?"

Deirdre looked around the empty cathedral, trying to hold herself together. She'd infused a forced cheerfulness into her voice, but her throat was so tight now that she doubted she could do it for much longer.

Where is Gavin?

The two dead guards outside were gone, along with the six horses the men had ridden. Inside, rocks and sticky mortar covered the floor in big, messy piles. She even thought she saw blood in certain spots.

She swallowed, blinked her eyes dry, and called out again. "Hello? Is anyone here? Master Builder?"

"I'm here."

She turned and saw the sullen-looking master builder coming down the stairs. He had rock dust in his hair and on his clothes. "Good day, Master O'Rourke. I told my husband that I would meet him here. Have you seen Laird MacKinnon this morning?"

"Aye, he was here."

"Oh." Furrows of confusion marred her forehead. "Did he leave, then?"

"You could say that."

"What does that mean?" She almost yelled the question, her control slipping. "He wanted me to speak to you about the cathedral, to help determine the cause of the stress fractures."

He reached the bottom, maneuvered around some piles of rocks, and carried on toward her, not slowing his stride.

She stepped back nervously and continued talking—babbling, really. "I noticed when we were here earlier that some of the stones where set unevenly, so the weight is not being distributed properly. You'll have to remove all the blocks and re-mortar using—"

O'Rourke lifted his arm and hit her across the face with the back of his hand—so fast and hard she barely had time to defend herself. She screamed in shock and pain and fell backward onto the stone floor, scraping her elbow.

"Deirdre!" she heard Gavin call out faintly from upstairs.

"Gavin!" she yelled, pressing her hand to her jaw. The pretense was over, and she rose from the floor, grabbing some rocks—but O'Rourke shoved her back down and kicked her in the thigh.

She cried out again in pain, fear crawling up her spine as more men appeared—big, tough-looking men. What could she possibly do to save Gavin or to save herself? She was one woman against a room full of warriors.

O'Rourke yanked her up roughly. "What a stupid

besom you are, coming here to tell me what to do." He pushed his face into hers, his expression vicious. "Now we get to have some fun. And not just the men here. The new arrivals will surely want a piece of you too."

"Nay!" a voice commanded from the top of the stairs, and O'Rourke tensed. "Bring her here but blindfold her first."

O'Rourke ground his jaw, and she could hear a few rumblings from the gathered warriors. The force was at least twenty-strong down here, possibly more behind them and upstairs. A force large enough to overtake a castle in a sneak attack. She wondered if they knew yet that Father Lundie had jammed the portcullis.

Then O'Rourke grabbed the bottom of her skirt. Her momentary satisfaction fled, replaced by fear and panic. Were they going to rape her after all?

Instead, O'Rourke ripped off a long strip of wool from her hem, tying it roughly around her eyes. The band was tight, only the smallest crack of light visible at the bottom.

She was jerked forward and had a hard time staying upright as she was dragged across the debris-littered floor. The other men were closer now, voices louder and their talk crude. She tried not to listen and prayed again to Saint Michael for help to vanquish her enemies. Surely God would be on the side of peace and justice?

At the top of the stairs, she was transferred to someone else, whose grip was much gentler. "Lady Deirdre," the man said, his softer voice almost warm.

"Please, can I see my husband?"

"Aye, but, lady, you must know his death is inevitable. Use the time to say goodbye. I will save your son if I can and keep you safe, but Gavin MacKinnon will not survive this day. War does not treat women and children kindly, I'm afraid."

"Which is why my husband and his allies fight for peace and justice in the Highlands!"

"A noble cause, for sure, but I canna afford the luxury of being noble. I will make sure you're cared for, and your son too, but none of the lairds will survive today. Our forces are too strong."

He turned her away from him and placed his hands on her shoulders, pushing her forward step by step. "'Tis a brave thing you did, coming here. How did you get past my men?"

His men? So, he was the leader, the one who had sanctioned her return to Boyd and had given the go-ahead to murder Ewan. No matter how kind and remorseful he seemed to be now, she had to remember he was a blackheart of the worst kind.

"A man attacked me. I fought him off."

The blackheart's fingers tightened on her shoulders, and he pulled her back against him. His cheek rubbed gently across her hair, almost lovingly. She swallowed the bile that rose in her throat.

"Did you kill him?" he whispered.

"I doona know. I ran to find Gavin, but then I remembered he was coming here to speak to the master builder. No one was in the castle and the gate was up. It was easy to get out."

He loosened his fingers on her shoulders and rubbed them soothingly, then guided her forward.

"You may remove the blindfold when I'm gone. Say goodbye to your husband, Lady Deirdre."

She heard a door close behind her and the muffled sound of something being jammed against it. Deirdre shoved the blindfold back. She was in a large room with stone walls and a wooden floor. Gavin was slumped against the far wall.

"Gavin!" She ran to him. One side of his face and body was covered in blood. "Oh no. Oh no!" She put her fingers to his neck on the uninjured side and tried to feel for his pulse. For a minute she couldn't feel anything, but then the vein bumped beneath her fingers as his eyes fluttered open.

She laughed and cried at the same time and gently cupped his face in her hands. "You're alive, dearling! I was so worried about you."

He squeezed her hand. "I canna fight, Deirdre. I canna protect you. You shouldn't be here."

"Your arm?"

"It's broken, but that's not the problem. 'Tis my head. I'm concussed. I canna balance; I canna swing my sword. I canna even stay awake for more than a few minutes."

He tried to get up, and she forced him back down. "*I'm* taking care of *you* this time, Gavin MacKinnon. I have a plan."

"What can you do against them?"

"A lot. I've already saved Ewan and Annag, and enlisted Father Lundie to jam the portcullis, so the gate canna be lifted. And I rode that bloody mare all the way here."

He smiled and she leaned forward to kiss him.

"We're going to make it, Husband. Doona lose hope."

"If the gate is jammed, my brothers and Gregor willna be trapped inside and taken unaware. You'll be safe with them, *if* we can find a way for you to get out of here. You can raise Ewan." He placed his hand over her belly. "And maybe another bairn too. The MacKinnons will survive. Our family will survive."

She frowned at him. "*You* will survive."

Unfastening her plaid, she loosened her chemise and pulled out three of Gavin's daggers she'd found in their room, followed by a leather sheath that she'd fastened around her waist. Her breasts swung free near his face when she laid the weapons on the floor between them.

"If that doesn't get me up, nothing will," he said.

She snorted as she pulled up her skirt to unfasten another leather sheath wrapped around her thigh that held three more daggers. He laid his hand on her leg. "Nay, you keep that one. I'll just take an extra dagger."

He pulled a knife from the sheath on her thigh and gave it to her. "Put it in my left sock. And then tie the band tight at the top." He tugged her skirt back down. "This man will try to woo you—'tis a game for him. Ne'er forget, no matter what he might say or do, he is the enemy. And tell my brothers and Gregor that Clyde is a spy. He killed Lorne."

She closed her eyes as despair rose within her. When would the betrayal and lies stop?

After refastening her chemise and plaid, she reached for the leather sheath that she'd laid on his lap. She couldn't imagine it would fit around *his* waist. "Where does this go?"

He held out his broken arm. She raised horrified eyes to his. "I'll hurt you."

"Aye, but I'd rather be hurt than dead. It has to be this arm, so I can throw with my left."

"You can do that?"

"We train on both sides for exactly this reason."

She gritted her teeth and then strapped the dagger-filled sheath around his broken arm. He closed his eyes, clenched his jaw, and she almost wished he would pass out like he had before, if it would spare him the pain. When she finished, she kissed him. "I'm going to look for a way out. Can you move at all?"

He grimaced. "Slowly. I willna be any help to you."

"I need to get onto the roof."

"The roof? Nay!"

"Aye. I know where the structure is weakest. I can take out all of the warriors by loosening one stone."

"And what happens if you're on top of it? You'll go down too."

"I'll step back, Gavin."

His jaw worked furiously, and then his eyes slowly closed and his body went slack.

"Gavin!"

His eyes fluttered open moments later, and he slowly focused on her. "Was I out long?"

"A few seconds."

His brows lifted. "It's getting better then. Help me up."

"You need to rest."

"There's no time. Look—Master Cameron wanted

to leave spaces for stained-glass windows up here. Instead of shutters, he piled stones in the voids to keep out the wind and rain, but he didn't mortar them down. If we remove the rocks, we can see up to the roof, maybe find a safe way up."

"Where are they?"

"Help me up and we'll find them. Together, Deirdre."

She stared at him for a moment before she kissed him. "Aye."

Gavin breathed deeply and tried to calm his pounding heart as he stood up—with Deirdre's help. The blackness closed in on him, but he kept it at bay by sheer force of will. The nausea too. He pointed to the wall that faced the castle. If his brothers and Gregor were coming, he wanted them to see Deirdre on the roof and know something was wrong.

He leaned heavily on his wife, practically useless, and when they reached the wall, he ran his fingers over the rocks, trying to feel the change. "Here," he said.

She waited until he was leaning against the stone and then raced for a chair that was tucked under the table and brought it back for him to rest on.

"You're right!" she said excitedly as she wiggled a rock. "It is loose."

She'd pulled about half of the stones out of the window when the bar on the outside of the door slid open. Gasping, she turned to face the intruder. Gavin cradled his broken arm with his good hand. He leaned his head back, closed his eyes, and breathed deeply.

O'Rourke saw them and drew his sword. "You're dead, MacKinnon."

"Nay!" Deirdre cried as the spy marched toward them. She darted between him and Gavin, but the man shoved her out of the way.

'Twas all the distraction Gavin needed. He lunged forward into the master builder and shoved his dagger deep—a killing blow.

They fell to the floor. Gavin stayed on top of him as the man gasped for breath—and died a much quicker death than he deserved.

"Gavin!" Deirdre kneeled beside him.

He rolled toward her. "I'm alright. See if the bar can slide across on the inside."

She ran to the door. "It does!"

He heard her struggle with the heavy piece of wood, and when she cried out triumphantly, he smiled.

"'Tis not as strong as the castle doors, but it will give us more time. Can you move?" she asked as she returned to his side. She did not look at O'Rourke.

Gavin wanted to stay where he was, despite the body bleeding out beside him, but if anyone broke in and he was still on the floor, he'd be worse than useless. He nodded and she helped him back to the chair.

He closed his eyes again and leaned against her as she pulled the rest of the rocks out of the window. He knew he wouldn't see her again after this, and he breathed as much of her scent into his body as he could.

She would survive and raise their children—aye, he believed they'd already made another bairn—and eventually stop grieving him.

He kissed her waist and she held him close. "I love you, Gavin. You and Ewan are everything to me. We're going to survive this."

"I love you too, Deirdre. So much."

He rested back against the wall as she leaned out. "How much farther to the top?" he asked.

"I need to be higher. Another foot maybe."

"We'll use the chair back as a ladder. Help me up."

She brought him to his feet and then picked up the chair and fed it through the opening. The leg braces rested on the windowsill and gave it extra height.

"Tie your skirt between your legs. That's what Maggie does before one of her adventures. Then climb up on the sill using the back of the chair for balance. When you feel steady, use the rungs on the back as a ladder. I'll hold the chair in place. I willna fail you."

She nodded and then wrapped her arms around him. "I'll be back before you know it. The falling rocks will injure most of our enemy, and the others will be too afraid to stay. The crashing noise will surely bring your brothers and Gregor back to investigate."

His throat was too tight to reply. He kissed her head and nudged her to get going. When she tied up her skirts, he moved into position and she climbed up on the sill, as quick as a wee mouse. "Are you there yet?" he asked as she scaled the wall.

"Almost!"

"I'm going to lift the chair, Deirdre. Hold tight and climb over as soon as you're able."

"Nay, Gavin! I doona want you hurt."

"Climb, Deirdre!" He braced himself and used one arm to lift the chair. His pulse pounded in his temples as his muscles strained. "Go!" he grunted. Black began to encircle his vision. The weight lightened suddenly as Deirdre scrambled up, and Gavin crashed to the floor next to the dead man. The chair fell beside him. His last thought before darkness engulfed him was that he hoped he hadn't killed his wife.

Deirdre moved as quickly as she could toward the soaring arched roof. In her mind, she pictured the cracks she'd seen from both inside and outside the cathedral, and she knew exactly where to go. When she started to climb the dome, she slowed, carefully moving higher.

She let out a happy squeak when she spotted the crack, exactly where she thought it should be. Following the seam upward, she was careful not to step directly on it—not yet, anyway. At the pinnacle of the arch, she pulled out one of Gavin's daggers and began working down the cracks to loosen the mortar even more. Once at the bottom of the first crack, she moved to the second, then the third and fourth.

She was exhausted by the time she'd done them all, and it had taken much longer than she'd hoped. She moved back up to the very center, to the capstone. Her heart pounding and mouth dry, she began to loosen the key on which the arch was built.

It shifted!

She scrambled back toward the edge and waited… but nothing happened. She returned, digging out more of the mortar around the capstone. It shifted again, but this time she stayed where she was, fighting her urge to retreat to safety.

When it didn't shift far enough, she stabbed the knife into the crack, frustrated, angry, and afraid. Chunks flew out as she tried to dig deeper and harder, and she was sure the stone would fall through, but it didn't. Crawling right on top of it, she crouched low, her hands holding on.

She jumped on it.

The only warning was a soft, cracking noise. The capstone fell out, plummeting to the cathedral floor a hundred feet below, and the rest of the roof crumbled after it. Deirdre jumped back, trying to get to safety, and she tripped, tumbling down the side of the dome.

She would either go over the edge of the cathedral or fall through the widening hole in the center.

She no longer knew what was up, what was down, or where the edge was—suddenly she was falling through empty air, despair engulfing her.

This is it. My life is over. I love you, Ewan. I love you, Gavin.

She closed her eyes and was jerked out of the air, dragged against a big, hard body. Gavin fell to his knees, squeezing her tight, but he managed to keep them both on the outer ledge as the roof fell through to the floor before.

The crash was deafening. Surely the sound would travel for miles. The other lairds would hear it. She had won.

"We need to get down," Gavin said. "I canna balance for much longer."

She stood up carefully and then helped him up. God help them if, after everything they'd gone through, he fell at the last minute.

They skimmed the edge of the gaping hole cautiously, the stone beneath their feet no wider than the span of Gavin's hand, the rocks loose in places and uneven. She kept her eyes glued to her feet so she wouldn't miss a step—or see the piles of fallen rocks on the cathedral floor, knowing crushed bodies lay beneath.

Behind her, she squeezed Gavin's hand, hoping that would somehow keep him upright.

When they finally made it to safety, they collapsed on the section of the roof that hadn't fallen, arms wrapped around each other and trembling. Emotional tears mixed with the blood that covered Gavin.

"What happened?" she asked. "You're even bloodier than before."

"I doona know exactly. I think I blacked out after lifting you and fell into O'Rourke's blood that had pooled on the stones. When I awoke, both of us had been tossed outside a door onto the roof over there." He pointed toward a flat area. "The blackhearts must have broken into the room and assumed I was dead as well and disposed of me alongside him."

Deirdre snorted and then began to laugh and couldn't stop. Gavin laughed with her. It was either that or cry. They weren't out of the woods yet, but it felt safe up here in the moment. And surely reinforcements would come soon.

When the laughter finally faded, a heaviness settled in her heart. "Did you see if it worked? Were the… enemies still in the cathedral when the roof fell?" Her voice broke at the end.

How many people did I just kill?

He embraced her gently. "A good number of them were still inside, I think. I didn't see them leave. I canna imagine the remaining men will stay. You saved us, Deirdre. You saved Ewan and the rest of our family. You saved the MacKinnons."

She nodded, unable to speak. Finally, she released a big sigh and said, "Is it over, then?"

"Nay, I don't think so, but we canna do much until my brothers and Gregor arrive. O'Rourke was signaling from the turret toward the forest, not the cathedral. There may be more warriors waiting at the quarry. Once they're vanquished, we'll go to war with the MacIntyres and MacColls."

"He told me another wave of men was coming."

Gavin shuddered and pulled her close again. "I canna believe the danger you were in."

"And I canna believe how close I came to losing you and Ewan."

A horse whinnied down below, and a man appeared, riding at full speed toward the forest. His black hair streamed out behind him. Gavin rose to his feet and peered at him until he was indistinguishable. "That's the head of the snake," he said. "The man behind all of this—and the attacks against my brothers." He swayed on his feet and she helped him down. "Did you see his face?" he asked.

"Nay. They blindfolded me. I'm surprised more people aren't escaping with him."

Gavin sighed. "He's attacked us before. And when the attack fails, he always kills any witnesses, even if they're his own men. I suspect he's done the same here so no one can identify him or speak of his future plans."

They fell quiet, just holding each other, amazed to be alive, stealing a moment of joy and contentment.

"Are you feeling better?" she asked.

"I am, but I'll leave the fighting up to my brothers and Gregor for the next week. I've seen how deadly head wounds can be."

"We can lie in bed and recuperate together."

He pushed back her hair and kissed the side of her neck. She could feel his smile against her skin. "I was hoping you'd say that."

A low, distant rumbling slowly increased in intensity until she felt it shaking through her bones and muscles. They looked over to see a group of riders racing toward them from the direction of the castle.

She tensed, and Gavin rubbed his cheek on the top of her head. "Doona worry, love. 'Tis Gregor and the lads. Shall I tell them to go home? I doona need their help, because you've already saved me—saved all of us."

"How could I not? You were all worth saving. Besides, 'tis what a lion does."

"You know what else a lion does?" He pulled her closer and began nibbling on her ear.

She shivered. "Lays about in the sun all day?"

"Aye, that too. Preferably without any fur on."

Deirdre laughed and then sighed. "Chases off all the other lion lasses?"

"There are no other lion lasses to chase off. Ever."

"What does she do with her time, then?"

"She kisses her mate."

Now it was her turn to smile against his skin. "Aye, love. I can do that."

Epilogue

Two months later…

Laird Boyd MacColl's lifeless body hanged from a rope looped around his neck in the middle of his bailey at Castle MacColl. Gavin estimated he had been there for two days at least, and the crows and rats had begun to feast on his dead flesh.

It was a fitting end for a deviant who'd preyed on young girls.

By all accounts, he'd been imprisoned and then executed by his eldest sister's husband when Boyd had come crawling home weeks ago.

Alone.

Somehow, he'd managed to escape murder at the hands of the master conspirator and scurry away from the battle in the quarry.

Or so Gavin's foster brothers and father had told him.

Gavin had been relegated to his sickbed for weeks after he'd been injured at the cathedral, and he'd missed the battle that had really been more of a rout. His men and allies had descended upon the quarry in force, and they'd all but obliterated several hundred MacIntyre warriors hidden there. They'd tried to take Laird MacIntyre alive, but he'd already been killed by a dagger in the back.

As soon as he'd been well enough to fight, Gavin and the other lairds had marched on Clan MacIntyre. Even without their laird, the warriors had fought well, sealing up the castle.

Gavin and his allies had endeavored to defeat them with as little carnage as possible—and they'd succeeded.

A gust of wind swung Boyd's body, dislodging the crows, and Gavin clenched his jaw as a another burst of rage hit him. He wanted to kill the man all over again for the things he'd said and done to Deirdre when she was a child. And he wouldn't have hanged him. Nay, Gavin would have dispensed justice by taking Boyd's head—after every person in his clan had had the chance to bear witness, if they wanted, to his crimes.

A woman approached him, and he knew who it was immediately, but he couldn't dredge up a smile—not after the way Deirdre's family had treated her and the damage they'd done.

"Laird MacKinnon, dear brother," she said. "I'm Muireall, Deirdre's eldest sister. 'Tis good to finally meet you."

She bowed her blond head and curtseyed perfectly, which soured his stomach further. He wouldn't take her head for the cruelties she'd imposed upon his wife, but he wished his sister, Isobel, were here to teach the viper a lesson.

When she raised her eyes, he could see her resemblance to Deirdre, despite her being so slender and fair. It made him miss his wife all the more. He'd been away from her for over five weeks now, and her absence was a constant pain in his body. Aye, part of his heart had been left behind at Clan MacKinnon with Deirdre and Ewan.

He looked back at Boyd. "Did you wait to hang him until you knew we were approaching?"

Muireall hesitated, then simply said, "Aye. He's my mother's son."

Gavin returned his gaze to her and saw her lips tremble before she tightened them. She either grieved her brother or was frightened that Gavin would proceed to hang her. Or both.

"We willna harm anyone who wasn't a part of Boyd's plans or enabled him in his deviant desires. I understand you doona live here any longer?" he asked.

"Nay, I came back for my father's passing. My other siblings and my mother left when we heard of Boyd's treachery. I am the eldest, and if the clan will have him, and you, of course, my husband will be laird. He's a good man. Much better than my father. Or Boyd."

Gavin nodded. He suspected that was true from the reports he'd received.

He looked back at Boyd, his anger rising again. He wanted to tear down the body and drag it through the forest behind Thor. "Did you know your brother was an abuser of children?"

"Nay," she whispered. "At least, I was never confronted by it. I think a part of me knew, but I left a year or so after Boyd returned from being fostered. I didn't see my family for years."

"Neither did Deirdre. No one seemed to care."

Muireall sighed. "My mother was a cold woman. She still is. And my father was mostly absent. I didn't understand that love could be freely given until I married my husband."

Gavin raised his brow. "Deirdre understood that."

"Aye, she was softer than the rest of us. I'm sorry for any harm I caused her. If I were to see her again, I would tell her."

He grunted and then whistled for Thor to be brought over. "I'll mention your sentiment to my wife. She has a kind, forgiving nature. I couldnae be more grateful to be her husband."

Muireall's eyes lit up. "Oh! You love her. How wonderful!"

Gavin mounted Thor and looked down at her. "She and Ewan hold my heart. I would return today if I could convince my brothers and foster father to leave."

"I'm all for that," Kerr said, riding up behind him. "But we need a few more days here at least."

Gavin nodded and looked at Boyd once more. "Take down the body and burn it. He willna have a proper burial."

Muireall bobbed a curtsey again—not so perfect this time. "Aye, laird. I will tell my husband immediately." She looked up at him and smiled a little shyly this time, warmth exuding from her eyes, rather than obsequiousness. "I am glad my sister found you."

"She didn't find me," Gavin said. "She saved me."

She nodded and then hurried toward the keep.

Kerr urged his horse forward, his eyes glinting devilishly. "Maybe I could get the lads to leave in only one day. I wouldnae want your heart to wither and die while it's in my cousin's hands."

Gavin considered clobbering him, but if Kerr could get the lairds to leave tomorrow he would kiss him instead. "Fall will be upon us sooner than you think, Brother, and then we'll all be back at our separate clans as winters rails against us. Let's hurry back—to my wife *and* my sister. You have a lot of work to do if you doona want to be inside your stone walls alone this year."

Kerr's brow furrowed, then he turned his horse around and yelled, "Gregor!"

Gavin almost punched the air in victory. Kerr was like a dog with a bone. If anyone could get them home faster, it was him.

He closed his eyes and sent out a message to Deirdre, imagining she could hear him, see him.

We're coming home, love.

Acknowledgments

As always, I have many people to thank for helping me bring this book to life—my editor, Cat Clyne, who shepherded me through the editing and production process; Hilary Doda, who is the first eyes on the book and gives such great feedback; and a huge shout-out to Dawn Adams and the art department at Sourcebooks, who have outdone themselves yet again with such a fantastic cover.

Smooches to all of you.

As per usual, thanks go out to my writing tribe: Kari Cole, Melonie Johnson, and Layla Rayne, who often message back and forth with me past midnight as we're each racing to meet our deadlines (or bemoaning the fact that we might miss them!). To my Mermaids, and all the fun times we have at conference, and to the supportive hive mind of the Golden Network—I love you guys! And new this year is all the love and support to be found at the Casablanca Authors messenger group—what a lifesaver you all have been! Thanks in particular to Sharon Wray, Diana Munoz-Stewart, and Maria Vale. Sisterhood at its best!

And mostly, I want to acknowledge my husband, Ken, who's been so sick this past year and just pushed through it as best he could despite pain, stress, and fatigue. You are loved, you are cherished, and I am forever grateful I get to walk through this life with you. You always make me laugh. Here's hoping for an easier year ahead!

Read on for an excerpt from the first Sons of Gregor MacLeod book

HIGHLAND PROMISE

Gleann Afraig (Fraser territory)—The Highlands, Scotland
Twenty Years Later

DARACH MACKENZIE WANTED TO KILL THE FRASERS. Slowly.

Lying on the forest floor, he peered through the leaves as his enemy rode single file along the trail at the bottom of the ravine. Midway down the line, a woman, tied belly down over a swaybacked horse, appeared to be unconscious. Rope secured her wrists, and a gag filled her mouth. The tips of her long, brown hair dragged on the muddy ground.

In front of her, Laird Fraser rode a white stallion that tossed its head and rubbed against the trees in an attempt to unseat him. The laird flailed his whip, cutting the stallion's flanks in retaliation.

To the front and behind them rode ten more men, heavily armed.

The King had ordered the MacKenzies and Frasers to cease hostilities two years before, and much trouble would come of helping the lass, let alone killing the laird. Still, the idea of doing nothing made Darach's bile rise.

"You canna rescue her without being seen."

The whispered words caused Darach's jaw to set in a stubborn line. He refused to look at his foster brother Lachlan, who'd spoken. "Maybe 'tis not the lass I want to rescue. Did you not see the fine mount under the Fraser filth?" Yet his gaze never left the swing of the lass's hair, her wee hands tied together.

"Fraser would no more appreciate you taking his horse than his woman."

"Bah! She's not his woman—not by choice, I'll wager."

They'd been reaving—a time-honored tradition the King had not mentioned in his command for peace—and could easily escape into the forest unseen with their goods. They'd perfected the procedure to a fine art, sneaking on and off Fraser land for years with bags of wheat, barrels of mead, sheep, and horses.

Never before had they stolen a woman.

He glanced at Lachlan, seeing the same anger and disgust he felt reflected in his foster brother's eyes. "You take the stallion. The laird willna recognize you. I'll get the lass."

Lachlan nodded and moved into position while Darach signaled his men with the distinctive trill of the dipper—three short bursts, high and loud pitched. The MacKenzies spread out through the heavy growth, a nearby creek muffling any sound.

The odds for a successful attack were in their favor. Ten Fraser warriors against Darach, the laird of Clan MacKenzie; his foster brother Lachlan, the laird of Clan MacKay; and three of Darach's men: Oslow, Brodie, and Gare. Only two to one, and they'd have the element of surprise.

As his enemy entered the trap, Darach mounted his huge, dark-gray stallion named Loki, drew his sword, and let out a second, sharp trill. The men burst through the trees, their horses' hooves pounding.

Two Frasers rode near the lass. Big, dirty men. Men who might have touched her. He plunged his sword into the arm of one, almost taking it off. The man fell to the ground with a howl. The second was a better fighter but not good enough, and Darach sliced open the man's side. Blood and guts spilled out. He keeled over, clutching his body.

Farther ahead, Lachlan struggled to control the wild-eyed stallion. The Fraser laird lay on the ground in front of Darach, and Darach resisted the urge to stomp the devil. He would leave the laird alive, even though he burned to run his sword through the man's black heart. Fraser's sister's too, if she were but alive.

In front of Darach, the mare carrying the lass thrashed around, looking for a means of escape. The ropes that secured the girl loosened, and she began sliding down the beast's side.

Just as her fingers touched the ground, he leaned over and pulled her to safety. Dark, silky hair tumbled over his linen léine. When the mare jostled them, he slapped it on the rump. The animal sprang forward, missing Fraser by inches.

Damnation.

Placing her limp body across his thighs, Darach used his knees to guide Loki out of the waning melee.

Not one Fraser was left standing.

~

They rode hard to put as much distance as possible between them and the Frasers, and along game trails and creek beds to conceal their tracks as best they could. When Darach felt they were safe, he slowed Loki and shifted the unconscious woman so she sat across his lap. Her head tipped back into the crook of his arm, and he stilled when he saw her sleeping face, bruised but still lovely—like a wee dove.

Dark lashes fanned out against fair cheeks, and a dusting of freckles crossed her nose.

She looked soft, pure.

God knows that meant nothing. He knew better than most a bonny face could hide a black heart.

Slicing through the dirty gag, he hurled it to the ground. Welts had formed at the corners of her mouth, and her lips, red and plump, had cracked. After cutting her hands free, he sheathed his dagger and massaged her wrists. Her cheek was chafed from rubbing against the side of the mare, and a large bruise marred her temple.

His gut tightened with the same fury he'd felt earlier.

Lachlan rode up beside him, the skittish stallion tethered behind his mount. "If you continue to stare at her, I'll wager she'll ne'er wake. Women are contrary creatures, doona you know?"

Darach drew to a stop. "She sleeps too deeply,

Brother. 'Tis unnatural. Do you think she'll be all right?" Oslow, Brodie, and Gare gathered 'round. It was the first time they'd seen the lass.

"Is she dead, do you think?" Gare asked, voice scarcely above a whisper. He was a tall, young warrior of seventeen, with the scrawny arms and legs of a lad still building up his muscle.

Oslow, Darach's older, gnarly lieutenant, cuffed Gare on the back of the head. "She's breathing, isna she? Look at the rise and fall of her chest, lad."

"I'll do no such thing. 'Tis not proper. She's a lady, I'll wager. Look at her fine clothes."

Lachlan snorted in amusement and picked up her hand, turning it over to run his fingers across her smooth palm. "I reckon you might be right, Gare. The lass hasn't seen hard labor. 'Tis smooth as a bairn's bottom."

Darach's chest tightened at the sight of her wee hand in Lachlan's. He fought the urge to snatch it back.

"She has stirred some, cried out in her sleep. I pray to God the damage isna permanent." Physically, at least. Emotionally, she could be scarred for life. His arm tightened around her, and she moaned.

"Pass me some water." Someone placed a leather flagon in his hand, and Darach wedged the opening between her lips. When he tilted the container, the water seeped down her cheek. He waited a moment and tried again. This time she swallowed, showing straight, white teeth. Her hand came up and closed over his, helping to steady the flask.

A peculiar feeling fluttered in Darach's chest.

When she made a choking sound, he pulled the

flask away. Her body convulsed as she coughed, and he sat her up to thump her on the back. Upon settling, he laid her back down in the crook of his arm.

"Christ, we doona want to drown her, Darach—or knock the lungs right out of her. Maybe you should give her to one of us to hold for a while?" Lachlan's laughing eyes told Darach his foster brother deliberately provoked him. Another time-honored tradition.

Gare jumped in. "Oh, aye. I'll hold the lass."

"You?" Brodie asked. "You canna even hold your own sword. Do you think those skinny arms will keep her safe? I'll hold the lass." Brodie was a few years older than Gare and had already filled out into a fine-looking man. He was a rogue with the lasses, and they all loved him for it. No way in hell would he be holding her.

"Cease. Both of you," said Oslow. "If anyone other than our laird holds the lass, it will be Laird MacKay. If she be a lady, she'll not want to be held by the likes of you."

Darach glowered at Lachlan, who grinned.

Then she stirred, drawing everyone's attention. They waited as her eyelids quivered before opening. A collective gasp went up from the men, Darach included.

He couldn't help it, for the lass staring up at him had the eyes of an angel.

They dominated her sweet face—big, round, innocent. And the color—Darach couldn't get over the color. A piercing, light blue surrounded by a rim of dark blue.

A shiver of desire, followed by unease, coursed through him. He tamped down the unwelcome feeling.

"Sweet Mary," Gare whispered. "She's a faery, aye?"

All except Lachlan looked at Darach for confirmation. He cleared his throat before speaking, trying to break the spell she'd cast over him. Not a faery, but maybe a witch.

"Nay, lad," he replied, voice rough. "She's naught but a bonny maid."

"A verra bonny maid," Lachlan agreed.

Her throat moved again, and Darach lifted the flask. Opening her mouth, she drank slowly, hand atop his, eyes never leaving his face. He couldn't look away.

When she'd had enough, she pressed his hand. He removed it, and she stared up at him, blinking slowly and licking her lips. Her pink tongue tempted him, and he quelled the urge to capture it in his mouth.

Then she raised her hand and traced her fingers over his lips and along his nose, caressed his forehead to the scar that sliced through his brow, gently scraped her nails through the whiskers on his jaw.

A more sensual act he'd never experienced, and shivers raced over his skin.

Finally, she spoke. "*Par l'amour de Dieu, etes-vous un ange?*"

Caitlin stared at the beautiful creature gazing down at her. He was magnificent, with flashing brown eyes and a fierce scar. Wavy, chestnut-colored hair framed his face and glinted with red highlights in the sun, emphasizing his tough jaw and soft, touchable lips.

For some reason, an overwhelming sense of peace spread through her. She must be in heaven, and he was a warrior angel. Maybe Michael or Gabriel, sure to wreak justice upon the men who'd abused her.

"*Non, ma petite. Je suis seulement un homme.*"

A man. Her angel said he was but a man.

Beneath her, a horse moved, and she realized she sat on the warrior's lap. The man's strong arms and powerful chest cushioned her. Protected her. She felt like a child held close to his big body.

Nay, not a child. A woman.

He watched her quizzically, and she realized something was amiss. Where was she? Had she been taken across the sea by the man her uncle had given her to?

She glanced at the forest above her. Afternoon sunlight poured through the leaves, but the air was still crisp. "Am I in France?" she asked. The words spilled out in her native Gaelic.

The man looked surprised, then replied in kind. "Nay, lass. You're in the Highlands of Scotland."

"But you spoke French."

"Only because you spoke it first."

"I did?"

"Aye."

Why had she spoken to him in French and what had she said? She tried to remember, but her head ached. Pain radiated down her face. Oh, aye—she'd asked if he was an angel.

"I spoke French because I couldnae remember Latin, and Gaelic seemed too coarse for an angel. English even worse. What angel in his right mind would appreciate being spoken to in English?" She stopped when she realized she was babbling.

The man smiled, and to her delight, a dimple formed in his cheek. "What angel, indeed."

Then a thought occurred to her, and she frowned. "Maybe a fallen angel. He would like the English devils, now wouldnae he?"

Another man laughed, and she realized they weren't alone. Shifting her gaze from the warrior's face, she found herself looking at another handsome Highlander astride a horse. Tall and broad shouldered, his light-brown hair was tied by a leather cord at the nape of his neck. Dark-blue eyes smiled at her from a finely formed face—though not nearly as fine as the man holding her.

"Doona startle her, Lachlan. She's still confused," her savior said gruffly.

"I'm all right, angel. Doona fash."

A young lad leaned forward on his horse, as skinny as he was tall, with a face covered in pimples. "Why'd you think him an angel, lass?"

Two other men on horses gathered 'round. Every one of them stared at her, concern etched on their faces. For the first time since the fire, she felt safe, even though they were strangers.

"Because he saved me. You all saved me." She swallowed and took a deep breath. "And he's so bonny, of course."

The lad went from looking proud to horrified. "Our laird isna bonny. He's fierce and intimidating."

"Oh, aye, I'm sure. But he has such bonny eyes, doona you think? And his hair glints red in the sun. 'Tis verra pretty."

The man named Lachlan laughed again, causing her warrior's brow to furrow. She reached up and massaged it with her fingers. "Doona glower so. 'Twill cause lines. You doona want to look fierce all the time, now do you?"

The man's eyes widened and the wrinkle disappeared. He appeared uncertain, an emotion she was sure he found bewildering. For some reason, it pleased her.

"What's your name, lass?" he finally asked.

She hesitated, not wanting to give too much away. "Caitlin. What's yours?"

"Darach MacKenzie, laird of Clan MacKenzie." He indicated his men. "This is Oslow, Gare, and Brodie. You're safe with us."

The truth of his statement settled in her bones with a certainty, and the fear and anxiety she'd been living with for the past three years slipped away, leaving her almost giddy.

She could barely contain her happiness as she waited for him to introduce the other man, the one he'd called Lachlan. A familiarity lay between them that did not extend to the others, and she wondered if they were related.

When it became clear Darach had forgotten, she asked, "Are you his brother, then? Lachlan MacKenzie?"

"Aye, we're brothers. Foster brothers. Two of five reared together by the great Gregor MacLeod. But I'm not a MacKenzie. I'm Lachlan MacKay, laird of Clan MacKay." Then his eyes twinkled. "Do you want to ride with me, lass? It's been suggested Darach may be getting tired."

Caitlin clutched Darach's léine. "Am I too heavy for you, Laird MacKenzie?"

He made a loud, dismissive sound and tightened his arms around her, telling her in no uncertain terms where she would ride.

"I'm not your laird, Caitlin. You will call me Darach."

"Oh, aye. Darach." It was a good name. Soft yet hard. Strong yet gentle. Worthy of the warrior. And the way he said her name—rough and deep—caused warmth to spread through her chest.

"What clan are you, lass?" he asked. "We'll make sure you get home safely. How did you come to be so abused by the dog Fraser?"

The heat inside Caitlin turned to ice, and she stiffened. He wanted to give her back? Nay. 'Twas unthinkable. She'd just escaped.

She closed her eyes, knowing they were the windows to her soul and allowed anyone to discern her thoughts.

"Caitlin?" The worry in Darach's voice compelled her to look at him. "Are you all right?"

She nodded, lips pressed together lest she blurt out the horrible truth and they took her back to Fraser. Or her uncle.

Her clan, her real clan, was dead. That was the truth. By all that was holy, she didn't belong with her uncle or Fraser. She belonged...she belonged... Where did she belong? Maybe she could find her mother's people in France?

Surely she'd be safe there. Her uncle and Fraser wouldn't travel so far to find her.

"I doona rightly know," she said, her heart skittering as she shifted her eyes downward.

"Is it your head, lass?" Oslow asked.

"Aye. 'Tis thumping like a rabbit's back foot when the fox nears."

It was true enough, and she heaved a sigh. Surely exaggeration would not be considered a mortal sin. Besides, she could barely keep her eyes open.

She peeped at Darach through her lashes to see he watched her skeptically. Aye, just like her da—although he didn't feel like her father. And at times he had a look in his eye she'd never seen in her father's eyes. It made her want to burrow into his embrace.

"I've seen these things happen," Oslow continued. "Men taking a blow to the head and not rightly remembering. The lass may ne'er remember, Laird."

Darach exchanged a glance with Lachlan. The MacKay laird shrugged, and Darach returned his gaze to her, expression bland.

"Is that what's happened, Caitlin? You canna remember anything? Other than your name, of course. And how to speak French?"

"Well, things are a bit foggy. Maybe in the morning, my mind will be clear."

Darach stared at her before answering. "Maybe." Then strong fingers gripped her chin and tilted her head.

To her surprise, his eyes had darkened. He released her and traced his fingers over her face, following the same path she'd taken earlier on his face. Her heart swelled and something filled her deep inside.

When he spoke, his voice was grave. "I promise to keep you safe, sweetling. You'll come to no harm while there is breath in my body. I pledge this on the honor of the MacKenzies."

About the Author

Alyson McLayne is a mom of twins and an award-winning writer of contemporary, historical, and paranormal romance. She's also a dog lover and cat servant with a serious stash of dark chocolate. After getting her degree in theater at the University of Alberta, she promptly moved to the west coast of Canada where she worked in film for several years and met her prop master husband.

Alyson has been nominated for several Romance Writers of America contests, including the Golden Heart, the Golden Pen, the Orange Rose, Great Expectations, the Molly, and the Winter Rose.

Her self-published works in contemporary romance include her Sizzling, Sexy, Santa Barbara series—*The Fabrizio Bride*, *The D'amici Mistake*, and *The Berrucci Rules*. *The Fabrizio Bride* was nominated for the RONE awards.

Alyson and her family reside in Vancouver with their sweet but troublesome chocolate lab named Jasper.

Please visit her at alysonmclayne.com and look her

up on Facebook (facebook.com/AlysonMcLayne) or Twitter (@AlysonMcLayne). She loves chatting with her readers!

HIGHLAND PROMISE

Wattpad author Alyson McLayne delivers bold, exciting Highland romance in the first Sons of Gregor MacLeod book

Darach MacKenzie vowed never again to let a woman near his heart after his betrothed betrayed him. It sparked an intense clan feud, and now he can't be distracted...especially not by a sweet, charming lass who needs his help.

Caitlin MacInnes vowed never again to let misery rule her life after escaping a hell of her uncle's making. Darach has saved her, and she's desperate to stay safe. But when Caitlin is caught up in a rival clan's trouble, Darach will need all his brawn and brain to save her life—even if it means losing his heart.

"What a fun read! A true page-turner."

—Wattpad user Lucianologna

For more Alyson McLayne, visit:

sourcebooks.com